A PASSAGE IN THE NIGHT

SHOLEM ASCH

A PASSAGE
IN THE NIGHT

G. P. Putnam's Sons, New York

Part I

CHAPTER ONE

IT all began with the holiday which Isaac Grossman, head of Grossman and Grossman, owners of a chain of hotels and nationwide real estate operators, spent on the Atlantic coast of Florida, at Winter Paradise, the firm's most recent acquisition.

Among the former glories of the establishment was the Ambassador Hall, the exact copy of the original Hall of Ambassadors in the Alhambra of Granada; here, twice weekly, were held the cocktail parties which were the great attraction of the new resort.

The great alcove under the baldaquin, where the caliphs had supposedly received the emissaries of foreign lands, was a luxurious bar; it was steeped in delicate blue-rose light which cast warm, heavy shadows. In the second alcove, the meeting place of the vizier and his ministers, was the buffet, with the long white tables and their burdens of appetizing hors d'oeuvres: miniature troughs of Russian caviar, cut-glass dishes of Strassburg *pâté de foie gras* heaped up in pyramids, a dozen variety of cheeses laid out symmetrically, cold cuts, marinated fish, salads. From the bar, where the experts in white jackets shook their decoctions, and from the buffet at which the quick-handed servers filled the trays, a stream of waiters in gala uniform carried the supplies to the guests at the little tables ranged along the walls of the hall.

The smooth floor, covered with arabesque designs and glittering under the crystal candelabra pendant from the high ceiling, was reserved for dancing. The nationally famous jazz orchestra was hidden in a third alcove, behind a miniature forest of tropical plants. The flood of light played on décolletés and headdresses, and on the latest creations of the fashion world. Mingling with the guests were a number of models whose bodies carried on display the gowns and furs and jewelry on sale at the shops in the foyers;

3

in the shimmer of robes, the glitter of diadems, bracelets and necklaces, swirling to the music, it was impossible to tell which were guests, which models.

The cocktail parties of Winter Paradise were not closed affairs; they were intended to draw, and they did draw, crowds of visitors from the other hotels, from Hollywood, Palm Beach and Miami Beach. Here was to be seen not only the newest in dress and jewelry design, but the loveliest in womanhood.

Isaac Grossman had picked out for himself a half-hidden corner of the hall, where he sat, incognito, with his secretary. In person he was known to none but a few intimate friends, the top members of the staff, and a few waiters who had been instructed to respect his privacy. Hour long he would sit in this corner, seeing but unseen, sunk in thought, abstracted completely from the gaiety, the lights, the music, and the dancing. And Rose, seated opposite him, asked herself again and again, what was it that had happened to her employer to plunge him into these long, unwonted, meditative silences.

On this evening in particular there was a painful contrast between the riotous merriment in the hall, and the somber, withdrawn heaviness of the owner of Winter Paradise. The guests were in unusually high spirits; the drinks, the sparkling music, the rhythmic circling of the dancers, had lifted them to a mood which was ready to find amusement in any trifle—and as it happened, the trifle was there, in the person of an old gentleman who became the center of attention. He had a shock of white hair which fell back almost to his shoulders; his mustache, too, and his thick eyebrows, were white as snow. But his behavior was that of a youngster. He did not miss a single dance, or omit a single lady in his group. He danced with everyone, all the complicated steps of the old and the new dances; and at every pause he was loudest in his applause, shouting impatiently, "Encore! Encore!" His partners and the musicians were both exhausted, but he remained fresh. The guests were delighted with the spectacle of this youthful oldster, and encouraged him with shouts of "Bravo!" And the old man, red-faced, radiant, became intoxicated with the applause and capered with renewed agility. Finally the guests formed a circle around him and watched him gliding and skipping with a young woman who could hardly keep up with him.

4

"They say he's over eighty, and he tires out all his partners," said Rose to her silent, abstracted employer.

"Yes?" returned Grossman.

"You ought to be interested, Mr. Grossman. Why don't you learn to dance?"

"I?"

"Yes, you, you. All your life you've been building hotels and resorts and movie houses, amusement places for others, and you've never learned how to have a good time."

Grossman came out of his stupor for a moment, looked at her without seeing her, and remained silent.

"Look at that old man there!" said Leonard the headwaiter, as he passed by Grossman's table. "He's liable to drop dead any moment, without knowing what happened."

"Why?" asked Grossman, startled.

"Blood pressure. The doctors have forbidden him to dance, but he pays no attention. I don't know how to stop him."

Grossman suddenly remembered that he too had to be careful. Dr. Markowitch had warned him more than once. He too could drop dead at any moment, without knowing what had happened. He muttered to himself: "God! Can it really happen to me?" And he sank deeper into himself.

"What is it you're thinking about?" asked Rose. "Business?"

"I'm not thinking about business," he answered, brusquely.

"What else can it be? What? Ever since we got here you've been lost in your thoughts. And frowning to yourself all the time. Thinking and worrying, as if all your ships had gone down. Tell me what you're thinking about, tell me."

"I'm thinking—I'm thinking—how did all this begin?" he answered, with a strange, forlorn smile.

"What do you mean—all this?"

"All this—the theaters, the hotels, Winter Paradise—all of it. It began with him—with him—but I'm not through with him, with this Kovalsky."

"Kovalsky? Who's Kovalsky?"

"Kovalsky?" Grossman started back in confusion and astonishment. "Did I say Kovalsky?"

"Yes. That's what you said. Kovalsky. Who is he?"

"Who?"

5

"This Kovalsky you just mentioned."

"I don't know who he is. Did I mention the name? It doesn't mean anything. It slipped out just so. No, I don't think I mentioned that name."

"You did, Mr. Grossman."

"No. I don't know anyone with that Polish name. Forget it, Rose, and don't bother me any more. Listen, it's time to go into the dining room. They're serving." And Grossman stood up.

Rose followed him, her eyes fixed on the floor.

Winter Paradise was one of the triumphs of Grossman and Grossman, but it had begun rather as a personal ambition than as a business venture. The transaction had not been undertaken with a view to large financial returns. The elder Grossman, head and founder of the firm, had had a poor opinion of the enterprise; it had really been initiated and carried through by his son Lazar, vice-president and treasurer, who had charge of this side of the operations, and who sometimes pushed them through without his father's consent, or even knowledge. And what the younger Grossman had originally had in mind was, in reality, an act of personal satisfaction, to possess this fashionable palace, where the gloomy snobbery of the international aristocracy had once reigned when it was known as the "Hundred Club"—for Grossman and Grossman to possess it, against his father's will.

Isaac did not like his son's overweening ambition, forgetting his own, and he nourished a secret desire that the project should be a failure.

To make this undertaking a success was a challenge to the younger Grossman. His intentions at the beginning had been confused, the practical aspect of the enterprise had been secondary, an afterthought. Now he threw himself into it with a furious determination to make good. Within six months he had the palace remodeled, exploiting every foot of space for the accommodation of all who could afford to pay. There would be no difficulty in finding room for five hundred where only one hundred had been spread before in the old club. Later he would extend the premises, and raise the capacity to a thousand. Most of the spacious foyers, vestibules, corridors, and boudoirs which consumed space in the main building and in the guesthouses were converted into bedrooms and

6

bathrooms. The new plan called for a number of shops—women's fashions, shoes, jewelry, flowers, perfumes, a beauty parlor, an extra restaurant, a coffee shop, and a magnificent bar. What before had been ostentatiously wasted space was now put to use and served some solid purpose, not, however, without a degree of luxury. He applied the same principles to the remodeling of the alleys and swimming pools. Nothing was for empty show—everything for intelligent use. Certain of the original features were left intact, so that the place might still lay claim to the title of the American Alhambra; but he cleared out of the dining rooms the tasteless imitations of Moorish and Renaissance furniture which someone had manufactured for American millionaires in love with Spanish period pieces. He threw away the ugly, iron-edged tables, and the uncomfortable "Inquisition" chairs, with their suggestion of termites and decay. He removed the huge, pretentious pieces which had kept light and air from the bedrooms, turning them into torture chambers, and replaced them with the simple and gracious furniture of the modest Colonial village period. He covered the walls with cheerful designs, and the windows with curtains which admitted the sunlight. The cold mausoleum became a warm and pleasant home. As for those who were still looking for the old Alhambra—and they were after all entitled to something they supposed they were paying for—they too could find what they wanted in the foyers and vestibules and halls which he had left intact.

He engaged a new staff, the kind that would suit the new clientele; people who would work willingly for guests who appreciated and rewarded service. All were new—gardeners, masseurs, cooks, porters, chambermaids, bellboys—and he inspired them with his own energy as they prepared to receive the first five hundred guests. The resort was open to anyone who was able to pay between thirty and forty dollars a day for a bedroom and bath, and ready to tip the service generously.

The day before the opening of Winter Paradise the son announced joyously to the father: "Governor, we're booked up solid for the next six months. America is a big country."

The father stared at his son. The voice—that too was his own. He saw himself as if poured into his son; and yet the son seemed to be a stranger. Perhaps that was because he was a stranger to himself.

7

Was Isaac Grossman jealous of his son? If there was jealousy and envy, it was unconscious; and what provoked it was the simplicity and matter-of-factness with which his son confronted every task; he took all difficulties in his stride. It had not been so with the father. He had had to break his way through, and he had emerged only by the skin of his teeth. What a long and perilous and bitter road it had been to the first foothold; what thorns and thickets had ripped his flesh before he had found a little space about him! And even from that vantage point on, what obstacles had stood in his way, and with what grim persistence he had had to push to right and left with his sharp elbows! He still bled from the splinters which had imbedded themselves in his body. True, he was seldom aware of the pain. The momentum which had carried him through all difficulties to his goal—what that goal was, and how he was to reach it, he had never stopped to consider—that inner momentum had bred a kind of forgetfulness in him. It was only during rare and transient intervals of tranquillity that the pain arrested his attention—the pain of an old wound. But then he would soothe himself with the promise that soon, soon, he would reach the goal—whatever it was—and then all the crooked things would be made straight, and everything that had been awry in his life would be set right. Such an interval of tranquillity, a pause which would let him catch his breath, he had found in the Winter Palace of the rich which his son's vigor and initiative had transformed into the Winter Paradise.

With all his achievements, with his place of honor in the business world, with the son and the grandchildren who had risen to social levels he had never dreamed of, Isaac Grossman was a lonely old man. Loneliness had descended on him for the first time when his wife—the only person whom he had truly loved, the only one who had been able to stand up to his will—had died, a year before the buying of the Winter Palace. The nearest to him now was another woman, not of his family, a complete stranger it might even be said—his secretary, Rose Rosenberg. There was a strong bond between them, but she could not penetrate to the heart of his loneliness.

Rose had never known another family relationship, another love, another friendship, than that of Grossman and Grossman, as personified in her employer, Isaac Grossman. She had come to the

8

firm when she was still young. The firm, too, was young. Isaac Grossman was in the full tide of his powers, and he had only just begun to reach out with his mighty arms and take an unshakable grip on what the world offered. He was in the late thirties, an impressive figure of a man with the build of an athlete, though he had never gone in for any sports—his occasional golf games, clumsy and amateurish, hardly deserved that title—and rarely showed an interest in them, unless it was to attend a baseball game now and then, more out of sociability than inclination. His thick black hair stood up in bristles on his head, despite the lotions and the hard brushes with which he tried to subdue it. He dominated every business conversation from the first word, if only by his physical presence, his broad, powerful chest, his mighty arms, his ringing, metallic voice. At home they used to call him, only half in jest, "the bear"; and that indeed was the impression which he made on everyone. And yet, for all that, the effect of massiveness came not so much from the man's physique as from his spirit, from the dark, grave, heavy-laden soul.

Little black-haired, dark-eyed Rose, with her childlike face, was carried away by his dominating personality. One might say that he swallowed her up. Not that there was ever even a suggestion of an improper relationship between them. The thought of an infidelity to his wife, whom he loved deeply, never crossed his mind. On the other hand, it could not be said that his attitude toward his secretary was only that of the employer. Despite his bearlike massiveness, despite his heavy-handedness, there was in him a certain softness, a kind of childlike helplessness, in his relationship toward women. It was a touch of gallantry which women became aware of at once, and instinctively; but it was not something acquired, it was not a self-conscious pose toward the other sex at large; it was something native, related to an inborn and concealed nobility. It was this gentleness and gallantry which really established his dominion over Rose.

As soon as he had become convinced of her ability he showed her every mark of confidence. He kept no transaction secret from her; occasionally he discussed with her—as if seeking advice—matters which he even concealed from his son. And he did it with such seeming helplessness, such naïveté, as if among all the people in his entourage she was the only one who could help him. He

9

consulted her on all his problems, and especially on those which arose from shady business offers. Nothing is more apt to win a woman's heart than the confidence which a man shows in seeking her advice. To have this powerful man, Isaac Grossman, pouring out his heart to her so soon after she had entered his employ, to have him come to her with this childlike helplessness, awoke in Rose all the natural instincts of a mother. At first she made an effort to resist, clinging to her personal life outside the office. But the magic of his personality, his frankness and friendliness—also the little gifts he made from time to time, the occasional glance or word which acknowledged her importance to him, and which caused the blood to rush into her face—these things bound her closer and closer to him, so that before she knew it she suddenly found herself isolated, cut off from all contact with the outside world, her hopes ended, her dreams extinguished. Every corner of her life, as it was emptied of its old content, was filled up with the new one, which consisted of the firm and her employer, Isaac Grossman.

He saw to it, of course, that she was adequately compensated for her diligence and devotion. Her future was secured. At first she received a modest bonus at the end of the financial year; later, when she become a genuine necessity to him, as indispensable as she was reliable, he gave her a number of shares in the firm. He planned it all in such a way that she should become entirely dependent on Grossman and Grossman, should be unable to think of severing her connection with him; and it was done with great skill, so that she did not notice how all her security, all that she had saved and relied on, was gradually absorbed into the firm, to which she was thus bound for the rest of her life.

While his wife still lived, and throughout the entire period of her long illness, Rose had assumed toward her employer the obligations which are expected of a daughter, a wife, and a nurse, not of a secretary. In time she became so much a part of him that whatever affected him she instinctively accepted as affecting her own existence. She could tell, the moment he entered the office in the morning, whether he had slept well or badly. She always had a supply of medicaments on hand, antacid powders, pills to soothe his nerves, and the like, which Dr. Markowitch, his physician, had prescribed. She trembled over her employer as a mother trembles over an only child. Without looking at him she could sense, as through some delicate instrument operating at a distance, all the variations of his moods. Without saying a word, without even glancing at him, she would suddenly get up, go to the office medicine chest, take out a pill and place it, together with a glass of water, before her employer.

Then Grossman would look at her like a spoilt child, would make a piteous grimace, and ask, "Must I take it?"

"Certainly, Mr. Grossman. You've done it again, eaten something you shouldn't have eaten. You've got those yellow spots under your eyes."

"Must have been that chopped liver. I had lunch at Lindy's, with Zeitlin and Kenig."

"You're really like a naughty child, Mr. Grossman. You know how often Dr. Markowitch told you to keep away from chopped liver. It's no good for you," she said, quite sternly.

"I know, I know."

"You'd better take the four-twenty home. You need a good night's sleep."

"How can I? I've got that appointment at four o'clock with Hochberg. And I want to see the late afternoon mail."

"No, no," she insisted. "I'll let Hochberg know that you can't see him today. And I'll look after the mail, Mr. Grossman."

"Are those the boss's orders?"

"Yes, Mr. Grossman. And no highball, and no roast beef, to-night. I'll call Frances to prepare rice and milk for you."

"Rice and milk, boss?"

"No cream tonight, Mr. Grossman; and no whisky. You don't want me to call Dr. Markowitch, do you?"

"All right, boss, all right."

On his wife's death it was generally expected that Grossman would marry his secretary. His son Lazar favored the idea, and was prepared for the event. Isaac Grossman was still a vigorous man, whose temperament and appetites were still strong. He frequented Jewish restaurants, and ate the spicy dishes to which he had become accustomed in his early years—livers, stuffed fish, heavy roasts. Even in his home in New Rochelle, from which he commuted daily to New York, they had to prepare the heavily salted and peppered meals he loved, although they knew that the

II

doctor had forbidden them. He suffered from inflammation of the gall bladder, and every fit of excitement was apt to be followed by very severe pains. Only two persons had ever been able to discipline him: his wife, whom he obeyed out of pure affection and, after her death, his secretary, whom he obeyed from force of habit, almost automatically.

When he was left alone, without his wife to control his appetite, his son Lazar was genuinely frightened for him, not trusting him to follow a sensible regimen. He was also afraid—and of this perhaps more—that in his loneliness his father would take up with some undesirable woman who had an eye on his money. You never knew with a man like Isaac Grossman; his uncurbed temperament had often been a great trial to his son, who hoped that Rose would, after the marriage, be an even more salutary influence in his father's life. But the elder Grossman surprised everyone; he made it clear that he did not intend to marry his secretary. He lived a lonely widower's life in the big house in New Rochelle.

Rose herself was not wounded by his decision, and her attitude toward him underwent no change. She even found it in her heart to justify him for wanting to remain as he was. Her devotion and submission were unaffected; or perhaps they were even deepened. It was as if new wells of motherly compassion had opened in her for her employer; she did whatever lay in her power to make his loneliness more bearable, to bring a touch of cheerfulness into his life. Isaac Grossman was not so dull-witted, or egotistical, as to remain unaware of her affection and her unreflecting devotion. He was touched by her humble goodness, by her self-denial, which seemed to flow from her without effort. He became more bound to her than ever, she became indispensable in a sense he had never experienced before. Rose was now the only living person toward whom he felt something more than a blood-relationship. And still he refused to bind his fate to hers in the bond of marriage. In part this was due to the conscious memory of his beloved wife, and in part—the greater part—to an innermost modesty and decency which he had inherited with the blood of his parents, a conservative sense of propriety which none of the trials and temptations of his stormy life had ever been able to overcome. One could think of it as an innate gift of tactfulness, a certain thoughtfulness in regard to his bearing. He could not contemplate a desecration of the pure bond between himself and his dead wife, and it would have been in some way a desecration to bring another woman into his life, to live with her in that last degree of sacred intimacy which he had known with his wife. Everything else—friendship, trust, mutual care, devotion, but not that. And indeed, it had come to such a pass that he could not have existed physically without Rose. She exercised the same care over his home life as she did over his office life —for in the end she even came to live in his house in New Rochelle. And when his son Lazar persuaded him, after he had suffered an unusually severe attack, to come down to Florida for a rest, he found it as natural to have Rose with him in The Winter Paradise as it now was to have her in his home in New Rochelle.

The Golden Suite of Winter Paradise, and the garden of the Lion Fountain on which its windows looked down, were also among the features of the "Hundred Club" which young Grossman had chosen to retain. It was in this suite that Grossman and his secretary were lodged. That night, as he lay on the huge Spanish Renaissance four-poster bed, under the baldaquin of red damask, Grossman had a frightful dream; no, not really a dream but a waking hallucination. He was not asleep when the visitation came; his senses were alert; and that was what was most horrible about it —that he knew himself to be awake all the time. In this nightmare, or vision, he knew himself to be who he was, namely, the chief owner of Grossman and Grossman, and he knew also who he had been. But he suddenly found himself on a street which he had never seen before. It was not an American street—definitely not an American street—perhaps it was a street in Poland, in some city or village which his father had known. And perhaps it wasn't a street at all, it was a canal, a passage, an alleyway, very narrow, because it was dark though the time was midday. It was a twilight darkness. The street, or alley, or whatever it was, had no opening on either side, it stretched away from him, stretched away endlessly. There were queer people about, the place was crowded with them, people in a hurry. He too, Grossman, was among them, and he too was hurrying with the rest, hurrying to deliver to some place the tremendous pack he was carrying on his shoulders. Everyone was loaded like himself, some with big packs, some with small, and his was the biggest. It was not the size that mat-

13

tered, though, but the weight. It was crushing him to the earth. It was as if a mountain had been lowered onto his shoulders. But he had to carry it to some place, without knowing where the place was, for the street along which he was dragging himself had no outlet, it was a dead end. He did not know where he was to unburden himself of the terrible weight. And all the time it was growing heavier; his body was bathed in sweat, his hands were trembling with weakness.

The pack threatened to slip off his shoulders, but he did not dare to let it happen, he must under no circumstances let go, he had to carry it to some destined place, the whereabouts of which he could not discover. He plodded on, and on, and on. His backbone was cracking, he would fall any moment. But he must not fall. He must go on, like the others, with the burden on his back. They too, the others, were covered with the sweat of their anguish. He heard them groaning, muttering to themselves, but they did not drop their burdens, and they did not stop walking. And suddenly the canal was transformed into one of the East Side streets of New York, and he was working in a clothing store. It was a familiar street out of his young years. The hour was between day and night, the season winter, snow was falling. It was dark, as though above him there was not a sky but a thick canopy. Electric lights and gas lights shone out of the show windows on either side of the street, and the hoar frost on the panes was melting. The side streets were heaped high with the snow which the city snow ploughs had thrown there. A tremendous traffic poured through the streets, the sidewalks were crowded. Suddenly he saw a horse pulling at a cart piled high with bales of cloth. The horse was covered with the frozen, glittering dewdrops of its agony, and icicles hung down from its jaws and flanks. It was tugging with all its strength at the cart which was stuck in the ploughed up, frozen mud. The neck strained forward, the eyeballs bulged, but the wagon did not move. The driver wielded his whip unceasingly, the horse lunged and scrambled, but there was no motion. He wanted to run up to the horse, help it to drag the wagon out of the mud, but with him too there was no motion. He wanted to shout to the driver to stop lashing the horse, but no sound issued from his throat; he was shouting, and yet nothing was heard. He felt on his own skin every

14

lash of the whip as it fell on the horse. Or rather, he himself was suddenly the horse. He was pulling at the cart, tugging, tearing himself in two. He tried to scream, but there was only a wailing and moaning which he heard within himself.

"Mr. Grossman! Wake up! Wake up! What is it, Mr. Grossman? Wake up!"

From her bedroom Rose had heard the ghastly sounds of his nightsweat, the choked gurgling, the howling, as of a tortured animal. But even before she had actually heard them, she had felt instinctively that her employer was in torment. She stood over him now, holding a candle in one hand, and with the other shaking him feverishly, to pull him out of the labyrinth of his hallucinations.

"Rose! Is that you?" Grossman had started out of the horror. He was glaring at her with astounded and uncomprehending eyes; his hair was drenched with sweat.

"What is it? A nightmare?"

He thought for a moment. "Yes. A nightmare." And then, to himself: "It has to do with that miserable Pole."

"Kovalsky?"

"Yes."

"In God's name, who is this Kovalsky?"

"It's a man who has a complaint against me. We'll have to find out where he is, and straighten this thing out . . . once for all."

"But who is it, who?"

"I've just told you. He has a complaint against me. I met him when I was a young man." He talked to someone behind Rose. "He's in the right, too."

"Good God! Is it such a serious thing that you have to have nightmares about it?" asked Rose anxiously.

But by now Grossman had come to again; he withdrew into himself. His tone changed.

"Forget it. It's nothing."

"Nothing! And it doesn't let you sleep? Is it so serious that you can't straighten it out with money?"

"Yes, you could, you could. As a matter of fact, it has to do with money. A small sum, which I didn't attend to when I should have done, while there was time. I'll do it now. But we've got to find him first. Now go to bed. It's late. Good night."

15

"I'm afraid to leave you alone. You were moaning as if you had terrible pains, as if someone was torturing you."

"Give me a glass of water, and go back to bed."

"Shall I give you a sleeping pill?"

"No, no. I'll sleep now. If you go back to bed I'll sleep like a log."

CHAPTER TWO

BUT he did not sleep through the rest of the night "like a log." In fact, he did not sleep at all. And this was not because he was an habitually poor sleeper. He had always had the wonderful faculty of falling asleep as if on command, at home, on trains, in hotels. No matter what problems plagued him, he only had to lie down, close his eyes, say to himself "I'm going to sleep," and he slept. This had been one of the sources of his strength, perhaps the most reliable standby in his tumultuous life. Only here, in the luxurious rooms of Winter Paradise, sleep fled from him for the first time. He had brought no business worries with him; he had let himself be persuaded to come down for a rest, to "hibernate," in the favorite word of the hotel's advertisements; and nothing outside of himself kept him awake. But there it was. He *dreaded* sleep. And it was this dread that kept him awake. Here, in Winter Paradise, which he could legitimately claim as the climax of his career, the triumph which would justify a pause, a period of quietude and restful satisfaction, he fell a victim to the night hallucinations which had once haunted him in his younger years, when he had registered his first successes. But many years had intervened since then; he had thought about the episode intermittently, at long intervals, without special anguish. And now, all of a sudden, the old hallucinations returned, for no discoverable reason, to torment him with a new fury.

He was quite clear in his own mind as to the source of his torments. He traced it back to a certain incident, and to what his father had told him about the indescribable punishments which God reserved for one who had committed a theft, and who had not repented and made reparation to his victim while there was yet time. It came out of one of his father's books.

He could see his father now, he could see the apartment in Essex

Street, in downtown New York, where he had spent his first years. He saw the pushcarts, the swarms of people, the buying and selling, he heard the uproar of innumerable voices.

He saw himself as a young boy, and there came to his nostrils the acrid fumes of burning garbage as they poured out of the cans which he had set fire to. He smelled the pickles, the tomatoes, the sauerkraut and herring in the barrels and boxes spread out on the pushcarts and on the sidewalk before the cellar doors. He remembered how his mouth had used to water. For he had always been hungry as a young boy. How often he used to sneak up behind the women, and when the pushcart owner turned her head, snatch a pickle, or tomato, or even a herring, and withdraw like a flash into the crowd! He didn't think it was a sin. He was hungry, and he wanted to eat. And if the woman who kept the pushcart happened to look round at the last moment, she too did not take it too much to heart. She would raise a cry—"He's robbing me, the young villain, he's ruining my children!"—but she would soon quiet down.

It was different with the baker; one had to be more careful there. The baker with the yellow beard, which was always half white with flour, and who always wore a white paper cap, kept his merchandise on stalls in front of a grocery: small loaves, poppy-seed rolls, onion pancakes, bagels piled on long sticks, and, on Fridays, yellow-golden Sabbath loaves. If the baker caught him with his hand in one of the baskets, he was not content with words; he would leave black and blue marks on his ribs, he would snatch the hat off his head and fling it away into the middle of the street. Once he even stripped the shirt off him. And when bystanders saw the baker hitting the youngster for trying to steal a bagel, or a roll, they would side with him, and not with the baker; and sometimes they even interfered and pushed the baker away.

"Look at him! All that row about because a hungry kid tries to snatch a bagel! As if there wasn't a Jewish heart in him, but a stone, instead."

Once he succeeded in filching a large Sabbath loaf, and took it home to his mother; not all of it, because he could not resist pinching off a piece, but most of it. He found his mother, as usual, at a household chore. He could not remember her except as working at something; in vain did he try to picture her, after all these years,

18

at rest, not occupied with cooking, washing, cleaning, or mending dresses, pants, shirts—"They just fall to pieces," was her eternal lament. And when she was done with the house, she would turn to the "bundle" which she had from her neighbor, Mrs. Krepliak, who got the work from a subcontractor, to do at home "in her free time." His mother was a heavy woman who was always complaining about her feet; evenings she used to soak them in hot water, into which she had stirred a rheumatism powder. Why had his mother been so heavy? It must have been her troubles; she had become blown up with troubles.

There were five children in the house, three boys and two girls. The two older boys had been born in "the old country." The oldest was Gabriel; they used to refer to him as "the old one." The next to him was Sam—but that was his American name; in the old country he was called Zebulon, and that was the name his father still used. Isaac was the first to be born in America, and he was followed by two girls, Dora and Ethel "the baby." Ethel's real name, the one which her father reported to his congregation, was Esther Rachel, after one of his grandmothers; but Mrs. Krepliak, the neighbor, told Mrs. Grossman that Ethel was a much better name, because no one in America would be able to say a mouthful like "Esther Rachel"—so Ethel it remained. The baby was the only child Mrs. Grossman fed with a bottle. Two more children had been born before the youngest, but they had died in infancy.

The first thing Isaac remembered about his brothers was that they attended the *cheder,* the one-room Hebrew school of his father's congregation. But Sam was always playing truant. In fact, he ran away altogether from the *cheder* and enrolled in the public school on Delancey Street. It was then that he changed his name to Sam; and that was how he was inscribed in the school. Isaac was too young at that time to enter public school; and he too rebelled against the *cheder.* His father took him there, to learn to say his prayers, but he ran away. There was nothing to be done about it; you couldn't talk to the child, and blows were useless. Isaac remembered clearly how it all went. His father led him to *cheder* early one morning. The entire premises of the congregation consisted of a single room with windows which were nailed down. They made him sit on a long bench, before a table, together with many other children, and a Jew with a big beard sat at one end.

A few moments after his father had left, Isaac slid away from the table, opened the door, and ran away.

On Sabbaths, unable to escape, he had to go with his father to prayers; but he found it almost unbearable. He stood among his brothers, near his father, and had to be told when to say "Amen." He loved the open street. Closed rooms were a torture. His father could not force him; father was a weak and sickly man, and any kind of excitation was dangerous for him. Little Isaac knew this very well: "Father is a sick man, and you mustn't cross him." But what could he do? It was impossible for him to sit in a room with nailed-down windows; and the rabbi with the thick beard was just as hateful as the room. There was nothing to be done with Isaac in those years; and he knew all the time how much unhappiness he caused his mother. He cared about that—he did not care at all about his father—and yet he could not help himself.

Before he was old enough to go to public school his father managed to teach him some of the prayers at home. That would be on odd evenings, but mostly on the Sabbath. When his father came home from work, his first words, even before his wife had handed him the towel, would be: "Isaac, did you say your prayers?"

He hated the question, and therefore hated *"davenning."*

"Yes, I did. Mother saw me *davenning*. Did you, Ma?"

"Yes, yes, he *davenned*." He was only a youngster, wasn't he? He would be better when he grew up.

He could see his mother, he could see everything in the kitchen, the sink, the gas stove, the meter, the crockery shelves, the sewing-machine. Whenever he saw his mother, he had to see the kitchen. He could not see them separately; he could not take her out of the kitchen. He saw the colored bedspread which curtained off the doorless room in which stood two collapsible iron cots and two dressers. One of the cots would be put up in the kitchen, for Reb Zvi Hirsch, the pious Jew from father's home town, whom mother had taken in, mostly out of pity, because he could not live among strangers where the food might not be *kosher*. He felt safe in Mrs. Grossman's kitchen. The few dollars a week which Reb Zvi Hirsch paid for board and lodging were also welcome. Mother cooked for him, did his laundry, mended his clothes. He was a very quiet man; you hardly noticed that he was there. He came only to eat and sleep, and he left the house very early, even before

20

mother had got up. He would fold the bed, put it quietly away behind the colored curtain, and go to work, or to morning prayers at father's congregation. The second bed which was set up in the kitchen was for the three boys, Gabriel, Sam and Isaac. Father and mother had their standing bed in the "dead alcove." Past the alcove there was another room; that was supposed to be for the bath and the toilet, but the two girls slept in it. There was no window in the alcove, only a door which was now nailed to. The room on the other side formed a separate apartment. Above the door in the dead alcove there were two shelves. On one of them father kept the books he had brought with him from the old country; the other was for mother's brass candlesticks, the wine bottle, and the sugar bowl, all of which were put on the table when Sabbath came around. Under the shelves, behind a white sheet, mother kept a variety of things: the linen, her Sabbath dress, her mantle, father's Sabbath suit, in which he went to prayers, his gabardine, his winter overcoat, and a pair of new shoes which mother had bought for a certain Passover and had never worn because they made her feet burn.

The only window in the apartment looked out from the kitchen into a yard where the pushcart peddlers kept their merchandise. When the window was open the smell of the pickles and herrings made the boys frightfully hungry. But you couldn't get at the wooden lockers, because the door to the yard was locked and made doubly fast with heavy iron bolts. Mother was able to hang her washing there on a clothesline which went over a wheel fastened into a pole in the middle of the yard. At the window stood the only table the family possessed.

The table served a multitude of purposes, sacred and profane. Early in the morning, when the rest of the family still slept, it was father's study. Lying now in the immense Renaissance bed under the red damask baldaquin, Isaac Grossman could still hear the melancholy chant with which his father accompanied his studies in the sacred books, could still see his father's shadow swaying to and fro on the wall. On the same table mother placed the candlesticks which she took down from the shelf every Friday evening, and made her benediction over the Sabbath lights. The boys did their homework there, Sam intent on his public school assignments, Gabriel intent on his Jewish studies. On some evenings, and on most Sabbaths, there would be lessons from the prayer book for Isaac and Sam. Here they ate, of course; and here mother ironed the family clothes and sorted the bundles she got from her neighbor.

It was at this table that Isaac still saw his mother's frightened face when, that Friday forenoon, he came home with the Sabbath loaf which he had stolen from the baker's bench. He did not think he had done anything terribly wrong. Other boys did the same thing. Willy, Mrs. Krepliak's boy, had often boasted to him that he knew a way of hiding to one side of a pushcart and working a bolt of cloth out from under a heap, right under the pushcart man's nose. And he not only boasted—he had really done it, too. Isaac thought he was performing a good deal, bringing home a whole Sabbath loaf, with only one corner pinched off.

"Look, ma, what I brought you."

Mother was standing at the table, measuring off a big patch which she was going to sew into Sam's trousers. Little Dora stood on a chair at the sink, helping her mother out with the dishes, and baby Ethel was asleep in the cradle. Mother looked up from the piece of cloth, and when she saw the loaf which he was holding in both hands, her face—Isaac Grossman remembered this vividly— changed color. Her long cheeks became gray, as if someone had spread ashes over them. The strands of hair which crept out from under the colored headcloth she always wore also became gray, at this moment for the first time—so it seemed to him—gray, and stiff, like wires. Her eyes, which had always been full of smiling tenderness for him and remained tranquil and assured under the wide brows, no matter what he did or how he behaved himself, suddenly seemed to be starting out of their sockets. She wanted to say something, but no sound issued. She gripped the table edge, as if she were about to fall, and slowly let herself down into father's chair at the head of it. She sat thus for a long while, still looking at him, before she found her speech.

"Where did you get that?"

He knew now that he had done a terrible thing.

"Somebody gave it to me," he stammered.

"Who? Tell me. Who?" She had risen to her feet. She took hold of him by the shoulders and began to shake him violently.

"I took it," he confessed.

22

"Where from? The baker's stall?"

He could not answer. He only nodded dumbly.

She grabbed the table edge again, and again lowered herself stiffly into the chair. She stared away in front of her, as if looking into the remote distance, and murmured, almost under her breath, "Ephraim Gombiner's grandson a thief!"

Her eyes flooded with tears.

"Mother, hit me, but don't cry," he implored. He came close to her, touched her knee.

"Why should I hit you? Is it your fault? It's my fault, the way I've managed things in America."

Only now did the well of her tears overflow, and the big drops coursed down the furrows of her cheeks.

"Mother, don't cry. I'll never do it again," he pleaded.

"Your father mustn't know about this," she murmured.

He understood that. Certainly. His father must not know about it. Anything rather than that.

"No, mother. You won't tell him, will you? I'll never do it again." And now it was he who burst into tears. "Only don't cry, mother." Again he took hold of her knee, but she pushed him away, and wept quietly.

Then, as if on a sudden resolution, she rose. For a moment Isaac thought she was going to punish him, and he felt happy. But she did not touch him. She took down a towel, wetted it in the sink, and wiped away her tears. Then she wiped Isaac's face, straightened out his shirt and hat, and threw a shawl over her shoulders.

"Dora! Look after the little one, and see she doesn't fall out of the cradle."

Without addressing herself to Isaac, she picked up the loaf and thrust it into his hands. Then she pulled him after her by the arm and went out of the apartment. With rapid steps she went through the crowded streets till she reached the baker's stall. There the man was, with his yellow beard half covered with white flour.

"My boy took a loaf from you, and didn't pay. How much is it?"

The man looked at her in astonishment. Then his eyes fell on the boy, and lit up with recognition."

"That's the one! A loaf? A dozen loaves. He's been stealing

23

from me for weeks. He's taken a couple of dollars' worth of my good bread."

"I haven't got a couple of dollars. Here is all I have." She rummaged about in her handbag, and brought out all the coins she could find. "Here. God will have to pay you the rest."

The man took the coins. "Tell him not to steal any more."

"No, no, he'll never do it again."

That evening, when father and Reb Zvi Hirsch came home from synagogue, and everyone was seated round the table, mother placed on the table a loaf and a herring, and said: "This is all the Sabbath meal I have. My meat got burned."

CHAPTER THREE

VERY, very different were their normal Friday evenings. Mother seemed to have a magic way of making the kitchen bigger for the oncoming Sabbath. It looked like another place, not the one they knew. And the preparation! He could see his mother, holding one of his brothers—or perhaps himself—at the kitchen sink, washing his head under the running water while she kept an eye on the oven where the stuffed fish was sending forth that delicious, sharp Sabbath aroma. She issued orders to her little helper, Dora—this dish off the flame, that one on, wipe here, dust there, the tablecloth, the wine carafe, the sugarbowl, the candlesticks. And then father's footstep on the stair. No, before he heard his father's footstep he heard the cough. Father came in very quietly, and first stood at the door for a moment as if he wanted his shadow to go in ahead of him. He came home early on Fridays, for he had his preparations to make, too. But first came the familiar words:

"Has Isaac *davenned?*"

He never asked whether Gabriel had *davenned,* or Sam. With Gabriel he was sure; his oldest son went to the Talmud Torah, and had taken to Jewish ways. Sam had become a hopeless case. He had no time for Jewishness; he was busy with his own affairs. There had been trouble at home because of him; father had blamed mother for letting the boy have his own way. Now it was no use even asking whether Sam had *davenned.* But with his youngest one father still persisted; perhaps he would get him into the habit of *davenning* every day. And because father was so persistent, Isaac learned to hate the word *daven* and everything connected with it.

"He's *davenned,*" said mother, almost under her breath; and as soon as father came in she left everything else—sometimes Isaac would have to wipe the soapsuds out of his smarting eyes—and ran to look after her husband. Father had collapsed into a chair, and was holding his hand to his breast. He was soaked in perspiration. The scarf which he wore winter and summer was soaked through and through; so was his shirt. He had taken off his coat and laid it across his knees. He was breathing hard, and his black beard, which seemed to be gummed onto his cheeks, rose and fell with his breathing, while his Adam's apple bobbed up and down. Mother stood over him, her eyes filled with anxiety and compassion.

"Tired?"

"A bit."

In a corner of the kitchen there was a bowl of ice, which mother kept covered with a cloth. It helped to keep food fresh during the hot summer days. Isaac was the one who always brought home the ice. Mother always protested; she would not have it; she would tell his father. But Isaac had his own way. He waited for the iceman as often as he could. Sometimes he wheedled a piece out of him; sometimes he stole it. But there was ice in the house nearly every summer day.

Mother kept in the icebowl a bottle of what she called "honey-water." It was a mixture of honey and lemon, her special recipe for father's cough. As soon as father had an attack, she ran to the bowl and poured him out a glassful of the mixture. She did it now. But as she drew the cloth off the bowl, father saw the half-filled bottle of milk standing near the pot of meat. He pointed, and said through his coughing, "Milk and meat together. *Treif*. Impure. We can't eat it."

"God help me! Dora! Why did you put the bottle of milk in the icebowl?" Mother ran over and snatched away the bottle as if it had been filled with poison. "It's only been standing there a minute," she explained to father. "The bottle didn't touch the pot. The meat is still *kosher*. Shmaya, I swear to you the bottle didn't touch the pot. Now drink the honey-water, that'll stop your cough."

Father held the glass in his hand, and thought back. Had he eaten meat, or anything that had touched meat, in the last six hours? The honey had been standing with milk, or it had turned milky. There had to be a full six hours between the tasting of meat and the tasting of milk.

26

"It hasn't turned milky," mother assured him, reading his thoughts.

Father carried the glass to his trembling lips, and mother turned back to the rest of her Sabbath preparations.

Father's workshop was owned by an orthodox Jew, and the very word "union" was forbidden there. The hours were long; in fact, no one really kept track of them. As against this the workers were given time off for afternoon prayers, and work was stopped early on Fridays so that they could go home and prepare becomingly for the Sabbath. As a rule father went to the ritual baths on Friday afternoon—they were on Essex Street, close to the house. First he came home and rested a while. Mother would then give him a laundered shirt and underwear and a pair of socks, and he would leave in good time. But sometimes he was too exhausted, and if a fit of coughing came on him, mother would dissuade him from going.

"You haven't the strength for it, Shmaya. You'll fall down, God forbid. Come, I'll help you to wash at home."

She would prepare a bowl of hot water, take off her husband's shirt, his shoes and his socks, and she would wash his head, his body, his feet, as she had done with the children.

Always, somehow—at least this was how Isaac Grossman remembered it—father was a different man later on Friday evenings. And somehow, in spite of rebellion, the habit of attending synagogue with father on Friday evenings had remained an unbroken practice with the boys. They too were different on Friday evenings—that is, until father began his homilies. They had put on clean shirts; their clothes were mended, the missing buttons replaced. Only the shoes were unmanageable. Mother scraped and cleaned and polished them as well as she could, but she could not straighten out the heels or patch the holes through which the stockings were sometimes visible.

"Shoes!" mother complained. "I can understand holes in shoes. It's natural. But how do you get holes in your caps? You don't walk on your heads, God forbid." And she would mend their caps too, for without these they could not go to synagogue.

The synagogue of father's congregation was nothing more than an upper room in a Jewish community house which served a large

27

variety of clubs, orders, brotherhoods, and political associations. It was precisely on Friday nights that the social life of the community house was at its liveliest, for it was then that most "affairs" were held. There would be dances, dramatic performances, a lecture by a freethinker or anarchist, a conference of youth organizations or *Lansmanschaften*. And the pious Jews of father's congregation, who shared the tiny synagogue with the equally pious "Moses Montefiore Lodge," had to push and elbow their way through the corridors jammed with noisy young people. In the narrow room there were two little windows which were never opened. The spiders' webs on them were seldom disturbed. On the walls hung portraits of the Presidents of the lodge, decorated with flags and ribbons. The sacred Ark, and the bookcase with its sacred volumes, were pushed into a corner on weekdays, and concealed behind a curtain; they were brought out for the Friday and Sabbath and Festival services, and placed by the pulpit. This synagogue was used by most of the pious Jews of the neighborhood, for whom the bigger or orthodox synagogues were too far away. The praying seemed interminable to the young people; it was as if they would never get out of the place. Only Gabriel never complained. It seemed that he liked it as much as his father. Very often Sam and Isaac would sneak away from their father's side, especially when he was absorbed in the Prayer of the Eighteen Benedictions, and go downstairs for a while to watch the dancing couples. Sometimes this was impossible.

And when it was over at last, they had to thrust their way again through the jammed corridors into the street, and in the street the crowds milled about the pushcarts with their blinding flares. But when they got home—father and Reb Zvi Hirsch leading the way, the boys following—what a transformation! It all seemed to have happened with mother's magic while they were in the synagogue. How spacious the kitchen had become! The sheet in front of the alcove was snow-white—mother always hung up a fresh sheet for Friday evenings. The table seemed to have expanded, too. It was like a banqueting board. The Sabbath tablecloth, white, with yellow embroidery, was spread over it. The polished brass candlesticks twinkled, the candle flames danced. The Sabbath loaf was covered with a white cloth. And there mother was, on the other side of the candles and the carafe of wine for the Sabbath benediction, a Sab-

28

bath apron covering her dress. She had baby Ethel on her knee, and little Dora, in a new-washed dress, stood at her side.

Outside, in the streets, it was pandemonium. The riot of noise came up faintly; one could feel it beating at the walls. On Friday nights there was a frenzy of buying at the pushcarts, and the shouting of the hucksters made the night hideous. But inside, in mother's little kitchen, it was Sabbath. It was if the Sabbath, driven away by the whole East Side, had taken refuge here.

On weekdays father came home late, and exhausted. He had barely strength enough to say his evening prayers. It seemed that he fell asleep after his supper, and muttered the grace after meals in his sleep. Mother had to help him to undress. On Friday nights it was different. After the meal he said the grace clearly, and with concentration. And when that was over he never failed to deliver a little homily, and to question his sons on their behavior. Had they missed their prayers? Had they eaten without saying a benediction first? Had they eaten meat and milk without a six-hour interval? Had they told any lies? Had they deceived or swindled anybody? Had they desecrated the Sabbath? Father warned them —he knew all about it—of the punishments which awaited such transgressors. Sitting there with his skullcap on his head, in his gabardine which was too big for his frail body, the little book in front of him, he would sway back and forth and tell them about hell and its torments, as if he wanted to make sure that they would remember for the rest of their lives, when he would be gone from them. He would close his eyes, and from his thin lips would issue terrible descriptions of the hereafter. He told them of the Angel of Silence, who waited for the dead man, and who asked him, the moment the earth covered the grave: "What is your name?" He would tell them of the judgment, and of the two angels, the Prosecutor and the Defender. There was a great book, in which were written down all the good deeds and all the sins of the dead man, whatever he had done throughout his life. The good deeds were written on one side, the sins on the other. The prosecuting angel turned the pages and reminded the dead man of time and place and occasion: at this and this hour, in this and this place, he had omitted the benediction over food; at this and this hour, in this and this place, he had swindled this and this man. He had failed in

29

reverence to his father and mother; he had skipped passages in the prayers; and, worst of all, he had desecrated the Sabbath.

And then father went on to speak of the punishments, the burning, the roasting, the boiling, to which the sinners were subjected. Father's homilies were directed chiefly at his second son, who had refused to go to the parochial school, who had left the path of Jewishness, who did not say his prayers and did not wash his hands before a meal. Young as he was, he had shaken off his father's authority. He had become independent. He sold newspapers, carried parcels for the groceryman, washed the floors for the butcher. He gave the money to his mother—but in all other ways he behaved as if he acknowledged no authority. When he was not working, he was always in the public library on Rivington Street. There was a girl there who showed him what books he ought to read. She helped him with his schoolwork, and sometimes, when he was short, she would give him money for a sandwich. And right in the middle of father's homily, Sam would get up and leave the house. Where had he gone? Perhaps to desecrate the Sabbath by working, by carrying parcels for the groceryman. And father went on talking, to Gabriel and little Isaac. Gabriel didn't need these homilies; little Dora was too young to understand; and anyway she and her mother, being women, did not carry the same responsibilities as men. . . . And so all the stories of hell were finally focused on little Isaac. It was as if all the paraphernalia of hell, all the punishments for skipping prayers, forgetting benedictions, deceiving and—above all—desecrating the Sabbath, had been invented especially for him.

And he, little Isaac, already had so many sins for which to be roasted and boiled in hell! He listened, and his soul rose in rebellion against God's judgment. It was neither the fear of God, nor reverence, nor any of the things that his father sought to implant in his heart—but secret hatred of a God who could decree such frightful punishments for such little transgressions as omitting to wash the hands before a meal, or carrying a package on the Sabbath. He knew all the people who were outside, in the street, on Friday nights, doing business, buying and selling on the Sabbath. He knew the baker with the yellow beard, and the pushcart woman who sold pickles, and the Jew who sold remnants—he was

30

the one with the loudest voice. All of them would burn, they would be boiled in big cauldrons over white-hot fires for such a little thing as buying and selling on the Sabbath. But didn't they have to make a living? They had to sell things—and they sold them. If he had had anything to sell, he too would have sold it on the Sabbath.

Mother had already taken the dishes off the table; she stood at the sink, washing them, and father did not like that. Mother, too, was dissatisfied. You could tell that by the way she handled the dishes. They always rattled more when she was discontented. She would say nothing to her husband; he was a sickly man, and if she irritated him he would have one of his coughing fits. But she could not entirely repress her feeling of discomfort and uneasiness; she said, at last:

"Why don't you tell him those wonderful stories out of the Books of Moses, about Abraham, and Isaac, and Jacob, and Joseph, instead of frightening him with those terrible things about hell. He has time to learn about that later. He's only a child."

Father became silent. He did not answer her. He became sad. And how sad father could become! It was heartbreaking just to look at him. His eyes clouded, the lids dropped halfway down; he made you think of a chicken which the *schochet* held across his knee, drawing its throat back for the sharp knife. He breathed heavily, and his lips moved, but he said nothing. And such a gloom settled on his hollowed cheeks that mother at once regretted her words. She trembled lest he get another coughing fit.

"I didn't mean any harm, Shmaya. I'm only a foolish woman. I was thinking that nice stories from the Holy Books would have more effect on a child."

"Nice stories, nice stories," moaned father. "A world is going down to destruction, the whole Jewish world; the Sabbath is desecrated openly; there is no Sabbath, there is no God, there is no judgment and there is no Judge."

"But you won't change America, my husband. God will have to accept his American Jews as they are."

"My sons, my own sons, I'm thinking of my own sons. If I don't set their feet on the right path, who will? They will grow up like gentiles in America."

31

"Don't eat your heart out, husband," said mother, and she came and stood over him, as if to caress and soothe him with her words. "Your children will be like other Jewish children in America. Have faith in God!" She spoke to him as if he were a little child.

CHAPTER FOUR

AND now, some time later, father lay on the folding bed, which mother set up for him in the kitchen. He could not sleep any more in the alcove. He choked there.

On summer days when the sun shone on the entrance to the house, mother would lead him carefully down and have him sit there on a cushioned chair, wrapped up, so that he might get some fresh air. But when the weather was bad father had to lie in the kitchen, with a spittoon at his side. And near him on the chair there always stood some boiled milk and sugar candy, to take when a fit of coughing came over him and he could not catch his breath. Father no longer went to work. Reb Zvi Hirsch had had to move out, and the family got four dollars a week from the charities; but they could not manage on this, so mother took more and more bundles from her neighbor. She worked at the sewing machine every spare minute, often till past midnight, and little Dora helped her out. Gabriel was not living at home; he was a student in a Yeshivah, a Talmudic seminary. Before he took to his bed father had run around from rabbi to rabbi until he had managed to place Gabriel, who now lived in the Yeshivah and only came home week ends to visit his father. Sam was no longer at home, either. He had not been able to stand his father's everlasting preaching and reproaching. He was somewhere in the Bronx, boarding with people to whom he had been recommended by the girl in the library. He worked all day in a grocery, and studied in the evenings. Sam would visit the house now and again, and would leave something with his mother, sometimes a dollar, sometimes less. He did not talk with father, because every conversation between them ended in a quarrel. Father always got angry—and started to cough. You had to be more careful with him than ever.

And so Isaac was the only son at home, and his mother fought

33

with all her might to keep him on at public school. But he had not the strength or the inclination to attend to his studies. He had to neglect his homework because money was needed, and he had to give his afternoons to that. He was not interested in school. (What a pity, he thought afterwards, what a pity! He regretted it all his life.)

What had he not already tried in his childhood years, before he had reached the age of thirteen! He remembered well the approach of his thirteenth year, because father was after him to learn how to put on phylacteries and say the appropriate prayers. When he was very little he had sold newspapers; then he had made himself a shoeshine box and had haunted the restaurants and the saloons; after that he had taken Sam's job with the groceryman and the butcher, carrying parcels for the first and washing floors for the second. Mother wanted to teach him how to use the sewing machine, so that he might help with the bundles. But that he could not stand. He wanted to be outside the house. Finally he found a steady job.

There was a Jew on Hester Street who kept a couple of mangles in a cellar. Women came from nearby houses with bundles of washing to mangle and dry. Isaac knew the place because he had often carried his mother's washing there. The mangles were worked by hand. Some of the women paid a few cents and did the turning themselves. Isaac too had done it for himself. But there were some women who had not the strength to turn the big wheel, and they would pay extra to have someone turn it for them. There would always be youngsters, and even adults, hanging around the cellar to earn a few cents in this way.

They paid five cents for a moderate-sized bundle, ten for a large one. The money was paid to the owner, and the owner paid the boys. Once, seeing Isaac turning the wheel for his own bundle, the owner looked at him approvingly and said, "You look like a strong boy."

"Look at my muscles," said Isaac, pulled up his sleeve, and bent his arm.

"Would you like a steady job here?"

"I certainly would," answered Isaac.

"It's not easy."

"I'm not afraid. I've done harder work."

34

"Will your parents let you?"

"I've got to earn a living. My dad is a sick man."

"Try it. I'll give three cents for the middle-sized bundles, six for the big ones."

At first it was much harder than he expected. After three or four bundles, blisters formed on his hands and his neck felt as if it was going to break. He had to set his teeth to go on. But when he came home with a whole quarter for his mother—and that for only a few hours' work—he forgot all about the pain. Mother made him a hot compress, and the swelling on his hands went down. In a few days he became accustomed to the work, and sometimes he brought home as much as fifty cents.

It was then, while he was employed by the mangling machine Jew, that he went through a dreadful experience which helped to set a stamp on the rest of his life. It had to do with the work there, and with what his father told him after a certain thing had happened. And yet the thing itself was such a trifle, so meaningless. . . . Bundles of wash would occasionally be left overnight in the cellar, sometimes out of forgetfulness, sometimes for convenience. A woman would come in with a bundle, ask to have it mangled, and say she would return in an hour or two, then fail to turn up. She would not come the second or third day. The bundle lay there on a shelf, gathering dust. If the woman did not return after ten or twelve days, the owner of the cellar would simply appropriate it and that was the end of it. Isaac saw this happen a few times and said to himself: "If he can do it, why can't I?" He had his eye on a certain bundle which had been lying on the shelf for more than a week; it had new pillowcases, bedsheets, towels, men's shirts and women's chemises. Mother would be thrilled with such a present. Father's bed-linen had to be changed very often now. Every evening his mother had to patch the bedsheets and pillowcases, they were so worn through. And so, one evening when no one was about, Isaac slid the bundle off the shelf and ran home with it. He would take a chance. If the mangling machine owner asked about it he would say the woman had called for it. And suppose she actually turned up? He would not think that far ahead.

The very instant his mother saw him come in with the bundle she understood. She wrung her hands and cried, "God help me!

35

What have you done? Do you want to ruin us all? Take it back! Take it back at once."

"Mother, a lady forgot it. She isn't coming back for it. It doesn't belong to anyone. If I don't take it the boss will."

"Let him! I don't want to have anything to do with it. It's theft! Ephraim Gombiner's grandson a thief! No, let me die first. Take it back this minute."

His mother took the bundle off the table and threw it into the hallway.

And Isaac went back with the bundle, and managed to replace it. But in the excitement he had forgotten that his father had witnessed the incident.

When he came running home again he found his father in a horrible coughing fit; his face had turned blue, and he could not draw breath. Mother was trying to force honey-water into his mouth. The two little sisters sat crying in a corner.

Finally, when the cough had let up, and mother had managed to soothe the children and was sitting down for a rest, Isaac heard his father's weak, croaking voice:

"Come here, Isaac. I want to tell you something."

Isaac did not want to approach the bed. He would rather have gone out into the street. But his mother got up and pushed him toward the bed.

"Go to him. He wants to tell you something. He is sick."

When he drew near, father stretched his hand out from the bed. He remembered that hand! Nothing but bone covered with shrunken skin. The long, lean fingers were like continuations of the network of blue veins which covered the withered skin. And when father took hold of Isaac's hand, and held it tight, it seemed to Isaac that his own hand had become like father's. He still felt the unexpected and terrifying hardness of the fingers that closed round his. Father held him tight, as if afraid that he would tear himself away any moment; and he had to sit down on the bed, and listen to everything his father had to say.

Father did not speak only with words; there was something more than the sounds coming out of his withered lips. The eyes spoke too, the deep-sunken, blazing eyes. It seemed to Isaac that he was being held by the terrible eyes even more than by the bony fingers fastened on his hand. For a while his father was silent; he

36

only breathed raspingly through his fluttering nostrils. Then he spoke:

"My son! Two months from now you will become *bar mitzvah,* you will be confirmed as a man in the congregation of Israel. I don't know if I'll live long enough to see it, but from that day on you will be responsible for all your deeds, and God will ask an accounting from you when the hour will come. Whatever wickedness you've done till now God will forgive, because you were a child, and not yet *bar mitzvah.* But promise me that after you are *bar mitzvah* you will never, never take what belongs to another. And if the thing should—God forbid—happen to you, if you should stumble and sin, then promise me that you will repent, and make restitution while you live, and return what you have stolen. Do you promise me?"

Father looked frightful, with his exposed hairy chest, his burning eyes, his huge Adam's apple.

Isaac stammered, "Pa, I didn't take it. . . ."

He had spoken in English, and his mother cried out: "Speak to your father in Yiddish."

He repeated, in Yiddish: "I didn't take it. I mean, it wasn't his, it wasn't the boss's. It wasn't anybody's."

"I am not talking about the parcel now. I tell you that whatever sins you've committed till now, God will forgive. You were not responsible for yourself. I was responsible for you. But from now on, from the day of your *bar mitzvah* on, do not stretch out your hand to what is not yours. No matter how slight; no matter if it is only the thread of a coat. And if you should be tempted, and fall, make good the theft. Do it while you live. For as long as you live you can make good the crime. Thereafter it is too late. Do you hear me?"

"I hear you, pa."

"Do you promise?"

"Yes, pa, I promise."

"I repeat it for you. Make good the theft while life is still in you. I can't make you swear to obey me, because you are not yet *bar mitzvah,* and therefore your oath is not binding. But remember it, in God's name. Remember it."

"I'll remember, pa."

"For you must know, my son"—and here father slipped unconsciously into his Talmudic study chant, "you must know that the sins a man commits against the Holy One, such as not saying his prayers or, God forbid, desecrating the Sabbath, such sins are forgiven when we pray on the Day of Atonement. But the evil which we do to our fellow men God has not the power to forgive. Only the man against whom you have sinned can forgive you. Thus, if you borrow money from a man and fail to return it, if you take something from a man, whether by violence, he knowing it, or by theft, he not knowing it, you become that man's debtor, whoever the man may be. And if you do not repay the debt while you live, you will have to repay it after your death; you will have to return and make good to the man you have robbed or to the man from whom you borrowed but whom you did not repay. And you will not be free until your debtor has forgiven you."

Father paused, but he did not relax the bony grip on Isaac's hand. Then he began again:

"And know, my son, that men who have died without having made good their thefts have been forced to return to earth in the form of animals, in the form of horses, and have had to work off the wages of their restitution. And they did not obtain release until the creditor had spoken his forgiveness. It came to pass once—this is told in one of our holy books—that a man possessed a horse, which labored hard, pulling great weights. On a certain day the owner of the horse chanced to find in a drawer a debtor's note, from a man who had died without repaying the debt. And the creditor thought to himself: He is dead, is he not? And his orphans are poor. I will forgive him his debt. . . . In that same instant the horse fell dead in the stable. And when the man went into the stable and saw what had happened, he said: 'Reb Mordecai'—that was the name of the debtor—'Reb Mordecai, I forgive you the debt.' Now if this be the punishment for a man who has not paid his debts, how much heavier is it for one who has stolen?"

But now even mother could not bear it any longer.

"Shmaya," she implored him, "no more of those stories."

"I must tell him, as long as my soul is in my body. Who will tell him when I am no longer here?" moaned father.

And so he went on, telling more stories of men who had been sent back to earth after their death, because of thefts they had not made good; and he told of the burdens they had had to carry, great

38

heavy loads, huge, leaden. Once—father said—he himself had recognized a dead man on the streets of Warsaw, in the guise of a harnessed horse.

"No more," cried mother, and she came over and freed the boy's hand from father's grip.

"What did I do?" wailed Isaac, the tears running down his cheeks

"Nothing, nothing," said mother. "Father means it for your good. Here—" she fumbled in her apron and brought out a nickel. "Take this—go and buy yourself chocolate."

"Chocolate—foo!"

He took the coin and ran down into the street. Isaac Grossman remembered how, at that moment, he wanted to do something outrageous. He would spend the nickel on cigarettes. No—that was not frightful enough. He would have liked to go into a saloon and buy a glass of beer, but he knew that he would not be served. Besides, that too was not outrageous enough. He wandered round to the pushcart market. This time he would not steal a pickle, or a loaf. That was kid's stuff. He glided through the clamoring women toward one of the remnant pushcarts, looked about him warily, and waited for his chance. When it came, he snatched a roll of cloth from under the heap and ran off with it. But he was sure that he had been seen, and he expected a hue and cry. But no one ran after him, so he went back, threw the roll of cloth onto the pushcart, and as he ran away a second time, he shouted:

"Hey, mister, that's yours. I stole it from you."

He spent the five cents on chocolate after all, and took it home to share with Dora and Ethel. Mother said proudly to father: "You see? He's a good boy."

"Oh, yes, I'm a good boy!" crowed Isaac, mocking his mother's tone; and he ran back to the street.

CHAPTER FIVE

ISAAC GROSSMAN sat with Miss Rosenberg in the cabana which fronted the sea. It had needed a lot of skillful coaxing on her part to get him there. He had not wanted to stir from his apartment. He had brooded over breakfast, his face showing the strain of the sleepless night; and the strain grew worse because he was fighting the memory down. He muttered to himself, not about Kovalsky, not about the night's hallucinations, but about plans for the future, great enterprises, achievements which would astound the world, show everybody who he was. He began to talk about a project which, as Miss Rosenberg knew, had been beckoning to him for some time—the biggest he had ever put his hand to. He would create, around Winter Paradise, a new city, a modern city. He had his own ideas about the layout, the shopping district, the residential streets, the cinemas, the gasoline stations. The potentialities of the site, commercial and otherwise, were limitless. The hotel now called Winter Paradise would of course be completely transformed and enormously enlarged; prices would have to come down considerably. The name Winter Paradise would be transferred to the city itself. *Here* was something big, which would lift the reputation of Grossman and Grossman into a class by itself. "I want Frankel the architect to come down here, at once," he said excitedly. "And some of his assistants." Then he collapsed, and muttered figures to himself. She watched him, at her wit's end for counsel.

She began again: "Mr. Grossman, what's wrong with you? Can't you take it easy for a few weeks? You came down here for a rest. Is this your idea of a rest? Or are you trying to run away from last night? What is it? Why don't you tell me?" She spoke urgently, almost angrily.

"Trying to run away?" he repeated. "I've nothing to run away from."

"Why do you hide it from me? In God's name, take yourself in hand, get rid of this thing once for all. Is it something so terrible that there's no way of making it good?"

She went on urging, and he answered her evasively, and with weakening conviction.

"This business of Kovalsky—tell me about it. What did you do to him that frightens you so?"

"I?"

"It's on your conscience. Tell me, Mr. Grossman. Perhaps I can help you. We've been in tough spots before, haven't we, and we've got out of them."

Grossman fell into a long silence.

"Maybe you're right. Maybe I ought to tell you about it. I've never told it to anyone. And maybe you're the only person that could help me. Yes, yes, I ought to tell you about it."

"But I don't want you to make a big tragedy of it. I'm sure it's really nothing. You've simply been brooding over it. It's all the result of your sick liver. The doctor's warned you against these moods; they come from your liver and your gallstones. They make you exaggerate things. You imagine you've got all sorts of diseases; or that you've committed some terrible crime. Mr. Grossman, why should we sit here? Let's go out into the sun. We came here for that. You're charging people forty dollars a day just for sunlight, and you don't enjoy any yourself. Come out on the beach; or into the cabana."

"I think you're right," he murmured, and he followed her out of the suite.

In the private cabana on the seafront, with its wide-open doors and windows, Grossman half sat, half lay, on a deckchair and opened his heart to Rose.

"What was the terrible thing you did to Kovalsky?" she asked suddenly, keeping her eyes on the crossword puzzle in the morning paper.

"I robbed him."

"Robbed him?" repeated Rose, and almost bit her tongue for fear of saying the wrong thing.

"Yes, I robbed him."

41

There was an interval of silence. Rose kept her head down.

"How did you happen to do that?"

"Very simply, as a matter of fact. I was working in a cheap clothing store in the Bowery—secondhand and new men's clothing. My father lay dying in Monticello. He was dying for seven or eight years; after my childhood all I remember about my father is —that he was dying. He had tuberculosis. The Charities didn't know what to do with him. The doctors said father had to get away from New York, into the hills somewhere. In the end they lent mother some money, and father's congregation got together a little sum, and mother opened a boardinghouse in Monticello. So besides having father on her hands, mother had to cook and clean for I don't know how many people. During the summers she made enough to live on. But the winters were brutal. There she was, with the girls, in the big, cold house, and not enough to eat. We lost touch with my brothers. Gabriel, the older one, had become a rabbi in some little country town. Sam, the next to him, had taken to politics, and was a Socialist. I was maybe fifteen or sixteen years old when mother and the girls went to Monticello with father.

"I'd always been a money-earner, from earliest childhood. Never had the chance to study. I worked for years at whatever I found, and at last I landed at this job in the clothing store. It was very poorly paid—all I got was a small percentage on my sales. I was a puller-in. I stood outside the store in the heat of summer, or the cold and wet of winter, and pulled customers in. I made barely enough for food and lodging. And yet I tried to send mother a couple of dollars during the winter. And I was always dreaming of something better. I felt certain that I'd make a good traveling salesman. I'd heard from some friends that children's clothing was a good thing to travel with, and there was a firm, Salzman Brothers, which was just beginning to rise. I don't know exactly how long I'd been at this job, but I know I was eaten up with ambition; and there was nothing I wanted more than to be a traveling salesman for the Salzmans. Well, I went at last to see the younger Salzman—he was at the selling end—and asked him to try me out. He listened—and he looked. He looked at me quite a long time. I wasn't too well dressed. Where was I to get the money for a decent suit of clothes? And you didn't need a decent suit of clothes to be a puller-in. Then Salzman asked me if I had any letters of recommendation from previous employers. Of course I didn't. I had no acquaintances in the business world, either. I explained everything to Salzman; told him where I was working; told him I couldn't get anything better because my father had no connections in the business world. Salzman told me to come back in a couple of days. I don't know whether he made inquiries about me, or whether he was pleased by my frankness, but when I came again he said he would give me a chance. He would let me go out of town as his representative, but at my own expense. I had to come back to him and show him twenty-five dollars, to cover my first expenses until I could send in some orders. He would trust me with the samples.

"Where was I to get twenty-five dollars? There wasn't a single friend or acquaintance whom I could approach for such a sum; and there wasn't any prospect of my being able to save up that sum from my earnings. Even if I cut down on my food, and didn't send mother anything, it would take me months to save that up, and by then that particular spring season would be gone, and I'd have to sweat through another summer in the Bowery. It was no use pleading. Salzman was very friendly—but hard as a rock. 'A boy who can't save up twenty-five dollars,' he said, 'can't win my confidence. Show me the money, and you can have the samples. That's all I have to say.' I gave up. I didn't want to lose his good will by making a nuisance of myself. But I just didn't know what to do next.

"And then one day, soon after, I was standing outside the store, keeping my eyes open for someone I could drag in. It was a mean, rainy day—I remember the month, it was March. There was filthy snow on the sidewalk, and the wet seeped into my shoes. I was frozen, through and through. It was dark—the electric lights were on everywhere. I stood there, on the alert, knocking one foot against the other and eaten up with one thought: Where could I get twenty-five dollars? I really had no hope of getting a customer that day; my boss didn't expect one, either. But he let me stand outside, and he sat inside warming himself at the big belly of the stove. And suddenly there was a man looking into the store window. I'd missed him. It was as if he'd risen up out of the ground. I can see him now, as I talk to you. A man of medium

43

height, dark, with black hair, and two big black mustaches in the European style. He had little black eyes, restless and frightened. I remember the eyes particularly, because he looked at me for quite a time before he spoke. His English was very poor. I had him by the sleeve, of course. 'You want a suit? Come inside. We've got a big choice. First-class goods, by first-class firms. Come inside, friend.' He shook his head, and found words at last. 'Yes, yes, suit —not new—secondhand.' 'Certainly. The best secondhand suits. And overcoats too.' 'No, no overcoat. Secondhand suit, good suit, strong.' He had a Slavic accent, and he stumbled over the English words. I had him inside in a few seconds, and was already taking off his overcoat, coat, and sweater. I tried suit after suit on him, until I found one that fitted, and that he liked. He liked it very much, I could see from the way he stroked the cloth. 'Strong,' he said, nodding, 'very strong.' After that came the bargaining. 'No money,' he kept repeating. 'I work mechanic Yale factory. No good wages,' and he smiled all the time, as if asking my pardon. We settled for twelve dollars and fifty cents. I helped him to put on his old sweater and overcoat. I remember asking him if he didn't want to put on his new suit, but he shook his head. 'No, no. A wedding. My daughter have a wedding.' I wrapped up the new suit, and he put his hand in his back pocket for the money. He didn't find it there. He looked up at me and felt in the other pockets, then in the sweater, and the overcoat. His face turned gray. He turned out his pockets again and again. No wallet. His eyes widened, his forehead became damp. He cried out in Polish, 'Boga, Boga'—I knew that word, 'God, God! My money! That store on Grand Street. They got my money. I forgot money in Grand Street.' He smiled like an idiot—and he was gone.

" 'There's our day's profit,' my boss said.

" 'And my day's earnings,' I said.

"I began to replace the suits on the racks.

" 'Just a trick, I'll bet,' the boss said. 'I don't believe he had a wallet to begin with. Polack!'

" 'I don't think so either,' I answered. 'I didn't like the man in the first place.' And as I lifted one of the suits, there it lay—the wallet—right in front of me.

"It was on the tip of my tongue to cry out 'Here it is!' Maybe

44

I actually said something, but not loud enough, because the boss, who was at the other end of the store, mumbled a question. But in that instant there went through me, like an electric shock, the thought: Here's your chance. I picked up the wallet and slipped it into the pocket of one of the hanging coats. I made a mental note of the rack and the color of the coat.

"About ten minutes later the Pole came back. He had shrunk to half his size. The idiotic smile was fixed on his lips. You couldn't tell, though, whether he wanted to laugh or cry.

" 'No found?' he asked me.

" 'No found.'

" 'You never had a wallet,' the boss called from the other end of the store.

" 'Yes, boss, I have wallet. Wages, all week wages, and ten dollar more. Five I borrow in pawnshop, to go to wedding. My daughter, she have wedding. And five dollar more I save up. Twenty-seven dollar fifty cent.'

"That was the sum I found in the wallet—twenty-seven dollars. And that was how I got my chance. That was how I became a traveling salesman for Salzman Brothers."

Isaac Grossman was silent. Rose waited, her eyes apparently fixed on the crossword puzzle in her lap. Grossman could not see her face; all he saw was the thick black hair, streaked with silver; it was parted severely in the middle and gathered in a bun at the back. All the time he had spoken she had given no sign; she had not lifted her eyes from the paper. But Grossman knew she had been listening intently, compassionately.

At last, still without lifting her head, she asked mildly, almost indifferently, "And you never paid back the loan?"

"Loan?"

"What then was it?" She looked at him now, her black eyes full of gentleness. Only round the lips there was a line of pain. "You intended to pay it back, didn't you? At the first opportunity."

"I haven't thought about it like that. Sure I intended to pay it back at the first opportunity. But I didn't do it."

"Why?"

"Because I didn't know at the time—and I certainly don't know now—how to do it. At first I was afraid. He might find out that

45

I'd stolen the money, and have me arrested. Afterwards I was ashamed."

"Ashamed? Of what?"

"Of having been able to stoop to such a thing. Maybe I wanted to deny to myself that I, Isaac Grossman, was guilty of such an act. I thought, perhaps, that by denying it I could think it out of existence, as if it had never happened. But I couldn't think it away, and I couldn't forget. It would come back to me, stand right in front of me...."

"But in heaven's name, why did you neglect it so long? Why didn't you get rid of the whole business?" she asked, a note of impatience creeping into her voice.

"I've told you. I kept the pocketbook by me for months. His factory card was in it—and the name ate itself into my memory. Yan Kovalsky. And there was another name written down, but I could only make out the first two letters, M-A. Yale factory, lock department. His address was there, too. Strawberry Hill, Springbrook, Connecticut. I kept on thinking, too, that one Sunday I'd go out to Springbrook and straighten the matter out. But the moment I really tried, I got frightened. He'd have me arrested. Or he might put the thing in the hands of a lawyer. He might even try to blackmail me, if the lawyer happened to be dishonest. My hair used to stand up at the thought of it—they'd victimize me for the rest of my life. I thought of sending him the money by mail— I'd have been glad to send him twice the amount; but I wanted to make sure he'd get it; and when I went to the post office to get a money order, they wouldn't give me one unless I filled out the name of the sender. I couldn't do that. It would be evidence against me. I kept on devising ways of sending him the money anonymously, while being able to check that he'd received it. That went on for a couple of years. And the more successful I became in the job I'd gotten through his money, the more scared I was to do anything that would jeopardize the job. Then more time passed, I met Clara, I went into business with my future brother-in-law, and I was ashamed as well as scared. I fell into a cold sweat thinking they might learn what I'd done. But I was even more ashamed before myself. Oh, sometimes it's harder to be ashamed before yourself than before others. That's how it was with me. I couldn't confess it to anyone, not to my partner, not to my lawyer, and

46

least of all could I confess it to myself. You see, I had the hope that I could wipe it out, destroy the memory of it." These last words Grossman uttered in a high-pitched voice.

"Wait," said Rose hurriedly. "You are doing what I asked you not to do. You're making a big tragedy of it. You're taking it too hard. You've helped out plenty of Kovalskys in your time. Hundreds. If that isn't good enough, give a thousand dollars for charity in Kovalsky's name and be done with it. Let dead things be."

"Dead things?" asked Grossman, startled.

"Certainly. Kovalsky has long been dead and buried. Forget him."

Grossman stood up suddenly, ran to the other end of the room, and faced her. His eyes were distended; his face had gone white, his hair a shade grayer. "Dead?" he stammered. "What are you talking about? He can't be dead. Kovalsky has to be alive."

"Isaac!" She called him by his first name. "You frighten me." She ran over to him, took his arm, and tried to lead him back to his deckchair. "You mustn't! You'll work yourself into an attack. Perhaps I'm wrong. Perhaps he's still alive. And if he isn't alive, there are surely children, grandchildren, heirs. We can tell them you owed him the money—you don't have to explain anything. Why are you doing this to yourself?"

"Oh, no, Rose, Kovalsky can't be dead. He mustn't be."

She almost forced him back into his seat, then drew her chair closer to him and spoke earnestly.

"You talk as if without Kovalsky all your life would have been different; as if you owed everything you've achieved to that one chance. Do you think you wouldn't have been Isaac Grossman without those few dollars? Would you have been someone else, a failure, or even a smaller man? You were bound to make your own opportunities, one way or another."

"Rose, everything that I am now, everything I have, I owe to Kovalsky. That one opportunity led to my success and my happiness—to the one happiness I was destined for."

"What was that?" she asked thoughtlessly, and then changed color. In a lowered voice she said, "Let me attend to this thing for you. I'll go to Springbrook and do whatever's necessary. Not that I see it the way you do. But I'll do it for your sake, so that your mind will be at peace."

47

"No, Rose, we'll go together. It's my debt, and I have to pay it."

"Have it your way, then. But promise me you won't excite yourself again, you won't even think about it."

"I'll try."

CHAPTER SIX

WHAT a relief it was to have shared his secret, at last, with another person! Isaac Grossman felt as if a load had been taken from his shoulders. He was younger, fresher, and lighter. It seemed to him, too, that Miss Rosenberg had shared in the renewal; and the confidence had brought her closer to him than ever before.

Rose was astounded by the effect on her employer, but she was also troubled by it. For Grossman, in a return of his former vigor, seemed determined to plunge back at once into his business affairs. It had occurred to him that this, his first long vacation, was beginning to look like a prelude to retirement. Until he had come down to Winter Paradise, the work had been divided between himself and Lazar. The management of the hotel system was Lazar's department. Purchase of land, new developments, had been under the older Grossman's direction. But for weeks now he had been out of touch with his own department. He had not checked on new transactions which had been pending when he left New York. By a long-standing agreement he had not looked into the direction of Winter Paradise. The management here, as in other hotels and resorts of the Grossman and Grossman chain, avoided business discussions with him on instructions from headquarters. He was a guest among the guests, although a special one with special privileges.

Now he stepped outside the rules. He called in the manager and began to question him on the affairs of Winter Paradise. He wanted information on which to base his plans for the expansion and reorganization of the hotel.

The season was in full tide. There was not a single vacancy at the resort. It happened to be the season when the fashion had turned toward beach and bathing costumes in flaming colors. The men looked as if they had escaped from a fire and had snatched

49

up, to cover their nakedness, the portieres and the slip covers off the furniture. The beach was dotted with cabins in the form of Turkish field tents. What with the tents, the costumes and the flags, the broad beach looked like a Turkish battlefield, and the half-naked people like dervishes who had been captured in their underwear. Or else one might have thought that a huge circus was in full swing, with its variety of attractions. Here an excited group was gathered in front of a large cabana on which a man was posting the results of horse races. In another section there was a parade of beauties in the latest bathing costumes. There were athletes, diving exhibitions, water sports—the golden stretch of sand rioted with joyous activity.

Only Isaac Grossman would have none of it. In vain did Miss Rosenberg plead and coax. It was not his world. Dressed in a white linen suit, he would permit himself to be dragged into a walk through the naked crowd, a curious figure out of keeping with the hundreds about him. He scarcely noticed what was going on. His thoughts were turned in on himself, on calculations and combinations and risks.

They had returned to their private suite above the lion well, to change for the cocktail party, when the telephone rang.

"New York," called Miss Rosenberg. "It's for you, Mr. Grossman."

"Hello! Governor!" He heard his son's cheery voice. "How are you enjoying the life of a playboy?"

"Don't care for it!" answered Isaac Grossman. "I'm too old to learn. Glad you called, Lazar. How are things?"

"First class." And the younger Grossman made as if to bypass the subject of business, but Isaac Grossman would not have it.

"What do you mean first class. What's the report from Chicago?"

"They're having a big season," Lazar explained, a bit impatiently. "Morris has had to hire a lot of new help."

"And Los Angeles?"

"O.K., dad, O.K." Lazar slipped from "governor" to the earlier "dad" whenever he became excited with his father. "Listen, you're not supposed to be bothering with business now. You're on vacation. Remember the Grossman Resorts slogan? 'A vacation is an important investment in time and money. Make the best of it.' You've got to set an example."

"Sure, I've got to set an example. But I'll tell you something. I'd like you to send Frankel down here. You know that project I've been mulling over—changes down here—I want to talk to Frankel about it. I was going to phone him."

"Dad, leave it alone now. There's loads and loads of time when you come back. Just take it easy. Say, are you backing any horses? I've got an inside tip on a horse—Victory! Number One. Try it."

"No, no, Lazar. I've got to get started again. That project— it's bigger than we realized till now. I've got it all worked out."

"Governor, dad—" it was as if Lazar was hopping from one foot onto the other. "Did you ever try deep-sea fishing? Do you know the Mishkins are in Miami now? They've got that wonderful yacht. Call them up. Or I'll call them. And by the way, there's a couple of things I've got to ask you about some of your—your beneficiaries. The Old People's Home, what do you call it, the Montefiore Home for the Aged, who got ten thousand dollars from you in grandfather's name. They want to make you honorary president, they sent a committee to me to ask permission. I've promised them to talk with you. We have to buy a couple of houses next door to the home, and build a new wing. And the Sanatorium. I have a letter from them. They want to name one of the pavilions the Isaac Grossman pavilion. They say it'll help them to raise money, having your name there."

"No," growled his father. "I don't want to have my name in all the papers. I hate that kind of thing. And you know it."

"O.K. I'll put them off." Lazar changed ground again. "Listen, dad, I'm thinking of sending Katherine and Louise down to you. They'll be good company for you. And they've got some nice things to tell you."

The older Grossman was silent for some seconds. Then he answered, a little sharply, "I'll be glad to see them."

Lazar must have felt that he had gone too far. As if to make amends, he added, "Oh, yes, listen, there's a piece of business I wanted to talk over with you. I think you'll like it. We got a wonderful offer for your property in Springbrook. They want to build a big supermarket there, with a movie next to it, and a

51

garage. The neighborhood's growing fast. We'll stay in with the corporation. I'll send you the terms—"

Isaac Grossman did not let his son finish.

"Springbrook isn't for sale," he said abruptly.

"You don't get me, dad. A ninety-nine-year lease, and a substantial guaranteed income."

"I've told you. Springbrook isn't for sale."

"For heaven's sake, how long are you going to hold on to it? It's just frozen capital."

"I'll see about it when I go up there."

"You're going to Springbrook? When do you reckon to go?"

"Maybe pretty soon."

He could see his son shrugging. "All right, dad. As you say. I'll call you again tomorrow. But forget all about business. Let me talk to Rose. Good night, dad."

"Good night."

Rose picked up the receiver.

"Rose?"

"Yes."

"How are you?"

"All right."

"Can the governor hear you?"

"No. He's gone to change."

"Listen, Rose. I don't like the way dad spoke. He's all excited. I could feel it in his voice. Can't you take his mind off business? Rose darling, we've got to do something for him. I'm worried."

"It'll be all right, Lazar. He's a lot better than he was. He wants to go to Springbrook."

"In heaven's name, what for? Is he homesick for a sight of snow? Connecticut's buried under five feet of snow."

"I don't know why he wants to go there. But I'll go with him. Don't worry. He's a lot better."

"Rose, try to keep him down there, will you?"

"I'll do what I can."

His good humor lasted for several days. He enjoyed his meals, as he had always done. He sat through the cocktail parties, commenting shrewdly on guests as they entered and left. It seemed

52

that he had managed at last to suppress the name of Kovalsky, and for this much Miss Rosenberg was profoundly grateful.

It was only a brief respite.

He had gone to bed in the expectation of his usual good night's sleep. And indeed, it had begun well. He had fallen asleep without effort, simply, sweetly, like a child whose eyes have been kissed by a loving mother.

Then it was all gone.

How long had he slept? And who was it who had tapped on the window and had said quietly, sternly, "Wake up"?

It was a light tap, but imperious; and there he lay, helpless. Sleep was like a bird he had just been holding safely and cozily in his hand, when suddenly it had flapped its wings, and there it was, perched on the windowsill, teasing him, challenging him to recapture it. The tide of his thoughts had set in again; they rolled through him, uncontrollable. He did not want to think. He did not dare to think. He knew it to be dangerous. The flood could carry him away, drown him. And yet, there was no way of escaping from the thoughts. They poured into the chambers of his mind, they danced about him, they tugged. There was nothing to be done but surrender.

He gave up the hopeless struggle, and lay there. It was Kovalsky still, Kovalsky again. Suppose he was dead? But surely he was dead, after all these years. And he, Isaac, could have made restitution—he had had a thousand opportunities. He had been on the verge of it a thousand times. Why had he let the opportunities slip away from him. Oh, he knew very well that what his father had told him was just foolishness. His father was old-fashioned, came from the old world; he was a fanatic. He, Isaac Grossman, didn't believe that God was so pitiless, and that there were such cruel punishments after death. Never. He, Isaac Grossman, was a modern, an American, a thinking man. If there were a God, He could not be so hard. In fact, even father had said that God was quite forgiving as far as He Himself was concerned. Yes, but God did not or could not forgive on someone else's behalf. That was what father had said. No, no, it was better to forget all that, not to think. But perhaps Kovalsky was still alive; if he was, there could be restitution, they could reach an understanding, whether there was a God or there wasn't.

53

His thoughts were like hooded torturers who kept thrusting the picture of Kovalsky before his lidless eyes. He could not stand it any more. He would turn his eyes away, he would force other memories to come up, he would take refuge in them—other memories, pleasant ones, healing, friendly, smiling memories. He would cover himself with them, like a man fleeing into a grove to protect himself from a blazing sun. With an immense effort he set himself to creating another panorama, beginning with the question: How was it, exactly, that I met Clara? How was it that the real upward slope of success began?

By sheer will power he succeeded. He saw himself in a train speeding along a lakeside—it was Lake Erie, his destination was Cleveland. Yes, it was a Friday again. He had an appointment the next morning with the head buyer of Kohn and Kohn, the department store. He was now one of the most successful salesmen employed by Salzman Brothers. His third year. And he had the exclusive rights to the Middle West. Salary and commission. But his ambition had only just been awakened. Kohn and Kohn were his biggest account. Why shouldn't he transfer the exclusive agency for the Middle West to Kohn and Kohn, and free himself for new areas? That was what he thought about as he sat in the Pullman and the train flew along the lakeside. He looked into the timetable, to check again on his arrival—and suddenly it flashed upon him that he had forgotten something. *Kaddish* for his father! He would get to Cleveland too late for a synagogue service. He would miss, for the first time, the sacred memorial prayer. This was the anniversary, the day for *Kaddish*. When he had gone up to Monticello for his father's funeral he had sworn to his mother that as long as he lived, as long as he lived, he would observe the anniversary, he would say *Kaddish* with a congregation of Jews. He had sworn that nothing would stand in the way; wherever he was, whatever he was doing, he would turn aside, enter a synagogue, and repeat the Mourner's Prayer. And here he was on the train, and he would get to Cleveland when all the services were over.

He had kept his word till now, often with difficulty. Now it was as if the Devil himself had taken a hand. He would get to Cleveland at nine-thirty, hopelessly late. What was to be done? He began to toy with the idea of missing *Kaddish* for once.

54

A fat lot of good it would do his father, wherever he was. Still, the old man would have liked it. Besides, there was his mother. He had sworn to her. He looked again into the timetable. The next stop was a little place called Lakeview. It would be half past six. A few minutes before sunset. They went to synagogue earlier in the little towns. Still, he would be in time for *Kaddish* toward the end of the services. Lakeview. He knew of the place but had never stopped there. About fifteen thousand inhabitants, rubber industry, an up-and-coming town. There was certainly a Jewish community, however small. And what about Kohn and Kohn? There was a later train, a milk train, starting out from Lakeview at midnight and getting into Cleveland at some ungodly morning hour. No Pullman. Well, it would have to be Lakeview. His samples had gone on ahead; he would pick them up in the morning. He would be very tired, not really fit for that important conference. "I'll miss it for once!" he decided. What harm would it do—just once? And then he reversed himself again. He would get off at Lakeview, come what might. And he did it, barely in time, clambering with his suitcase out of the train just as the doors were being closed.

He jumped into the station buggy. "Take me to the synagogue."

"Synagogue? What's that?"

"You know, the Jewish church."

"Never heard of one in this town. I'll take you to the Putnam Hotel. They'll know."

At the hotel he found out that he still had time to wash and change. The desk clerk, himself a Jew, told him that there was in fact no synagogue in Lakeview; but a quorum of ten Jews held services Friday nights in a rented room. The clerk was due for *Kaddish* too, in memory of his mother. He would take Grossman along.

They arrived in the midst of the prayers, in good time for the *Kaddish*. When the service was ended Grossman was about to leave, but was stopped at the door by an eldery Jew with a broad, smiling face, and a graying beard which spread over half his chest. The Jew held out his hand, and said *"Sholem Aleichem"* heartily, and almost without waiting for the response, asked: "What are you doing this evening?"

55

Grossman answered the question with a question: "Why do you ask?"

"Well, it's my guess you're waiting for the midnight train to Cleveland. Where do you reckon to spend the evening?"

"How do you know I'm waiting for the midnight to Cleveland?"

"Well now, what else would a stranger be doing in our little town? You've certainly got no business here."

"Right," said Grossman, and smiled in turn. "I got off the train here to say *Kaddish* for my father, God rest his soul. And I'm waiting for the midnight train."

"In that case you'd better come and wait in my home. You see, we have a family get-together Friday evenings. Don't be afraid of being bored. There'll be a young crowd."

Grossman stared, and could not overcome his astonishment.

"I'm a stranger here," he said, embarrassed, "and you're asking me to meet your family. You've never met me, you don't know who I am."

"Listen, Mr. Traveler, I wasn't born yesterday. A young man who breaks his journey here to say *Kaddish* for his father, knowing he'll have to sit up half the night in a milk train, is no stranger to me. Come along, you'll pass the time pleasantly."

When he came with his host into the commodious, brightly lit provincial home, he found the family assembled. There they were: Clara, who was to become his wife, Matilda, his sister-in-law to be, Harry her husband, with his comical little mustache, all the youngsters. The house was filled with happy laughter. He stood at the door, touched, shy, uneasy.

"Dora," the Jew sang out. "I've brought a guest, to taste your Sabbath cooking. What's your name? I forgot to ask your name."

"Grossman," he said, and then added apologetically to the company, "He made me come with him. I went to the synagogue to say *Kaddish,* and your father absolutely insisted on bringing me home. It's not my fault."

"Can you imagine, Dora? This young fellow got off to say *Kaddish* and he'll have to sit up all night for it. Here. Let me introduce you, Mr. Grossman. That's my wife, the busy lady over there, bless her; my daughters, Matilda, and Clara, and Reisel, and Rachel; and that's my son-in-law, Harry Schwartzkop."

"I hope you'll excuse me," stammered Grossman.

56

"Why, it's a Jewish custom," said the mother. "You meet a stranger, a wanderer, in the synagogue on a Friday evening, you bring him home for the Sabbath. Clara, make room next to you for Mr. Grossman."

He remembered little of the meal. All his memories were concentrated on the conversation—and on Clara. The first words she spoke to him, the beginning of their lifelong association, were:

"What are you doing in this part of the world?"

The first words—and something in her voice, an echo, a shading, went straight to his heart. A curious, sweet, birdlike quality. There was a suggestion of wings about her. Her voice carried an intimation of her quiet strength, the counterpoise to his type of energy, which made up their destiny.

He glanced at her hastily. She was not beautiful, at least according to his conscious taste. There was something unsettling at first in her big, dark eyes, in the openness and directness of her gaze; and against it there was reassurance and warmth in her smile—the first smile, it seemed to him, that he had received from a woman.

"I'm a traveling salesman," he said, awkwardly.

"From New York, I suppose."

"I'll bet two cents he's got an appointment with Kohn and Kohn tomorrow morning."

"How did you know?" asked Grossman, astounded. He looked round. "Your father seems to know everything about me. The moment he saw me in the synagogue he knew I was going to Cleveland."

"My husband likes to guess," said the mother. "He's been guessing all his life."

"And guessing right," put in Harry.

"There's no trick to it," said the father boisterously. "Did you ever hear of a traveling salesman going to Cleveland and having no business with Kohn and Kohn?"

"Well, your father's right. I'm seeing the head buyer tomorrow morning. I'm traveling for Salzman Brothers, New York. Children's clothes."

"Salzman? We've got their line. And who do you think supplies us? Kohn and Kohn," said the father.

"I'll do some guessing," cried Harry. "I'll bet that now Mr. Grossman will make Lakeview one of his regular stops, and sell us

57

direct. We're a growing town, Mr. Grossman. We doubled our population in the last two years."

Grossman nodded. "Tires," he said.

"Two factories, three shifts, all year round. There's a whole industrial section springing up. We'll need another movie house. And we'll need it fast, before someone else comes in."

"Harry has the movie house here," said the mother. "I don't suppose it's as big as those you have in New York. But it's big enough for us."

"I'll tell you what," said the father. "Take Mr. Grossman along tonight, Harry. You're all going, I suppose."

"Come with us, Mr. Grossman," said Harry. "There's a new picture every Friday evening. We're having a Western tonight."

"I don't want to miss my train," said Grossman.

"We'll look after that," said Clara.

He glanced at her again. She was wearing a black and white check dress with a small, embroidered white collar. Her hair was parted neatly. Her neck was long, and it seemed to him that the soft, musical, birdlike voice came out of her without disturbing her lips. Everything was grace and delicacy, but behind these an intimation of strength.

She added: "We always finish well before midnight. We'll take you to the train in the family buggy."

"You're terribly kind to me," he stammered.

And after the meal the whole crowd of youngsters tumbled out of the house, leaving only the two old folks.

"Dora," said Grossman's father-in-law to be (he himself had reported the conversation years later to Isaac Grossman), "I think that what happened with King Saul is going to happen with this young man."

"What happened to King Saul?"

"He went out to look for his father's lost asses, and he found a kingdom. This young man went out to say *Kaddish* and he found—"

She did not let him finish. "Bite your tongue off! You're always guessing."

"And I'm always guessing right."

CHAPTER SEVEN

THE rest of that evening was like a dream within a dream, an innermost area of memory which had its own character because he had conjured it up so often. The cinema—a converted barn, with huge doors opening outward—the garish electric lights—the shrill, multicolored posters—the crowds milling before the doors, young and old—and Clara near him always. Harry's voice, her voice, other voices—a double world in which there were two realities, the reality of Clara, the reality of the rest. Or rather, one reality, Clara's, beside which all the rest were unreal.

"Look," said Harry. "See that mob? Half of them won't get in. If I had two more places like this I could fill them both. They've got to have their amusement, it's just as important as bread."

The benches were so jammed that even the owner could not keep his party together. Isaac Grossman found himself separated with Clara, their bodies pressed against each other, around them a human mass as close-pressed, they a part of it, and yet not of it. He watched the screen and saw nothing. A tiny hand had crept into his huge fist, and through the contact flowed something that brought a thick beating into his heart. He had been born, he had grown up, he had become strong, for this moment, that the tiny hand might rest in his, assured, protected. And after a while—they did not know how or when it happened—her head was on his shoulder, and his arm was around her, and they were whispering to each other.

"When do you think you'll come back?"

"Come back? I don't want to go away."

She flashed a look at him in the half-darkness. He saw the white glimmer of her eyes, and the tenderness of the line of her lips. He was in love with her at once, as he was to remain forever after. He saw in the eyes and lips all the years of his happiness with her.

White glimmer of eyes, red line of the lips, tenderness, and a teasing playfulness.

"I don't even know your first name."

"Isaac."

"Your hand is so strong, Isaac."

"You say my name just the way my mother always says it."

"Your mother! How is she?"

"She's well now. She's been through a lot. My father was sick for many years. She looked after him and the children. She brought them up by herself. She lives in Monticello now, a little town in the Catskills, in New York. She has a little hotel. My two brothers are with her now."

In whispers she drew him out, pressed close to him in the mass of bodies.

"What was your father?"

"Worked in a sweatshop. Then he was sick a long time. You want to know everything, Clara? We've only just met."

"Have we? I feel as if I'd known you all my life. I feel as if I'd been waiting for you all my life."

It was incredible that she should feel exactly as he did. He could not speak for a while. And when they spoke again it was in this strange, unrestrained, unfaltering way, beyond all shyness and uncertainty.

A long, long time afterward the picture ended, the lights went on, the crowd rose, and they were back in this world. Harry came up to them. "Time to go," he said. "You'll find us in the car outside."

They lingered, paralyzed by the thought of leaving each other, and at last followed the stragglers.

"I don't want to leave you," he muttered, his voice dry.

"I don't want you to leave," she answered. "But I'll come with you to the station." And suddenly she said an astounding thing: "Will I see you again?"

"What?"

"Do you need me? You, with your strength. What will you do with me?"

"I—" he struggled for words, and said, oddly, "I will swallow you up." Then he caught himself. "No, I don't mean that."

"I want you to mean it."

They had reached a dark corner, and suddenly he turned, caught her to him, and pressed his lips to hers.

"Sweet!" she said, trembling.

They hurried out, and Harry began again with his enthusiastic prospects.

"What do you think, Mr. Grossman?"

"What?"

"About this cinema business."

"This cinema business? Yes, it's good. Certainly. You could have another two theaters here."

When they were seated in the buggy, and he had emerged from his trance, he asked, "What do you need, how much capital, to start a place like this?"

"Cash? Five thousand dollars, tops."

"Is that all?"

"You rent one of these barns, nothing down. You need the cash for fixing it up. You don't have to lay it all out, either. The bank'll go along with you."

The last moment on the platform. "Good-by, Mr. Schwartzkop, good-by, Mrs. Schwartzkop, good-by—" he could bring himself to call Clara by her name. "Thanks for everything. Many thanks."

He had been sure only of one thing—of Clara's place in his life. The rest? He had imagined nothing. A cinema in Lakeview, in Monticello, in Omaha, Nebraska—a chain across the country. That had not been in his thoughts at all. He had gone into the Lakeview venture for Clara's sake. The rest followed, of itself, once the model had been created. For it was always the same pattern. You always began small. You looked for rising little towns beginning to industrialize, little towns with empty lots. You drew in local capital, sometimes a bank, more often people you'd met in business.

It was pleasant to dream of those first steps, just as it was pleasant to remember the first kiss he had given Clara.

There had been great changes in the condition of the Grossman family since Isaac had gone to work for Salzman Brothers. After her husband's death a new life had begun for Mrs. Grossman. She stayed on in Monticello, still taking in boarders; but now a crushing burden had been removed, and she could attend, for the first time, to a business. She could give her boarders her full attention;

61

she could prepare their meals decently. Somehow, despite the poverty of her married years, she had caught the trick of cooking; her simplest dishes were a delight—her desserts of stewed carrots in honey, her stuffed chicken necks, her meat patties, her cheese blintzes; one would have thought she had never lacked the ingredients. Her name became a household word in Monticello, and each boarder recommended two others. Within a year after her husband's death she was having new rooms added to her house. Isaac lent her some money, and she got a little more from the local bank. The girls were now able to take a hand. Isaac felt that there were big possibilities in the boardinghouse. There was a large summer clientele of orthodox Jews in the Catskills; they liked good food, and they wanted it *kosher*. And mother became known in these circle as Shmaya Grossman's widow. That was the name she took, from that time on, for her house: "Grossman Widow's Kosher Home." Not long after, Isaac half persuaded, half bullied his two brothers into joining their mother, and then the firm became "Widow Grossman and Sons." Gabriel was already married; Sam, the Socialist, left his socialism and entered the partnership. The boardinghouse graduated into the hotel class. Instead of workers, there were shopkeepers and professionals as guests.

Isaac's affairs also prospered. He had learned early not to rush bullheaded at big earnings; he knew that the best investment was in friendships and a good reputation. He won the confidence of his customers by his genuine interest in their enterprises; he could seek out the weak side and suggest improvements without giving offense; sales were secondary, or rather they were the natural consequence of his attitude of concern, his knowledge of what a locality needed. He was willing to spend time, thought, and energy with his customers, and they learned to look on him as a kind of unofficial partner, as much concerned with their success as with his own.

On his second visit to Lakeview, when he timidly asked for Clara's hand, he brought with him twenty-five hundred dollars to invest in Harry's second theater. This was his first independent venture, the beginning of his career as a theater owner. From that moment he never looked back.

For further ventures he had the backing of Morris Kaplan, first vice-president of the State Bank, where he kept his money. One of the Salzman brothers had recommended him, with the words: "Keep an eye on this young man. He'll go far. He's got drive and initiative." And initiative was what he showed in his new venture. Whatever town he visited as a traveling salesman he now investigated with an eye to a cinema; and wherever the prospects were favorable he talked his customers into joining him. Shopkeepers who had never dreamed that they could do anything more than stand behind a counter discovered that there were other ways of making a living. Step by step, with the help of customers, some of them quite wealthy, others in moderate circumstances, but all of them convinced of his honesty and reliability, Isaac Grossman spread out his net of cinemas. Before long he had to leave the Salzmans and devote himself to the building up of the machinery of his theater concern. The times were with him. All he had to do was put in initiative and energy; America did the rest.

How much of that initiative did he owe to his love for Clara? He could not have answered that question. He only knew that she was an inextricable part of him, that her dominion over him was a necessity in his life. There was a profound joy in being dominated by her fragility, in acceding to her wishes in small matters as in great. The sound of his name on her lips never lost its magic power over him. To yield to her seemed to him a sign of his strength. And he understood best the place she had come to take in his life by her effect on his memory of Kovalsky. When he had told Rose that to be ashamed before himself was even bitterer than to be ashamed before others, he had referred in his mind to his wife. She had lifted him to a level which made the memory of the Kovalsky incident intolerable. It was inconceivable that he who was loved by this woman could carry the stain of such a repulsive act, that he had been able to steal from a wretched worker the few dollars he had saved up to marry his daughter off. Clara could not have such a husband. And Clara's son could not have such a father. And the higher he climbed the less conceivable it all became, the more intolerable. In the end restitution, which would have been an admission of the ugly misdeed, also became unthinkable. It would have meant, also, that he owed everything, his career, his life, his triumph, his happiness, to a piece of baseness, to the act of a pickpocket. It would appear that all he had could be traced back to this disgusting beginning, it was all built on this

63

foundation of meanness. That was an impossibility. The moment
he took that view his initiative and energy would disappear. And
so there was nothing for it but to uproot the wretched Kovalsky
from his mind, so that it would seem that no such man had ever
existed. There were a thousand ways of beginning a career, were
there not? It was not just a question of opportunity, for there were
thousands of opportunities, but of what you did with it. In this
respect he had nothing to reproach himself with.

And so, thinking back now, he saw that Rose was right, and he
blessed her for having put it that way, for having mentioned his
"debt." He had repaid the debt a hundredfold, he was still repaying it. And who, after all, was this Kovalsky, that he should
threaten the moral existence of Isaac Grossman? Some wandering
drunkard. That was it. A drunken vagabond. There were details
of that miserable encounter which he had not told Miss Rosenberg;
details which were really too sickening. When Kovalsky returned
from his fruitless search in Grand Street, he said, among other
things:

"I go jump in the river, I drown, I finish."

"Why?" asked Grossman, terrified.

"They no believe I lost money. My daughter say I get drunk.
She say her father get drunk, not come to wedding."

He spoke heavily, as though he had in fact been drinking.

"Maybe you're already drunk," called Grossman's employer.

"No, boss. I no drunk. I no drink today."

For one agonizing instant Isaac had wanted to snatch the wallet
out of the hanging suit, and throw it at the Pole. But it was too
late. He would certainly have lost his job. And the same instinct of
self-preservation had kept him from revealing the incident to anyone, or from revealing all of it even to Miss Rosenberg. He had not
told her, for instance, that he had conceived a deadly hatred for
Kovalsky, who had returned into his life from time to time to torment him, and to poison his happiness. For of course he had never
managed to uproot the memory. The man was forever there. And
since to annihilate him was impossible, he did the next best thing;
he annihilated the man's character. It was of a piece with Kovalsky's behavior that he should lose his money; it was proper, it was
fitting; he was just the kind of drunkard who would fail to turn up
at his daughter's wedding. He would have failed even without

64

Isaac Grossman. Hadn't the man said it himself—that his family considered him a drunkard? This last baseness, this destruction of Kovalsky's name and claim, was perhaps an even viler thing than the theft, and he had not been able to descend to that level of himself in confessing to Miss Rosenberg.

There were also other ways in which he tried to belittle the incident. Why was Kovalsky more important than the hundreds of other victims who strewed Isaac Grossman's path, as they strewed the path of every successful man? Those that break their way through the jungles of life come out scarred—but they leave scars on others. He had wounded and bruised God knew how many, far more severely than Kovalsky. Yet with respect to them his conscience was clear. Why should Kovalsky alone, of all of them, haunt him without remission, and embitter his last days?

CHAPTER EIGHT

HE was floating in darkness. He knew that actually he was lying in his stationary bed, but he felt that he was being carried from point to point of darkness. It was a kind of flight, a search for a point of refuge and security; and the motion was only in his memories, among which he sought justification; but the feeling was so vivid that it was imparted to his body.

He was among the memories of the Miami episode. He saw the city after the great crisis; not a city, but a ruin.

It was the development of the hotel in Monticello which had led him to Miami Beach. Mother's Kosher Home had become the best known orthodox resort in the area. She had established its reputation for good food, and for strict observation of the dietary laws. Gabriel, the pietist and man of learning, had added distinction to it. Sam, the modern member of the family, had catered to the young people, putting in a swimming pool and tennis courts. The place prospered and expanded, so that in the winter season mother and Isaac's two sisters could afford a vacation in Miami Beach. That was how the contact began. At first it was vacation and nothing more, a deserved rest after the strenuous summer. Later these hotelkeepers of the Catskills began to open hotels and boarding-houses and restaurants in Miami Beach. Very often they catered to the same clientele in both places, summers in the Catskills, winters in Miami Beach. It became an all-year-round business.

Those were the first years of the great prosperity, the days of the first World War, before America had entered it. The war industry was beginning to boom, and everywhere, in its wake, men were becoming wealthy. Dealers in junk who a little while before had been driving down country roads buying up rags or rusty iron from farm houses blossomed into big buyers and sellers of steel. Wool, leather, cotton, everything that could be turned into military

66

supplies, was in demand. The market was insatiable. But the big fever, the frenzy of prosperity, came, after a brief pause, in the years which followed the war. Those were the Coolidge days, the days when prosperity poured down like manna from heaven. Not only merchants and manufacturers, but workers and small shopkeepers were carried by that tide. Merchandise passed from hand to hand, becoming dearer in transit but never failing to find a consumer. The demand for luxuries became more and more insistent. Workers who had known no summer vacations except such as they had spent on the hot fire escapes of their tenements discovered that there were beaches, mountains, lakes, woods. The summer resort became the fashion; the winter resort was a close second. It was by no means only the upper economic levels which began to move in on golden Florida, and on the island which had been rescued from the sea, on Miami Beach, drained of its swamps and turned into the Land of Renewed Youth.

Finally the hysterical get-rich-quick stage was reached, the Florida real estate hysteria, and thousands of almost maniacally possessed speculators streamed into the peninsula, bringing with them their life's savings, certain that they would become millionaires overnight. Isaac Grossman put a restraining hand on his brothers. "You're not in the real estate business," he said. "You're in the hotel business." It was only when the crash came, when buyers lost their options or failed to meet a second or third payment, when the life savings of thousands were wiped out, that Isaac Grossman stepped in.

He came with cold cash to a city which was in ruins, which was indeed one single ruin. The skeletons of unfinished houses stood up starkly against the blue Florida sky. Many houses had risen no further than their foundations; some, with walls half erected, had been blown down by the great hurricane. Streets, in being or projected, were littered with bricks, steel girders, cement, hewn stones, tin, wire, beams. No one cast a second glance at these materials which, only a few days before, had been worth their weight in gold. People wandered bleakly among the heaps and ruins which now represented the totality of their possessions. Some had not even this to look at: only vacant lots, to which they had lost title. This had been their triumph, their hope, and the security of their latter years. They walked about with glazed, unbeliev-

67

ing eyes, like mourners in a cemetery in which the uncompleted houses were the fresh gravestones. They wandered about hungry, literally hungry, without the wherewithal for a decent meal.

Isaac Grossman bought up mortgages. The banks, anxious to unload their bad debts, accepted almost any bid. Grossman acquired seashore land, because there the hurricane had wrought the greatest havoc. "When *we* build here," he said, "we'll build solid. We'll be stronger than the sea."

He saw himself in his rented office. The millionaires of the day before, men with names, men who had lived in the finest sections of the city, stood before his desk. They came with their wives, their married children, with sons-in-law and daughters-in-law, pale, red-eyed, their hands trembling.

"You've got our life's savings for a tenth of their value," said one of them. "Our blood. You can't rob us like that. We have a right to a decent deal. You can't do this to us."

He looked at the man and answered him quietly, courteously, but within he was as hard as stone: "I've made my deal with the bank. I have no other responsibility, and nobody else has a claim on me. All I'm prepared to do is give you your fare home."

The ashen faces, which became even grayer at his words, swam around him in the darkness. Yes, he had taken their life's savings; he had left them hungry, naked, helpless. Had he not committed a greater crime against them than against Kovalsky?

It was this Florida deal which had given him his real lift, had placed him in the top class. That was when he had founded the firm of Grossman and Grossman. That was when he had begun to buy, with Kaplan's help, his chain of hotels. That was when Lazar had given up his studies at Columbia, to be taken into his father's business. Why, as he thought about it now, he could see that Kovalsky had nothing to do with it! Miami, not Kovalsky, had been his first real opportunity. Why this ridiculous preoccupation with Kovalsky? That unimportant start didn't count at all. If his conscience was going to bother him, Florida was the thing, not the Pole. The fortunes he had taken away from so many people were the real foundation of his wealth. This was Grossman and Grossman. What did it have to do with a forlorn little drunkard?

But the queer thing was that Florida had never been on his conscience. He had never felt a twinge of remorse because of those whom he had stripped in the Miami transactions. Miami had been a tremendous gamble. Everyone had gambled. If he had not bought up the mortgages, others would have. Had he gambled at the wrong time, had he bought during the hysteria, he would have been in the same position as his victims. Any one of them would have done to him what he had done to them.

He regretted nothing in connection with Miami; he regretted none of his other big transactions. He had followed the rules honorably, he had stayed within the law, he had administered, as he would have accepted against himself, the justice of the business world.

What was the good of fooling himself? Kovalsky had not been part of that game, had not been subject to its laws. He had robbed Kovalsky, stolen from him as if from a child, taken away his last penny, driven him to thoughts of suicide.

"God, help me," he muttered in the darkness through which he swam. "God, help me."

It was a long, long time since he had uttered such a prayer.

CHAPTER NINE

WHEN he came out of his bedroom the next morning Rose, who was waiting for him for breakfast, could not repress a visible start. He seemed to have aged ten years in that one night. His eyes were lightless, as if they had been squeezed up out of the flabby bags which hung under them. His cheeks were hollow, and his neck had gone stringy. He was trembling. When he lifted his cup of coffee he spilled the liquid on the tablecloth, and when he set it down it was with a rattle.

Rose made up her mind to do no more coaxing. She maintained a hard silence throughout breakfast, so that finally Grossman became uneasily aware of her displeasure. He looked at her several times, as if imploring her to comfort him. But she kept her eyes on her cup of tea, which she hardly tasted, and obstinately fought off his supplication.

"What's the matter?" he asked at last.

"Nothing."

"But something is the matter."

"Mr. Grossman, how is this thing going to end?" she asked sharply.

"I don't know what you mean."

"You know very well."

"How can I help myself?" he asked, desperately.

"How? By taking yourself in hand. You've got to stop indulging your moods."

He waited, hoping she would soften, but she said no more.

"What do you want me to do?" he asked, at last.

"If I tell you, will you do it?"

"Yes," he answered firmly. "I will do it."

"Then I'll tell you. First you must put this thing out of your mind for a month. It's out of the question for us to go up to

Springbrook before another month. Lazar simply won't understand why you should leave Florida for Connecticut at this time of the year. It won't make sense to him, and it doesn't make sense to anyone else. Do you want him to suspect that something queer is attached to your visit?"

Grossman shook his head.

"Is that clear?"

"It's clear, yes."

"I promise you we'll go up in April and do whatever's necessary. But until then you mustn't waste one moment thinking of the matter. You've waited so long, you can wait a month longer. Turn your mind away from that man. If you don't, you'll eat yourself up, you'll worry yourself into a breakdown."

"You're right."

"The second thing I want is to send you off to the races at Hialeah today. The Jacobsons—you know, the shirt people you sold that plot to in Jersey, for their factory—are having a lunch party at Hialeah. Lazar phoned them and asked them to take you along, and they'll be delighted. It's the big event of the season. It'll pull you out of yourself. There's a wonderful field today—Black Prince, Hurricane, My Kentucky, and lots more. There'll be millions bet on them. So you can put your couple of dollars with the bookmakers, too. What do you say, Mr. Grossman?"

"First-class idea," he said, with forced heartiness. "First-class. You're coming along, aren't you?"

"I will if you'll let me bet, too. I don't want to be an outsider."

"But you'll have to let me pick the horses."

She felt him struggling to put on a spirit of playfulness, and she tried to encourage him. "Here's my money—" she threw her handbag over. "And bring home the bacon, if you know what I mean."

"Don't need this. How much do you want to invest?"

"Fifty dollars."

"No, ma'am. Twenty-five's my limit—for the two of us. And we'll go fifty-fifty. Let's see now." He opened the handbag and rummaged inside. "Hey, what's this? One dollar, two, three— nothing but one-dollar bills—and not enough of those. Big-time gambler!"

"All right, I'll bet you haven't more in your own wallet, and if I don't give you any you won't be able to bet either."

71

"You're right at that, boss."

"Here, you look at the forms while I go out for a swim." And she threw him *The Racing Gazette.*

"Don't believe in those things," he said. And as she was going through the door he called out to her, "Did you say Lazar phoned the Jacobsons?"

"Sure. Why shouldn't he?"

"He's a good boy. Always thinking of his old father."

And Miss Rosenberg could not make up her mind whether it was said in all simplicity or ironically.

Not least among the amusements at Winter Paradise was the horse racing. "Amusement" is perhaps a misleading term; it was a serious, even a grim, occupation. One might have thought it was the livelihood of the guests. They began in the morning, when they turned first to the sports pages of the newspaper left at their doors, or to the racing bulletin which was deposited with it; and they talked about it throughout the day. They talked about it—men, women, and children—with immense seriousness, with exchanges of information, with canvassing of opinions, with comparisons of records. The genealogical table of every important horse was widely known; so was its history; so was the record of every prominent jockey. Children advised their parents, and parents were proud to take the advice of such intelligent and thoughtful children; and boasted to each other about the precocity and reliability of their offspring. The bookmakers' cabana on the hotel beach, with its announcement board and frequent reports, was always surrounded by an excited mob of half-naked enthusiasts who watched intently as the attendant chalked up the results streaming in telegraphically from various parts of the country.

This was not a peculiarity of Winter Paradise; it was a general feature of the Florida area. The season was in full tide. The North, from New York to Chicago, was in the last bitter grip of winter. Many cities were snowbound, and trains were stalled. Whoever had the means escaped from the inclement weather to the warmth and sunlight of southern Florida. Hotels, boardinghouses, and resorts were packed. Every other private house became a hostelry. And everywhere, in luxurious palace and humble home alike, they played the races. . . .

Hialeah Park, near Miami, was filled with an immense crowd drawn from every part of the United States and besprinkled with representatives from Cuba and Mexico. The air was tense with expectation, and the deep murmur that ascended to the skies was compounded of anxiety and hope. Notes and impressions were exchanged, the latest rumors concerning the conditions of the favorites and the leading jockeys, tips that came direct from the stables, remarks attributed to famous trainers. The box in which the Jacobsons were giving their luncheon party was a special focus of excitement, for some of the young men were obviously important experts, and there was a constant coming and going of bookies and trainers, and of acquaintances who were looking for inside information. Grossman was making a gallant attempt to simulate interest; he pretended to listen earnestly to the advice which was generously showered on him, he made notes, he discussed odds; but it was obvious that his heart was not in it. Miss Rosenberg was chagrined and alarmed; he was not living up to his bargain with her. She was particularly disturbed when, shortly before the principal race, Grossman made a polite excuse and withdrew from the box.

He had yielded to a sudden impulse to get a closer look at the horses which were to run in the principal race. He could not have explained the impulse; and he could not have explained why he did not resist it. He pushed his way through the crowds to the row of stalls, and went from window to window, fascinated all at once by the sight of the high-strung animals. They were alert, filled with anticipation, restless with the premonition of competition, and bursting with explosive vitality. One of them, however, not among the favorites, attracted his attention by its contrast with the others. It was a brown animal, with a large white asterisk on its forehead, and white hocks. It did not prance like the others, it was not aquiver with impatience, it did not twitch. It stood there tranquilly, its long muzzle steeped, one would have said, in meditation. The brown eyes were sad, but determined. It seemed to be concentrating in its own way, a more conscious and responsible way, on the forthcoming contest, as if aware of the obligation it had toward its owner. Grossman could not take his eyes off the animal; and while he stared the animal turned slightly and looked back full at him; and Grossman had the strange feeling that it was addressing itself to him, communicating with him. He felt an incomprehensible sympathy for the dumb creature, and what was more, a kind of understanding. It was as if there was a personal relationship between them, between him, Isaac Grossman, and a being which had been transformed into a horse. The number on the jockey's blouse was seven, the color was yellow. Grossman went up to the bookmaker's window and put all his day's gambling money on the horse, making an inward note: Number 7, yellow, white hocks. He returned to the box in time to see the start.

The race began with a throb, followed by a brief lull. As the horses separated out the excitement began to rise, and Grossman was inundated by a torrent of sound and motion. About him men and women shouted, gesticulated, hopped up and down, called out to the horses as if their voices would really carry across the field and be heard by the animals: "Come on, Blackie! Hurry up, Virginia!" Grossman was silent and motionless. He followed with his field glasses the flight of the yellow blouse and the white hocks; now they were lost in a swirl of bodies and dust, now they emerged to his view. The excitement which gripped him was very different from that which found expression in the yelling crowds about him. There was something deeply personal, intimate almost, in his interest. Before he was aware of it, he was clenching his teeth, and a light sweat had broken out on his forehead. Seven was in third place, behind two favorites, Three and Five. Seven was apparently saving himself, holding off; it was quite clear—at least to Grossman—that Seven could have put on more power and have drawn alongside or even ahead of Five, but chose instead to bide his time. This restraint cost Seven his place as third, for at the curve Eleven, one of the favorites, suddenly drew ahead of him, amidst a roar of approval from all over the field. Now Seven, aware of having waited too long, and perhaps provoked by the triumphant shout of Eleven's backers, flung himself ahead, cutting through the dust like a light boat through water, shot past Eleven and came almost alongside Five. Again, another effort, a smooth, rocking forward thrust, and he was a neck behind Five. Now Seven was giving all he had; his hoofs skimmed rather than touched the ground, neck and flanks were almost in a straight line. It was too late. As Seven distanced Five, Eleven glided past both, drew up to Three, and

74

inched past him as they came to the tape. Grossman's Seven finished up third.

Grossman wiped the perspiration from his forehead, looked around at his fellow guests in Jacobson's box, and smiled apologetically:

"Well, he came in third, didn't he?"

"Third? Is that what you backed? Fortune? Why he's a complete outsider," said one of the young experts contemptuously, offended that Grossman had not listened to his advice, and pleased to see the offender fittingly punished.

Everyone else was astonished at Grossman's choice.

"Mr. Grossman has his private sources of information," said Miss Rosenberg, delighted to see her employer so absorbed after all.

"Come, Rose, we'll pay him a visit," said Grossman.

"Pay whom a visit?"

"Fortune, our favorite. I had no idea he had such an interesting name. I think he did everything that could be expected of him, don't you?"

"He's cost me all my gambling money, all my savings," grumbled Miss Rosenberg.

"He'll make it good someday, take my word for it. Let's go and cheer him up. He needs it."

In the stable court boys were rubbing the horses down under the supervision of the trainers. The sweat still poured down the bronze flanks, and the animals still panted with the anguish of their effort. A happy group was assembled around the winner and his owner, congratulating him and the jockey; there was a smaller group around Three, the runner-up. Fortune stood on one side, attended by two boys who plied cloths and brushes under the eyes of the trainer and the owner. The latter was a young dandy in typical Miami Beach costume—a motley silk shirt, red slacks, and a kerchief with weird African designs round his neck. He was talking disgustedly to the trainer, a little man with a brown, wrinkled face, who kept stroking and soothing the horse. It was clear from the look on the owner's face that he had an extremely low opinion of Number Seven. Fortune was drenched in sweat, like all his competitors, and the hide twitched spasmodically on his massive body. But his long, equine face was still earnest and

75

meditative, as it had been before the race. Again it seemed to Grossman that the horse was trying to convey something to him; the humble, supplicating animal eyes seemed to be saying "Thank you for your sympathy, for your good thoughts. Forgive me if I didn't live up to your expectations. I did everything in my power. I gave all I had. I'm not a wonder-horse. I'm not one of those fiery space-eaters. I just gallop as hard as I can." Grossman talked back in the spirit: "But still, you see, with your decent gallop you did achieve something, you did come in third."

"You're eying that nag as if you'd like to buy it," said the owner suddenly, only half in jest.

"My son might be interested," said Grossman, "but not me. It's not my line. I only bet on him."

"Now what made you do a thing like that?"

"He looks like an honest horse to me."

"An honest horse?" asked the owner, astonished. "What kind of a horse is that?"

"He isn't one of those wonder-horses, those show-offs and fire-eaters. He does an honest job, the best he can."

"And what good does that do me if he doesn't win? Let him be a show-off, if that's what wins races."

Something in Grossman made him want to answer sharply, but Miss Rosenberg sensed his mood and feared a passage between the two men. She tugged at Grossman's sleeve. "Come on, they're waiting for us."

"That halfwit doesn't keep horses for sport, but for exploitation," muttered Grossman. "Quick returns—that's what he wants. The people who own horses nowadays!"

His momentary good humor had dissipated. He went back to the Jacobson box to thank his hosts, and left quickly with Miss Rosenberg before the traffic jam began. All the way home he wondered darkly at the queer, confused notion that the horse meant something special to him, that he was in some way close to it, that he was not unlike a horse himself.

CHAPTER TEN

THESE alternations of mood persisted, and his nights were a
torment. Sleeplessness was no longer merely the absence of sleep,
a negative thing; it had become an affirmation, an authority which
had stretched out its hand over him. During the day he was his
own master, and could make his will prevail; could control his
thoughts, and present whatever front he chose. He could pick out
an undesired thought as one might pick out a faulty grain of wheat
from between the millstones, and throw it away. But in the night
it was that new authority which took over and chose his thoughts;
it also sat in judgment on him, and demanded an accounting from
him for whatever was false in his life. So he would lie and ask
himself everlastingly what it was that had prevented him from
straightening out the great error, and he reviewed in hot fantasy
phase after phase of the past.

Hunger and poverty had eaten into his bones, and had remained
part of him long after his childhood years. It is said that men who
have passed through one long famine never shake off the inner
effects. So it was with the hunger of Grossman's childhood, and
the poverty of his mother's home. On the surface it was only a
far-off memory; underneath it was an integral part of him. It
manifested itself in an incurable fear for his material security
on earth. Fear of the morrow accompanied him into affluence;
it did not diminish, it grew with his increased possessions; and
with this increase had come the step by step alienation from his
family.

In the very midst of his triumphs his fears became stronger.
The opportunity which had offered itself in the Florida crash had
its reverse side. He was by then the owner of a string of theaters;
he had been able to step in and buy up the ruins of other people's
lives. But by that very token, by the very memory which he

77

carried away of yesterday's "millionaires" coming to him for railroad tickets to be able to return home, by that very token he knew the insecurity of his own position.

And the extraordinary thing was that Clara, with all her physical frailty, walked through life as upon a massive iron bridge. Calm, untroubled, she accepted everything as her natural right, as though she knew that it had been prepared for her, and that more would follow with the same tacit certainty. Where had she acquired this self-assurance, this aristocratic balance? Where had she learned to manage her big city life with such grace and decision? Perhaps she had dreamed of all these things in her little home town, had prepared herself by a sort of mental rehearsal. She was always far ahead of him; she occupied his positions for him in advance. It was she who had taken the big apartment on Riverside Drive—almost without consulting him—when they had returned to New York after the wedding. The rent alone was about a third of his income. When he hinted that he was only a traveling salesman—it was no more than a hint, a subdued murmur, an embarrassed smile—she had answered him frankly, openly, not hinting, or murmuring, or smiling in embarrassment, but with sweetness and assurance: "My darling, do you think you're going to remain a traveling salesman all the days of your life?" But of course she was right, and he knew it. For he himself foresaw better things; and when the number of his movie theaters made it inevitable that he should leave the Salzman brothers, he knew that not only had Clara been right but that her attitude had been no little factor in his advance. She had furnished the large apartment with taste, and she played the hostess in a manner which left a profound impression on his business acquaintances. They, and their wives, felt it a privilege to be invited to the cocktail parties in the Grossman home. And he did not cease to marvel at her bearing, her tact, her grace, her way of putting guests at their ease, her way of handling the help in the house. She was to the manner born.

A friendship sprang up between the Grossmans and the Kaplans. Hitherto Morris Kaplan, vice-president of the State Bank, had been Grossman's patronizing superior; now the women brought the men together. Clara and Mrs. Kaplan were active members of the sisterhood of Temple Jeshurun, which was then

78

under the leadership of the brilliant young Rabbi Dr. Ornstein, already well known for his progressive ideas. Membership in this reform Temple was not Isaac Grossman's idea of participation in Jewish religious life. He joined for Clara's sake, and she joined for the sake of the charitable and cultural activities, the lectures, concerts and amateur dramatics. Around Clara and Mrs. Kaplan were grouped the wives of the most prominent members of the Temple, leading Jewish families of New York. These were people whom Isaac Grossman would never have dreamed of having as his friends.

If it was the hidden hunger, the unrealized fear, that drove him in the first instance, the second force which came to increase his success was Clara's ambition. But Clara's ambition meant a division of his life between past and present; every advance meant a more decisive interval between himself and his family. That which he had been before he met his wife, and that which was now, had less and less to do with each other. They ceased, as it were, to be on speaking terms.

There were specific causes as well as general reasons. There was for instance the question of *kosher* food. Isaac's mother stopped coming to his house because she did not dare to take as much as a drink of water there. How did she know what had been done with the various dishes, and even with a glass, whether it had not contained some forbidden fat, whether it had not been contaminated and never purified? Grossman himself found it difficult to accustom himself to the non-Jewish type of cooking which Clara, in spite of her Jewish home surroundings, introduced from the beginning. He found the dishes flat and unappetizing. He would sneak away occasionally to an East Side restaurant and refresh himself with a really Jewish meal, *kosher* and tasty. Clara did not like that, and so he strove to adapt himself to her in the matter of food too; but it was a long time before he became half-way reconciled to the un-*kosher* cooking, and to pork. Meanwhile her persistence drove away his mother; Gabriel too could not taste anything in the house; and for Gabriel's sake, and mother's, Sam too stopped coming to the house. And this was what Clara had wanted.

When his mother's boardinghouse in the Catskills was transformed into a flourishing hotel, and she had added the hotel in

79

Miami, she wanted her youngest son to join her in business, together with his two brothers. She wanted to hold the family together, around herself. Also, she was frightened by Isaac's daring. "Those theaters of yours, here, there, everywhere, they make me dizzy," she said. "You don't have to swallow up the whole world. You'll never eat two suppers on the same day." She was concerned, too, for her grandson Lazar, who was being brought up without any Jewishness, did not even learn to say a Jewish prayer, and was encouraged to find his friendships among non-Jewish children. Clara sent little Lazar to private school—she could not bear the thought of public schools. Old Mrs. Grossman had nightmares of Lazar growing up into—God forbid—apostasy. She thought that if Isaac could only be persuaded to come into the family business, the general effect would be to keep the child, too, in a Jewish world. But to Clara it was as if Mrs. Grossman was asking Isaac to go back to the pickles and tomatoes of Essex Street, taking her and the child with him. And even Isaac smiled at his mother's naïveté. The break became decisive when Clara bought a house in a gentile section of New Rochelle. She said to her husband that New York was no place in which to bring up their little son—a remark which Isaac did not understand, but did not challenge.

Clara did not want to have a second child, and Lazar grew up without brother or sister. There was a certain time when the older Mrs. Grossman went back to New York and lived there between seasons; Isaac occasionally took the youngster to see her. Although he was a member of Temple Jeshurun, he never set foot in the place. He prayed twice a year, once when he had to say *Kaddish* for his father—his mother never failed to remind him with a telephone call when the day approached—and once at *Kol Nidre* on the eve of Yom Kippur. But then he went to an orthodox synagogue on the East Side, which Gabriel attended. It was supposed to be, in spite of expansion and chance of locale, his father's synagogue, and Isaac Grossman was a generous contributor to its funds. Sometimes he would come to his mother's house on important festivals, taking Lazar with him. There the family would be assembled for the eve of the Passover, which Gabriel would celebrate with all the ritualistic details of a Chassidic believer; there it would also be assembled on the New Year. Now and then

80

Isaac would not wait for the excuse of a special occasion, and would drop in at his mother's house on a Saturday night. The youngster had a vague notion about his father's family, and understood that somehow this was his father's origin. When the younger Grossmans moved to New Rochelle, this contact was broken, and little Lazar forgot his grandmother and his uncles and aunts. He grew away from them—and at the same time he grew away from his own father, too. There was nothing in common in their origins, and next to nothing in common anywhere else. They could only exchange perfunctory remarks about something in the newspaper, or about a baseball game—the kind of remarks that might have passed between the most casual acquaintances.

Very early Lazar began to display the characteristics of his mother—an instinctive urge to social advancement, and the capacity to achieve it. He had no inclination to make friends with youngsters who came from "lower" circles; he was drawn, one would have said by instinct, to families of wealth and standing. He made efforts to be worthy of "good" friends, to acquire a sort of distinction. His bearing, and his athletic physique, were natural aids; he loved sports; he had excellent taste in clothes, and even as a child could distinguish between the flashy and the discreetly attractive. He was given the privilege at an early age of choosing his own suits, and he always went to the best tailors; at a comparatively early age, too, he was given, at his mother's insistence, a car. He had from his mother a natural tact in dealing with older people; and his friendly smile came from feeling, not from pretense. He was warmly welcomed by the parents of his friends, and often he chose these among non-Jews who, if their attitude toward Jews generally was hostile, found Lazar Grossman a winning exception. But Lazar was accustomed to think of himself as an exception. He belonged to sport clubs in which he was the only Jew. His gentile friends, visiting his home and received warmly and graciously by his mother, did not feel that there was anything different, anything Jewish, there; it was an American home like any other.

It was when they moved to New Rochelle that Clara was at last able to manage things completely after her own heart, and she created a home in which the owner felt himself more and more a stranger. There were times when it seemed to him that not only the distinguished guests, but his wife and son, had a curious, off-handed, perhaps even snobbish attitude toward him. His surroundings became more and more remote from him. Clara spent large sums on the remodeling, adding a large veranda and converting the place into a replica of a Colonial home. She engaged a famous interior decorator, a woman who was all the rage at that time, and replaced all her New York furniture, which had been in the Spanish style, with the Colonial. All the pieces—acquired for the decorator by a Jewish firm of Boston—belonged to the late eighteenth century; it was, and looked, costly.

Clara also developed a passion for French modern paintings, and spent enormous sums on Matisses, Monets and Degas. She also went in for the younger schools—Picasso and his contemporaries. The latter was just coming into his own. When Isaac stared at the bills, she advised him that the paintings were, among other things, first-class investments; everybody with any knowledge of such matters would tell him so. And "everybody," meaning the art dealers, did indeed tell him so. The Grossman house in New Rochelle acquired a reputation. Pictures of the drawing room, with its Matisses and Picassos, and with its magnificent, carved balustrade, appeared in journals dealing with the decorative arts. It became also the most distinguished social symbol of New Rochelle. Here the rabbi of the Temple met the minister of the Congregationalist Church, a nationally known liberal. Clara was a member of the Temple Sisterhood and of the Women's Auxiliary of the Unitarian Church. She was active in the Community Chest and in the Jewish Philanthropies. She even stormed the citadel of the Harmony Country Club, the members of which, German Jews, were more snobbish toward the East European Jews than many exclusive Christian circles. There were soirees in the Grossman house which were open only to small cliques—the leading families of the vicinity, nationally known in financial circles.

More remarkable than her gift in such matters was her energy. Grossman wondered over both. She grew more frail with the passing years. She often had to spend whole days in her bed. But there were two telephones at her bedside, and the maid was there to hand them to her. She would call up the secretary of the organization which was arranging the garden party for the Nirenbergs for the benefit of the Children's Home, and go over the list of the guests;

she would revise, remove, add. On the other telephone Monsignor Macray was waiting to consult her about the drive for St. Joseph's Hospital. There would follow a half-hour talk with Mrs. Sanders about her daughter's debut; and here was a request from someone else—would Mrs. Grossman kindly call back about a very important matter, which turned out to be the question of the proper dress at the social event of the season. So it went, hour after hour; and in the evening Clara would come down to dinner, to meet the handful of carefully chosen guests.

Her simple dinner dress was made by the most expensive fashion house in New York; a single string of pearls shimmered on her albaster-white throat; her black hair was drawn back, and parted in the middle; her little slippers peeped out under the folds of her dress, in the manner of a Goya portrait; and all was lightness and graceful motion, as if in her delicate veins flowed not blood but a rarefied quicksilver. They were waiting for her as for some celebrity, and her entry filled the room. She smiled out of her lively black eyes at a giant of a man who seemed to melt at her glance, while she held out her hand to be kissed by another guest. Here she called to one side one of the younger women, to whisper some advice to her, and here she was introducing another to a professor of music, or a Congressman, or a Senator. There was always some distinguished person to surprise her regular guests. She had a style and skill all her own, and there was rarely a dinner in the Grossman home which was not the talk of the vicinity for many days after.

And amidst all this distinction Isaac Grossman felt himself an alien. In his own home, at his own table, he looked about him and wondered what he was doing there. It was not the irksomeness and stiffness of the discipline imposed on him by Clara, who insisted that he dress for dinner whether or not there were guests. It was not a feeling of inferiority in the presence even of the wealthiest and most distinguished of their guests—the merchants, bankers, lawyers, churchmen and politicians. He knew his own worth, and was prepared to stack it against anyone's. They, for the most part, were indebted to the good luck of being born in well-to-do families for their advantageous start in life. He had no one to thank for his success. Without money, without prestige, and without education, he had arrived where he was. Nor did he feel any inferiority of character. If he was aware of a touch of snobbery here and there, that did not disturb him. On the whole he knew he merited—whether he obtained it or not—the respect of these men and women. It was true that now and then he displayed a lack of polish, but that was in minor matters. He had balance, independence, tact; he was never flustered or taken off his feet. No, his feeling of alienation sprang from the form his life had taken. He had brought with him out of the wretchedness of his childhood an imperious demand for security. At bottom, the demand was a modest one, and if his furious energies more than met the demand, and he had more than security, that was irrelevant.

But something had happened: in the successful flight from insecurity he had cut his own life into two parts, he had severed the connection with his own past, with everything that he had regarded as right, and becoming, and proper, in the setting of his childhood world. His wife and son were moving with ever increasing speed away from the world he had known, and he was dragging himself after them. Like almost all men who have known want and upon whom hunger had set its mark, Isaac Grossman had a natural fellow-feeling for the underdog; it was a native impulse with him to stretch out a hand to the suffering. He did not become a Socialist, like his brother Sam. His mind did not work that way. His reactions were more primal; he could not think the matter through. He did not brood on it. He was too occupied with himself to go into the needs of others systematically. He only knew that his sympathies were with the poor, not with the rich. He went so far as to contribute to the funds of socialist and radical groups on the East Side, and it was known that Isaac Grossman was a "sympathizer." Party representatives called on him occasionally. First they approached him through Sam, who, though he had become part owner of a *kosher* hotel in the Catskills, had never divorced himself entirely from his socialist past. Later they came to him direct, and he never sent them away empty-handed. Nor were they the only ones. There was the synagogue; there were other orthodox institutions. He had struggled to overcome the handicaps of his East Side childhood, but there was a feeling of home attached to it nevertheless; and the richer he became, the greater the separation from the East Side created for him by his family, the more he remembered it with nostalgia, the more he felt the need to maintain some link with it.

At a certain time in his career, when he was withdrawing from his theater enterprises to concentrate on hotels and real estate, he had even played with a housing project for the low income groups. He remembered the apartment in Essex Street, and he knew, he remembered bitterly, what a disproportionate part of their income the poor expend on rent for their wretched quarters. He remembered the miserable corridor apartments, the half-ruined structures, the firetraps, the rooms without light and air, without toilets, the rat-infested, insect-ridden homes of the poor. The project came to nothing; he was pulled along in venture after venture; here, as in his private life, the process he had begun had become his master. Momentum carried him now, not original purpose. Only from time to time did he remember this project, always with a feeling of frustration, always with the dim belief that someday he would reach a goal, *his* goal, and then he would do the things he had neglected and follow his heart's desire.

In the meantime he was the prisoner of the forces he had set in motion, forces which he could not fight. Often he had to listen, in his own home, at his own table, to sentiments which outraged his inmost feelings. Observations were made about the world he came from, his East Side, his flesh and blood, the poor, the workers, the radicals, which froze him into speechlessness, so that the most fitting thing would have been for him to get up and walk out on his guests. Hot fury coursed through his veins—but he kept his peace, always.

Or almost always. For there was at least one occasion when it became too much for him.

It was the time of the great prosperity in America—the prosperity which, President Coolidge assured the country, had come to stay. It was the time of the great financial and moral inflation. Half of America was buying and selling on the stock market. In the shops and factories the talk was all of stocks, bonds, dividends, Wall Street, and profits. Shopgirls, machinists, cap-makers, waterproofers, gambled their savings—and as much more as they could borrow—on the market. It seemed to many of them downright foolish to work for a living when a day's winnings in Wall Street amounted to more than a week's wages. And suddenly, without warning, like a bolt from the blue, the crash came.

The catastrophe began with the collapse of one of the largest banks in Wall Street—a Jewish bank. Its stockholders and depositors were all Jews. This bank had originally been started as a semiphilanthropic public service. In the days of the great Jewish immigration many little banks had sprung up on the East Side, founded by stockbrokers and speculators. They were intended to serve the Jewish immigrants, transmitting money for them to their relatives in Europe and giving them the opportunity to buy ships' tickets on the installment plan. Free from all government supervision, these banks would often fold up and disappear as mysteriously as they had sprung up. One day the depositors would arrive as usual with their week's savings, only to find the doors locked and the windows shuttered behind the screaming placards, in English and Yiddish: WE WILL SEND YOUR MONEY FOR YOU TO EUROPE. The East Side needed a solid and reliable financial institution, and as such this bank was founded by one who was himself an immigrant who enlisted the support of Wall Street bankers and the Jewish press.

The affairs of the bank prospered mightily along with the rest of the country. It ceased in time to be a service to immigrants and became a general financial instrument for rising Jewish manufacturers. In the Coolidge era it had achieved a dizzy place among the most spectacular successes, and its shares were selling at many times their justifiable value. Deposits amounted to hundreds of millions, and its turnover to billions. Vast numbers of New York Jews had deposited or invested their entire possessions with the bank—that is, their future, their old age security, the dowries of daughters, and the provision for widows.

And on a certain day rumors began to circulate, and crowds began to assemble before the doors: men, women, children, manufacturers, merchants, workers, shopkeepers, newspapermen, actors. It was an outpouring from every class and every level of New York, eddying in stormy pools at the doors of every branch of the bank. And before long they found the doors locked, the windows shuttered, just as, not many years before, they had found the doors and windows of the fly-by-night immigrants banks locked and shuttered. But there were no screaming placards on the win-

86

dows: WE WILL SEND YOUR MONEY FOR YOU TO EUROPE. There was only the dignified, discreet bronze plaque with the proud name of the bankrupt institution: BANK OF THE UNITED STATES.

At one of Clara Grossman's dinners, in the superb dining room decorated with the costly works of French painting and the rare flowers grown in the Grossman conservatory, a few guests— among them two or three younger Wall Street men and their wives—discussed the day's affairs; namely, the failure of the Bank, the universal theme of conversation. Heartrending stories were told of individual tragedies. One girl, for instance, had taken poison on the very doorstep of the Bank: another depositor had blown his brains out—and so on, and so on.

Mark Nirenberg, son of the founder of the Wall Street firm of that name, recounted, at the end of the meal, the story of a conference called by a group of Wall Street bankers for the purpose of pulling The Bank of the United States through. The extent of the great crash was not yet appreciated; and it seemed to many that by stemming the rush on this one institution they could do something to avert the bankruptcy of thousands of small firms, and the ruining of thousands of individuals, thereby stemming a rush on all the banks. In particular it was the garment industry which was threatened. It seemed that the affairs of the Bank were not hopeless, and that with some good will they could be brought in order. Certainly the deposits of the little people could be assured, and their infectious panic quieted. It appeared, in fact, that some such action was practically agreed on, when one of the bankers— he was not named, but it was known that he was an aristocrat of the old school, filled with the pride of his family's standing in the "old country," to wit, Germany—had taken the floor:

"For my part, gentlemen, I think it serves the East Siders right. Every shoemaker and tailor has become a Wall Street speculator, buys and sells stocks, and this is what has brought chaos into the market. They themselves are responsible for the crisis, and it's time they learned their lesson, and their proper place. Workers belong to the factory, not to Wall Street."

"These few words were enough to decide the fate of the Bank. The meeting broke up without taking action," ended young Nirenberg.

"I'm in thorough agreement with that view; I haven't the honor of knowing who the gentleman quoted is, but my opinions are his. It was a sound, realistic approach. That bankruptcy will turn out for the best; it will clear the air, and put a stop to the speculative craze on the East Side," said another of the guests, an elderly man with a white carnation in his buttonhole, and a general perfume of Eau de Cologne about him.

"I myself can't quite see why shoemakers and tailors haven't the same right to speculate in Wall Street as bankers and financiers," said Isaac Grossman, quietly. "Isn't America the land of private initiative and equality of opportunity? None of us here came over on the Mayflower, I take it. My father, too, was one of the East Side tailors. It's true that he didn't speculate in Wall Street; he got tuberculosis, instead. That was his reward. But as it happens, my father's tuberculosis led to our first family venture. You'll wonder how, no doubt. My mother had to open a little boardinghouse in Monticello, so that my father could get the fresh air of the country. That was the beginning of the Widow Grossman's hotels in the Catskills and Florida. And that is American equality of opportunity. It seems to me that it would be much more proper to take away the privilege of speculating in Wall Street not from the tailors and shoemakers, but from the big financier just quoted—that is, if he has been quoted correctly. And do you know why? Because he doesn't belong to us, to America. With those reactionary ideas he belongs over there, where he comes from, he belongs to Germany."

Grossman did not seem to notice the silence which had fallen on his guests. He went on playing with his fork, and continued in the same quiet tone:

"If that aristocratic financier and philanthropist who was so anxious to teach the shoemakers and tailors of the East Side a lesson is the gentleman I have in mind, I can assure you, my friends, that he knew enough to sell betimes the shares of The Bank of the United States which he had taken over from his predecessor. He sold them on the open market, at the highest price, before he came with his excellent counsel to the conference. And that was what every member of his financial group did. It wouldn't be inaccurate to say that a considerable part of the possessions of those poor shoemakers and tailors who are now storming the doors of the bank found its way into the pockets of the lofty dispensers of good advice. I have heard more than one report to that effect."

Clara said nothing to her husband when the guests were gone. She did not become hysterical, she was not seized with spasms. But in the middle of the night she had a heart attack, and Isaac sat at her bedside through the night while she hovered between life and death.

CHAPTER ELEVEN

SHE came to slowly, very slowly, under the treatment of their family doctor. Isaac Grossman was shattered by the experience. He displayed, throughout those weeks, a tenderness and sensitivity which no business acquaintance would ever have suspected in him. He went late to the office—some days not at all—and returned early; he spent all his waking hours at her bedside. He had Dr. Markowitch bring in the leading specialists, and he kept a relay of three nurses. When Clara was out of danger and on the way to recovery, he still left the house reluctantly, and every half hour he telephoned home for a report.

That attack brought a change into Clara's life. In some manner it quieted her, took the edge off her social activity. She undertook less; her dinner parties became smaller; she withdrew gradually into a limited circle of friends. And she found a new interest—literature. She read a great deal.

Grossman thought only of her happiness, and was forever seeking ways of pleasing her. He knew that she loved roses of flaming colors, so he arranged with a florist to have a bouquet delivered every morning, with all shades of red, coral, carmine, crimson. One day he had an inspiration: he would surprise Clara with a rose garden. It so happened that a vacant lot next to his house was put up for sale. He bought it secretly, and without saying a word to Clara hired a gardener to plant a rose garden there; moreover, he promised him a large bonus if he could produce a new variety, which would be named the Clara.

This outpouring of his was not caused by any feeling of guilt toward his wife. It sprang from a profound love. He realized again how much he was in love with her. It was a deep physical love. Her frail, marmoreal-white elastic body, her slender throat which always moved him to compassion, her singing voice, awakened and sated his desire. Those eyes which, despite her dominion over him, always expressed timidity—but was it not this timidity which was her dominion?—appealed to him with a kind of sadness; and in that mournful shrinking from his strength there was a tender provocation, and the deepest satisfaction.

Rose Rosenberg, who had now been Grossman's secretary for several years, was a little jealous of her employer's wife; but it was a sweet jealousy which stilled in some measure the repressed, the scarcely acknowledged love which she felt for him. She understood well his fidelity to Clara, the unforced exclusion of all other women from his life; and herself beginning to take on the characteristics of an old maid, she found a romantic pleasure in the picture. She was happy to give it her own touches. She reminded him to call Clara whenever, pulled along in some exacting transaction, he had forgotten to do so; she also knew when to call the bedside number, and when to use the downstairs telephone in case Mrs. Grossman was resting. She arranged matters so that Grossman could get away early; she helped him to choose flowers for his wife. She wanted to keep alive and alert the love of one who, she felt, was better and luckier than herself. And Grossman was dimly aware of this play of emotions, and was glad that Miss Rosenberg had this secret source of muted happiness.

It was not long after Clara's recovery that he came home quite early, and entering, called out: "Clara, where are you?" He thought he had lowered his voice, but apparently it had been louder than he intended, for when he entered the living room he saw her lying on the couch, her wide eyes fluttering as if with fear, like a bird that had been frightened in its nest. He forgot what it was that he had wanted to tell her; he could only stammer, with a woebegone expression on his face, "I frightened you, Clara!"

"Darling," she murmured, "you came in so suddenly. I didn't expect you yet. Come, sit down near me."

It seemed to him that he could have picked her up in his huge hands and made a single mouthful of her. He was afraid to sit too close; his very proximity was crushing. He stretched out his hand to caress her frail shoulder under its light shawl of black silk, but he refrained, from the same fear; his hands were like the paws of a huge bear. But she, as if she had read his thoughts, stretched out her hand to his.

"How was it in the office today? Hard?"

"So-so. And how was it here at home?"

"So-so." She smiled. "I was in the garden a little while, I read a bit, I listened a bit to music." Then suddenly her face became serious. "Isaac, I have something to tell you."

He was startled. "What is it?"

"Nothing terrible. Lazar is bringing his girl to dinner. I want you to be nice to her."

"Why shouldn't I be nice to her? What am I? A wild animal?"

"Oh, darling, you're the gentlest person in the world.... You see, she isn't of our faith."

"What has it to do with me whether she's of our faith or not?"

"Her name is Katherine Evans. The Evans Engineering Company—that's her father. Lazar knows her from Columbia. They're good friends."

"I still don't see what that has to do with me."

"They're engaged."

"What?" Grossman had turned pale. He mastered himself and stammered: "Lazar has never said a word to me."

"He was afraid to tell you because she isn't of our faith. She's a Quaker.... Isaac, we're modern people, worldly people. The children love each other. We're not going to ruin their happiness for the sake of an old superstition. If there is God He's the God of all of us, of Jew and of Christian, isn't He?"

"Yes, God is the same to all of us, but people are not the same," he answered through half-closed lips.

"Oh, I know what you feel, my dearest," and she squeezed his hand with all her might. "I know what it means to you ... and to your family.... But we can't help ourselves. We can only spoil things. Lazar is a grown-up person; so is Katherine. They will marry whether we want it or not. We can only alienate the children from ourselves, and you surely don't want to do that."

"No, I don't want to do that," he said mechanically.

"And they've settled the question of religion. Lazar told me that he's spoken with the rabbi, and Rabbi Silverman said that if he hasn't already changed his religion he can still remain a member of the Temple. Lazar certainly doesn't want to leave it. I don't know what Katherine is going to do. But they've decided that the children won't get any religious instruction until they're grown up and can choose for themselves. Don't you think it's a sensible arrangement? You see, Isaac, young people nowadays know how to get round these religious difficulties. Don't you think so?"

"Yes, Clara."

"Are you satisfied, Isaac?" And she squeezed his hand still harder.

"What is there for me to be satisfied about? As long as Rabbi Silverman is satisfied."

Isaac Grossman, like most men of his type, did not have a personal God. He had the God Whom he had inherited from his father; but he could not say that he had been much occupied with Him. He had neither the time nor the inclination for it. Yes, certainly, he believed in Him, for he feared Him. He did his best not to anger Him, but rather to placate Him. He tried to be decent to people. In business, of course, he acted toward others as they acted toward him. It was a battle, a contest; but it had its rules, one played fair. If one didn't, there was the law; and what was perhaps more important, there was your reputation. Once you'd lost that, you'd lost everything. Though of course if you were successful much was forgiven you. That was how others acted toward him, that was how he acted toward others. He gave as good as he got. The street had been his nursery, life his mentor. This was the law of life, and it had nothing to do with God.

But there was one virtue which Isaac Grossman could claim. He did not look upon himself as being hand in glove with the Almighty. He did not consider himself a favorite. He recognized that, as it was, God had done more for him than he for God, and therefore he was the debtor. He knew that though business was something else again, his actions there—whatever the business world might think—were not what God accepted. For God could see through and through a man, knew all man's deeds and thoughts, and would demand an accounting beyond this life, or perhaps even in this life. So his father had taught him; and Isaac Grossman did not feel justified in God's eyes. He would be called to judgment, and the thought frightened him. The hand of God had often been laid upon him, and had held him back from many actions which even the law would have condoned. It pushed him away from evil, it caused him to make restitution for wrongs he had done; it held him to the right path.

93

He knew further that if there were a God He could not be bribed with trifles, with little charities and gestures, with the presidency of a synagogue, or being active in a congregation. You had to be straightforward with Him. "You've got to play ball with Him," he often said to himself. And so he had not sought the honors which people were ready to thrust on him. Not even when his wife and son had assured him that the presidency of the Temple would be good for business. He gave generously to all sorts of institutions, homes, synagogues, hospitals, Red Cross, but he did it in the name of the firm, avoiding publicity. Sometimes a charitable organization would approach him, as a prominent real estate dealer, to help it buy a piece of land. He did it gladly, without charge, sometimes at a loss, but quietly, and he was relieved when he could avoid official thanks. He had the same attitude toward individuals; he was glad to help, and he was glad when none but the beneficiary knew of the helping hand he had extended.

This was a hard blow, this that his wife had just told him. He felt his mother's milk freezing in him; and there rose before him the picture of his dead father. The dead father and the living mother. But more than the dread of what it meant to them, was the dread of what it meant to himself. He could deny with utter sincerity that he had even the faintest negative feeling toward other faiths; he had never thought of non-Jews as being better or worse than Jews. He knew he was a Jew, though he did not pray more than twice a year, did not observe the dietary laws; he knew that he would be prepared to die rather than deny his Jewishness. He felt he would endure the most unthinkable tortures, rather than apostatize. And this was the sum of his Jewishness. The rest did not matter. Outside of it he was an American, and that was the end of it.

Nor could he have anything against the girl who would become the mother of his grandchildren, for he had never met her; and he was sure that if Lazar had chosen her, and Clara had given her consent, she must be a good child—certainly as good as his own. And yet he was frozen from head to foot, and he was filled with dread. He felt that with this marriage something was brought to an end, something infinitely precious. He himself was being erased from the book of life, and with his son something was beginning toward which he, Isaac Grossman, had no relationship.

94

But he also knew what the limitations of the situation were. He realized at once that Clara had been right; there was nothing he could do. There was no way of preventing the marriage. To try would be not only useless, but dangerous. There was his wife's health, which could not stand such a strain; there was his only son, whom he would alienate forever. And even his business would suffer. He said to himself, as he always did in an extremity: "I have no alternative."

An event of this kind could not be kept a secret long; the families were too prominent—especially the Evanses, of the Evans Engineering Company. The marriage was a quiet one, celebrated privately—"because of the delicate condition of Mrs. Grossman's health," newspapers reported—and it was noted that neither rabbi nor minister officiated. But the pictures of Lazar Grossman and his bride appeared in *The New York Times*, and there was a short list of the guests who had attended the ceremony.

A few days later Isaac Grossman received a telephone call from his brother Gabriel, telling him that his mother was seriously ill, and that he was to come to her.

Since the time when Clara had bought the house in New Rochelle the relations between Isaac Grossman and the members of his family had become even less intimate than before. But he had not broken off with them. He met his mother, and his brothers and sisters, from time to time; he had been in contact with them in Florida. "Shmaya's widow," as she was still called by the older, pious guests of her hotels, had never come to New Rochelle, and therefore the others had kept away too. But Isaac visited her occasionally in her apartment on Washington Heights, where she was to be found between seasons, and sometimes took a meal with her. His mother would give him stuffed fish, chicken-noodle soup, and other home dishes, and would look at him with tears in her eyes, saying: "Eat, my son, you can't get this kind of food at home." And she would add, sighing: "Those gentile dishes—how can they have any taste? Where should they have learned how to cook? They eat all sorts of worms and impurities. Eat, my son, it will do you good." However alien from her her son's wife and child might be, he was still, after all, the glory of the family. "The whole world is ringing with your name," she said fondly, "but what do you get out of it all?" His brothers, too, were proud of

95

him; and they knew that his name was helpful to them. Nor did they hesitate to call him or see him at his office when they needed advice, or more substantial help, even though by tacit agreement they did not come to his home.

Isaac Grossman knew well enough why his brother had telephoned. He also knew what kind of reception to expect. But again he said: "I have no alternative," and he went.

At first he had believed that the report of his mother's sickness had been only a device. He did not remember his mother ever to have been ill. Everyone in the family had a right to take to his or her bed—but not mother. It had been so on the East Side, it had been so ever since. Mother was there not to be sick, but to tend others in sickness. She might suffer with pains in her feet, but she never rested them. But this time Isaac Grossman found her in her bed, her head bound in a white kerchief from under which strayed wisps of white hair. He had never seen her hair before; she had always worn, night and day, the peruke of the pious Jewess, and so he had always thought of her as brown-haired, even in her old age. Now it was as if she did not care how he saw her, for nothing mattered any more. It did not even matter whether she would suffer hell-fire or not. Those gray-white wisps told him more about his mother's condition than her furrowed cheeks, and her deep-sunken eyes, and the blue tinge which had appeared on her lips. He marveled, in the midst of his distress, that a person's face should have been able to alter so. But it was the white hair which shattered his spirit, more than her face and eyes, and more than the stony looks on the faces of his brothers and sisters assembled about the bed.

"I can't help myself, mother," he pleaded, cowering before her eyes. He lowered his head and repeated, in Yiddish: "There's nothing I can do."

"What are you in your family? A workhorse? You work for them, you give them your life, and your word counts for nothing?" asked his mother, biting her lips.

"A horse?" he said, confused, and something flashed through his mind.

"Yes, yes, a horse which works for its owner and has no say over its own life."

Why was she talking about a horse? He felt the blood coming

96

into his eyes. "If you must talk to me like that, I can't stay," he said, and he turned to his silent brothers and sisters. "I've told you I can do nothing. It's out of my hands. My son is an adult, a grown man, not a child, and we are in America, a land of freedom. We're not in the old country. Here a man can't tell his son what kind of wife to take. Here, in America, where we live, it's all one, Jew or Christian. We're all human beings, and if there is a God He's everyone's Father. There are no stepchildren of God," he added excitedly.

"That's all very well, but you're ruining our business. What orthodox Jew is going to stick his nose into our *kosher* hotel if one of the Grossmans marries his son to a gentile girl!" cried Sam.

"Is that the Socialist talking?" asked Isaac, with a bitter smile.

"What's socialism got to do with business?"

"God, God, God," came the mother's moaning voice. Isaac looked round. His mother was sitting up in the bed. The covering had fallen from her head, and she was tugging at her white locks. She went on, in a voice that tore at the heart: "I will cry out to God and the world.... Who dares to speak of business? Over there," she lifted her hand wildly, "they are driving your father out of his place in paradise.... He has been shamed in the congregation of the saints ... and his children talk of business." She wrung her hands, and her body was shaken by spasms of agony.

They tried to comfort her, but she wept bitterly into her hands, muttering into them, again and again: "Shamed in the congregation of the saints. They all turn away from him, the learned ones, the pious ones, the holy ones, who were his companions in paradise."

The daughters, too, burst into tears. The men were wiping their eyes. Isaac felt his head swirling. Then he pulled himself together, came closer to his mother, and said quietly:

"I've told you I could do nothing about it, and that ends the matter. We'll have to wait till this hysteria is past, and we can talk like reasonable human beings." He stepped away from the bed and turned to the door.

His mother took her hands from her face and in a clear, commanding voice, such as she had used to him when he was a little boy, called out to him: "Isaac, come here."

Automatically he turned again, and approached the bed. His

mother looked at him long and quietly, and then, without agitation, said, "Do you think your father will have nothing to say about this?"

"What?"

"Do you think he will take it quietly that you should have shamed him before his companions in paradise?"

"I have not shamed him. I don't know what you want me to do."

"But *he* knows what he wants you to do. He told you before he died that you bear full responsibility for your acts. You have not lived like a Jew, and he will come to you to demand an accounting for the disgrace you have brought upon him. Remember."

These were the last words his mother spoke to him.

CHAPTER TWELVE

HE clung to his wife now as his last refuge, the one place where he felt safe from the pursuit of his implacable conscience. She was the sole object of his existence; and the frailer she became, the greater grew his love. Nor was it a love grounded in compassion for her. Its foundation was desire, the hot-blooded desire of man for woman. The fragility of her body, which awakened his longing, and compelled him at the same time to treat her with the utmost tenderness and care—as if she were a delicate vase—the whiteness of her skin, the fine network of veins showing through the transparency, were an inexhaustible joy to him; and she, touched by his complete surrender, responded with a passion which had its own provocative character, flowing from the restraint placed upon it by her failing strength.

In the period following his mother's death he flung himself into business activity with new will power. This too was a flight, so that business became an end in itself. It became impossible for him to see a vacant lot, an undeveloped area, without imagining what could be done with it. He had begun with the Miami purchases before his mother died; despite the crisis he extended his interests and bought hotels in many parts of the country. He joined slum-clearance projects; he was part of the group which transformed derelict areas of the East Side, the former locations of stables, and slaughterhouses, and shanty towns, into modern apartments.

He found in Lazar a magnificent partner. The boy—he was in his early twenties and had left Columbia without finishing his economics course, impatient to get into the active world—seemed to have passed into complete manhood at a bound. He brought into the new firm of Grossman and Grossman a freshness of energy, a freedom of mind, which contrasted strikingly with the older man's weighted psyche. Lazar was a pragmatist. He had

99

come under the influence of John Dewey's practical philosophy. He was Young America, unhampered by ancient timidities and terrors, free, energetic, convinced that the world stood open before him. His gift for making friends became a great business asset. He moved among politicians, and soon came to know what was being discussed in City Hall. He belonged to both camps, for in New York he stood with the reform Republicans, while nationally he was an ardent Democrat. And he had a flair for what was afoot in the world of finance.

Isaac Grossman had never gambled with stocks; he was a creator, not a gambler. The liquid capital of the firm was always invested in government bonds, and whatever purchases it made, in Miami or elsewhere, it backed with cash. But what Isaac Grossman had lacked was a sense of system, a bent for organization. This was what his son, young though he was, supplied. Lazar was always and completely aware of what he was doing. His marriage with Katherine Evans had indeed been the outcome of a genuine love, which had had to meet a certain opposition on the part of her parents (they had no religious scruples, it was the social standing of the young man that disappointed them); but Katherine brought him a considerable fortune, a legacy from her grandfather over which the parents had no control. Lazar invested the legacy with his father and became an equal partner in the new firm of Grossman and Grossman.

Side by side with his business drive, Lazar carried on an intense social and philanthropic activity. That was a time when men had begun to doubt the solidity of the very rocks which sustained the island of Manhattan. On the sidewalks of the world's greatest city the furniture of dispossessed families—beds, dishes, Gramophone records, pails, brooms—seemed to proclaim the collapse of a world. Shops and factories discharged their hands by tens and hundreds of thousands, and the unemployed roamed the streets like shadows. The soup kitchens of the Salvation Army, and of other charitable organizations, were thronged with factory hands, white collar workers, former shopkeepers, among whom there wandered, doubly forlorn, the rich of yesterday: pale, frightened faces, eyes red with weeping and sleeplessness, bodies racked by hunger. It was a period of nomadic movement. People slept in subways and under bridges; they stormed churches and schools; they stole the

100

mattresses of the dispossessed lying in the streets. The banks failed, one after another, and honorable businessmen with well-established reputations were to be seen selling apples in Times Square. It was as if a dreadful, chilling mist had descended on the city and obliterated the heavens.

During that time Lazar Grossman was one of the leading figures in the relief organizations. He called meetings of rabbis, ministers and priests, and organized a huge distribution apparatus. He opened public kitchens in synagogues and churches; he headed —a boy wonder—a deputation to Albany to petition the governor for a moratorium on paying rent, even though his own firm was going to suffer thereby. He helped found a women's organization for the distribution of milk and bread in the schools. Above all, he fought for State and Federal Relief action, and had a prominent place in a second deputation, which went to Washington.

In the matter of these deputations to the governor and the President he met with considerable opposition in his own circles, which showed no inclination to relinquish any privileges and held with President Hoover that relief was something for philanthropic institutions, not for the government. It was not, they said, in the American spirit, which saw government and philanthropy as two separate concepts. America was the land of free opportunity, and the government had to guarantee that freedom; but after that every man was responsible for himself. The crisis, they said, was temporary; it was the squeezing out of the superfluous water from the stocks. It was necessary to become "realistic" again, and teach people to live more modestly. The place of the workers, they said, like the financier at the conference, was in the factory, not in Wall Street.

Lazar Grossman was one of the small group who believed that the crisis would last a long time, and that it had its source in the inequity of the division of the fruits of labor, itself caused by the complete lawlessness of private initiative and by the conspiracies of the trusts. In the crisis they saw an opportunity for the cleansing of the American mind and the American economy, the beginnings of a new social life following the awakening of America's conscience. Men would begin to see that the Federal government would have to be on the watch, in peacetime not less than in wartime; in peacetime against the attack of the internal enemy, hunger.

It was the business of the Federal government, they believed, to see that the population was protected in work and food no less than against foreign enemies. These were new and revolutionary thoughts in Lazar's circle, which was predominantly Republican. And he felt himself an outsider there.

He did not let his ostracism discourage him. He threw himself into political work, and became one of the first disciples of the New Deal, bringing into the movement his talents as a speaker, as well as his organizing ability. He was recognized as one of the men who had done a great deal toward getting Roosevelt into the White House.

Under the Roosevelt administration Lazar Grossman attained national importance. He refused an official post, but he was widely known to belong to the inner circle of economists, businessmen and professors with whom the President consulted on his New Deal reforms. He was a member of powerful committees which transformed the economic structure of the country. He became a symbol of the forward-looking, progressive young American businessman. His picture appeared frequently in newspapers and magazines, and a great future was foretold for him.

Isaac Grossman had every reason to be proud of his son, and he was as proud of him as Clara was. Nevertheless he had a feeling of discomfort, contemplating his son's extraordinary career. There was not the slightest touch of envy in his discomfort; he had never been affected by Lazar's type of ambition, or Clara's. If there was anything for him to envy in his son it was rather his self-assurance, his unreflecting and tacit acceptance of life. His son had not brought with him, out of his past, a secret burden, a divisive anguish. Perhaps there was fear in Isaac Grossman's heart. Perhaps his son would some day find out that one particular, crushing secret which neither he nor Clara remotely suspected. The higher Lazar Grossman rose, the greater grew his father's dread, so that he became like a man who had committed an undiscovered murder.

Lazar, on the other hand, came closer to his father as he grew older. He had a genuine respect for his father's character and achievement; and after his one negative step, his marriage with Katherine, showed himself firmly attached to his Jewish faith and origin. He became an active member of a Temple in Long Island, where he had settled shortly after the birth of his first child.

Isaac Grossman had had many unspoken misgivings about his future daughter-in-law before he met her. They turned out to be unfounded. Despite her background of wealth and aristocracy Katherine was a simple, straightforward girl. She was natural, friendly, and open; and from the first she put herself out to win her father-in-law's confidence and affection. She must have known something of the unhappiness which her marriage had caused him and his family, for she avoided with the greatest care any mention of religious questions, or of other matters which might remind him that she came from another world.

When Katherine gave birth to her first child, a son, the question of the covenant, or circumcision, rose painfully in Isaac Grossman's mind. But it was Katherine who took the first step to put him at ease. The second day after the confinement Lazar drew his father aside in the office, and told him that Katherine wanted to have the boy circumcised according to the Jewish ritual.

"Why?" asked Isaac Grossman, stammering in his astonishment. "Does she want it for my sake? It's her son. I don't want her to do something she—and the child—may regret in later years."

"Well, it's not a question of ritual, exactly," said Lazar. "It's a question of hygiene. The child would be circumcised anyhow. Lots of non-Jews believe in it. But if he's going to be circumcised, why shouldn't it be done according to the ritual? Anyway, Katherine believes that the religious Jews have greater experts, and more experience—" This last was added in a lighter tone.

No; Lazar, despite his early inclinations, was not ashamed of his Jewish origin, and in no way sought to deny it. He only refused to make a tragedy of it. He intended to take it lightheartedly. He was fond of telling in company the story of his father's outburst at the dinner party—the outburst which had been occasioned by the reactionary remarks of the German Jewish Wall Street financier, and had nearly cost Lazar's mother her life. However, for all that, Lazar faked a little when it came to his family history. His grandfather was not a poor worker in a sweatshop, where he had contracted the proletarian disease, tuberculosis; he was, to be sure, a poor man, but a great scholar and Talmudist, and a rabbi in a poor orthodox congregation. The rest he left untouched—the story of Monticello, the boardinghouse, and the origins of the hotels in the Catskills and Miami.

The times were changing, and humble origins were no longer regarded as a blot. New winds were beginning to blow in American life generally, and in American-Jewish life in particular. The crisis of 1929 was something more than an economic portent; it was the awakening of the American conscience. A breath came from the American Revolution, from the spirit of Franklin and Jefferson, and the air which had been fouled by the activities of the "robber barons" began to clear.

The old saying, "like Christian, like Jew," could well be applied to those days. Something entered the social life of Jewry which cleansed it almost overnight of the German-Jewish aristocratic snobbery which had dominated it. The atmosphere became democratic. The German Jews who had set the tone for Jewish life were deposed from their leadership when Germany ceased to be a *Vaterland* to boast of. Here and there the old spirit lingered, in "The Harmony Club," and in the country clubs, which excluded "East European Jews"—the Jews of Poland, and Russia—not less rigorously than did their gentile opposites; but in public life the luster of the German Jews was extinguished.

The brief and ghastly reign of Hitler dawned. The thousand-year-old heritage of German Jewry was obliterated, and with it the genius which it had so lavishly contributed to Germany's phenomenal rise. Outlawed in their own country, rejected with contempt, the German Jews found themselves beggars and wanderers. The property of the Jews became the spoil of gangsters. Jewish families with a record of tens of generations of service to the Fatherland were uprooted like weeds.

A wave of self-consciousness passed over American Jewry. First there came universal fear: Could it happen here too? Many of the big industrialists, bankers, and merchants of German-Jewish origin suddenly perceived to what an extent they too had been tainted with the pathological Hitlerian outlook when they had denounced every effort at reform, every move toward greater freedom, as communism and bolshevism. With the decline of German Jewry, the East European Jews came into their own. Many of them were in the Roosevelt camp. Not only the children of the immigrants, but actual immigrants, such as had crossed the Atlantic in the holds and had worked in the sweatshops on the East Side, became the leaders of powerful labor organizations, and played a role not only in the economic field, but in government as well. "East Side" ceased to be a term of opprobrium; it was something respected not only in the Jewish world, but in America at large, wherever big industry had its labor movement.

Like many others of his kind Lazar Grossman became, under the impact of the Hitler catastrophe, a "spite-Jew"—his Judaism motivated by resentment and wounded pride. He had always been a member of the Temple in his Long Island town; now he also joined a prominent Temple in New York. "If Hitler comes," he said, "he'll know where to find me." He became one of the leaders of the movement for the relief and rescue of Hitler's victims. He traveled throughout the country making passionate speeches to Jewish communities. He helped bring thousands of refugees into the safety of America. And again like many others of his kind, he drew nearer to his people.

As it happened, his wife Katherine shared his sympathies completely. Brought up in the spirit of America, in the atmosphere of tolerance which had pervaded her home, where no religion was ever decried, Katherine reacted to German anti-Semitism as vigorously as her husband. It led her to emphasize to her children their roots in the people which Hitler was determined to exterminate. She would have regarded it as cowardice if now, when Jews were being persecuted by a madman who wanted to infect the whole world with his insanity, she should disassociate herself or even her children from the persecuted. Hers was the reaction of a sound, free American. Moreover, she was deeply under her husband's influence, and deeply in love with him, too, so that she was ready to follow him in all his actions.

Robert, their son, whom they had intended to bring up without religion until he was old enough to choose, himself raised the subject betimes. He and his sister Louise had received no formal, systematic religious instruction; religion as such was never discussed in the house; and when as tots they had posed the usual questions, prompted by what they had heard elsewhere, they were put off with vague generalities. But the boy, growing up, returned to the subject; he became persistent; his interest in the words *God*, *Church*, and *Synagogue* grew rather than diminished under his parents' evasive responses. He embarrassed Katherine and Lazar by his blunt and reiterated demand for an answer to the question:

What are we, Jews or Christians? "But what makes you ask that question? Who told you to ask it?" his mother asked in turn. "Why," he answered, "in school, I know some of my friends are Jews, some are Christians." "We are human beings," answered his mother. "We believe there is one God for all human beings. It doesn't matter how you pray to Him, in the Church or in the Temple. That's why we go to both. When you'll grow up, you'll choose for yourself if you want to pray only in one of them."

But Robert did not want to wait till he was grown up. He wanted to know there and then whether God was a Jew or a Christian; and what was the difference between the Jewish God and Jesus. He was immensely attracted by whatever religious ceremonial he came across, whether it was Jewish or Christian. Once, in his grandmother's house in New Rochelle, he saw candles burning on the table. It was Friday evening, and the habit of lighting candles was something that Clara had brought with her from her home in Lakeview; it was pure reflex action, had no religious meaning, and was not accompanied by prayer or any other formula. But Robert thought the candles beautiful and asked his mother to light candles on Friday evenings, the way he had seen his grandmother do. And Katherine did it, to please him. She had no feeling for the distinction between Jewish and Christian ceremonials, although, loving her husband as she did, she was inclined toward the Jewish. Perhaps she also found them a little exotic and was stirred by them when she encountered them in the homes of her friends. She observed Christmas and Easter, and attended the local Congregational Church. Robert began to plead to be taken along, and he returned from his first visit full of the experience, delighted by the sights and sounds, the altar, the flowers, the lights, the prayers, the hymns, the choir—everything had delighted him. He came home with the same enthusiasm from the first Yom Kippur service to which his father took him. He loved the cantor and the choir, the prayer shawls of the congregants, the festive air, the Ark of the Covenant: to the boy the Temple was like a Church and the Church like a Temple. He could not make up his mind which was better. They were both places in which you prayed to God. But what he could not understand was why he was being held off from both of them, Church and Temple alike. He was not being sent, for that matter, to either Sunday school, that of his mother's

Church, or that of his father's. But the children of Jewish and Christian parents did go to the Sunday schools.

Thus, instead of growing up with no religion, the boy actually grew up with two. In Lazar's home, especially after his Jewish self-consciousness had asserted itself, both sets of festivals were celebrated. There was the Christmas tree, with its presents, and all the ceremonies customary in an American home. In New Rochelle, Isaac Grossman now observed some of the Passover; he went through the *seder* ceremony on the first evening; that is, to the extent that he remembered his father's traditional ritual. On that evening Katherine, Lazar, and their children were present. There were *matzos* on the table, and there were Jewish dishes proper to the occasion, supplied by a Jewish caterer. But at the same season of the year, sometimes earlier, sometimes later than the Passover, Katherine would be celebrating Easter. She liked to get together the Christian children of the neighborhood and have them join in the search for the Easter eggs hidden in the large garden. The grass was already green, and the flower beds were in bloom. On Easter Sunday Robert and his little sister would accompany their mother to the Church, which, like the garden, was filled with the spring, with lilies and other blooms which adorned also the Temple and the home. All these symbols and adornments filled his heart with joy, and he was happy in his earlier childhood with both religions, his father's and his mother's, and felt no contradiction between them.

This time of reconciliation and happiness was brief. How his disillusionment came about, whether it was a quiet snub, or whether, in the infection of Hitlerism which spread here and there in America, he was suddenly confronted with hatred and contempt, his parents did not know; but he suddenly became aware that he was an outsider; he belonged nowhere, neither to the Jews nor to the Christians. He came home one day depressed and silent, and after long coaxing and vain questioning, burst into tears: "Pa, who are the Jews? Why are they hated? And what are we?"

"Don't cry, son," his father answered. "Boys don't cry—only babies cry. Go and wash your face, and then we'll talk it over."

When Robert returned with a washed face, his father drew him to his side on the couch and began:

"You asked me three questions: Who are the Jews? Why are

they hated? And what are we? Here is my answer: Jews are people, just like other people. They belong to the white race, and they have their good side and their bad side just like others. We are hated because we are a minority. They aren't afraid to hate us —I mean the ones that do the hating. If they were to hate a Christian, or hit a Christian, they'd have to defend themselves against too many. But when they hit a Jew, there aren't many people to take his part. The Jews haven't anyone to defend them. Sometimes people are like animals in the forest. They take advantage of the weakness of the Jews to attack them, and rob them, and take away their means of making a living. You want to know what *we* are. Mama is a Christian, I'm a Jew. Mama and I agreed that you and Louise should wait till you're both grown up and understand these things better, and then you'll choose to be whatever you think better for yourself—Jewish or Christian. But I see you haven't the patience to wait, and you want to know now. Why? I suppose it's because someone stronger than you said something to you, and you feel insulted. Now you go into your room, and sit down by yourself, son, and think it over. You're getting to be a big boy—you're nearly thirteen. Among us Jews a boy of thirteen is considered a man; he can decide things for himself; and you can decide whether you want to be with the stronger ones or the weaker ones. On your father's side you're a Jew, on your mother's, a Christian. You can choose which to be. You have the right to be either. And if you choose to be a Christian, nobody is going to criticize you, or reproach you, for having gone from the weaker to the stronger side. Go and think it over well. Then come and tell me what you've decided. You needn't tell me today, or tomorrow, or the day after. Take your time—a week, or two, or more. I want you first to calm yourself, so that you can think quietly and know what you're doing."

The boy stood up, but instead of leaving, remained there, sunk in thought, indecision written on his face. He was struggling to find words, and finally said, "Dad, tell me: why did God divide people into Jews and Christians?"

"God didn't divide people into Jews and Christians. People themselves did it. And Christians too are divided into different groups, which they call denominations. And the Jews are also divided into orthodox and reform, as they call them. All these groups are often unfriendly to each other. Why that should be so, I can't tell you, I don't know. You'll have to ask a rabbi, or a priest—and I don't know if they could give you the right answer. We've got to take people as they are, and love them as they are, because they're human beings just like us. A man has to live among people; he can't live by himself, he can't achieve anything by himself. Man is a social animal, he has to live in society. And we must do everything we can to adapt ourself to our fellow human beings."

And Robert made his choice. Before a week had passed he stood before his father and said, "I want to be a Jew, dad, like you, and like your father, and like his father. I don't want to wait any more. Because while I'm waiting I'm nothing, and I'm afraid of being nothing."

And Robert, with Katherine's consent, placed the boy under the guidance of Rabbi Glicksman, to prepare him for his *bar mitzvah*, which was duly celebrated in their Temple.

Isaac Grossman was overjoyed by this turn of events. He saw in this choice of Judaism by his grandson a veritable miracle. And when the next Day of Atonement came, Robert remembered how his grandfather used to take him to the synagogue on the East Side where *his* father had prayed, and he asked to be taken there again. These bearded Jews, swathed in their prayer shawls, made a profound impression on him; he saw them in a new light. And Isaac Grossman, seeing his young grandson standing near him in a prayer shawl, felt as though no break had taken place in his life. The long thread which reached back to his father, and to generations of the past, was being spun further into the future through his grandson.

For his grandson's sake, old Isaac Grossman turned more toward religion. The whole family was similarly affected. Katherine went oftener to Church, and Lazar himself became more active in the Temple. The times were favorable to such a change. A strong bond was created between old Grossman and his grandson—a bond closer than the one with his son. The grandson, too, was drawn to the grandfather. In grandfather's house the candles were lit on Friday nights, grandfather now said the Friday evening benediction over the wine. He did it as it were to celebrate Robert's choice

of the Jewish faith, and the boy seemed to know it and was
attracted more strongly than ever to the religion of his choice.

Now, if ever, Isaac Grossman should have been happy; and on
the surface he did achieve a certain happiness. He had healed the
breach in his life, or rather his grandson had done it for him. The
unpleasant episode—that was how he referred to it whenever he
remembered—sank away into its proper perspective. He looked
into his early years through the medium of his grandson, and he
was no longer afraid of them. There was nothing really evil nor
ugly in his life. There had only been poverty, suffering, hunger,
father's sickness, mother's struggles; but, with this, honest work,
decency.

But that was only on the surface. Deep within there was a fester-
ing wound which did not heal. He turned his gaze away; he would
not let this obscure evil infect the happiness of his family life.
Sometimes he dreamed of hands which were stretched out in the
darkness to take hold of him, drag him away somewhere. He
fought them off. He fought off the melancholia which sometimes
assailed him in the night, and he thought of his wife, his son, his
grandson. Those obsessions were only the result of his gallstones.
Dr. Markowitch had warned him to stick to his diet; he was too
old to be operated on.

It was all the easier for him to practice this deception on himself when, with the war years, Lazar was drawn deeper and deeper
into national work, and the full burden of the firm fell again on
Isaac Grossman's shoulders. The day after Pearl Harbor, Lazar
had tried to enlist; he was rejected because of his age. Instead of
service at the front, he was given a position of high responsibility
in Washington, and directed the erection of army camps throughout the country. He was released, with the rank of lieutenant general, only with the ending of the war.

But before that came, Isaac Grossman suffered a shattering loss.
Clara, his refuge, his hold on life, came down with a second heart
attack, and this time she did not come around. Months passed and
she remained bedfast, with nurses in constant attendance. During
that period Isaac Grossman never left the house before he had
given Clara her breakfast, and he did not stay at the office a
moment longer than was essential. Week after week he watched
her fading, and with her his security and his reason for living.

Dr. Markowitch was now more concerned with Isaac Grossman than with his wife. He struggled to keep her alive as much for her husband's sake as for hers. But he knew the struggle to be hopeless, and he warned Lazar Grossman that with the death of his mother he must be prepared for a serious threat to his father's life.

But the threat did not materialize at once. One would have said that Kovalsky waited to make sure that Isaac Grossman had lost his wife's protection. It was not until that long vacation which Isaac Grossman spent in Winter Paradise that Kovalsky moved once again into the foreground, this time not to be driven away.

CHAPTER THIRTEEN

THE day following the visit to Hialeah, Miss Rosenberg announced a totally unexpected visitor—Isaac Grossman's older brother.

"Gabriel!" exclaimed Grossman, in astonishment.

"I asked him to come up to your suite. He's waiting in the other room. I offered him refreshments, but he very politely refused. I'd forgotten."

"Ah, yes, neither he nor mother would taste anything in my house—or in one of my hotels." Isaac Grossman went into the reception room of his suite with outstretched hand.

"Gabriel! What a pleasure!" Then he stopped short, a little confused at the sight of the aged Jew, with the sparse little beard and the timid eyes. He would not have recognized him without the warning.

Many years had passed since they had seen each other. Shortly after their mother's death a quarrel had arisen between Sam and Gabriel, who had taken over the two *kosher* hotels of the widow. Sam had wanted to convert them into what he called modern resorts, *Kosher Style*—which would mean that guests who wanted ritually pure meat would get it, while others would be served on request with anything from ham to steaks cut from the forbidden parts of the animal. Gabriel would not have it. He insisted on *Strictly Kosher*. The thought that under his roof swine-meat would be cooked in his utensils, or that butter would be served together with meat at one of his tables, was intolerable to him. The quarrel continued until Gabriel discovered that his brother was encouraging the surreptitious introduction of un-*kosher* foods into the rooms of the guests. Sam protested furiously that in America the customer was always right, and that if the Widow Grossman's hotels were to stay in business, they would have to come out of their old-fashioned habits. Gabriel refused to listen, and they broke. Isaac was called in to arbitrate, and he arranged the details of the separation. Gabriel opened a small hotel and restaurant of his own, where he continued the tradition of his mother of blessed memory, with all the minutiae of the ritual strictly enforced. Sam was to pay him off over a period of years. Since that incident Isaac had not met his brothers, nor heard from them, and he had not gone out of his way to get news of them. And here Gabriel stood before him, and Isaac's heart gave a sudden throb. It might almost have been his father: the sparse little white beard, which trembled with every word which Gabriel uttered, the long, scraggy neck, the dancing Adam's apple, and the thin, sloping shoulders on which hung the oversized topcoat.

"You know, Gabriel, you look almost like father now, God rest his soul."

"Well, father was a Jew, and I'm a Jew, and all Jews look alike," said Gabriel, smiling.

"Do you hear from Sam? Is he paying you out regularly?"

"I don't want his money."

"What do you mean?"

"I don't want to profit from his unclean food. I don't want to be a partner to it. It's not the same as your hotels. You don't pretend to be *kosher,* you don't fool anyone, and you don't help anyone to fool himself. But a hotel which says *Kosher,* or even says *Kosher Style,* and serves pork—no, I won't take anything from him."

"How's your own hotel going?"

"So-so. What do I need? My children are on their own, God be praised; they can look after themselves. There's only myself and my wife. It doesn't take much to keep us. And as long as we stay Jewish..."

"But it's a shame to lose your part of the inheritance. I don't know how the matter stands, whether you've lost your rights or not. I'd like to talk with my lawyer. Sam ought to pay you off. You were equal owners. It isn't right that he should take everything away from you."

"I've told you," said Gabriel obstinately. "I won't touch a cent of his money that way." And he made a gesture as if he were shaking something dirty off his coat.

"As you say," answered Isaac. "But you came to see me about something. Can I help you in any way?"

"Yes. In that same matter, actually. I've been thinking and thinking, all these years. I can't let this thing go on. I haven't taken his money, so I'm still a part owner of the hotels. I want you to talk with Sam, and see whether we can't have the hotels go back to the truly *kosher* rules, as they were in mother's time, God rest her."

"*I* should talk with him?" Isaac lifted his shoulders in amazement. "He'll laugh at me. What have I got to do with *kosher?* He'll tell me to make my hotels *kosher,* first."

"Don't you care at all," asked Gabriel, "that mother can't rest in the other world because in the hotels of Shmaya's widow the food of abomination is served and eaten?"

"How do you know that mother can't rest in the other world?"

"Oh, I know it, I know it well," answered Gabriel, sighing bitterly. "And not only mother—father, too, of blessed memory. He has no peace in paradise. Imagine! Pork being served in the restaurant which flaunts the pure and pious name of his wife. Why, they'll punish *him* too, God forbid."

"Yes, yes, I remember mother talking just like that when Lazar married Katherine. But do you know what happened, Gabriel? My grandson Robert, Lazar's boy, turned out to be a good Jew. Would you believe that? No one persuaded him, his parents didn't force him, he chose it of his own free will. It's a pity mother didn't live to see it. She might have had an easier death."

"Ha!" cried Gabriel triumphantly. "And who do you think did this for you, if it wasn't father and mother? Can't you see it? They didn't rest, they ran from saint to saint and from patriarch to patriarch, to get God's intercession for you. And they didn't stop, the two of them, until they had obtained their wish, that their great-grandchildren should be Jews. But you—you don't even want to do this much for mother, and see to it that her name should not be besmirched by Sam."

"Gabriel, it's ridiculous. I bear the Grossman name, and my hotels are as un-*kosher* as Sam's—more so. I don't observe the ritual myself."

"I've told you, you're different. You don't pretend. You don't fool anyone, and you don't help others to fool themselves. But

114

Sam calls it *Kosher Style,* and the world remembers Shmaya's widow, and it's a desecration. She came to me and told me to have it stopped; she bade me go to Sam and tell him that he must return to real *kosher* regulations."

"She came to you?" repeated Isaac, baffled.

"Certainly. She came to me in a dream. She wrung her hands, she wept bitter tears. It was heartrending," said Gabriel quietly.

Isaac was silent, not knowing how to deal with his brother. He said, at last, "You really believe all that?"

"What do you mean? How else can it be?"

"It certainly isn't right, either," muttered Isaac, half to himself. "The hotels still bear mother's name. I don't know whether you haven't a case there. I'd like to find out; we may be able to do something. I didn't want any part of the legacy myself, but I did expect that the hotels would be conducted the way mother wanted it. That was how you understood it, too. Do you think Sam would really pay attention if I spoke to him?"

"He's afraid of you, Isaac. He knows you can hire the best lawyers, and make it hard for him. Me he thinks a schlemiel."

"I'll think about it. I'll talk to my lawyer."

"I knew it!" said Gabriel gratefully. "I knew I wouldn't come to you in vain. You'll do it, if not for my sake, then for mother's."

"Yes, for her sake," said Isaac slowly. "Tell me, Gabriel, you really think the dead know what the living are doing, and are interested in us?"

"Do they know? And how they know! They follow all our deeds, the good ones and—God save us—the bad ones. And from the good deeds they derive joy in paradise, and from the bad, misery and shame."

"No, brother," said Isaac, suddenly and decisively. "When you die you die."

"If that were so, what would be the sense of life? What would be the point of all our suffering for the sake of life? What interest would it have for us? If it's all to end like that, let another Hitler come and take everything from us. Let *him* live, in that case. If there's no afterlife, and no Judge, and no judgment, nothing is worth the trouble. Brother, there is a God, there is a judgment, there is an afterlife. There is a hand that writes, and a balance that weighs. The world is not a lawless place. There is reward and

115

punishment for every one of our deeds. Sometimes we need the help and merit of our fathers and forefathers, because we have so tangled ourselves in evil that our own strength can't get us out. Take yourself, for instance. Who do you think brought your grandson back into the Jewish fold? You? His father? His mother? No. It was mother and father, peace be upon them, who interceded for him. They could find no peace because of the thread that was cut, because of the generations which were lost. Do you understand? And wait; they will yet do greater things. Yes, they will bring you and your son back into the fold." And Gabriel, as he talked, began to sway back and forth, like a pious Jew at his prayers.

"My son and I have never ceased to be Jews," said Isaac.

"God forbid that you should have done, and I do not say it. But you and your son have been so much occupied with yourselves that you have never had the time to be occupied with God. And while we are young it matters less, because we can still rectify the error. While we are young we think this world is everything. But in the latter days, when we see life running out between our fingers, running out like the water from a broken cask, we know it is not well for us not to have prepared for the second life which is before us."

"My son and I have done our best. We have tried to be just, to steal from no one, to be decent and honest. And it seems to me that for an ordinary mortal that is enough," said Isaac, in uncertain self-defense.

"Yes, yes, these are good things, who will deny it? But each one of us needs God's help and must pray for it, if we are to have strength enough to stay on the right path and not tremble with fear and shame when we stand before the judgment seat. And each of us must bethink himself whether there isn't some deed which even in our old age it is not too late to make amends for. For did not our sages say that a man should repent at least one day before his death? Farewell, brother, and God keep you in health."

When Gabriel left the room Isaac could have sworn that the shadow of his father had passed before him.

Isaac was really driven to believe that Gabriel had been right, that the dead father and mother were giving heaven no rest for

116

the salvation of the youngest generation. This was how he felt when he heard the news from his daughter-in-law Katherine—the "good things" Lazar had mentioned on the telephone.

Katherine, however, came alone, to Isaac Grossman's disappointment. He had a curious, intense, painful affection for his granddaughter. The child had not "chosen" like her brother. She simply remained close to her mother, and therefore was in the habit of attending church, and the Quaker meetings. She showed no special interest in her father's religion. Isaac Grossman had often wondered how this was going to affect the relationship between the brother and the sister; but for the time being the house remained harmonious. Lazar and Katherine were scrupulously faithful to their promise; they had their personal preferences, but they remained neutral with regard to any choice by the children. This was easier for Katherine, for she took her Christian faith as something self-understood, which did not call for explanation; but her love for her husband was more active, and one could have said that that was her real religion. Moreover, a profound resentment of Hitler had made her think of herself and her daughter, Christian though they were, as special targets of the religion of hate. Through them Hitler sought to strike at her husband. All this gave a poignancy to Isaac Grossman's affection for his daughter-in-law and his granddaughter.

And again, in the latter, there was a vivid reminder of his dead Clara. As so often happens, the resemblance had skipped a generation, and it was not Lazar, but Lazar's daughter, who came near to being the replica of Clara.

"Where's Louise?" was the first question Isaac Grossman addressed to his daughter-in-law. "Lazar said she was coming with you."

Katherine laughed delightedly. "Mayn't I come without her?"

This trim, glowing woman in the early forties, with unrouged lips and young, flashing eyes, looked more like a bride than the mother of grown-up children.

"Rose, did you hear the greeting?" she went on, and threw up her hands in mock despair.

"Now, now," said Isaac hastily. "That isn't nice of you. I knew you were coming, but I was expecting Louise, too. She's also got a place in my heart."

"Well, if you want to know, Louise has something better to do with her vacation than spend it with us old people, even under the Florida sun. She decided to go up to New Hampshire for the skiing with the Hanover children."

"The Hanovers—who are they?"

"Hanover, Goldman and Co. Now do you know?"

"Oh—those—the Wall Street people? What has she to do with them?"

"She must have quite a lot to do with them," said Katherine teasingly, "if she prefers to be with them in the ice and snow of New Hampshire, rather than with us in the warm sun of Florida."

"Skiing," muttered Grossman uneasily. "That child, with her delicate doll-legs. She oughtn't to be allowed."

"There's nothing to be afraid of. There's someone there to look after her. She's in good hands. There's Margaret, her special friend, and there's Felix."

"Felix? Who's he?"

"Felix Hanover, of course. Her fiancé, if you want to know."

The old man meditated, with a faraway look in his eyes. "So that's it?"

"Yes, sir."

"When did that happen?"

"We don't know. It seems the children have known it for a long time. Louise and Margaret were friends at school, and Felix came quite often with his sister to visit us. They played tennis together, they were all friends at camp. Well, just as I was preparing Louise to come down here with me, she comes in with that long youngster—I don't think you've ever seen him—and begs me and Lazar to let her go to New Hampshire with Margaret and Felix. And when we looked a bit disappointed, Felix came out with it. Louise and he are in love with each other, and they want our blessing. You should have seen our Louise while Felix was telling us—knee-high to a grasshopper, standing by his side. You see, Felix is going to be called up pretty soon, and he wants to be married first." Katherine had tears of happiness in her eyes. "How terrified the boy was! He held her hand, and he stammered, and he begged, and she encouraged him. It was so comical —and so heartbreaking. And when Felix pretended to look very grave and stern, you should have heard her pipe up: 'Pa, we love each other *so* much!' "

Isaac Grossman listened, and it seemed to him that he could see Clara, frail, delicate, childlike, at his side, and he could hear that singing, birdlike voice. He hid his feelings behind a matter-of-fact demeanor and asked, as it were skeptically, "And what about his parents? What do they think of it?"

"They had dinner with us a few nights ago. Lazar knows Felix's father, Alex Hanover, from the work on the Relief Committee. They were as friendly and as charming as could be. They know Louise and they like her a lot, and they're really happy at Felix's choice. They put only one condition: the wedding must take place before a rabbi, in a synagogue. You know, the Hanovers are traditional Jews, and they insist that Louise's and Felix's children must be brought up in the Jewish faith. I believe the Hanovers have had famous rabbis and scholars in their family. They're from Germany."

"Yes, yes, I know." He was thinking: The Grossmans had come a long way.... Shmaya Grossman's great-granddaughter marrying into the Hanover family.... Shmaya, of Essex Street. ... Aloud he asked, "And Louise agrees? I mean, the Jewish upbringing of the children."

"What do *you* think? What don't they do for love? Sure she agrees. I'm the only one who doesn't agree—" And as she said this her eyes laughed up at the old man.

"What a funny little person *you* are, Katherine."

"Am I? Why? What's funny about me?"

"I don't know. You're a queer soul. I can't tell you why."

"You can't talk like that without an explanation."

"You're the loyalest person in the world, Katherine. You'd go through fire and water for those you love."

"You're an old flatterer, father."

"I mean it."

"I know it, so I forgive you. Yes, Louise agrees, and she's more than happy about it."

"So this is the good news Lazar said you'd have for me," mused Grossman.

"Isn't it good news? Aren't you happy that your grandchildren have both come back to your people?"

"Indeed I am, indeed. And this marrying into the Hanovers. I am very happy. What do you hear from Robert?"

"We had a long letter from him—I mean Lazar did, and I've brought it with me for you to read. He's become a kind of assistant to a chaplain, and he says he wants to stay on in Germany as long as the chaplain does. Can you imagine our Robert an assistant chaplain? But it's a very sad letter. I didn't want to bring it, only Lazar insisted."

Grossman stretched out his hand. "Give it to me."

"Father, it's terribly sad."

"Never mind. I can imagine what it's about."

"It'll break your heart."

"Others have paid a heavier price for being Jewish. Let me have it, Katherine." And as she took the letter from her handbag he added: "I'll go into the next room for a while. Rose, take care of Katherine."

"She has, father. The nicest suite in the hotel. She's looked after everything."

"Imagine," grumbled the old man, "with those delicate limbs of hers, skiing in New Hampshire, in this weather." He was thinking again of Clara as he left the room. He wondered whether Felix Hanover would tremble over little Louise's well-being as he had done over Clara's.

"How is he, Rose?" asked Katherine in a low voice, indicating her father-in-law with her eyes.

"He has his bad moments. The nights aren't good. He doesn't sleep. Your visit ought to help a lot. You should have been here long ago, Katherine. He has to have his family around him."

"But, Rose, you're family too. He's so used to you."

Rose flushed. "I mean, his own flesh and blood. Sometimes his fits of depression frighten me."

"Lazar is worried. He had a talk with Dr. Markowitch again, and Dr. Markowitch said he's beginning to wonder whether this thing doesn't go much deeper than he suspected. Something very deep, out of his far-off past, coming up now and destroying his peace of mind. Perhaps we ought to consult a psychiatrist."

"I think it's too early to talk about that. Besides, that kind of talk would only upset his nerves more. I'm wondering whether it wasn't a mistake to tear him away so completely from his work.

120

He feels better when he's in harness. If he were to take up his work again he might forget."

"Forget what?" asked Katherine, eagerly.

Rose hesitated. "It's a trifle, really," she said at last. "I mean, it's a trifle in itself."

"So he told you?"

"You know what a hard life he had as a boy," answered Rose evasively. "It was a long, difficult struggle."

"But the thing itself is not serious?"

"What thing?"

"You mentioned it—a trifle, you said."

"You have to remember, Katherine, he was brought up in a strictly orthodox home, his parents were fanatically religious; they had queer beliefs. You know how sensitive he is to any idea of wrong, how he reacts to an injustice."

"Yes, that's the wonderful thing about him. Lazar is the same. And I wouldn't have him different. But there's a limit. There's his health."

"I think I can straighten this out. Not that it's serious; I mean straighten it out as far as he's concerned. He'll be calmer after that, I hope."

"Do you know whom it concerns?"

"Yes, he told me."

"Rose darling, don't put it off. We're frightened for him."

"I'm going to attend to it as soon as we get home."

Meanwhile Isaac Grossman, in the next room, was reading his grandson's letter. There were passages which he could not grasp, but what he did understand shook him profoundly:

Dear Father:

Something has happened to me in these last two weeks that I feel I must write you about. I have been on a tour, with our chaplain, of the sites of the former concentration camps in our part of the occupied territory, the places where Hitler put to death so many thousands of our brothers. And it seems to me that I have grown old in these two weeks. I suppose I should have understood before; maybe I was too young; maybe some people have to be on the spot to be able to see. I saw these places, and I heard—it seemed to me for the first time—the ghastly story: the starvation, the tortures, the degradation, the slaughter, the gas chambers, the ovens. It seems to me that I shall never be the same again.

I can't describe my feelings to you just now, but I have to tell you this: I don't believe that these horrible things were the work of one man, Hitler, or of one people, the Germans, or Nazis, or whatever name you want to give them. The evil doesn't come just from one source. It comes from many sources, and from many ages; it's an accumulation of generations and generations of injustice, oppression, crimes against God and man; and all of us have been guilty. All of us have been living materialistic lives, egotistical, sinful lives which have turned us into wild animals. I remember, dad, you once told me that people can be like animals in a forest. The strong attack the weak, and that's why we Jews are persecuted: not because we're better than the others, but because we're weaker, and our weakness awakens the blood lust of the hunter.

I've seen it here, in the remnants of the concentration camps. But I've seen it in America, too; not as something exceptional, but as part of our daily life. I've seen it in our "economic struggle," as we call it, but that's only a high-sounding name for our brutal treatment of each other, our exploitation of each other's weakness. We've become so accustomed to the evil, that all we think of is the bite of food we can snatch out of the other's mouth. I'm thinking of my own family. I never knew grandfather's father, but I know that he worked in a shop, in an orthodox Jewish shop, a sweatshop, and there he got tuberculosis. He worked for the sake of the hour or two of freedom which it got him, so that he could study the Talmud and praise God. He worked because he had to, it was the only means by which he could enjoy some spiritual freedom. But grandfather and you (forgive me for saying this, father) have turned your work into the sum of your spiritual life; your work is your worship and your faith. And you've never felt how enslaved you've become to materialism, the modern Moloch. I ask you again to forgive me for these

122

words. But a great change has taken place in me since I've had my eyes opened to the materialism into which we've been led.

I don't know whether I'll go back to college when I come home. If I do, it won't be to continue the course you persuaded me to take; all you had in mind was its practical value when I join the firm. I don't want to study economics; I don't want a law course. I don't want "practical" and "useful" courses. If I study at all, it'll be something not practical and not useful. It'll be something that will feed my soul, not my body. . . . I know I'm young, but I feel like an old man who has reached the end of the road, and stands before a blank wall. What kind of world is this that you brought us into? What kind of world is it that the older generation hands on to the younger generation? It's the practical world, the world of realism, of usefulness,— the school, the home, the thoughtfulness of our parents—it all adds up to the same thing. Such a world can perish, for all I care. I want to be impractical, unreal, even fantastic, if you want to put it that way. I don't believe in the leaders we've had till now. They've brought us to the concentration camps—to the economic and spiritual concentration camps. I need a God I can believe in.

There was much in the letter that eluded Isaac Grossman's understanding; but what he did understand startled him by its resemblance to what he had heard his brother Gabriel say:

"You have been so much occupied with yourselves that you have never had the time to occupy yourselves with God. You have thought only of yourselves."

Part II

CHAPTER ONE

THE Old Poland Restaurant in Springbrook, Connecticut, was a survival out of the last century, when the town had a physiognomy of its own—this was before New York had discovered Springbrook and turned it into a suburb of the metropolis—the physiognomy of a hard-working New England industrial town. The restaurant occupied one of the old buildings on Main Street, remodeled and with two wings added, a concession to the spirit of progress. Old Poland was particularly popular among the Irish of Springbrook. A group of Main Street storekeepers met there regularly for lunch—more out of habit than liking—and had their own tables. This too was a survival out of the more leisurely past, before New York had swooped down on the city. Even during the noon hour Old Poland retained some of the easier tempo of a bygone age; it was a little island of retreat from the frenzy of the present. One felt here the homey atmosphere of well-known customers. Everyone knew everyone else—owner, waiters, diners alike—since childhood, and everyone called everyone else by his first name.

As the noon hour passed, the people in a hurry were filtered out—the professionals, the lawyers, dentists, insurance agents—and Old Poland reverted more visibly to a previous age. It was a little like a European coffeehouse for people with no other occupation than to pass the time chatting, drinking coffee, glancing at the newspapers. There was, however, a difference. The oldtimers who made a long lunch of it, and the bookmakers who also had tables of their own, now settled down to the serious business of their existence—horses. And Mike the headwaiter was the presiding genius.

It was to Mike the headwaiter that the white workers came through the front door, the colored workers through the back door, to place their bets. They sidled up to him, whispered something into his ear, thrust something into his hand, and disappeared. Everything was done rapidly, with a minimum of words, without interruption of Mike's more respectable professional activities. For Mike served his favorite customers while he supervised the serving by other waiters and took bets and reported them—all with marvelous alertness and agility. He would come out of the kitchen balancing on one hand a tray of Irish stew prepared Polish fashion, with salad, vegetables, bread and butter, while with the other he received and pocketed the bets, remembering everything until he had transmitted it to the right bookie. He would do more: coming from the kitchen, and returning to it, he would pause here and there to answer a question, offer advice, report the odds, settle a dispute, recall a name; he would greet customers entering, say good-by to those leaving, take a new order, pacify someone impatiently demanding dessert, recommend a dish —and all of it neatly, acrobatically one might say, so that he seemed to be everywhere simultaneously.

He was a pleasant-looking man, and he put one in mind of the singing waiters of the old-time Bowery. He was, for all his amazing energy, somewhat plump, and a good deal older than he looked. His eyes were black and lively, his hair black, too, whether by nature or art could not be said. He had a thick black mustache, always lustrous, and an ingratiating voice. If he was not literally and physically everywhere simultaneously, he was everywhere simultaneously in the spirit. He would be pausing at one end of the restaurant and apparently overhearing what was being said at the other end, for he would call across, or slip by, and put in a relevant observation as if he had had nothing to do but eavesdrop. He had the complete picture of the restaurant before him at every moment: someone signaled behind him—he knew it without turning round; someone wanted a drink, Mike nodded without looking. He issued commands to the other waiters, knowing better than they who should be served out of turn, and who could be kept waiting, who was important, and who did not matter. Meanwhile he served, listened, took bets, threw in a word here and there.

"Hey, get a place ready for Mr. Goldman, don't you see he's just come in? The big table wants to pay. Mr. Nelson over there is in a hurry. Take Judge McMillan's coat. Step it up, there!"

Mike was weaving his way choreographically to one of the tables when he sensed, rather than saw, that a lady had entered. Very definitely a lady, because by her dress it was obvious to Mike that she was a New Yorker—black suit, small beret—and if she was from New York, she was a lady to Mike. What was she doing here? A meal? Certainly not. She was looking for someone? Very interesting. It was of course Mike's business. Everything was Mike's business. The lady did not sit down at a table. She went up to the desk, where Miss Yadviga, the daughter of Pan Zaslavsky, the owner, sat behind the cash register. Mr. Zaslavsky was at the bar, putting the bottles in order. He came over to the cash register, where Miss Yadviga and the lady were in conversation. The lady was asking for someone, and Mr. Zaslavsky called out.

"Hey, Mike!"

But Mike was already there.

The lady turned directly to Mike. "Do you know anyone by the name of Kovalsky?"

"Sure I do. There's lots of Kovalskys. Which one do you want—Mike, Yan, Stepan? There was a Yan Kovalsky, a dishwasher—"

"Mike!" Mr. Zaslavsky interrupted impatiently. Or perhaps it was in a tone of warning.

"I didn't say he was here. I can't tell the lady anything, unless she tells me first which one she's looking for."

"I can't tell you that now," the lady answered cautiously. "The Kovalsky I'm looking for used to work for the Yale Company."

"Oh, that must have been Stepan," said Mike. "What does the lady want him for?"

"I can't tell you that now," she repeated. "I've got to see him first."

"The lady can't see him. He's in the cemetery. He's dead."

"Is there a widow? Or are there children?"

"I think there's a widow. What does the lady want her for?"

The lady showed impatience. "That I can only tell the Kovalsky family, not a stranger."

"I'm no stranger to the Kovalskys," said Mike. "Stepan Kovalsky was my uncle by marriage, he was my mother's brother-in-law."

The lady stared in turn at Miss Yadviga, Pan Zaslavsky, Mike.

129

What was going on here? She made a visible effort to remain calm, and went on: "I'd like to talk to your aunt."

"I don't know whether my aunt is the one the lady wants to talk to. There were several Kovalskys," repeated the astonishing Mike. "If the lady would tell me what it's all about, I'd know which Kovalsky she means. But the lady doesn't want to talk."

The lady passed her tongue over her lips.

"Can I meet Mr. Kovalsky's widow, or a son, or a daughter?"

"Who sent the lady here?"

"We were sent here by Mr. Silverstein."

"Ha! Pop Moses. I thought so."

"He told us to ask here."

"Us? Who else is looking for Kovalsky?"

"What is the difference? Where can I find the widow?"

"Can't tell you unless I know what it's all about. The lady will have to excuse me. The customers are calling me."

It was true enough. There was a chorus of "Mike, what's happened to you?" and "Hey, Mike, come over here" from all over the restaurant. Miss Rosenberg stood at the desk, a dumbfounded look on her face.

"Who is that Mike?" she asked.

"Mike? Everybody knows. Mike is Mike. He's our headwaiter. He's been here a long time. He was here before I came."

"Do *you* know a Kovalsky?"

"Mike will tell you. He knows the whole town. If he doesn't know the man you want, nobody does."

"Did you have a Kovalsky here once, a dishwasher?"

"My dear lady, don't you see I'm busy?" Mr. Zaslavsky's politeness vanished. "Mike will tell you everything." And Mr. Zaslavsky went back to the bar.

Miss Rosenberg sat down grimly at a table. She was going to wait this out. She watched Mike flitting back and forth, between the tables, to and from the bar, in and out of the kitchen, carrying trays, breaking in on conversations, issuing instructions. He was obviously keeping an eye on her too, as if to make sure that she was not leaving. Every now and again he passed by her table and threw a few words at her.

"Well, does the lady remember which Kovalsky she's looking for?"

130

Before she could answer he was gone. A few moments later he was back.

"I've told you. The Kovalsky I'm looking for was a mechanic. He worked for the Yale Company."

There was another interval. Mike answered, passing, "Lots of Kovalskys were mechanics and worked for the Yale Company." And he was gone again.

This went on a while, a cat and mouse game. Miss Rosenberg had long since caught on. The man was an obvious twister and intriguer; he thought he could come in on something; it was impossible to trust him. She would tell him nothing more; she would only try to get whatever information she could out of him. She would be patient. That was the main thing.

She asked, "Who was the Kovalsky who was a dishwasher here?"

"Didn't say he worked here," he answered, as he flew by. Then, on another trip, he stopped briefly, and with a cunning look added, "Didn't you see the boss doesn't like to have him mentioned? The boss is a distant relative of that Kovalsky. He was no good. See what I mean?" Mike swayed a little, imitating a drunkard.

When he returned again Miss Rosenberg ventured a little more information. "This Kovalsky," she said, "married off one of his daughters, and just before the wedding he went to New York."

"Oh?" Mike pursed his lips shrewdly. "Married off a daughter? Went to New York just before the wedding? Is that so? Say, where can I meet you, lady, so we can talk. It's no good here—" and he indicated Mr. Zaslavsky.

"Silverstein's store, tomorrow afternoon, at three o'clock."

"Why Silverstein's? If the lady would let me know what hotel—"

"Silverstein's," said Miss Rosenberg abruptly.

"O.K., O.K., lady. Three in the afternoon. I'll have all the information for you."

The chorus rose once more: "Mike, what's keeping you?" "Mike, you're wanted." He disappeared again, with a knowing wink at Miss Rosenberg. She stood up, shuddered slightly, and went back to The Springbrook Inn, where Isaac Grossman was waiting for her.

She found him as she had left him, seated in an armchair and staring out of the window. A low, penetrating mist had descended, and swirled about the steeple of the church opposite the hotel. Isaac Grossman stared into the mist and said nothing as she entered. He turned toward her, and the white mist was reflected in his eyes. Miss Rosenberg, convinced that both Kovalskys mentioned by Mike were dead, was afraid of the effect the information would have on her employer. She burst out:

"I don't believe a single word that man told me."

"What man?"

"That Polish waiter Mike that Mr. Silverstein sent us to."

"What did he tell you?"

"He said there are lots of Kovalskys. He himself is related to one of them, and he knows another. These Kovalskys are dead. But the man's a liar, a swindler. He's fishing for something."

She had expected to see Grossman leap to his feet. He remained sitting and asked quietly, "What about widows, children?"

"There's a widow living, with a daughter. But Mike's cagey. He won't take us there unless he knows what our business with the widow is."

"It's the Kovalsky whose widow is still living," said Grossman.

"But Mr. Grossman, how do you know that's the one?"

"I just know, that's all."

"Oh, what's the good, Mr. Grossman? You're guessing, and Mike's a liar and a faker. He says it's Stepan's widow, not Yan's, that's alive. And we're looking for Yan. What's more, Stepan worked at the Yale factory, but Yan was a dishwasher, and a regular drunkard. Mike claims he's a nephew of Stepan's widow; but Yan was related to Mr. Zaslavsky, the owner of Old Poland. You daren't talk about Yan when Mr. Zaslavsky's around—he doesn't want to hear his name mentioned. He was a bad lot."

"That's the man," cried Mr. Grossman. "Mike has it all mixed up. I can see it now. That's the man I ruined."

"Ruined?" asked Miss Rosenberg, shocked.

"Certainly. Don't you see it? It was because of me that he became a drunkard—perhaps a thief, too." Grossman became silent.

"But you can't believe a word Mike says."

"What's that got to do with it? It's absolutely clear to me.

Didn't he say, 'They won't believe me. They'll say I spent the money getting drunk.'?"

"Isaac!" Miss Rosenberg used his first name, as she always did under great stress. "You've promised to give me a free hand. I want to warn you, if you interfere I'll drop it all, and return to New York. Do you want the whole town to be talking about this? We're dealing with a crook. I'm convinced he's a crook."

"Yes, yes, we've got to be careful, that's true enough. But I have to do one thing, you understand." Grossman's voice trembled, and his eyes filled with tears. Miss Rosenberg had never seen him in this condition before.

"What's that?"

"I want to tell the widow that Kovalsky didn't spend his money on drink that day. I want to tell her that he came to buy a suit, yes, and he lost his money, it was stolen from him. That's the one thing I've got to do." He sat down again in the armchair, and covered his face with his hands.

"Very well. You'll do that. But only when you've made sure that you're speaking to the right person. Don't fall into the hands of a swindler."

"Yes, that mustn't happen," whispered Grossman, nodding.

"Tomorrow we'll meet Mike at Silverstein's. He'll have the widow's address. We'll go there. If that's the woman, we'll know what's to be done next. And now will you be calm?"

"I am calm. Why do you say I'm not calm?" asked Grossman; and his eyes were like those of a hurt child.

CHAPTER TWO

IT was the GI's who had given Moses Silverstein the affection-
ate name of Pop Moses, but he had been a well-known figure in
Springbrook long before. To Jew and gentile alike he was known
as the man to go to when you were in trouble. Not that he was
attached in an official capacity to any philanthropic organization;
no such body had appointed him or paid him a salary; perhaps it
would have been accurate to call him a one-man philanthropic
enterprise. If a Polish or a Jewish woman came into his stationery
store, weeping and wringing her hands because there was not a
piece of bread in the house to see them through till the next pay-
day, or because a child was sick and there wasn't the money for
the medicine which the doctor had prescribed, or because a son
had got into trouble and there was no one to guarantee bail, or
because an aging father or mother needed to be taken to a hospital,
or into an old folks' home—if they came with this or other similar
miseries into Moses Silverstein's stationery store, they knew they
would not be turned away. Moses Silverstein would take them
into his "office"—the courtesy name for the narrow, windowless
room at the back of the store. It was illumined by a single gas jet
at all seasons, and warmed in the winter by a little gas stove on
which stood a tin tea kettle always on the boil. There was also a
desk covered with old papers, dusty books, and merchandise.
Moses did not sit on the rocker which stood near the table; he had
quicksilver in his feet, and springs in all his limbs. His long, lean
figure hopped, strode, skipped, turned, as if the plaintive words
of the women set the springs inside him dancing. His head, set
on a long, lean neck, shook in every direction, as if inside his
neck, too, there was a spring. He nodded continuously, and as he
did so, the little goatee danced along, and with it the glasses
balanced on his eagle-beak of a nose. The glasses had an incredible

134

way of dancing on his nose without ever dancing off it. Instinctively you stretched out your hand to catch them, but they never fell. It was as though they were attached with invisible wires to the bridge of his nose; they could dance just so far and no further. When the woman had finished her story, Moses expressed his sympathy, not in so many words, but in a few extra spasmodic movements of his body, his head, his beard, his limbs; and having done so, he would proceed to action. He would pick up the telephone on the dusty table.

And when Moses was on the telephone, in action on one of his cases, his little store could be packed with clamoring customers, there could be riots in the street, war and pestilence might threaten mankind—Moses would not leave the telephone until he had completed his self-imposed task. He broke through locked doors, through steel walls, into forbidden places. Everyone knew Moses; when Moses called it was useless to try to get away. Father Murphy of St. Vincent's, the Reverend Neilson of the First Presbyterian Church, Rabbi Silman of the Temple, Dr. Steinberg of the City Philanthropies, the Mayor, the aldermen, the Police Commissioner—they knew that voice; they knew the story. Moses wanted something; Moses was prepared to guarantee, with all that he had, and all that he was, the character and need and worthiness of the person he was pleading for. And if Moses got a refusal on the telephone, he would be around in person, with his case in tow. Moses guaranteed loans, contracted loans in his own name, pawned his possessions, and saw to it that the needy one was helped. Friends and relatives pleaded and argued—Moses paid not the slightest attention. Everyone in Springbrook knew Moses, those that needed help and those that could extend it. And Moses always got his way, in part because he was respected, but more because it was impossible to get rid of him.

When the GI's began to return to America from their overseas service, Moses took up their cause as a personal matter. Himself the father of an only son who had also gone overseas, but would never return, he became the father of the local GI's. Thus it was that the boys had given him the name "Pop Moses." But he did not relinquish his interest in his older clientele, and his was still the best known address among the poor of Springbrook. They came to him not only for help but for spiritual advice, too. More than one broken family had been made whole again in his "office." He was a domestic court, a counselor, an arbitrator, all rolled into one. Quarreling business partners, congregations at odds with their ministers, heirs at war over a legacy, sought him out and agreed to abide by his decision. He had an extraordinary faculty for listening without taking sides; and his favorite technique, after having heard all the details of the quarrel between husband and wife, was to lock them in his office and make them talk it out between them. Often a ferocious shouting was heard inside, but Moses did not interfere: "Let them yell," he said, "people have to spit their angers out, and then friendship returns." Sometimes the method succeeded, sometimes it did not.

The name of Moses had spread beyond the confines of Springbrook. Traveling salesmen had spread his reputation through the country; and strangers visiting Springbrook for the first time were liable to turn to Moses for advice and information. Grossman had known Moses Silverstein for many years, and from him he had often learned of vacant pieces of property which were about to be put on the market. Neither Lazar nor Miss Rosenberg had ever suspected that there was a special reason for Grossman's interest in Springbrook; they assumed that he had cast his eyes at the little city as one of the up and coming places around New York, and had made his big purchase there as he had made purchases elsewhere, in the expectation of a large profit. As it happened, it was one of his best investments.

In the days when Grossman made that purchase he had been moved by vague impulses toward the memory of Kovalsky; he had played with the notion of going into the matter again. But the pressure of Kovalsky's memory was fitful and intermittent. It had brought him to Springbrook, it had prompted him to buy the property, it had flickered up and had died down—and it had seemed to Grossman that he was in danger of making a fool of himself. He had, indeed, never gone so far as to ask Silverstein about Kovalsky; a warning prudence inside him held him back. And yet he had returned several times, always with abortive intentions. Moses Silverstein had begun to look upon him as a local resident—chiefly for the purpose of enlisting his help for his cases. Grossman became a contributor to the local charities, to the city chest, and to the Jewish drives—on top of which there were regular calls from Moses Silverstein for "specials." Perhaps through these benefactions Grossman was dulling the reproaches of his conscience; perhaps the mere contact with Springbrook gave him the obscure feeling that he was always about to straighten out the matter. But the fact remained that he had let it drift through all the years.

Now, when the pressure of it had become intolerable and he was determined to put an end to it, he had come with Miss Rosenberg to Springbrook, and they had turned to Moses Silverstein for information about Kovalsky. They did not say what they wanted of the man; Moses did not ask. He assumed that Kovalsky had once worked for Grossman and had disappeared without collecting some monies due him, and now Grossman was looking for the man, or his family, in order to make the payment. So he had sent them to Old Poland, and to Mike, who knew the Poles of Springbrook even better than he.

They found Mike at Silverstein's the next afternoon. He had been waiting there for half an hour; and he had, he indicated, the answers to all their questions.

Before he sent Grossman and Miss Rosenberg into the office, Moses said, in a low voice: "I ought to warn you—this man isn't to be trusted. Watch him."

"Thank you," answered Miss Rosenberg. "I caught on to that myself."

They sat in the inner room, Grossman in a corner, away from the flickering gaslight, Mike near the stove which drove away some of the damp chill. Miss Rosenberg sat opposite Mike, who had come to this important appointment in his Sunday suit, with a blue shirt and a multicolored tie. His mustaches glistened with a recent application of grease. He spoke freely, and with vigorous gesticulations.

"Sure I know the Kovalskys you mean. Why shouldn't I? My mother was a Kovalsky, and she married a Kovalsky, Stepan Kovalsky. No, not Yan Kovalsky. Yan was a distant relative, maybe a second cousin. At first the Kovalskys lived in Watertown, and worked on a farm. Then they settled in Springbrook. I'm talking about Stepan Kovalsky. He was a butcher. He didn't have his own butchershop. He used to take a pig, or a calf, off his farm and kill it, and peddle the meat to the farms round here. He used to make sausages, too, and liverwurst. Oh, he was good. He used to go round with a horse and cart to all the farms, and he made a good living."

"But yesterday you said he was a mechanic, and worked at the Yale factory."

"Sure. That was later, when he settled in Springbrook. You see, he lost his farm—I don't know how, because he was making good money. Then he came here, and he worked for the Yale Company. No, I'm remembering now. He wasn't a mechanic. He was a watchman. Or anyway, he was a watchman for some time, see? At first a night watchman, and then a day watchman. Sure, I remember. He used to stand at the gate and search the workmen when they left the factory. Any man he suspected, maybe he was carrying away a tool or something, he had the right to search him. They were scared of him. He was a big guy, big shoulders, and big arms. They gave him a policeman's badge, he used to wear it under his coat, like this, see? They let him wear a uniform, too, like a policeman's uniform."

"And there's a widow here, this Stepan's widow?" asked Miss Rosenberg.

"Yeah, that's my aunt. The lady can go and see her any time she likes, and the gentleman too. My aunt is expecting you, because I told her that a lady and a gentleman came special from New York to see her. She's living with a daughter, Mrs. Zaslavsky, it's not far from here, on the Post Road. The old woman's a bit deaf, and she's not quite right here—" He tapped his forehead. "The Zaslavskys have a lot of trouble with her. They want to put her into the city home, because they need the bed for the son who came back from the army; he's got a wife and a child. He wants a home. You can't get homes here in Springbrook, no homes, no houses, no rooms. And this boy who came back from the army, he got all upset, and he began to drink. It's hell there—I mean in the Zaslavsky home." Mike grinned.

"Why don't they take her into the city Home?" asked Grossman.

"They say she's not quite right in the head, so she ought to go to an institution, you know, lunatic asylum. And the lunatic asylum, they say they're not an old people's home. So she doesn't get anywhere. And Mrs. Zaslavsky—her name's Yadviga, like my boss's daughter—Mrs. Zaslavsky has it hard, with the old woman there and her husband drinking. He doesn't treat her right."

"Who is this Yadviga?" asked Grossman.

"I told you. She's my cousin. She's Stepan's daughter. Yadviga, that's her name."

"Does the old lady remember, did she ever tell the daughter, how the father went off to New York just before the wedding?"

"You better ask my cousin, lady."

"Did the father have business in New York?" persisted Miss Rosenberg. "Was there any reason why he should have gone there?"

"I can't tell you, missus." Mike had passed from "lady" to "missus"—a sign of growing familiarity. "You talk with my aunt, or my cousin. If the gentleman can't tell me what business he has with my aunt, I can't tell him what business my uncle had in New York."

"And what about Yan Kovalsky?" asked Grossman, suddenly out of his corner. "What became of him?"

"Oh, he was no good, mister. Yan Kovalsky was a boozer, drank like a fish. And a gambler, a terrible gambler. Horses. He'd sell his pants, the shirt off his back, his shoes; he'd steal; everything, to back horses. He was always hanging round the race tracks getting tips from jockeys, inside dope. Once he had a job as a stableboy and traveled to all the race tracks, Saratoga Springs, New Jersey, Long Island, everywhere. He was away for years. Then he came back to Springbrook, he had a game leg, he was half crippled. He said a horse kicked him in the belly. But that was a lie. We found out that a trainer caught him doping one of the horses before a race. We took him into the restaurant, just out of pity, gave him a job, a busboy, a dishwasher. But he was just the same. Drinking and gambling, drinking and gambling. We tried to cure him, yes, mister. We locked him once in a room, before one of the races, but that made him crazy, his hands were shaking, and he used to break dishes. Then he was caught stealing knives and forks and selling them to a junk-dealer, all for the races. He used to make a lot of trouble for the bookies. Used to tell the colored boys the bookies were swindling them. He got beat up a couple of times. Then we sent him away from the restaurant, so he broke in at night and stole a lot of whisky and sold

139

it to a colored restaurant. Everything for the horses. We had to keep him away from here. He was bumming around in the streets for a couple of weeks, and then I guess he did something real bad, because the police came after him. But they never caught him, and we never heard anything more about him."

"And his wife? His daughter?" asked Grossman, from his corner.

"Whose wife? Whose daughter?"

"Yan's."

"What are you talking about? He never had a wife, and he never had a daughter. He was always a tramp. The Kovalsky who had a wife and a daughter, that was my Uncle Stepan. That's the aunt and cousin you're going to see. Tomorrow, three o'clock like today, we'll go there. We'll meet here again, eh?"

Before they could question him further, he was gone.

Isaac Grossman did not let himself be put off by Mike's rambling account of the past. Yan Kovalsky was the man he had wronged. Yan Kovalsky had had a wife and daughter. Yan Kovalsky had worked for the Yale Company. And Yan Kovalsky had disgraced himself, and had been ruined. All that Mike said about Yan and his gambling and thieving was true. But it had happened after his return from New York. He had lost his job. He had become a dishwasher. He had taken to drinking, to gambling, to forget his misery.

All that night Isaac Grossman struggled with the man he had ruined. He saw Kovalsky sitting at the door of the restaurant kitchen, peeling potatoes, or at the sink, washing dishes. Grimy, ragged, haggard, unshaven, an idiotic smile on his twisted lips— that idiotic smile which Grossman had seen when the man came back, terrified, from Grand Street, without his wallet. But worse. Yan Kovalsky, the despised. Everybody knew about that incident. The waiters in the restaurant, too. They jeered at him, bullied him, made his life unbearable.

Grossman tortured himself reconstructing the events of that day of the wedding. He saw Kovalsky stealing into his own house in his old, tattered clothing. They were all waiting for him: the bride, the mother, the bridegroom and his family, all decent, respectable people. And the bride's father sneaked into the house like a fright-

140

ened thief. Kovalsky saw the bride turning pale, he heard the screaming of the bride's mother: "Drunkard! This is how you come back for your daughter's wedding!" And no doubt Kovalsky had actually got drunk, unable to face the family. "Drunkard! Get in there!" And his wife pushed him out of the living room, out of the kitchen, into a black hole under the stairs. "There's your place!" Kovalsky tried to stammer something, as he had stammered in the clothing store, "They'll say I spent the money getting drunk." Of course they said it. He *was* drunk. And from that time on he was never really sober again. He lost his job in the factory. They took him into the restaurant out of pity—that was the way it had happened.

Yan Kovalsky never recovered his self-respect, his ambition, his human dignity. He never recovered his self-control. He had to drink and gamble. And when he hadn't any money, he stole. They threw him out of the restaurant; he came back like a whipped dog, because he had nowhere else to go. Now and then they'd take pity on him. A waiter would throw him the remnants of a customer's meal, as one throws a bone to a homeless dog.

The picture became so vivid that Grossman began to think that he ought to get up from his bed and go out into the night and find Yan Kovalsky, who was no doubt lying at this moment on the doorstep of the Polish restaurant, a huddled figure soaked to the bone by the mist. Isaac Grossman fought with himself. These were hallucinations, dreams. But what are dreams? he asked himself desperately. Are they not the things we see at night which we are afraid to look at in the daytime? Undoubtedly he was seeing things more clearly now. For instance, that ludicrous, criminal notion of his that he could straighten things out with Kovalsky by returning the money, or returning it a thousandfold; or by explaining, after all these years, what had happened. What restitution could there be? What baseness it was to think of it all as a business transaction.

But surely Kovalsky was not there now, on the doorstep of the restaurant. That was utterly impossible. Was it? Was he saying "Impossible! Impossible!" because he didn't dare to face the man? That was it. On the other hand, he was imagining all these things only because he wanted to torment and punish himself. It was good and proper that he should be so punished, and therefore

141

he was conjuring up the picture of Yan coming home to the wedding, disgraced, Yan being thrown out of the factory, Yan becoming a drunkard and a gambler, Yan lying on the doorstep of the restaurant.

"I won't think of him any more," muttered Grossman to himself. But in the brief instant of denial he knew that he *wanted* to think of Kovalsky, did not dare to dismiss him. Kovalsky had become a necessity to him. And he relinquished the brief resolution and gave free reign to his hallucinations.

Suddenly he got out of bed and dressed rapidly. He was going out to the restaurant to find Kovalsky.

Miss Rosenberg, in the adjoining room, woke just as he got to his door. She sprang up, threw on her nightgown, and came in, to see her employer fully dressed, with hat and overcoat on.

"Isaac! Where are you going?"

"To meet him."

"Oh God! To meet whom?"

"Kovalsky. He's lying on the doorstep of the Polish restaurant."

She rushed over and placed herself in front of the door, falling back against it in fright and weakness.

"You're having nightmares."

"I'm wide awake. I know what I'm doing. Let me go to him."

"Isaac! For God's sake! Go back to your bed."

"I am not dreaming, I am not sick. They've thrown him out of the restaurant. I must go to him."

She took him by the sleeve and led him away from the door.

"Listen to me, Isaac. Kovalsky is dead."

He was stupefied. "Kovalsky, the dishwasher at the Polish restaurant? Dead?"

"All those Kovalskys are dead. They died many years ago. Go back to bed."

"Many years ago?" murmured Grossman. "Died many years ago. I was sure that he's alive, and waiting for me."

She helped him to undress, and when she went back to her room she did not lie down for fear of falling asleep, but sat at the door, listening.

It was clear to her now that her employer was sick. And now it occurred to her for the first time that perhaps there had never been a Kovalsky in his life, and no such incident as he had described.

142

Somewhere he had heard that name, perhaps here in Springbrook, to be sure; somewhere he had heard of some such incident. Perhaps a friend of his had told him the story, and somehow, in the way sick people have, Grossman had caught it up, brooded on it, injected himself into it, made himself a part of it. And now it was a fixation with him. The best thing was probably to tell Lazar all about it, to have Dr. Markowitch come in, before the story became public property. That was undoubtedly the best thing. Nevertheless, she hesitated. Had she the right to disclose, even to her employer's son, even to her employer's doctor, the secret he had entrusted to her, the secret he had kept from his own wife? She was the only one he had confided in. Perhaps there was something in it, even though it resembled in no way the tragedy Grossman had made of it. She trembled at the possibility that her "betrayal" of the confidence would only plunge her employer into deeper complications of hallucination. She trembled at the thought of what it might do to their relationship. He would think of her as treacherous; he would never trust her again. And yet, something had to be done. But what? What? She stood before a blank wall.

CHAPTER THREE

THE pattern of the days and nights which Grossman had established in Winter Paradise held in Springbrook. When he arose the next morning no one would have guessed that he had passed a sleepless and tormented night. Miss Rosenberg, who had fallen asleep late, was astonished when he awoke her. He was fully dressed, clean-shaven, fresh, smiling—the Isaac Grossman she had always known, radiating energy and waiting impatiently to begin a day's work.

"I knew that vacation would make us both lazy," he said. "Get up, lazybones. No more vacation, thank God. We're in Springbrook, remember? Not for pleasure, but for business. Get up!"

"What business?" She was a little frightened, as well as bewildered.

"We've got a piece of property here, haven't we, that my clever son is thinking of leasing to others. We're going to take a look at it. If others can use it, why can't we?"

Not a word about the Kovalskys. She looked at him uncertainly. Was Kovalsky just a night apparition, banished by the day? Had her employer been awake when he got up in the middle of the night, ready to go out in search of Kovalsky? Or had he been in a kind of trance, sleepwalking? But he had spoken with her. It was impossible to understand. Did he remember the conversation in the night? She would not try to find out; she would not mention the incident, or Kovalsky. She would play up to his present behavior. She answered cheerfully: "All right, Mr. Industrious. Give me a few minutes. Have you had breakfast?"

"Certainly not. I was waiting for the lady."

"Order for both of us. I want bacon and eggs, and tea. And I give you permission to have anything you like this morning."

"Make it fast," he said, as he left the room.

It was a typical New England spring day. Sunshine and clouds alternated, the streets were alternately wet and dry. The clouds raced across the sky, now throwing the town into shadow, now opening it to warm, exhilarating sunshine. There was liveliness and hope in the air, an awakening and a promise.

Isaac Grossman and his secretary, still wrapped in their winter clothes, walked energetically down Main Street. Miss Rosenberg was overjoyed by her employer's mood, though a nagging doubt of its stability worked at the back of her mind. But she hoped that the spring, the resumption of work, the excitement of new plans, would make a permanent change in him for the better.

Smith's Farm, the Grossman property in Springbrook, lay to one side of the town, where Main Street ended and the State road began. Main Street curved into the road, and farther on there was the new residential district. Springbrook was one of the oldest settlements in Connecticut, but apart from the wooden Congregationalist Church with its classical Colonial steeple, and a few buildings of the early nineteenth century, themselves mostly rebuilt and remodeled, nothing remained of the original architecture. The buildings on Main Street were either middle nineteenth century, put up when Springbrook was developing into a commercial and industrial center, or early twentieth—mostly two- and three-story structures, business and professional offices. Here and there, between the rows of shops, more massive buildings rose, in imitation Colonial style, in brick and wood. The city hall dominated the public square, opposite the Presbyterian Church with its arches in the Norman style. There were two Catholic Churches, with high Gothic arches and spires visible for many miles around.

Main Street, with its men's clothing, furniture, tobacco, hardware, and liquor stores, hotels, and restaurants, ran from City Hall down to Smith's Farm. There it curved into the ridges of the automobile road. A straight continuation of Main Street once led through Smith's Farm. The present odd development was due, it was told locally, to the obstinacy of a certain Smith, who had refused to abandon his farm in spite of fantastic offers, thereby causing Springbrook to avoid and then surround him. When Smith died there were complications in the will, much litigation, and still no sale. Finally the property had been released, and Isaac Grossman had come into possession, but he too had held on and done nothing except pay taxes. The older inhabitants of Springbrook remembered when cows used to pasture on Smith's Farm. Smith had had the right, in his day, of leading his cattle across Main Street—which at that time ran straight through—from the pastures to the milking shed. On either side of the road there had been a shingle: ATTENTION! PASSAGE FOR CATTLE. Traffic had to stop to let the animals cross. There was not a cow, or any other sign of life, visible there now. The farm was desolate and neglected, covered with weeds and thorns; young pines and elms lifted their slender branches into the cool spring air. The ruined farmhouse stood on a hillock, and the peeling barns and storehouses were surrounded by tangles of barbed wire. At the entrance to the farm was a sign: PRIVATE PROPERTY. NO TRESPASSING.

Grossman crawled through hedges, pushed aside barbed wires, climbed briskly, and dragged Miss Rosenberg after him. Finally they reached the summit of the hillock, and there Grossman paused, looked around grandly, and with sweeping gestures indicated his plans. Main Street lay on one side, and on the other, at a distance, the graceful residential area, surrounded by young trees just beginning to green. White, green, and red, the little houses seemed to be dreaming in light and shadow.

"My God! We can create a whole city here. Streets, squares, gardens. Look! I'll cut the main street through this way—a residential street, apartment houses, not high ones, two or three stories, Georgian style, red brick and white woodwork. The houses will stand behind big green lawns. Part of it I'll reserve for shops, in a uniform style, for this whole district; New England style, with big, wide windows; and lawns with flower beds in front of the shops. You see that slope there? It would be a wonderful place for a movie. Two stories, fifteen hundred seats. I'll use the rear for a parking lot and a gasoline station for the movie theater patrons. My God! At a time like this, with people crying for homes, to leave a place like this undeveloped." He was speaking to himself now more than to Miss Rosenberg. "And the way the town is growing! It's a wonderful location for middle class income people. They'll gladly pay the same prices here as on Long Island. Why, it's easier to get here, from Grand Central. Forty-five minutes, that's all. And no subway misery. No comparison between Long Island and Connecticut. From here you're in the open country in

146

five minutes, resorts, holiday places. You can charge the same rent here for three and four rooms with kitchen as in Forest Hills. And what with government encouragement, you can put up three hundred units here. And my wise son was thinking of giving it away, practically giving it away."

She let him talk on, happy in his absorption. This was her old boss, the one she knew so well, the one she admired and loved. He made her think of a fish—a powerful old fish who had been flung on the land, had nearly died, had floundered back into the water, had come to, and was swimming again vigorously in his own element. The nightmare was gone.

"We have to think of a name for the development, eh? Smith Village. How do you like that one."

"Why not Grossman Village?"

"Grossman Village! Grossman Village! I don't like to push my name. Well, we'll see. The important thing is to get moving. I'd like to have Frankel out here at once. We'll call the office. Get the surveyors busy. I'll tell Lazar my plans. But first—there's that meeting with Mike."

Her heart stood still. "Mike!"

"Certainly. Didn't we make an appointment with him for this afternoon?"

"Mr. Grossman," said Miss Rosenberg, dry-throated, "we're not going to meet Mike." She became vehement. "We're dropping that Kovalsky business."

"What are you talking about?"

"It's a delusion, do you hear? I just don't believe you ever had anything to do with the Kovalskys." She looked straight into his eyes.

"I see. You think I'm sick. I'm out of my mind. Tell me, Rose, have I been talking like a sick person?" He took her hand and looked back at her.

"No, you're not sick. It's just nervousness. Depression. You think often of Clara. And there's your liver. And childhood memories; and your father's stories of hell and hellfire. I just don't know where you picked up this Kovalsky delusion, but it *is* a delusion. If it keeps returning, you'll have to see a doctor. You've got to get rid of it before it really makes you sick."

"But what about Kovalsky? What's going to happen to him?"

"There is no such person. You've got to forget him."

"If I'm to forget Kovalsky, I have to kill you first."

She started. "Why?"

"Because you're the only person who knows my secret. You're the only one who knows why I'm looking for him. How can I forget my shame as long as you know about it? Every time I'll see you I'll remember it."

"Well, if it'll help you to forget, kill me," she answered, smiling. She took his hand and stroked it, but he went on repeating: "We've got to see Mike this afternoon."

She shook her head. "I'll have nothing to do with it. I'm not going to encourage your mania."

"Let me see him this once. Let me find out once for all whether I did meet that Kovalsky in New York," he pleaded, a note of cunning in his voice.

"Mike is a liar, a twister, a swindler. He'll supply you with a Kovalsky. He'll fool you."

"Will he? That Polak will fool *me?* It'll take a dozen like him to put one over on Isaac Grossman. Look, let's have no more such talk. We're going to Silverstein's. And Mike will take us to the widow."

"I'll have no part in it," said Miss Rosenberg.

"So you'll leave me. Just when I need you most. Very good. I'll go alone."

"I won't let you. You're pursuing a chimera, a nightmare."

"Let me find it out for myself. Isn't that the best way to get rid of it? I must get rid of it. It's torturing me to death."

What was the use? They could talk like this for hours, and it would lead nowhere.

"Don't be afraid for me, Rose. If this is a trick, I'll find out soon enough, and I'll send him packing."

Pity and uncertainty struggled in her with common sense. He might be right; perhaps it was best to see it through.

"Very well," she said. "I'll come with you. But on one condition —that you don't ask me to leave you alone with Mike."

Strawberry Hill lay outside Springbrook, not far from the city incinerator. Despite its aspiring name, it was a depression and formed part of a drained swamp. The smoke of the incinerator

148

hung low over it, and poisoned the air as far down as the shore of the lake. At one time the area had been occupied by slaughter-houses and tan-yards, but these had been removed further from the city. There remained the rows of tumbledown houses which had been occupied by the workers, long rows of two- and three-story dwellings. Every row had a continuous veranda, with a single flight of wooden stairs at one end. On the verandas most of the families did their cooking, and sometimes even their bathing, in full view of the neighbors; on these they also slept on the hot summer nights. The verandas made a common meeting ground, and intro-duced a social note into the lives of the workers, a touch of neigh-borliness. Here and there the veranda would be turned into a storage room for household possessions which found no place within: old baby carriages, iceboxes, bundles of frayed linen, col-lapsible cots which, with their pillows inside, looked like monster sandwiches. On the verandas was hung the wash, and coats and dresses which needed airing. There was a depressing monotony about the long lines of shirts, underwear, socks. Occasionally there was a touch of color—an Italian scarf, a Polish shawl, a Latvian headcovering. Sometimes it was a motley carpet, or a Sunday dress, or a winter jacket with a mangy fur collarpiece. Wire cages, with or without birds, hung from the rafters. And here and there a flowerpot added a wistful reminder of meadows.

They mounted the moldering wooden steps, made their way through piles of household goods, past domestic animals. From the open doors issued the heavy odors of cooking, of damp bedclothes, accompanied by the squalling of children and the angry voices of grownups. They came at last to the Zaslavsky home on the third floor. To enter, they had to push aside a heap of dirty laundry lying near a tin washtub. Bent over the washtub was an elderly woman. Her head, swathed in a kerchief, was thrust into the rising steam. She had not noticed their approach.

"Cousin Yadviga! Cousin Yadviga! You're doing the wash now? Didn't I tell Auntie I was bringing the gentleman and the lady from New York, the ones who are looking for the Koval-skys?"

The woman straightened up and turned round. One saw at first only two big eyes set deep in a hard, wrinkled face. Then one noticed the thin, compressed lips, and the sharp nose. The woman stared a while at the group, saying nothing, so that they became uncomfortable. Then she said, in a gruff voice:

"And suppose the lady and the gentleman are looking for the Kovalskys, will they help me to do the wash?" She turned to Grossman and Miss Rosenberg. "What do you want with the Kovalskys?"

"Yadviga, for God's sake come inside. The lady and the gentleman have something important to tell you. They came here specially from New York." Mike gesticulated at Yadviga, using eyes, hands, even legs, in the effort to convey the importance of the visit.

"Where will they sit down inside? There's no place."

"We'll find a place, good friend," said Grossman mildly. "We're not going to do you any harm, either."

The woman was right. When they came into the dim low room they seemed to perceive nothing but beds, ranged along the walls. Some of the beds were occupied, for heads were raised at their entry, and then fell back. When Grossman's eyes had become accustomed to the half-darkness, he saw a kitchen table in a corner. From one side of the table a long broad bench ran along the wall, covered with bedclothes, and under the bedclothes a figure half sat and half reclined. At the other side of the table was a coal stove, which overheated the room, and on the flat stove top were some pots and a huge tin kettle of boiling water. Gradually Grossman also made out a shelf bracketed into the wall and loaded with cooking utensils, and a small china closet. In a second corner, over the sink, there was a shelf with a razor, a brush, a shaving mirror, and a towel rack. Jammed in among the beds was a chest of drawers, and on it a lamp with a colored paper shade, a book, a sugarbowl, and a cracked mirror into the edges of which were stuck faded photographs. On the wall above the cracked mirror hung two sacred pictures, Jesus of the Bleeding Heart, and Our Lady of Chenstochova, both in Byzantine style, and both illumined by a tiny red electric bulb.

"Jerry, get up and go into your bed, so the lady and gentleman can sit down," said the woman, and snatched the cover off the bench.

A boy of seven or eight was curled up on the bench. He said, in a spoiled, obstinate voice, "I don't wanna." He threw an angry look at the intruders.

"Is the child sick?" asked Grossman.

The woman shook her head, and turned again to the boy. "Go on, get into bed."

"I don't wanna. Let them get into bed."

"Why isn't the boy in a hospital?" asked Grossman.

"He's not sick," said Mike. He went over, picked up the boy, and carried him to a bed.

"But he is! There's something the matter with him," insisted Grossman.

"It's nothing," said the woman sharply. She lifted the remainder of the bedclothes off the bench, threw them across a bed, and indicated a place for Grossman and Miss Rosenberg. "Now tell me what you want with the Kovalskys."

"You are a Kovalsky, aren't you?" began Miss Rosenberg. She had been standing, silent, observant, patient. Now it was obvious that she intended to get through with the business quickly.

"My father was a Kovalsky. Now I'm a Zaslavsky."

"Is your mother living?"

"Yes, she's there, in that bed. She can't get up. Do you want to see her?"

"Not now. Tell me, what year were you married?"

"I don't remember."

"You mean you don't remember how long you're married?"

"What should I remember for? I have more important things to think about."

"But try. Try and remember."

"Why should I? And what do you want to know for? Is it the police?"

"It has nothing to do with the police."

"If it's not the police, why should I answer you? Will it do me any good? Will it help me with my troubles?"

"It might," said Grossman.

"Tell them, Pani Yadviga," broke in Mike. "Tell them. It's for your good. The lady and gentleman are interested in you—and in all the Kovalskys," he added.

"I was married in nineteen hundred and ten," said the woman.

"Nineteen hundred and ten?" repeated Miss Rosenberg.

"Yes, what's surprising about that? Nineteen hundred and ten."

Miss Rosenberg threw a quick and meaningful glance at her employer. But Grossman either did not perceive, or refused to respond. He took up the questioning.

"Was it in the spring, in May?"

"Yes."

"You're sure? In May?"

"Yes. Is that bad?"

"No, no," said Miss Rosenberg, resuming the cross-questioning. "Tell me, did your father often go to New York?"

"I don't know how often. He used to go now and again. He had family there."

"Did your father take a trip to New York a day before the wedding?"

"I don't remember. I don't think he did. Why should he go to New York a day before my wedding?"

"Maybe to bring some of the family with him. Maybe to buy a suit for the wedding."

"Buy a suit? He didn't have to go to New York. Couldn't he get a suit in Watertown?"

"Why in Watertown?"

"That's where we lived. That's where we had the wedding."

"In Watertown?"

"Yes, is that bad?"

"No, it's not bad, but your cousin Mike said that you were already living in Springbrook, and that's where the wedding was."

"What does he know about it? He wasn't there at that time."

"Cousin Yadviga," cried out Mike, "didn't you tell me that the wedding was in Springbrook and your father went to New York the day before the wedding?"

She flew out at him. "You told me to say so if the people from New York asked me. But I never said it to you. My father didn't go to New York a day before my wedding."

"Isaac, come," said Miss Rosenberg, breaking in on the dispute between Mike and Yadviga. "Excuse us for having bothered you." She rose and went to the door, certain that Grossman would follow her. But Grossman did not move. He was sunk in thought.

"What else does the gentleman want?" asked Yadviga impatiently. "I've told him everything he wants to know."

"No, not everything," answered Grossman.

"Isaac, come!" pleaded Miss Rosenberg.

"I've got something else to attend to," he said. "There are other things I've got to find out about the Kovalsky family."

"But don't you see this isn't the Kovalsky you want?"

"Yes, I see, I see. I know. But I've got to find out other things."

"What does he mean?" asked the woman, of Mike. Mike silenced her with a gesture.

"I'm talking about your family," said Grossman. "If the boy is sick, why isn't he in a hospital? And if he isn't sick, why isn't he at school, or outside? How do you come to be living here, in this—in this place. I want to know everything about you."

"If you're not from the police, mister, maybe you're from the Old People's Home?"

"No. I'm finding out for myself."

"Will it help me?"

"I told you, it might. Maybe a lot. I'm interested in you."

"Tell him, tell him, Yadviga," urged Mike. "The gentleman can help you, and your mother, even if you aren't the Kovalsky he's looking for."

Miss Rosenberg returned reluctantly and sat down next to her employer on the bench.

"What does the gentleman want to know about the family?"

"How many are you?"

"There's myself, my husband, and my mother. And then there's my son and his wife, and Jerry, that's the little boy there. And then there's my brother-in-law and his wife, the Grabskis. It's really their apartment, not ours. They took us in, because my husband lost his job in the slaughterhouse. He got sick—his lungs— and the inspector said he couldn't work there any more, the animals would catch his sickness. Now he's got a job as night watchman. Thank God it's a night job, so he can sleep in the daytime. When the Grabskis took us in here my mother was still able to do some work, she could cook and wash for them. You see, my sister-in-law likes to go out. Now my mother is sick, and I can't attend to all the house. So they want us to move out. Where are we going to move? What am I going to do with my mother? I can't throw her in the street, can I? What can I do if they won't take her in the Old People's Home?"

153

"Why won't they take her?"

"She can't look after herself. She needs someone. She's old. You know how it is, you're not so clean when you're old. That's why the Grabskis don't want her around. My husband, too. The Grabskis say if it was their mother, well, they would have to. But it's not. Mrs. Grabski's not my sister, only a sister-in-law, because her husband's brother married my sister. And now my son came home from the army, and he's got no place to live. His wife and Jerry lived with us while he was in the army, now he came back. Where should he go with his wife and child? There's no apartment anywhere, and he can't sleep in the street, can he?"

"And you can't find an apartment?"

"I'd take anything. Let the gentleman try and find a place for us. Or only for my son. Because this is how all the trouble started."

"What trouble?"

"With my son."

"What's wrong with him?"

"He don't want to work. He don't want to do anything. We thought when he comes back from the army, he'll have a little pension, because he was wounded, and he got a medal, and he'll make out."

"Don't talk so loud," said Mike hastily, and indicated one of the beds with his thumb.

"He won't hear. They bring him home drunk, and he lies there like a stone. And let him hear, anyway. He'll understand, maybe, what my life is. He got his pension, sure, but every time he gets the money he spends it on drink. And when he's short, he bums from his wife; or he takes things out of the house and sells them. That's Michael. We were praying for him to come back; we would get an apartment, we'd move out of this hell. He was a good mechanic. He worked in a garage, and got good pay. That was before they took him in the army. All he does now is drink, and he won't listen to a word. He says only one thing, all the time: 'It don't pay! It don't pay.' And the doctors said he mustn't drink. His head goes round, and he falls down, and he has to lie in bed two days, three days, like he's lying now. And then when he gets over the drunk he grabs something from the house, and he disappears till they bring him home. And so now you know about the family, mister. Maybe if Michael had his own home, where he could be just with

154

his wife and the boy, he would stop drinking. But like this, he don't care what happens to him, as long as he can drink. And it's on account of him that the little boy got sick."

"What's the matter with the boy?"

"What do you think? His father used to be like a god to him, see? When the father was in the army, the little boy never used to stop talking about him. His daddy was a hero, he killed ten Germans, he took a hundred prisoners, he got wounded, he got a medal. And he waited and waited for his father to come home. He put on a soldier's hat, and he always slept with a toy gun under his pillow. And he said, when he grows up he's going to be a hero like his father. Well—the father came home, and what is he? A drunk. The little boy sees the police bringing home his father, dirty, sometimes beat up, a slob. And the little boy knows that his daddy steals mamma's dresses and sells them for liquor, while mamma goes out to work. Yes, if you want to know, his daddy just took his radio, and pawned it! You don't know how Jerry loved that radio. Well, what do you expect? That boy doesn't want to go to school, doesn't want to dress, doesn't want to play with other children. He stays in, just the way you see."

Suddenly Grossman felt a rain of childish blows on his legs, his stomach, his arms. It was Jerry, who had sprung out of his bed and thrown himself on the old man.

"You get out of here!" the child yelled.

"Jerry! Jerry!" exclaimed Yadviga and Mike.

"I hate him! I hate him!" The child's voice rose to a screaming falsetto.

They pulled the child away and threw him on his bed, where he lay sobbing.

"Who's that?" A hoarse voice came out of the corner, and Grossman, looking in that direction, saw a smudged, swollen, unshaven face, and pair of wildly glaring eyes. "Who's that?"

"It's a gentleman, Michael. He wants to help us." And the mother went over to the corner.

"Who the hell wants his help? Get out, before I break your goddam neck. And you, bookie!" The man sat up in the bed and shook his fist at Mike.

"Come," said Miss Rosenberg, trembling, and she pulled at Grossman's sleeve.

Grossman stood up, straightened out his clothes, and said gently to Yadviga: "I know all I wanted to know." Then he turned to Mike and said, in a changed voice, hard and decisive: "Bring Mrs. Zaslavsky to Silverstein's tomorrow, at four o'clock."

He took Miss Rosenberg's hand, and they went out of the house.

CHAPTER FOUR

"CAN it be an illusion, a chimera, as Rose says? Is it possible there was no Kovalsky in my life, that I invented him, or heard about him, and persuaded myself that I met him? But God, God, I saw him with my own eyes. I took that money, I used it for expenses on my first business trip. And I see him, right in front of me, he's standing there, alive, a little man, shaking, an idiotic smile on his face. His forelock sticks to his sweating forehead, his black mustaches tremble, like his lips, as he says: 'Now I must go drown myself, they say I spend that money for booze.' I see him. I feel myself almost saying to him, 'Here, here's the money, I found it,' but I hold myself back and I say nothing. I say nothing because this is my one big chance to get the job with Salzman Brothers, to become a traveling salesman. I see him, I hear him speak. What do they mean, he never existed? Why he's here now, standing at my bedside, looking at me."

Grossman stretched his hands out into the darkness, he wanted to take hold of Kovalsky, hold him. But the darkness was empty. He sat up and looked around.

"Is it possible I got the names mixed? No. How should that name have come to me? I see it clearly, typed on the card: Yan Kovalsky. Yes, and there's another name, beginning with an M. But I can't read it. Still, there's no mistaking the Yan. A machinist in the Yale Company, lives in Springbrook. I kept that wallet for a time, and the identification card. Then I ripped everything to little pieces, and threw them in a garbage can. My God, it's all as clear as if I just did it. On Grand Street—it was a rainy night. That name and address never faded out of my mind. Yan. And there *was* a Yan Kovalsky here, he was here in Springbrook, a dishwasher. And I'm here in Springbrook. And Strawberry Hill is here in Springbrook, just outside the town. I was there yesterday, wasn't I? I met his relatives, I met the woman whose maiden name was Kovalsky. Yes, they were all here, in Springbrook, and the family's still here, on Strawberry Hill. It's not a dream, a delusion. It's real and solid, as real and solid as myself. But the Kovalsky I want, the Kovalsky I wronged, has disappeared. Mike wanted me to believe that Yan Kovalsky isn't the Kovalsky I'm looking for. That's what he said. But Mike is a swindler. He knows where my Kovalsky is. He keeps him hidden somewhere, locked in a room, perhaps. He wanted that woman to pretend she was the daughter of the man I was looking for. She wouldn't swindle along with him. She didn't even want to talk to us at first. She told us she was married 1910. It doesn't fit. She's a decent person. Only Mike—he's bad, through and through. The way he talked about Yan. He knows where Yan is, he keeps him locked up. We've got to work out a plan to get the secret out of Mike."

He could not lie still. Something was lifting him, driving him. Again he wanted to put on his clothes and go out in search of Yan Kovalsky. But he knew now that Miss Rosenberg would hear him. She lay in the next room, on the alert.

"I'll have to do this without Rose. She'll only stand in my way. I'll have to get at Mike myself, and find out what he's done with Yan Kovalsky."

He fell asleep very late, out of sheer exhaustion. But then he slept long, and dreamlessly, like a child after it has wept itself out. When he awoke, Miss Rosenberg was waiting for him.

"I had no idea that the housing shortage was so frightful here," was the first thing he said.

"It's bad," she agreed.

"I can't get that Strawberry Hill out of my mind. And I'm building summer resorts, and winter resorts, apartments for a thousand dollars a month. Here people are living like herrings in a barrel, choking for air. Is it any wonder that the son took to drink when he got out of the army, and pawned the boy's radio? Is it any wonder he can't return to a normal life? Can you blame him? Would I have been any better?"

"Yes, you would," said Miss Rosenberg decidedly.

"What makes you think so? I tell you that in those surroundings, the ones we saw in Strawberry Hill, anything can happen—

even murder. No, there's something wrong in our rich country, in 'God's own country.' Horrible! Horrible!"

"Come. You haven't had breakfast yet."

"O.K. We'll have to do something about it."

"What do you mean?"

"Well, the first thing is to look after the Zaslavskys. They're not my Kovalskys—I know—but what's the difference? I can't get over that place, that woman. She's an honest woman. We'll have to do something big for her, get her out of trouble, fix things up for her son. We'll go over to Silverstein's and talk the matter over with him."

"Let's go easy, Mr. Grossman. I'm afraid of that Mike. He's got something up his sleeve, and he's absolutely shameless. No matter how many lies you catch him in—"

"You don't have to tell me. I don't trust Mike any more than you do. But Mrs. Zaslavsky is decent. You could see that. We've got to help her, and Silverstein will show us how."

Again Miss Rosenberg was relieved, and pleased. Her employer still had the Kovalskys on his mind, but his attitude was reasonable.

"What is the city doing for the GI's?" asked Grossman sharply of Silverstein, as though the latter were the responsible power.

Silverstein looked up, his beard trembling, his glasses dancing on his nose. He was too astonished to answer.

"I mean about housing. Yesterday I saw how people live here, in dirt, in ugliness, squeezed together. It kept me awake all night."

"Why do you ask me?" retorted Silverstein. "You're a builder, a real estate man, not I."

"Are they doing any building here?"

"Plenty. Country houses, resorts, palaces with swimming pools and tennis courts and flower beds and hothouses. They're remodeling old farmhouses, even barns, and turning them into grand homes. You'd better get around—you'll find out that Springbrook is doing more building than any other city its size. Sure they're building—for those who can pay."

"Where do they get their materials? Haven't you got any restrictions here? Don't they give preference to GI homes?"

"Not in Springbrook. Here the New York commuters are the privileged class. You get the idea? Pull, connections, politics. As much steel, and cement, and wood, as builders need for commuters. No shortage there."

"And is nothing being done for the GI's?"

"Why, yes. Who says nothing is being done for the GI's? They brought hundreds of tin huts from the recruiting camps and put them up on the damp earth, near the bay. The kind of hut where you roast in the summer and get rheumatism in the winter. They say it cost a fortune to dump the huts here. But the GI's won't set foot in them. No matter how badly they live now, it's not as bad as in the army huts. Would you like to see? I'll take you there."

"Tin huts. Yes, I want to see them. We'll have to look into this. Something has to be done."

"Ah, it's time a man like you did something, Mr. Grossman. *You* can start something here. Who am I? Honestly, when I saw you this time I was sure you had just this question in mind. I don't know how it is in other cities, but living conditions here are awful. I just can't describe them. Hundreds and hundreds of GI's are back, most of them got married either before they left or while they were in the army, and most of them have children. They dreamed of the time when the war would be over, they dreamed in the foxholes about the homes they would have—and where are they living? With in-laws, crowded together, getting on each other's nerves, quarreling day and night. And lots of them take to drinking. What keeps a man going, Mr. Grossman, if not his wife and child and home? It gives him discipline, and a purpose. You break that up, and the man breaks up too. They don't want to go to the barracks. They've had enough of that; they don't want to see their wives and children in barracks too. You can see the psychology of that, can't you? We've had many tragedies here because of the overcrowding. Families broken up, jealousy, yes, murder. It's a breakdown of morale. And the government only thinks of sending GI's to college. But not all GI's want to be doctors, and professors, and lawyers. There are plain, ordinary people who want to go back to their old, normal lives which the war interrupted. The first thing they need is a home, and that's what they don't get."

Grossman nodded. "I've got to do something about it."

"What about that land of yours, Mr. Grossman? Do you know there's room enough there to take care of all our GI's? I thought that's what brought you here. And all you're interested in is a Kovalsky. Mr. Grossman, is there only one Kovalsky in the world? You come with me and I'll show you hundreds and hundreds of Kovalskys, like the ones you saw yesterday. Why do you care just about one of them?"

Grossman felt the blood coming into his face. He swallowed, and waited a few moments. Then he said:

"That business with Kovalsky happens to be something special. It's a private matter. My assistant, Miss Rosenberg, knows all the details, and that's what brought us to you, Mr. Silverstein. I'd like your help in clearing that matter up. Yesterday I saw the way the Kovalskys—I mean the Zaslavskys—live. It's horrible. Mrs. Zaslavsky is a very fine woman, and I want to help her. It's because of a friendship I once felt for a certain Kovalsky, who was a member of that family. I want to help her, and her family, and you're the man to handle it for me. I want to arrange for Mrs. Zaslavsky to get a small pension, which will be paid out by my firm. Please talk it over with Miss Rosenberg, won't you?"

"Certainly. I'll be glad to. But we'll have to be cautious."

"And I also want to get Mrs. Zaslavsky's mother into a home. I'll pay whatever's necessary. The Old People's Home here can't take in that type of case, it seems. I want you to find the right kind of place. I want all the payments to be made through you."

"But in your name, of course."

"No, no, under no circumstances. I don't want her to know it comes from me."

"She'll guess."

"Tell her I got the pension for her from an institution. It's not from me personally."

"She won't believe it."

"Well, that can't be helped. I don't want to be in direct contact with them, that's all. And now, about the bigger question. I've got to get more information about the building situation here. I want you to show me the Quonset huts, and the other low income areas. We'll see what can be done."

That afternoon Miss Rosenberg and Mr. Silverstein worked out a plan for Mrs. Zaslavsky, and put down all the details on paper. Silverstein was to find an apartment for the family, get the old mother into an invalid hospital, see that the boy got a new radio

161

and began to attend school. Even Mike was to get a handsome tip for having brought Grossman and the Zaslavsky family together.

"And now," said Miss Rosenberg, coming into the hotel from Silverstein's, "we can go home, and forget the whole business."

"What's the hurry?" asked Grossman.

"This Kovalsky, that Kovalsky, the right one, the wrong one—you've done everything you could for the family, and I don't imagine your health will improve very much in this atmosphere."

"The family?" he asked. "I don't even know whether they are related to the real Kovalsky. I am helping a poor woman. That's all. Now I have to look for the real Kovalsky to whom I am indebted."

She did not answer. She only looked at him wordlessly, but the change that came over her face told him enough of what was going on within her.

Her face seemed to shrivel, as though in complete defeat. It became small, like a child's, but wrinkled, like an old woman's. She put on many, many years while he was still looking at her. Deep lines appeared, and an ashy discoloration spread over the skin. It almost seemed to him that the gray streak in her hair widened until it covered her whole head. Was it his own mood that he saw reflected in her?

"So you think I'm sick," he said, half jestingly.

She shook her head, though not too decisively, while she answered: "Not yet. But you're well on the way toward becoming sick. Your condition frightens me. I say we must get out of here. Every extra moment of delay is dangerous. You've done all you could do. And there never was a Kovalsky in your life. Not the one you're looking for. He never existed."

He answered slowly: "I am not sick, and I am not in danger. There was a Kovalsky. I saw him, and I stole his money. I ruined him, thrust him into the gutter." He spoke quietly, normally, without excitement. "I shall find him, Rose."

"So what are you going to do?"

"I'm going to remain here until I find him. Or until I'm certain that he's no longer alive. I must find his family, his real family. Then my conscience will be at peace. Either that, or I will become sick."

"But you see there's no trace of him. You've found his nearest relatives, you've done all that you can."

"I suspect Mike. He knows where Yan Kovalsky is," said Grossman earnestly, and he shook a warning finger in her face. "He's hiding Yan Kovalsky somewhere. I don't know what he's up to, this Mike, but he hopes to get money out of me. I won't rest until I've got to the bottom of all this."

"Isaac! Isaac! For the love of God, think what you're doing. You're digging a pit for yourself, and you'll fall into it, and your family with you—you and your good name and reputation. Get out, save yourself while you can. Don't stay here another minute. We'll have to save you in spite of yourself. We'll have to get a doctor for you. I can't hide this thing from Lazar any more. It was criminal of me not to have told him before now. I'm going to New York."

He seized her hand suddenly, pressed it with all his might, and looked sternly into her eyes.

"You will not tell Lazar."

"Why not? He's your son."

"You know why. Just because he's my son. Lazar dare not know. I won't want to live if he finds out what I've done. Do you understand?" His tone shook her. "Do you promise you won't tell?"

"I won't say anything if you come back with me to New Rochelle."

"I shan't go home till I've done all in my power to make restitution for my crime. You can go back, if you like. I shan't try to keep you. I have to remain. But remember: if you reveal my secret to Lazar, the secret which I kept from my wife, I shall not be able to go on living."

Miss Rosenberg clasped her hands in despair, and her eyes filled with tears. "But we've got to do something. We must find a way out. I'm lost, Isaac, I don't know what to do. We've got to talk it over with someone who will understand, someone we can trust. Listen! Will you let me confide in Silverstein? He is a friend, he understands."

"Silverstein? Moses Silverstein? Moses Silverstein?" Grossman repeated the name to himself several times.

"He already suspects something. He knows there was something unusual between you and Kovalsky. We can trust him, of all people, can't we? I'll tell it to him cautiously, I'll be very careful. Let me, Isaac. Let me talk with him."

"Moses Silverstein? Moses Silverstein?" Grossman finally looked up at her. "Yes! You can confide in him. And hide nothing from him. Do you hear? Tell him everything. He'll understand."

CHAPTER FIVE

MOSES SILVERSTEIN had not always had a wobbling head, and the pince-nez had not always danced on his thin nose. On the contrary, at one time they had been accustomed, in Springbrook, to a Moses Silverstein who walked erect, and whose head rose light and firm from his shoulders, like an eagle surveying the world with sure and rapid glance. He walked straight to his destination, his pince-nez set firmly on the bridge of his nose. And though he had always been in motion, and his bespectacled nose had been everywhere, finding out everything, interested in everything that was taking place in Springbrook, he was not afflicted by a nervous tremor. He was restless, eager, active, but at the same time self-controlled, even thoughtful. The affliction came upon him the day when he learned that his only son, Nathan, had been killed somewhere on one of the Pacific islands. His wife Malkah collapsed, and for a time her life was despaired of. She too was not the same person from that day on. Her eyes were seldom free from tears, and her voice never lost its note of lamentation. The meals she cooked for her husband were salted with her tears—but she cooked, and she washed, and she served for many hours every day in the store. She had no choice, for Moses was busy with more important things than his store. He had to attend to Springbrook. Moses did not lament, and he would not let others lament over him—not even when they came to him in the period of mourning. He accepted condolences as a grave general courtesy rather than as a personal offering. He needed no consolation for himself. He would answer: "Am I the only one? Millions of fathers have their sons in the war." But the tremor came into his limbs and head, and the pince-nez began their dance. His backbone bent like a relaxed bowstring. But he refused to see a doctor. He would say, when his friends expostulated, "I'm just a bit nervous. I'll get over it."

He had no time to mourn, to be sick, or to pity himself. His wife had her own way of putting it: "My husband doesn't serve in a store. He works in a trouble laundry. He's the mangling machine for all the troubles of Springbrook." When the war ended, Moses added to all his other customers the returning GI's. For the one son he had lost he acquired now many, many sons. Overnight, as it were, the word spread that the man to go to was Moses Silverstein. You could tell him all your woes, your most intimate secrets. He was not just a helpful friend, but a blood relative who understood. Many of the returning GI's had known his son. Nat Silverstein had been popular at school, and not only for his interest in baseball, which was deep and genuine, although he had not himself been a player on account of his shortsightedness. He had had his share in the game looking after the players, and seeing to it that they took care of themselves during the periods between contests, drank their milk, and went to bed at the right hour. Some of his friends had been with him on the Pacific island when he fell. Returning to Springbrook, they went to visit old Silverstein, and the store soon became a combination mess hall, casino and PX. Moses Silverstein became "Pop Moses." The problems of the boys became his problems, and he was drawn so completely into their lives that he forgot his own identity. He felt for them and saw into them. It was as if he had lived through their experiences, had known what it was to dodge a sniper's bullets, to feel like a hunted animal for whom death lurks in every tree, to shiver in the frozen foxholes, to shiver afterwards in a frozen and indifferent world. He was happy for those who were able to shake off the effects of the war and adapt themselves to civilian life; and he was close to those who were stuck fast in their horrible memories, like flies stuck fast in a spider's web. He was the unofficial finder of apartments and jobs, the obtainer and guarantor of loans. He could not bear to hear a GI spoken badly of, even when there was reason enough. It was as though he was standing by his own son, who would always be his son, no matter what he had done. "They took children, put guns in their hands, and sent them out into a jungle, where it was 'Kill or be killed,'" he would say.

The store was busier with GI troubles than with customers. His

166

wife Malkah pleaded: "One man can't do all that. You're not the United States government. And if the government can't handle it all, can you? Moses, it's going to knock you out." And once, when she was at him, he exclaimed: "I'm not doing it for the GI's, I'm doing it for myself." And she had no answer.

Pop Moses could listen for hours on end to the troubles of the GI, but with the troubles of Miss Rosenberg and Isaac Grossman he had no patience. She gave him part of the story, and he guessed at the rest; and when she was halfway through he interrupted:

"People are always up to the funniest tricks just to avoid going to a doctor. Yes, yes, I'll look into the matter, but for God's sake let him forget about Kovalsky, the real Kovalsky, or the imaginary Kovalsky. Every one of us has a Kovalsky to whom we can't make restitution. Let Grossman help where help is needed, and where all of us are guilty—I mean the GI's. They barely escaped with their lives. You could say they won their lives in a horrible bingo game. And whom did they risk their young lives for, if not us, the old, the sick, the rotten? We had our young lives, didn't we? We've known everything that youth can give. But they risked everything —life, joy, love, opportunity. They risked it all to save us from the Hitler curse. And what are we doing for them? Oh, I'll talk with Grossman; I'll show him where his debt lies, and for whom his conscience should be tormenting him."

When Miss Rosenberg tried to tell Silverstein about her employer's sufferings, he became quite furious. He stumbled over his words, the glasses danced more wildly than ever on his nose, and his Adam's apple bobbed like a cork in a storm.

But later in the day, when he conducted Grossman to the barrack huts, the "coffins for the living," as he called them, Moses Silverstein was all cheerfulness and good humor. This was what he wanted. He put great hopes in Grossman, and he did not mention a word of what Miss Rosenberg had told him. The effect on Grossman was that he too, seeing no change in the attitude of Moses, felt lighter and more cheerful.

The field in which the Quonset huts had been erected was still partly under water from the rains and the melted snow. The long rows of huts went up and down slopes, through the half swamp in the depressions and the mud on the hillocks. The doors and windows were low under the arches of the metal roofs, and the

167

water seeped in across the cement platforms. Here and there a hut had been blown down by the wind. Most of the huts were empty; a few were occupied by desperate GI's who had no alternative but to take shelter here. Barefoot children splashed about in the mud, bedsheets and blankets fluttered on the clotheslines.

"They look like mass-graves," muttered Grossman.

"Right! Mass-graves!" cried Moses, pleased with the word. "What the enemy couldn't do, we did. We saved them from mass-graves in the war to bury them alive in mass-graves here."

"How many live here?"

"I don't know. Certainly not a single one who can help it. They fight against coming here, but sometimes they have to give in. A man has to have a burrow to crawl into, hasn't he? They're trying to persuade the colored GI's. They have it worse, you see."

"Can there be worse?"

"My dear friend, there is no limit to human need, and there is no limit to what we human beings can endure, as long as we can hang on to this bit of life we have. And is it worth it?"

"It seems so."

"Yes, it seems so. God has planted in us this lust to live—God, or the devil?"

"Devil?" asked Grossman, astonished.

"Can God be so cruel?"

"Tell me, Mr. Silverstein, do you believe in God?"

"Have I any choice? I tried hard not to believe in Him, I fought against it for many years. For the rich and successful, belief in God is easy. But for us who have had to fight tooth and nail in this forest of life into which our mothers threw us, for us who have known only thorns and thickets, and no clear road, it isn't easy to believe in God, and especially in a good God. No, it wasn't easy. I quarreled with Him—but I had to come round in the end. I found Him again, and then I lost Him again. Could you believe in God when Hitler was rising, especially if you were a Jew and you saw your people doomed? The poorest, the unhappiest, and the most believing people in the world. Could one believe then in justice, in an eye that sees and lets these things happen, when the hand is there that could prevent it? No, no, no. And yet—what could one do? It's hard to believe in God, but not to believe in Him is impossible. You understand? A bad, cruel.

unjust God, if you like, but still a God. Because, you see, it's better that God should be unjust, than that He shouldn't exist. But then, I couldn't have it that God should be unjust, I accept His decrees with love, and have it that *I'm* unjust. We're bad, sinful, evil—though I don't see where we're any worse than the gentiles. In any case, *He* has to be just. Because, don't you see, if we were just, and God was not, what would become of us?"

Grossman thought a while, and then asked, in a low voice, "Do you think there is reward and punishment, as my father used to tell me? Another world, in which we are judged for our deeds in this one?"

"I don't know. I've never been in another world. But I believe in God, and believe in Him in the Jewish way, according to what the rabbis have taught us: we must serve Him, we must carry out His commandments *lo al menas lekabel pras,* not for the sake of a reward, but for the sake of the commandments. And they also taught us that we must cling to God, be one with Him, that is, take on His virtues. 'As God is good, we must be good, as He is merciful, we must be merciful.' And the rabbis taught us, again, that God said to the Jews: 'Would that you forgot Me, and remembered My Law.' If there is a God, I can't imagine that He would be wanting us to think always of Him, singing His praises day and night and carrying Him about as if He were an idol. It seems to me that the rabbis were right. And this is the only way. I don't believe that God wants us to be forever occupied with Him. Here we stand, in this swampy field where we've put up living graves for the best of our children. This is what we've prepared for them, after they risked their lives to save our freedom, our homes, our institutions—this is what we've prepared for those of them whose bodies haven't been left to rot there. Here we stand, and if I had the means for it, I know what God would demand of me. He would want me to help these boys, my sons and your sons, to bring their wives and children into decent homes, warm, bright homes, nests they can love. I know that that would be God's demand. And if I could obey, then I know that He would forgive me all the transgressions I had committed. He would not even remember them, He would know that all those little sins were irrelevant, they were digressions, they were not the true way of my life. Why, even the sins themselves would become purified, if they helped to lift a man to where he could help others."

Grossman listened, deeply absorbed. He understood the hint, and he was silent. He felt his heart beating, as if he stood before one of the great decisions of his life. Should he speak out to Silverstein? He did not know how much Rose had told him. Probably not all the ugly details, but enough to give him a glimpse. He was grateful to Silverstein because the man meant well. Still, he was evading the heart of the issue; he was generalizing the individual problem which was Grossman's own, personal anguish. He would speak up, be open now; and he said, in a clear, loud voice:

"Mr. Silverstein, is it not true, is it not according to the Jewish faith, that if you pray earnestly on the Day of Atonement, God can forgive you the sins you have committed against Him, but He cannot forgive the sins which a man has committed against his fellow men?"

"Who told you this?"

"My father."

"Yes, that is the Jewish view; and yet—it is not a hopeless situation. I know what is on your mind. You want to talk to me about your Kovalsky. I know something about it from your secretary. But this is not the place to discuss it. We're liable to catch cold. Let's go home, Mr. Grossman, and we'll talk it all over in my store."

"Yes, I want to have your opinion," answered Grossman, and signaled to the hired car which had brought them out.

"Mr. Grossman," said Silverstein, when the two were seated behind the locked door of the office. "I want you, first of all, to bear in mind that you aren't the only one who goes through life under that sort of burden. Every one of us who has had to make his own way in life is more or less in the same case. Like you, I had to start earning my living early, and like every one of us I encountered temptations and pitfalls. Well, I did certain things that I would certainly not do today. And yet, I don't let them tower up and overshadow my life. When you think of the education we got, of the universities—God help us—our fathers sent us to, we haven't come out too badly. Remember, we had to begin from the beginning, each one of us for himself, each one in his own way. Our sages tell us that for every creature God creates, He appoints its Angel of Death; but He also provides every creature with its own means to ward off the Angel of Death. For instance, the mouse has its Angel of Death—the cat. But against this He made it possible for the mouse to escape into holes where the cat can't reach him. And so every living thing has its own defense, its own gift, with which to cling to life.

"I am not a philosopher, and I am not a thinker—I have never had the time for it. And yet, in my younger years I did my share of reading; and even today there are moments when I can't resist the impulse to open the pages of a book, to see what new things have been discovered. To me, with my poor, primitive mind, it seems that God, or nature, gave man all the gifts and all the defenses of all the creatures, so that he might with these look for sustenance, hold on to life, and save himself from the Angel of Death. Yes, from the many Angels of Death who pursue him. You'll find in man the nature of every other creature. He's a summary of all of them. He has the courage of the lion, the cruelty of the tiger, the cunning of the fox, the lightness of the cat, the timidity of the mouse; he swims like the fish, he flies like the birds—and all so that he might find his nourishment, hold on to life, and continue his kind. But he differs in this, that God breathed into him a soul, so that he might be able to tame and control all these animal impulses and abilities, and be master of them. And this mastery, or authority, he has for the service of his higher nature. And so it depends how the man has used these animal impulses and powers which are lodged in him. If he has used them solely for himself, to fill his belly, to accumulate riches, to grab power, to dominate others, then he is worse than all the animals put together. For those have no soul, whereas he has. But if he uses all these animal instincts to do good, to be just, then he purifies all the animal instincts. He gives them a purpose and a meaning. He binds them to a higher sphere, and places them at the service not of his coarse physical self, which is doomed to rot in the earth, but of that part of him which remains, which he has in addition to his animal powers, and which is dedicated to the divine spark."

Old Grossman sat with head bowed, taking in the philosophic discourse of Moses Silverstein, which the latter delivered with the contentment of a sage who loves wisdom. This was the frustrated Moses Silverstein, the Silverstein that would have been if certain dreams had been fulfilled—the dreams of his boyhood, when he used to walk with friends in the evenings along the alley of chestnut trees near the castle of his native townlet, talking of things of the spirit.

After a long pause Grossman answered, tranquilly, without emphasis, as if in a trance: "That is what I have been thinking. If God cannot forgive me the sin I have committed against a fellow man, and if only the wronged man can forgive me, is not my soul in pawn to that man? It is no longer in my possession, but in his."

It was this quiet tone, this trancelike manner, which made a profound impression on Silverstein. It seemed to him that in the chair opposite was seated not Isaac Grossman of the firm of Grossman and Grossman, known to so many, but a shadow, while the man himself was elsewhere.

"Your soul in pawn? In his possession, not yours? Let me say this first: I don't believe that the thing happened as you now believe it did. I'm not convinced by any means that there's even a Kovalsky in it. Perhaps it happened somewhere, perhaps it didn't —but it didn't happen to you. Human beings like to torment themselves in order to appease their conscience. And man's conscience has an enormous appetite; give it a finger, it will swallow a hand. Our sages warned us against this. And second: our sages have declared that a man cannot testify against himself. If he comes before a court and accuses himself, his testimony is ignored. And our Chassidic rabbis have warned us against heaviness of spirit and gloomy thoughts. The greatest sin that man can commit against God is to decline into sadness, and—God forbid—into despair of the world. They have told us that it is a greater sin to dwell on sin than to commit sin. Certainly one must repent, and determine not to sin again; but one must repent and dismiss the matter. For if you yield to gloominess you lose the joy of life; then you do not acknowledge the goodness of the Eternal, you are not grateful for the life He gave you, and for the mercies He shows you every day. You bring an evil repute on His world, you become a Job, who cursed the day he was born; and you are angry with God because He created you. Thus, with your concentration on your sin, you sin greatly against God. God wants you to cast aside your gloom and to rejoice in His world and His creation, in the sunlight, in growing things, in the fruits of the field. That is why the rabbis commanded us to remember to utter a benediction whenever we taste fruit, or when we partake of any joy. Our enjoyment of life is itself a benediction and a thanks, which exalt Him and His work. But if we reject His work, and trample it under foot, we degrade it. Further, the rabbis told us not to speak evil of God's creatures; yes, a man must not speak evil even of himself. For a man is not his own property; he did not create himself; he belongs to God, being part of His creation. He may not accuse himself any more than he may accuse another."

"But I may accuse another, may I not, when I have clear proof against him? I may bring him to judgment, may I not? Why, then, may I not do it against myself?"

"You have no proofs. Your proofs are only self-delusions. And therefore your testimony is rejected."

"But the sin is there. The sin was committed. There was such a thing. I know it."

"Suppose I grant it, suppose the sin was there. It can be annulled. And there's the end of it."

"What do you mean, annulled?"

"Erased, wiped out. One says to oneself that it never was."

"May one do such a thing?"

"Yes. Now listen to this. It happened in nineteen hundred and five, in my village in Russia. Those were the pogrom years after the first Russian revolution. A band of hooligans broke into our rabbi's house and violated his daughter before his eyes. When the hooligans had finished their plundering and raping, the rabbi crawled over to his daughter, wiped the tears from her face, lifted her from the ground, and said: 'My child, nothing has happened. I annul it and turn it into nothing.' And he caused the *shofar* to be blown in the synagogue, while he proclaimed that wherever such evil deeds had been done against Jewish daughters, they were annulled and made void. A curse lay on the man that mentioned them, and it was forbidden to think of them. 'And he that transgresses against this,' the ban said, 'has committed mortal sin, in that he brings a bad name on the daughters of his people.' "

"Yes," conceded Grossman softly. "Had the sin been committed against me, I could annul it. Only the wronged one can annul the

173

sin. It is in his power, and he has the choice. But can he be forced to do it?"

"Yes, he can be forced."

"How?"

"He can be recompensed with good. And if he refuses, if he is obstinate, his debt can be flung back in his face. There is not a Jewish court of law which would not so rule for you."

"And what is to be done if the wronged one is no longer among the living?"

"Such cases have been known. We hear that rabbis have even summoned the dead to their court, and have compelled the dead to accept a judgment concerning the living. I don't believe in those things; I don't believe that the dead actually came into the court and spoke from behind a curtain, as those stories tell. These are old wives' tales. But I do believe that the dead, too, are subject to law, and they can't have their own way simply because they are dead. The court pronounces sentence and the dead must submit. Law and justice exist for the dead as for the living, if the dead wish to maintain connection with those who have survived them."

Grossman was absorbed in Silverstein's words; a new alertness was reflected in his face, which was now turned to the pallid gas flame.

"Have such trials and pronouncements taken place among Jews?"

"Assuredly. It is told of any number of Chassidic figures that they exorcised from the bodies of the living the spirits of dead men who had taken up residence there and refused to be expelled. The rabbi called forth the dead souls, forced them to take their place behind a curtain and state their complaints to the court. I say I do not believe these stories; and I don't believe, either, that when a man dies he becomes a higher creature who is of necessity in the right while the living are sinful and guilty. It is a human thing to die, just as it is to be born, and to beget. When a man dies and is released from his human obligations he is supposed to ascend to heaven and become an angel—but all that is outside of my knowledge, and I have nothing to say about it. But I do know that his earthly life was human, subject to all the laws and commandments of human existence, and we have the right to judge him according to our judgment, and to weigh him in our scales—

174

that is, according to our insights, our sense of justice, and our weakness."

Grossman started. "Mr. Silverstein, you know so much of Judaism, were you ever a rabbi? I mean, have you now, or have you ever had, the authority of a rabbi?"

"No, thank God. My father, God rest his soul, did want me to become a rabbi, and he kept me in the Talmudical seminary as long as he could—in fact, longer than he could. He was a very poor man, burdened with many children. I had to start earning money early; besides, the rabbinate didn't attract me. I was not strong enough in the faith. It was the time of the rise of socialism; and we could not see the Messiah coming down from heaven and riding in among us on an ass. We saw him riding on a gun carriage of the revolution, a red flag in his hand. I left the seminary and became a watchmaker. But I didn't give up all my studies. Why do you ask, Mr. Grossman?"

"Just so. You speak with authority, as if you were a rabbi."

"Do you think that among us Jews only rabbis may speak with authority on matters of faith? Every Jew has that authority. Every Jew has the right to interpret the law. We are a democratic people; ours was the first democracy in world history. Do you understand, Mr. Grossman? We proclaimed long, long ago: 'Every Jew has a portion in the world to come.' Neither prince nor priest can take it away from him. And it is further written: 'All Jews are brothers,' and 'Every Jew is responsible for his fellow Jews.' And when I see a fellow Jew with a broken spirit, embittered, ruining himself because of some foolish notion, because of some sin he committed in his youth, then, according to my Jewish faith, I must try to free him from his burden. It is my duty to speak freely to him, and to tell him that he is acting contrary to God's will, and there is no such thing as having one's soul in pawn to another being of flesh and blood, for the sake of a debt. We are in the hands of God, not of man. This I have the right to say, and the duty, though I am not a rabbi but a plain Jew."

"My father taught me otherwise. He told me that only he whom I have wronged can forgive me for it, after I have made restitution. Until then I am in his hands. My father was a pious Jew."

"I do not doubt it. Perhaps he was a little too pious. I do not know. Perhaps he tried to frighten you away from sin. But my

175

human reason and my knowledge of our faith tell me that you have
no reason to torment yourself as you do. You have done your best
to rectify the wrong, as you call it, which you have committed.
You sought the man, you sought his family, you sought out a dis-
tantly related branch of it—and you found some people, and
lifted them out of their dire distress. What more can you do in
respect to that particular man? But there is a lot you can do, not
for that man, but for a great many persons. You can do much for
our children, our hundreds of children, those who saved the world
from Hitler and re-established God's justice, which we once
thought destroyed. There you have a real debt, as all of us have.
Go out of here, Mr. Grossman, and use your knowledge and
power and skill on their behalf. Your son does not need your
help; and you yourself are no longer a young man. Forgive me
for being so outspoken, Mr. Grossman, but I say: build homes for
our boys. Put a roof over their heads, and make them and God
happy. Then everything that you have done will be cleansed of
its sinfulness, and your whole life will take on form and meaning.
And you will be doing something for this land of ours, to which
we owe so much; you will be doing honor to our people. What
more, in God's name, do you want? Here is the place. Build decent
homes for a hundred GI families."

"A hundred!" muttered Grossman. "Five hundred! There's
room here for five hundred, six hundred homes; and playgrounds,
and shops, and a movie house—a whole GI city. Comfortable
homes in spacious surroundings; and with government help, at a
price they can pay...."

"Well?"

"Do you think that this will content him?"

"Who?"

"You know who I mean—the wronged man."

"Why do you bring that up?"

"If I do it, it will be for his sake," said Grossman softly.

"Is that necessary, Mr. Grossman? I don't see the connection;
but if it helps your conscience, let it be so. What difference is it,
for whom you do it, as long as it's done?"

"How do I know that he wants it, and that he will be content,
and will forgive me?"

"Mr. Grossman, what you have in mind is a hundred times more

176

important, and a hundred times more pleasing in the eyes of God, than anything you can do for Kovalsky. And if there was such a Kovalsky, which I still doubt, and, living or dead, he is not contented, in this world or the other, with what you have done, then surely he is not worth a second thought, and then you sin doubly to poison your life for his sake. With this plan of yours you pay a debt not only to some individual, but your greater debt to society, and a debt to society takes precedence over a debt to the individual."

"Is that too the Jewish law?"

"It is Jewish law, and human law, and universal law."

Grossman reflected long in silence.

"I will think about it. Whatever happens, let me thank you for your words. I have learned a great deal from them."

CHAPTER SIX

WHAT was it that had awakened his interest in the Springbrook property from the first moment that he learned it was for sale? Why had he at once decided to buy it—and for himself, not for the firm? And why had he obstinately refused to sell it in spite of advantageous offers? Neither Lazar nor anyone else had been able to understand his pointless clinging to this particular parcel, his readiness to continue paying the taxes attached to it, and his freezing of a considerable sum of money. There had been sharp discussions on the subject between Isaac Grossman and his son, and each of them had had to exercise no little restraint to keep out of a serious quarrel. But Isaac Grossman himself would not have been able to explain his own behavior. It seemed to him that he had to have that property, that there was something personal about his relationship to it, something intimate, even. Certainly it was connected with the secret which he had kept from everyone, including his wife; but in what manner, and pointing to what purpose, he could not have said.

He had definitely not bought in the way of business, for profit. As he thought back now, it occurred to him that he had always intended to create, on this spot, something to make good the wrong he had committed against Kovalsky. Or was it something to the memory of his father? The two, he perceived, were indissolubly linked—his father, Kovalsky. For if he now sought to appease Kovalsky, it was because of his father. In his father that compulsion was rooted which now gave him no rest. And as often as he had tried, in his recent unhappiness, to thrust Kovalsky out of his mind, he had remembered the scene with his father: the old man with the haggard, dying face, the bony hand gripping his; he had heard his admonition. He could forget Kovalsky only by forgetting his father, and that was impossible.

In one sense Silverstein had done him little good, making light, as he had done, of both Kovalsky and of his father's admonition. Yet he had been of some help. He had suggested the way out—the social act which would answer the claims of both dead men. But now the question was, to whom should the act point, whose name should the enterprise perpetuate, Kovalsky's or Shmaya Grossman's? For surely, if a debt was being paid, the name of the creditor had to be attached to the transaction. In respect of the wrong he had committed, he was not in debt to his father; he had nothing to pay him, or his family. Kovalsky was the creditor, and such a name as Kovalsky Center would be fitting. And still—

He made up his mind that the less he talked about it, especially to Miss Rosenberg, the better. Let her think that he had shaken himself free of what she called his hallucination. He would play a game with her, and with Silverstein too. For the latter he had great respect, but it would not do to tell him of his intention. Sympathetic, wise, learned, Silverstein nevertheless did not understand. To him Kovalsky was mostly the product of Isaac Grossman's sick fantasy, and the moralizing of Shmaya Grossman had been rooted in excess of piety. And now Isaac Grossman found himself alone again, unable to confide in anyone. He suddenly felt his alienation from his son, whose assistance he would assuredly need in the fulfillment of his purpose. The whole family would be astounded—and outraged, too—at this dedication of the project to an utter stranger. It would seem insane to them. But he could not tell Lazar, could not tell the family. He felt his alienation from all of them—and in that "all" was included the memory of his wife.

"Why was I never able to confide in her? Why did I hide it from her too? If there is another life—as father believed—and Clara is there now, then she knows about it anyway."

But his mind was made up, and it was not in his character to shrink from difficulties. He was going to see the project through.

A few days after his talk with Silverstein he asked Miss Rosenberg to connect him with his son, in New York. She hesitated, uncertain of his intentions. Her employer had not yet reported to her the results of his conversation with Silverstein. He had spent his time visiting his property, making calculations, examining the adjacent areas. He had been thoughtful, but not depressed.

179

And he had not been in touch with New York. Now the way he asked to be connected with his son showed her that he had come to some sort of decision.

"Call Lazar?" she asked. "I thought we'd be going home today."

"No, not by a long way. I'm not through with Springbrook yet. You'll hear about it in good time. Hello, Lazar—listen, I've got something very important on."

"Hello, governor. How are you feeling?"

"Never felt better in my life. That property I've got here— I've made up my mind about it. I've got a project. The first thing is to send out Frankel, with a couple of assistants. I'm going to build."

"Is that why you've been dawdling in Springbrook? We've been expecting you back in town for more than a week. Don't you want to be at Louise's birthday party? Listen, governor: it's going to be more than a birthday party. It'll be your granddaughter's engagement, an alliance between the two families, Grossman and Hanover."

"Has it gone as far as that?"

"Yes, sir. Felix's calling-up has been deferred. He's remaining at Columbia."

"Don't you be afraid, Lazar. I'll be there. But I can't get away from here until I've settled this business. It's a big project. It's going to scare you."

"Governor, this isn't the time for big building projects. You've got that wonderful offer for your land. You'll never get a better. Take it, and be done with it. It'll be the best stroke of business you've done for years."

"This isn't business, Lazar."

"What then is it?"

"It's a great project. I've decided to use this property for a social purpose. I'm going to build a big GI village in Springbrook."

"A what?" gasped Lazar.

"You heard me. I'm going to build a big development for returning GI's. They need it. They've nowhere to live."

It took Lazar Grossman a few moments to find his voice. "Listen, governor. I think I'll come out to Springbrook tomorrow morning. Then we'll—"

"No, no, I don't want you to come out here. I want Frankel," and Grossman raised his voice excitedly.

"Let me finish," answered Lazar, in a disturbed tone. "The land you've got in Springbrook is too expensive for a low-rental project. The town is moving up in that direction. It's a place for business and shops. That's why that offer you got is so good."

"Lazar, this land is my own private property. I had my mind made up when I bought it, that it would be used for a social project. That's the way it was, and that's the way it'll stay."

"But dad, dad—"

"I don't want to listen. I want you to send out Frankel."

"Dad, will you listen?"

"No. I want to talk with Frankel. If he's in the office connect me with him."

"He's not in the office. He's up in Yonkers. I'll send him to you. Sure I'll send him to you. I'll let him know right away what you want him for. But listen to me before you take the first step and the thing becomes public. Will you listen?"

"All right, all right, what?"

"I've got nothing against your project. I think it's a good idea. I like it. Honest, I do. It's the kind of thing I expected from you. It'll be an honor to our family, and to our firm. I'm ready to help you in every way possible."

"I'm not doing it for the family. It won't be named after us."

"Why?"

"I have my reasons. You know I don't care for that kind of publicity."

"O.K., call it by any name you like. But before it becomes a public matter, think the thing through. We can't expose the family name, and the firm's name, to ridicule."

"What are you talking about?"

"I don't say it has to be that way. But I'm warning you, if you—if we—have to give up the project halfway through, for one reason or another, it'll be a black eye for all of us, and you can expect all sorts of rumors and gossip and slander."

"Why? I don't know what you're talking about."

"Let's not discuss it on the telephone. I've got to see you before you take the first step. You come home, or I'll come out there."

"I can't come home before I've had a talk with Frankel here, on the spot. I want to explain everything. And I don't want you to come out here. I've got my reasons. Whatever you have to say, you can say it on the telephone. Nobody's listening. Only Rose is here. Now, what's your objection?"

"Why must you have that project in Springbrook, of all places? Why not in Long Island, or New York? GI homes are needed everywhere. What have we got to do with Springbrook? None of us has ever lived there. Or done business there. It ought to be in some place with which we've been connected one way or another. Why Springbrook?"

"I've got my own reasons. They're private reasons. I don't have to tell them to anybody. And second, I have this piece of land, a big piece, and I bought it for this purpose. What's wrong with that?" And while he spoke with his son, Isaac Grossman kept glancing at Miss Rosenberg, as if he were speaking to her, too.

"But why can't you sell the property in Springbrook and use the money for a similar project somewhere else? Why, the difference in the cost of the land will be enough to cover half the cost of the project. Do GI's have to live so close to a business district, or in the heart of it, as it will be tomorrow? They'd much rather be out in the country, for the sake of their children. And for a project like that you can get land for nothing, or next to nothing. The city will buy it for you. For God's sake, dad, where's your business instinct?"

"I've told you, this isn't a business project. And I bought this land, this, not another piece, for this purpose. I'm not looking for profits on the deal. Can't I, for once in my life, act as if I wasn't a businessman? Haven't I a right to my own way of living, can't I do something without giving an accounting for it?" Grossman was beginning to shout, and all the time he kept glancing at his secretary, as if he was answering her unspoken objections, too.

"Sure you can, dad. I beg you, don't get excited. Do what you like. I'll be glad to help you. But for heaven's sake, don't take any steps before we've talked the whole thing over. There's time enough."

"Send out Frankel."

"Certainly. Dad, take it easy."

"I'm taking it easy. Miss Rosenberg, am I taking it easy or not?"

"All right, dad. I'm glad you're taking it easy. Good-by—and don't forget the engagement."

"Forget the engagement? What do you think is the matter with me? How is Louise?"

"Fine. But scared like a little rabbit."

"Scared of what?"

"Nothing. Expectancy. Excitement."

"Say hello to her for me. What do you hear from Robert?"

"Nothing new."

"Good-by, Lazar. See you soon." He turned from the telephone. "Well?" he said to the astonished Miss Rosenberg. "What do you think of my project?"

"You mean Silverstein's," she said tartly. "Is that all he had for you?"

"It's mine. I can see it now. That's what I bought the land for."

"Why in Springbrook?" she asked, as if she had heard Lazar's objections. "Because you happen to have a piece of land here? Grossman and Grossman have land in many places. You've got land in Yonkers, and in White Plains."

"Why shouldn't it be in Springbrook? What have you against Springbrook?"

"It's poison for you. You've got to sever your connections with this place."

"You mean *that* business? Forget it. Since I had the talk with Silverstein I see it in a different light. Have I mentioned Kovalsky to you in the last couple of days? Silverstein's a clever man; a wise man, too. And learned. Do you know that he once studied for the rabbinate? He knows all the laws of the faith. You should have heard him. He talked to me the way my father used to talk when I was a youngster, but in a different style, more worldly, more modern."

"What did he tell you?"

"To forget about the business. There wasn't anything, he says. I've talked myself into it."

"So what are we doing here? Why aren't we going home?"

"Because I have to set that project in motion."

"Oh, you mean Silverstein's project."

"It's mine, I tell you, not his. . . . I've long wanted to do some-

183

thing in a social way. . . . A memorial, so that people should remember that a Grossman once existed."

"Then why in Springbrook?"

"That's exactly what Lazar asked. Because I've got the land here, and because I dedicated it from the beginning to such a purpose, and I haven't the right to cancel that dedication. It's not in my keeping any more, it's in God's keeping."

"Yes? But a few days ago you had quite another use for that land. You were going to build a fine residential district, with shops and everything."

"I didn't want to tell you of my real intention. I know you dislike Springbrook because of what I told you. The truth is, I always intended to do something special here. That's why I bought the land out of my own funds, not out of the firm's funds. And that's why I turned down all the offers for the land. I wasn't sure what I'd do with it—a park, a hospital, a center—but it was going to be something special."

"So now it's a GI project. Now tell me you were thinking of that, too."

"No, that was Silverstein's idea all right. He took me out to the barracks they've set up for GI families. They're horrible. And I'll admit he turned my thoughts in that direction. Don't you see that with such a project a man can justify the whole of his life? It's an atonement for all the sins he's ever committed. How you got the money isn't so important as what you use it for, Silverstein said. He's a clever man. Yes, and what else did he say? He said that a man's life is one piece, a single block. There can be holes and cracks in a block, but if it's massive and solid enough, it can serve as the foundation of a building. It can be a cornerstone. In every man's life, he said, there are ups and downs, moral successes and moral failures; no one's life is perfect, especially among those of us who had only ourselves to begin with and to rely on. The main thing is what you do with your life. If you give it a purpose, then even its defects form part of the purpose. That's what he said, and it makes sense. It's wise. The man's a folk-philosopher. There he sits in his little store, sells writing paper, children's toys, birthday cards, and thinks up these things. Unbelievable, isn't it? He doesn't really invent them—he got them out of the holy books, the Jewish sources of wisdom, the sages."

And here Isaac Grossman forgot his strategy, and added: "He told me that this enterprise of mine, this project, would be an atonement for all my sins, not only for my sin against Kovalsky."

Rose started back. "There is no Kovalsky," she cried.

"That's very possible," said Grossman hastily. "It might be just my imagination. But if it's more than my imagination, then I'll have settled my account with him, and with his family. What's the difference, Rose? I don't think about him any more."

"Then for God's sake, why are we staying on in Springbrook?"

"Whichever way it is, that project will put my conscience at ease. I'll have to come back here from time to time."

"I want to go home," said Miss Rosenberg. "I'm dog-tired. We were supposed to stay here a couple of days, and it's more than a week. I haven't a decent dress to put on."

"Why shouldn't you go home, Rose? Go home for the week end, and bring me another suit, too. And some laundry. More than that, I'd like you to talk to Lazar, and explain the project to him, and calm him down. He seems to think I've gone out of my mind, I don't know what I'm doing. I can feel that's the way he feels about his father. What do you think, Rose? Don't I know what I'm doing? Have I gone out of my mind?"

"Now, please, don't get excited again," she pleaded. "It's Thursday today. Frankel won't be able to come out before Monday or Tuesday. Why shouldn't we both go home for the week end? I'll call Steve and ask him to come for us in the car. Go home, and be comfortable, in your own house; and eat decently. Frances has been phoning every day, asking when to expect us. Sunday we'll be able to go out to Long Island, you can see Louise, you can tell Lazar whatever you want to. What do you say?"

"No, I want you to go alone; and you talk with Lazar. I don't want to talk with him. We're liable to quarrel. I don't like his attitude toward me. He seems to think I haven't the right to do what I like with my own property. He wants—" Grossman became excited—"he wants to inherit me while I'm alive."

"No, please—be calm. Lazar has reason enough to be uneasy about the way you're acting. And you can be just as angry with me as with him. He means well by you, and so do I."

"Do as I ask you, Rose. You go and talk with him. I can't I've got to be on the spot. I want to look the place over again, I want

185

to test out some ideas. I want to prepare the material for Frankel. I have lots to do—I can't go home."

"It can wait, Mr. Grossman. It's waited so long...."

"You know how I am, Rose. When I start something I've got to go at it bullheaded. That's the only way I can get anything done. Once I start something I don't let go until it's finished."

"I don't like leaving you here alone."

"For God's sake, am I sick? And I won't be—unless you make me sick, you and Lazar. She doesn't like leaving me alone! What the hell does that mean? Call Steve and have him come for you."

"What will you do for two or three days?"

"I'll go dancing," he answered, wrathfully. "I'll find me a night club and a couple of girls."

"I wish you would. Honestly, I do."

"All right, give me a chance. But you're afraid to leave me alone."

"That isn't what I'm afraid of. You know what I'm afraid of."

The blood came into Grossman's face. "Rose!"

"I'm sorry. I can't stop thinking of him."

"I've told you that it doesn't bother me any more. I don't want you to talk about it."

"All right. If you feel so certain."

"And there's Moses Silverstein here, isn't there? We have lots to talk about."

She yielded, reluctantly. She would leave him alone for the next few days.

CHAPTER SEVEN

MISS ROSENBERG had scarcely left the hotel, to be driven back by Steve to New Rochelle, when old Grossman stole furtively out and made his way down Main Street in the direction of the Old Poland Restaurant. He had never been there before, and Miss Rosenberg had not told him where it was—she had been very careful about that. Nevertheless he had guessed at its location. He walked slowly, like a man strolling without a destination, stopping now and again to gaze into the shop windows. The streets were wet—for it was spring in Connecticut, raw, cloudy— but Grossman was indifferent to the weather. When he reached the restaurant, evening was coming on and the place was beginning to fill. He peered through the large plate-glass window which gave on Main Street, and observed the bustle within. Customers stood at the door, waiting for their turn, the waiters scurried about the packed tables. From the outside it seemed that the restaurant was filled with steam and smoke, and persons emerged from view, and disappeared from it, as the clouds parted and closed. Grossman stared for a while, then returned quickly to his hotel. He was going to change his shoes, eat dinner alone, and above all wait for Miss Rosenberg's telephone call from New Rochelle. She was sure to call him as soon as she got home, and he wanted to be in the hotel so as not to arouse any suspicions. Later, when the Old Poland would be emptying, he would return to see Mike—and perhaps someone else.

He was in the middle of his dinner, in his rooms, when Rose called. She only wanted to know if everything was O.K. "What do you mean, O.K.?" he asked irritably. She reported that everyone in New Rochelle was asking when he would be back. Tomorrow she would send out Steve with the car. There was a letter from Robert. She would also send some clothes and linen; and

Steve could stay on in Springbrook. "What for?" asked Grossman, with the same irritation. "What does he want to stay on for? I don't need a car. I can walk a little, too, can't I? Or do you want me to forget how to walk?" Rose tried to say something about his needing the car over the long week end. He softened. "All right, I'll see tomorrow. But don't bother me any more today. I'm tired. As soon as I've eaten I'll go to bed, like a good boy, with a heap of comics. Good night, Rose."

But he was thinking to himself that what he was about to do was a crime against his family, against Rose—the one person close to him—and against himself, too. He was deliberately walking into a trap. He knew it, and yet he could not hold back. He was drawn to the restaurant by his fixation as a murderer is drawn to the scene of his crime. He had to see the place where his victim, Kovalsky, had worked as a dishwasher. He was quite sure that the Yan Mike had spoken about was the one he had robbed. He simply could not shake himself free of this idea. Yes, Yan was still alive, and was to be found in one of the rooms off the restaurant kitchen. Mike was keeping him a prisoner there for some dark purpose of his own.

The Old Poland was emptying as Grossman looked in a second time. Here and there a belated customer was getting a check from the waiter. He saw Mike sitting at a corner table with another waiter, and the two were gulping down a meal. He went in. The air was heavy with steam and the lingering odor of the departed customers who had just filled it; an echo of the hullabaloo still hung about. With dripping overcoat and umbrella Grossman walked past the bar and made for a table from which he could watch the kitchen door.

Mike was eating rapidly; he was covered with perspiration, and the shirt under his waiter's coat stuck to his body, just as his hair stuck to his low forehead. He was hungry and tired, and he snatched at the food with wolfish impatience. But looking up, he saw old Grossman, and suddenly he stopped chewing, though his mouth was full. The mouthful seemed to be stuck halfway down his throat. His little black eyes lit up, and he called out, with a choked voice, *"Ola Boga! My God! It's the boss!"*

"What boss?" asked the other waiter.

Mike did not answer him. He gulped down the mouthful,

188

picked up the napkin, wiped the sweat off his forehead, stroked his mustaches rapidly, and came over to Grossman. He helped him off with his coat, hung up coat and umbrella and hat, and asked, in the manner of someone greeting an old friend, "Is the boss alone? Where's the lady?"

"What lady?"

"The lady who's always with the boss. I mean the missus I met."

"Miss Rosenberg? She's not here today."

"And the boss is alone?"

"Yes, I'm alone."

"That's good. Sit down here, Mr. Grossman. You see, I know your name. No, sit here, Mr. Grossman, it's more comfortable—" And he pointed to another corner, away from the kitchen.

"No, I prefer to sit here."

"As the boss likes. Can I serve the boss anything? Dinner?"

"No, I've eaten. You can bring me a glass of tea. Don't hurry. I have lots of time. Tell me first, why is it good that I'm alone?"

"Because I've got news for the boss. I wanted to see you. You know, I telephoned The Inn, but they wouldn't connect me. They would only connect me with the lady, with the secretary; they told me I would have to talk with her. But I didn't want to talk with her, because the news I've got is only for you, Mr. Grossman. I know you're going to be very much interested"—he winked—"and I know the lady isn't interested. But let me first bring you the tea."

"There's time for that. Tell me, what news have you got for me? Sit down."

"Wait, I want to see if my boss is around."

"What boss?"

"You know, from the restaurant. If he's here, I can't talk with you about those things. He understands. I'll have to tell the Pan, I mean, the mister, some other time."

Mike looked round carefully, went into the kitchen, returned after a few moments, and sat down, satisfied.

"No, he's not here. Now I'll be able to talk to you, Mr. Grossman. Only a little bit, see? Because the big talk we'll have to have someplace else, where we won't be interrupted. Because I've got good news for you, see? Now, you tell me where we can meet."

"Tell me what the news is. Can't you tell me here?"

Mike looked round nervously. "You don't know who's looking and listening, Mr. Grossman. . . . Can I call you by that name, or should I just say boss?" Mike sat on a corner of his chair and looked earnestly at Grossman.

"How did you get to know my name?"

"Why, who doesn't know Mr. Grossman? Everybody in town knows Mr. Grossman of Grossman and Grossman, who owns Smith's Farm. I heard lots about you. I know you're a big man, the boss of Grossman and Grossman. You're the father of General Grossman. Oh yes, I know plenty. Mr. Bornstein told me about you, too."

"Who's Mr. Bornstein?"

"What? You never heard of Mr. Bornstein? He's a very important attorney in the city. He knows all the judges; the Mayor, the District Attorney—all are his friends. He's going to be a judge soon. You should meet him, you got to meet him, Mr. Grossman. Because he wants to see you. He's the same religion as you, Mr. Grossman. He's a Jew."

"Why should I meet him? And what does he want to see me about?"

"Oh, he can help you a lot. It's good to know a man like him."

"He can help me in what?"

"Help you to fix that quarrel with the Kovalskys. He's ready to take that over."

"What quarrel have I got with the Kovalskys?"

"H-m—well, you know what I mean, Mr. Grossman."

"What? Tell me what you mean?" said Grossman, in a tone of command.

"The thing is like this. You knew right away, Mr. Grossman, when you met the Zaslavskys, that they aren't the right Kovalskys. Boy—you knew that right away! You smelled it! You said it right away, and so did the lady. I've got nothing against the Zaslavskys, and Mrs. Zaslavsky, she's my aunt. And you did a good thing for them, Mr. Grossman, you took care of a poor family. You should see how happy they are now, those Zaslavskys. You can be satisfied you did something good, even if they're not the right Kovalskys but only relatives, far-off relatives, of that Kovalsky. The real Kovalsky, he's somebody else, another man. I found that out only just now. Since you told me that was not the right Kovalsky, I made up my mind to find the right one. And I did it for your sake, to ease—what is it?—your conscience. And I have him now."

Grossman became white with anger. He lost control of himself, looked straight at Mike, and cried out, "I know you have him."

"You know it, Mr. Grossman?"

"Yes, sir. I've known it all along. From the first moment I saw you. I knew all along where he was, but you wouldn't produce him."

"I don't want to produce him?" asked Mike, stupefied. "Oh no, Mr. Grossman, I didn't know about him until just now. I found out a couple of days ago from a relative. I asked, and asked, and I found out. For you, Mr. Grossman."

"Where are you hiding him?" asked Grossman coldly.

"Who?"

"Yan Kovalsky."

"I'm hiding him?"

"Yes, yes!" And Grossman glared at him.

"I'm not hiding him. What should I be hiding him for?"

"Why, you say you know where he is. Tell me, where is he?"

"I can't do that right away, Mr. Grossman."

"Why?"

"Because I told Mr. Bornstein that I wouldn't settle the business with you alone, and without him. I'm leaving it all to him."

"Why?"

"He's my lawyer. He's Yan Kovalsky's lawyer, too."

"What do we need a lawyer for?"

"Oh, yes, we've got to have a lawyer for a thing like this. I'm advising you, Mr. Grossman, to talk it over with Mr. Bornstein. Bornstein's got lots of people out of trouble. He's got pull."

Grossman controlled his rage with a violent effort, put on a smile, and answered, "I'm not in any trouble, and I don't need anyone's pull."

"I only mean, when it comes to fixing up that quarrel with Kovalsky. Because after all, Mr. Grossman, you'll have to fix it up with the real Kovalsky. The Zaslavskys aren't the real ones."

Throughout the conversation Grossman had not taken his eyes off the kitchen door. Whenever the door opened he tried to see what was inside. But there was only the steam which came bursting out and concealed the interior. Nevertheless he was sure at the moment that his Yan Kovalsky was somewhere within, or near by.

"And you know where the real Kovalsky is?"

"I've told you I know."

"Where?"

"I can't say that without Bornstein."

"Is that so? Well, you come with me and I'll show you where the real Kovalsky is."

"Where?" asked Mike, startled.

"There. In the kitchen. That's where you keep him."

"In the kitchen?" Mike broke into a sudden laugh. "In the kitchen? All right, you come in there with me."

Grossman was already inside, Mike following him.

The kitchen swam in mist. Cooks in white stood over flaming ovens. Men naked to the waist were busy at a huge, steaming tank; Grossman saw the bronze torsos of Negroes who were scouring and scrubbing huge iron pots, and scraping heavy tables. There were no whites among these, but there were two old women with sacks who were picking up pieces of food from plates, and out of garbagecans, and thrusting them into the sacks. The plates moved automatically along a belt in the tanks, reached the center, rotated under the jets, and moved on under jets of steam.

"You get lots of dishes here after dinner, Mr. Grossman. You please excuse the noise and the mess, eh? This is cleaning time. We used to have dishwashers, and now we have, you see, a machine, which is cleaner. And it saves time, and money," Mike explained, as though Grossman were on a tour of inspection.

Grossman listened with half an ear. He walked back and forth through the kitchen and peered into every corner. He looked sharply at the Negroes over the tank, at the old women picking up the leavings. Then, in a corner, he saw two other old women peeling potatoes and peas, preparing heads of cabbage. There was also an additional Negro who stood over a wide table boiling and drying the cutlery which lay in large heaps. There was not a soul

192

present to whom he could attach the face and identity of his obsession—Yan Kovalsky.

"We used to have a lot more workers in the kitchen. Now, with the machines, we have less. We don't even have to cut the meat. Everything comes ready for cooking," said Mike, as if in further explanation.

"What have you done with Yan Kovalsky?" Grossman interrupted sharply.

"What have I done—"

"Where have you concealed him?" And Grossman raised his voice.

"Mr. Grossman, be so good, please, not to talk so loud. People will hear you; people will think a crime has been committed."

"But you have committed a crime. You are a criminal. Didn't you tell me yourself that you locked Kovalsky in a room near the kitchen? Where is that room? Show me, show me at once."

"What? You mean *that* Kovalsky, that drunk who used to wash dishes in our kitchen? But he's been dead a long time. No, no, I'm not talking about that one. He's certainly dead, been dead a long time."

"But what did you do with him?"

"I tell you he disappeared. No one knows what happened to him."

"Show me the room where he used to live."

"The room isn't here any more. I mean, it was changed into a storeroom."

"Let me see it."

"O.K. Come with me."

Mike led him through a door into a dimly lit corridor filled with milk cans, incinerators, empty tins, cardboard boxes containing empty bottles. There were several locked doors along the corridor.

"In one of these rooms," said Mike. "He had a straw mattress, and he used to lie there for days, even in the summer. You see, these used to be bedrooms. Some of the kitchen help slept here. They used to sleep even in the kitchen."

"And here is where you locked him in, eh?"

"Today it's forbidden, by the department of health. You see, it's not hygienic. You can't let anyone sleep in the kitchen now.

193

Yeah, it was dangerous to let him out when there was a horse race. He was crazy, sick, like a drunk."

"And what's here now?"

"I told you, Mr. Grossman. Storerooms. We keep canned goods in there."

"I want to see."

"I haven't got the key. I'm telling you, Mr. Grossman, Kovalsky isn't here. He isn't in there with the canned goods. If you want to know where Kovalsky is, you'll have to find it out from me. *I* know where to find the Kovalsky you're looking for."

"Well, how do you know which Kovalsky I'm looking for?"

"Listen, mister, I wasn't born yesterday. My name's Mike, and I've got a brain in my head. If a man like you, Mr. Grossman, comes here to town to look for a Kovalsky with whom he had something to do when he was a young man, and he spends a lot of his own money for somebody who is only related to that Kovalsky—just for the name, eh?—then it must be a very interesting business, eh? A feller can get cut in, maybe, eh? Because otherwise you wouldn't come to the restaurant to look for Mike, would you? Because Mike is the only one who knows where Kovalsky is. Mike has the key to the business."

Suddenly Mike felt bony fingers at his throat, bony fingers that clutched him like pliers.

"I'll kill you!" raged Grossman. "Tell me what you've done with him! I'll send you to Sing Sing. I'll put the best lawyers on the case, and I'll get you, you murderer."

Mike tore the hands from his throat. "Have you gone crazy? Who do you think I am? Kovalsky? You think you can do to me what you did to him?"

"What did I do to Kovalsky?"

"Oh, we know what you did to him. We know everything now. You robbed him. You took away his money—every cent. You drove him to drink, you ruined his life, and you became rich—from his money. We know it now."

Grossman was paralyzed into speechlessness.

"And now your conscience bothers you," Mike went on, insistently. "You want to make it up to him, but you can't find him. I find him for you, and what thanks do I get? You attack me, you want to strangle me. You threaten me, you'll send me to Sing Sing. Why do you treat me like that? I told you that Yan the drunkard isn't the Kovalsky you are looking for. That Yan was a stableboy, he was never a machinist, he never had a daughter who got married. He disappeared. Like he was drowned. You ask me to produce this Kovalsky. Where should I take him? The devil knows what became of him."

"Forgive me for what I did," said Grossman. "Where is that other Yan, the one you found?"

"I already explained to you, I can't tell you here and now. We made up, Bornstein should be our representative. If you want, I will come to you tomorrow with Mr. Bornstein, any place you like except Silverstein's. Mr. Bornstein doesn't want to have anything to do with that Silverstein. Just us three. And it's no good too many people should know about it. We can fix it up among ourselves. Mr. Bornstein will explain everything to you. I'll bring you to this Kovalsky, I mean to his family, and we'll finish the whole business, and that'll be the end of it."

"With his family? And what about him? Isn't he alive any more?" Grossman asked eagerly.

"I can't tell you here. Tomorrow, with Mr. Bornstein, you'll find out everything."

"And how do I know that this one that you found is the real Kovalsky?"

"You'll see, you'll talk with the people, you'll find out for yourself. Didn't you know right away that Mrs. Zaslavsky wasn't the daughter of the real Kovalsky? You tell me, now, where the three of us can meet. Anywhere you say, except Silverstein's."

Grossman reflected. "Tomorrow, ten in the morning, in my hotel, apartment two."

"Good. That's a date. You'll see, you won't regret it."

"I'm very sorry for what I did. Forgive me," said Grossman, in a low voice.

"Oh, never you mind that, Mr. Grossman, I know you didn't mean it, what you did and what you said. A man in a situation like that is bound to forget himself now and again."

"A situation like what?"

"I mean—excuse me—I mean when a man gets excited. Me too,

when I get excited, I'm liable to do something like that. Don't think about it any more. Shall I call you a taxi? It's raining pretty bad. And I don't want my boss to find you here. Nobody has to know what we arranged, isn't that right? We got to keep it to ourselves." He finished up on a note of conspiratorial familiarity.

CHAPTER EIGHT

STRANGELY enough, he slept well that night, a sweet, tranquil sleep, as if a stone had been rolled off his shoulders. When he awoke in the morning there was a smiling in his heart, as bright as the spring sunlight pouring through the window. It was obvious to him that his obsession about Yan Kovalsky, that Mike was keeping him locked up in a room near the kitchen, had vanished. Kovalsky was not there; he might have been there at one time, but now no longer. He might be somewhere else, still concealed by Mike. He was not interested in any other Kovalsky. But was the one he had in mind the real Kovalsky? In his imagination he saw so vividly the features of the dishwasher whom he had wronged that to transfer the wrong to anyone else would have seemed to him like an act of betrayal. Kovalsky the dishwasher of the Old Poland Restaurant had now become a part of him, had become identified for him with his father. And just as he could not let another take the place of his father, so he could not permit a substitute for Kovalsky. Now if this Kovalsky wanted to fade into a spirit, a myth, it would be impossible to drag him into the light of day; and he would have to be dealt with as a spirit and a myth; he would have to receive his compensation not in a material transaction, but in spiritual form. In the same way he could not do anything material for his father now; he had to content him with moral actions, with purity of behavior. And so the only way left to correct the error—it was error, now, not misdeed—of his youth was to follow Silverstein's counsel and create a humanitarian public institution in the man's name. He had to call it *Kovalsky Center*—right out, without evasion or circumlocution; and he had to do it in a way which would bring no glory or prestige to himself or his own family. This was his resolve, and he had to stand by it, outface all objections, do it in opposition, if

197

need be, to his son. "What do people matter to me? I must liberate my soul, before it is too late," he said firmly to himself.

He regretted now that he had arranged to meet with Mike and this man Bornstein, whom he did not know at all. He regretted, too, his outburst of rage, although the total outcome of the evening had been satisfying enough. He even felt well disposed toward Mike for having destroyed his delusion. He would have to compensate him for the insult, and for the rough treatment. He felt some discomfort at the thought of facing Mike; and more than discomfort at the thought of meeting Bornstein. He knew something about these shyster lawyers, attorneys for gangsters, bookies, con men and swindlers of all types. He considered for a moment whether it would not be better to leave word downstairs, in the hotel, that he was not to be disturbed. But he gave up the notion. He would have to see Mike, to make amends for his behavior. And as for the lawyer, he would give him a reception that he would remember for the rest of his life. Besides, it was just as well to make that shyster lawyer understand at once that Isaac Grossman was not afraid to see him.

The man was pretty much what Grossman had imagined him to be: in the thirties, wearing a double-breasted blue serge suit, a blue shirt, and a blue tie; two pencilstrokes of mustache under his nose, and a pair of restless, ratlike eyes: with a forced smile, with exaggerated politeness which slipped easily into familiarity. His first words expressed his great satisfaction at having the privilege of meeting face to face the distinguished, nationally known head of the firm of Grossman and Grossman.

Grossman remained seated, and interrupted the man's preliminary flourish in a cold tone: "What can I do for you?" He let him stand on the other side of the table.

"May I sit down?" the young man asked.

Grossman let several moments pass before he answered curtly, "You may. But not for long. I'm expecting some people."

"We shan't keep you long, Mr. Grossman. We know how precious your time is."

"What can I do for you?" repeated Grossman.

Bornstein glanced at Mike, who stood at the side of the table, and said, with a saccharine smile, "I thought we could do some-

thing for you, Mr. Grossman. My client here—" he indicated Mike
—"and I."

"And what is it you could do for me?" asked Grossman, very
seriously.

"My client had occasion to speak with you yesterday, and he
informed you that we, I mean, he, my client, has found the real
Kovalsky that you're looking for. The Kovalsky whom you compensated, so to speak, I mean whom you got straight with, is, as
you know, not the real one."

"How do you know which Kovalsky I'm looking for?"

"Why, everyone knows. The whole town knows that you're
looking for a Kovalsky whom you knew when you were a young
man, and with whom you had, let's say, a kind of argument, and
you want to make it good to him." The smile became a trifle uncertain; then he found the right tone again. "Mr. Grossman, we've
come here as your friends, especially I. I know who you are, and
whom you represent; I know your social standing, and the high
rank your son attained. I didn't come here, God forbid, to make
things harder for you. I am a friend, who has come here to help
you."

"Help me? Do I need someone's help?" asked Grossman, in
astonishment.

"I mean, in the matter of the Kovalsky you are looking for."

"I'm not looking for a Kovalsky, and I have nothing to
straighten out with any Kovalsky. You're wasting my time." And
Grossman made a motion as if to get up.

Bornstein looked blankly at Mike, who returned the stare.
Finally Mike stammered: "Mr. Grossman, didn't you come to my
restaurant yesterday and ask me about a Kovalsky? You were even
looking for him in the kitchen and the storerooms. You demanded
that I produce Kovalsky, as if I'd hidden him somewhere, and you
wanted to strangle me because I couldn't produce a Kovalsky."

"It's true, I'm interested in a Yan Kovalsky who was a dishwasher in the Old Poland Restaurant. If you can find him, or you
know where he is, bring him to me and I'll reward you. No other
Kovalsky interests me. That is all."

"But, Mr. Grossman, that Yan Kovalsky, the dishwasher, is
not the true Kovalsky you are looking for. I've told you so many
times. He was a stableboy, and he left no daughter. Now we've

found the real, the true Kovalsky, with whom you had that—er—dispute."

"I don't want to hear any more," interrupted Grossman. "You've heard what I said. If you can find the Yan Kovalsky whom you kept locked in a room in the restaurant, and whom you maybe tortured, too, I'll reward you. I don't want to hear about another one. And now, gentlemen, I'd like to be left alone." And he rose.

"Wait a moment, Mr. Grossman, wait a moment," said the attorney, who remained sitting at the table. He spoke calmly. "You are not interested, to be sure, in the Kovalsky my client has found. But this other Kovalsky may be interested in you. It so happens that I also represent the real Kovalsky, the Kovalsky with whom you had this—er—falling out many years ago. You finished up owing him something. But that isn't all. There are certain important and weighty facts involved, facts of a serious character which can reflect very unfavorably on the firm of Grossman and Grossman, and perhaps with unpleasant consequences for you. I'm not prepared to call these things by their right name—not yet; and I don't *have* to, ever. Mr. Grossman, you're a businessman."

"What? Blackmail?" said Grossman, seating himself again.

"Mr. Grossman, you do me an injustice, just as you did my client Mike an injustice when you threatened to have him sent to Sing Sing, and to prosecute him. You even assaulted him physically. He has blue marks on his throat, the bruises left by your fingers, as anybody can see. A doctor has examined him."

"And he tore the lapel of my service coat, a new black coat," added Mike.

"Tore your coat?" asked Grossman, surprised.

"Yes, you pulled at the lapels, and you tore one of them. You were so excited, Mr. Grossman, that you don't remember anything."

"We can quite understand it, and we, my client and I, don't want to bring it up again," began Bornstein once more. "A man in your situation can easily get excited. We want to forget about it. I tell you again that we came, my client and I, as good friends. In a delicate matter like this it's far better to reach a mutual accommodation, in a friendly way, than to go to court and let the whole matter become public property. We, at least I, certainly came here as your good friend, with the right respect for your good name and ready to help you in your difficulty, in this—er—let's call it unpleasant situation. And you call it blackmail? You are very unjust to me, Mr. Grossman. But I forgive you, because I know how you feel. I'll forget it, for the benefit of all of us."

"But I won't forget it, you swindler, I won't forget it, for the benefit of all of us," said Grossman, his expression changing suddenly. "Listen to me, young man. I know your kind, I know what you are. I've met many like you. A young man like you, who no doubt had quite a struggle to get a degree and become an attorney, ought to place his profession in the service of law and justice, ought to be useful to society, and ought to build himself a solid reputation; instead of which you stoop to the lowest transactions, you become the defender of racketeers, swindlers, even gangsters; you learn from them what justice is, and you don't hesitate to accuse innocent people baselessly, in order to blackmail money out of them by promising to hush up the accusation. That's what you want to do with me. I've seen what happens to your tribe. You go hand in hand with your clients to prison—or worse. Go back, young man, and turn to something decent. You're young, your family put much hope in you. Don't disappoint them, and don't make a mess of your life. And if you undertake to go on the right path, and you need help, come to me. I'll gladly help you. I'll be needing here in town, in Springbrook, the assistance of a lawyer in connection with a project I'm about to undertake. Not, of course, to represent the firm of Grossman and Grossman, but to work with our lawyers, so that you'll have the opportunity to be with honest people."

"What? You're trying to bribe me, Mr. Grossman?"

Grossman was astounded.

"Bribe you? What do you mean?"

"I mean the very thing that you meant. Bribe the other client's attorney." A faint, cynical smile appeared under the cat's-whisker mustaches of Mr. Bornstein.

"Young man, be good enough to leave this room at once, before I have you shown out."

"Very good, Mr. Grossman, I am going. But I'm still your friend and still ready to serve you. If you change your mind, before it's too late of course, you can call me. You'll find my number in the telephone book. I haven't taken offense."

201

"I know it," said Grossman. "Now be good enough to get out."

"Something else, Mr. Grossman," said Bornstein, his hand already on the door knob. "Regarding this project which you have in mind. If this project has anything to do with compensation for my client, I warn you in advance, in the name of my client, that he is not going to be satisfied with moral compensation, and your philanthropic undertakings have no interest for him."

Grossman looked at him penetratingly. He felt it distasteful to go on talking with the man, but his curiosity got the better of him. He asked: "Who do you mean by 'my client'? Him?" He pointed at Mike. "*He* won't be satisfied with my project?"

"Yes, Mike is also my client. Because of your assault yesterday. But I wasn't referring to him. I was referring to—" he glanced away significantly—"you know who I mean, the one who takes place number one in this entire business."

"And who is that?"

"Kovalsky and his family, toward whom you have the heaviest obligations. They have unshakable proof of that. Do you want to talk to the point, Mr. Grossman?"

"Get out, you miserable swindler," cried Grossman, and made for the door.

"This time I do take offense. You're my witness, Mike, that he called me a miserable swindler." He flung the door open and strode out.

"Hey, Mike, send my secretary a bill, a good, fat bill," called Grossman through the open door.

He felt sick when the two impostors had left the room. The air was foul, it was filled with the odor of decay. He felt lonely, abandoned. He wished that Rose had not gone home. And where was Steve? He should have arrived by now. Steve, and his wife Frances, the cook, had been with him quite a number of years. They were part of his family, like Rose. With Steve around he would feel safer. He felt exposed to enemies who lay about him, in ambush, like hunters for their prey. It seemed to him he heard the panting of dogs on his trail. He wanted to go out at once, but he had to wait for Rose's telephone call. He had been waiting for it since morning. Should he call the house? No, he must not show weakness, he must not betray his alarm. But to wait any longer

202

here was impossible. It was asphyxiating. He would go across to Silverstein's little store and ask him about this Bornstein. After all, he had to have some kind of protection, if only for the duration of his stay in Springbrook. He must engage a capable and decent lawyer. Bornstein's closing words, that he represented Yan Kovalsky, lying and improbable as they might be, had nevertheless hit home. He could not get over them so easily, not though he knew that whoever it was that the two impostors had got hold of, it could not be the real Yan. There was no doubt about that. His instinct would tell him who was the real Yan. His imagination placed the real Yan in the little room, and there he remained, not to be conjured out of the place by anyone. No, he would not accept any other Yan. And he had very definite proof: the real Yan had two names. As long as no one revealed to him Yan's second name, which he could not recall but which he would recognize at once, hearing it uttered—for it was there, within him, buried in his memory—just so long would he not accept another Yan. These impostors undoubtedly had found themselves a Yan Kovalsky; or they might have created one, picked up a man and hung this name on him; and no doubt they could back up his identity with forged papers. But they could not do anything with him. They did not know the exact circumstances under which he, Isaac Grossman, had committed the wrong against the man. No one knew the details except Rose. Silverstein did not know them. Rose had merely indicated the outline to him. Moreover, not a single trace of the crime had remained, not a scrap of evidence could be brought against him. Nevertheless it was necessary to obtain protection against the impostors; and that immediately, before they took the first step. They had to be frightened off before they brought the thing into the open. He would not wait another minute. He would go over to Silverstein and tell him what had happened. He would get his advice on how to protect himself against the swindlers.

He instructed the girl at the switchboard where he could be found in case of calls, and left the hotel.

But when he stepped out into the street and took a deep breath of the sweet, refreshing air, washed by the sunlight, he bethought himself: no, he would not think of those two men now. They had made the morning repulsive, they had besmirched him with their presence; he would cleanse himself, bathe in the purifying spring air. His restlessness subsided, the hidden anxiety which had started up when he heard the words "I represent Yan Kovalsky" dissolved. Here, on the very threshold of the hotel, as he fronted the morning, he was once again Isaac Grossman, secure, firm and determined. And suddenly he was seized with the desire to take still another look at his property. Yes, he needed to prepare material for Frankel, the architect. The map of the territory was, unfortunately, in New York. No doubt there was one in Springbrook. He would have to get a copy from City Hall.

He stepped up to a taxi outside the hotel and asked to be taken to Smith's Farm.

"Which side?" asked the driver, "Main or Elm?"

"Elm Street side first, then we'll see."

Smith's Farm lay, a large, irregular quadrangle, between Main and Elm Streets. The nearer edge was close to the business section, the further edge approached the residential area. On the other side of Elm Street there was a large sports ground. It was now covered with fresh green which had sprung up under a protecting mantle of snow out of the well-soaked earth. Here and there drooping willows were already showing tender buds of green. The field was starred with innumerable crocuses and daffodils; and though there were paths across the field, they too were covered with green, and they looked like marks in an unbroken carpet. From behind the little wood came the sound of rushing water; it was a brook, tumbling down the slopes of a hillock. It's heavy with the rains, thought Grossman. Along the Elm Street edge of Smith's Farm there was a row of elm trees, earnest, motionless sentinels casting their shadow on the grass. Looking over his property, Grossman did not, indeed, have a vision of dancing nymphs against an Arcadian background; but he did have a vision of young mothers with baby carriages, or with babies in their arms; or young mothers still big with the unborn. He saw them sitting in the shadow of the willow trees. He saw the fathers, young men of muscular build. They carried their children on their shoulders, up the hillock, to the source of the rivulet. Their faces, tired with the day's work, lit up with the joy and tranquillity of their homecoming. Happiness wiped the sweat off their faces. He heard the chatter of children's voices, mixed with the twittering of birds. He heard children laughing, shouting, crying. They danced about on the field, like birds hopping. They were here, they were there, they were gone; and wherever they left a footprint, a flower sprang up. He felt in his nostrils the presence of milk, and children's bodies. He heard the calling of mothers, the barking of dogs, the thud of footballs, the cries of triumph, all mingled into a harmonious and melodic theme.

Grossman's imagination was that of the builder. He could not see an empty lot without building upon it, at once, the appropriate structures and shelters. But until now he had, in actual practice, confined himself to the erection of theaters and of costly winter and summer resorts; he had filled empty lots with amusement places for the rich; he had provided for those who came in Cadillacs and Packards; in and out of his hotels and apartment houses went women in expensive furs. And he was thinking now of homes for the plain people; he saw the men pouring in overalls out of the factories and streaming toward their homes, their nests, their places of rest and renewal and affection. That was what he wanted to build now; and he would build generously, not squeezing extra rooms out of calculated square inches. He would have comfortable workers' apartments, which would make the mother's housework easier and the father's homecoming more pleasant. Three or four stories; wide corridors; small houses, with not more than twenty apartments to a house, the houses spaced with room for gardens and flower beds. Spacious kitchens, because the poor live mostly in their kitchens; the houses grouped in blocks, and every block with its own central laundry and clubrooms. In every house, individual storerooms. The windows would be on the Elm Street side, with a clear view to the sports ground. On the other side, toward Main Street, a central market with small individual stores, a bookseller, a drugstore, a cafeteria, and so on. There really ought to be a garage, too, but that was far too expensive, beyond the reach of these people. Parking space would be a problem for the city to solve. But a movie house was of course a necessity. And even more necessary was the sports ground. He would have to find out whether this belonged to the city or was private property; but whichever it was, it had to be acquired for the project. In fact the project was practically impossible without it.

A profound satisfaction filled his inmost being when he meditated on this project for GI homes. The bitter taste of the two impostors was washed completely out of him. He even felt grateful now for the Kovalsky incident without which he would never have come upon the idea of the project: the first plan he had ever had for homes for simple working people.

On the Elm Street side the property was thickly covered with bushes, weeds, and poison ivy; it was difficult to break a path through to the center. Grossman could only look across. Here and there he saw an elm tree lifting to the sun its bare branches on which the closed buds of leaves were beginning to swell. But he saw neither bushes, nor weeds, nor naked trees; he saw the red roofs of the houses, the red walls with the white trim, he saw the lawns and the flower beds. He saw the windows flashing like mirrors in the setting sun. He saw the peace and contentment and gaiety of the homes of the GI's.

CHAPTER NINE

IT was in a grateful and chastened mood that he entered Silverstein's little store. He found Silverstein actually at work! There he sat in his office over a pile of papers, his pince-nez in subdued dance on his nose, keeping time with the wobbling of his head.

"What?" laughed Grossman. "You work, too? I thought you lived on manna from heaven."

"I have a little job with City Hall. You know, I was once a printer—and so they gave me the job of looking through the printing work for the city. I know a bit of law too, I took evening courses—I once was quite an ambitious lad. I thought I'd be a second Untermeyer, or even Brandeis. It all wound up with this little store. I have no regrets, thank God. I know the Mayor, I know other people, so I got this job. Not much, but it helps me to make a living."

"You studied law once, eh? As it happens, I need a lawyer. I'd like to have a talk with you. Can you stop work for a few minutes and go into a cafeteria with me for a sandwich and coffee? I've been quite busy."

"Right. Only please wait until my wife comes. She'll be here any moment. Or no—never mind. We'll go right away and I'll leave this notice on the door: Back in a Few Moments. My customers can wait."

"Where shall we go?"

"There's a cafeteria a few doors down. You said a sandwich and coffee, didn't you—not a roast duck."

"Can you recommend me a good, reliable lawyer here in Springbrook?" began Grossman. "There's something I want done. I thought I'd be able to put it off till I saw the firm's lawyers in New York, but it looks now as if I'll need a local lawyer, immediately."

"What's the hurry?"

"There are several things. First, the sports ground on Elm Street, opposite my property. Do you know to whom it belongs? I've got to have it for my project. I've just been down there, and I'm working on the details. It's impossible to go on with the plan unless I have that ground for the mothers and children. Does it belong to the city?" Grossman spoke rapidly, munching on his sandwich.

"It belongs to the city. It was part of the grounds of a high school once, but the building decayed, and a new one was built in another part of town. There was some idea of turning the place into a professional sports park, but there were difficulties. The experts said it wasn't big enough, and there would be no room for parking space. Besides, the neighbors in the residential area objected. It would bring in a lot of noise. Then some politician persuaded the city fathers to give him a permit to build a factory there. But the park commissioner voided it, because the neighbors got wind of it and objected to that even more strenuously. So there the ground is, and nothing is being done with it. The politician still has an option on it. During the summer the kids of the neighborhood play there. I'm pretty sure the city will let you have it for the project. You've got to know where to apply, though, and you'll have to come to terms with the politician who has the option. But he won't be too difficult. You only have to find a good lawyer."

"Yes, that's what I have to find," said Grossman, with a cheerful smile. "A local lawyer, who knows the ropes. And then, you know, Mr. Silverstein, I've got to be free from city and state taxes. Why should the GI's have to carry the burden of taxes? Because only GI's will get those homes. I'm also thinking of the wounded and crippled GI's. I'm thinking of building two classes of houses, one class for those who've come back whole, and another for the wounded veterans. The second class will have to be more comfortable—and cheaper."

"Don't you think it might lead to quarrels and jealousies?"

"Who's going to be jealous of artificial hands and legs, or remodeled faces? I even think there ought to be a difference between the way we treat a GI who's been at the front, and under fire for months, and one who stayed home at a desk job."

208

"I don't know how the veterans' organizations are going to see that. There'll be protests."

"We'll leave that for later. Meanwhile I want to be sure of plenty of space, and light, and air. That's why I must have the sports ground. I guess we'll manage the politician."

"You ought to see Franklin and Davis."

"Who are they?"

"The leading lawyers in Springbrook. They do all the important business here. And they've a lot of influence in the city and the state."

"Good. Are they far from here?"

"No, right here on Main Street, next door to the State Bank. But what's the rush?"

"I've got something else for them—a private matter." Grossman leaned over, as if to impart a secret. "Are they ours?"

"What do you mean?"

"Jews?"

"Since when do you make this distinction, Mr. Grossman? I know you don't make it in your business."

"I've got a reason. This matter that I want to see them on—it's not particularly nice for us, I'd like to keep it between Jews."

"What do you mean, not particularly nice?"

"Do you know a certain Bornstein, a local lawyer."

"Bornstein? The shyster?" Silverstein was startled. "What have you got to do with him?"

"Something happened. Something unpleasant. He came to me on behalf of one of his clients—to blackmail me."

"He did? Well! We'll have to clip *his* wings immediately. He's a dangerous customer, Mr. Grossman. He came into Springbrook with a gang of bookies who made Springbrook one of their headquarters. They're a pest here. They've got several lawyers of their own. This Bornstein is a disgrace to us; he drags us down into the gutter. We'll have to get after him at once. I might as well tell you that Mr. Davis has been keeping an eye on him."

"Is Davis a Jew?"

"Better than that," answered Silverstein. "Franklin is a Jew, Davis is a Presbyterian. They're partners. When the Jews of Springbrook need something communal, they go to Davis, not to Franklin. Just recently we had a situation round the orthodox syna-

209

gogue—I'll tell you about that later—and who do you think we went to? Davis, not Franklin. Franklin keeps out of those affairs, so he shouldn't be accused of interfering as a Jew. Davis isn't afraid of that, of course. And Bornstein will be afraid of Davis, where he wouldn't be afraid of Franklin."

"I suppose you know the picture."

"You can rely on me. Let's go back to the store, I'll call up Mr. Davis. We've got to act at once, stamp it out immediately. With a man like Bornstein you've got to hit hard, and without delay. And you want to know how we get along, the Jews and the Christians here. Well, there's no distinction between Jew and Christian. There's only the distinction between honest people and dishonest people. And of course we have both sorts here, among the Jews and among the Christians. We have our Bornsteins, and they have theirs. There are Christian bookies and—God help us— Jewish bookies. And as against that, we have our Franklins, and they have their Davises. Franklin the Jew does his share for the Christian population. He's a member of the Board of Governors of St. Vincent's Hospital, and he's President of the Community Chest. His partner Davis is just as active in Jewish institutions. For instance, in the campaign of the United Jewish Appeal Davis organized the Committee of Christian Clergymen. If you want to know how we stand with the Irish, the Catholics, I'll tell you about the orthodox synagogue. Have you got a little time?"

"Yes," said Grossman, uneasily. "But you hung a notice on your door, didn't you? Your customers will be getting impatient."

"My customers? Aren't you one of my customers? I stand in my stationery store, and what do you think I sell? Stationery? My customers don't need stationery. Just now and again a Rosh Hashonoh or a New Year's card. Or a little present, a toy, for a child. Christmas is my best season. I tell you, the Jews ought to be grateful for Christmas. And apart from all that, my business consists of good advice, words of comfort, settling quarrels between husbands and wives, and a little help I get for people on the telephone. I'm the clearinghouse for other people's troubles. 'The Trouble laundry' my wife calls it. If I haven't got any of my own, I take in other people's. But you know, that's a real business, too. I heard tell of a Jew who once came to a market, and stationed himself in an empty booth. He had nothing to sell but prayers, charity, and good deeds. That's my merchandise, too. You're one of my good customers, Mr. Grossman."

"All right, Mr. Silverstein. But you were going to tell me about the orthodox synagogue. It's getting late."

"It will take me a minute. Listen to this: you know we have two kinds of Jews here, just like everywhere else; rich Jews and poor Jews. The rich have a temple for their prayers, the poor a synagogue. The temple of course is very handsome, with pillars and a broad flight of steps, a kindergarten, a Sunday school, a lecture hall, and what-not. The orthodox Jews had a little wooden synagogue on the side street where the chicken dealers and the butchers' stores are. During the last few years quite a number of pious Jews settled in Springbrook, some of them more or less well-to-do. They brought a Rav—a rabbi of the old classical type—into town, but no rabbi wanted to have a synagogue among the butchers and chicken dealers and feathers. So they undertook to build themselves an orthodox synagogue on a presentable street. They were envious of the temple, of course. They argued that if Jews who aren't pious have such a magnificent place of worship, the pious Jews ought to have something even more magnificent. They collected funds, they made public appeals, they got contributions from Christians, too. But the well-to-do pious Jews don't measure up to the well-to-do among the Reform, so they had to get a loan from the bank. And Davis, of Franklin and Davis, and others—the Protestants, as it happened—helped them get the loan. They built their synagogue, with a Hebrew School, and a house for the rabbi, and ritual baths—all the flourishes. They built the kind of synagogue they wanted—and went up to the ears in debt. They couldn't pay the interest on the mortgage, let alone the installments on the principal. So they began running around again for money."

"I know. They came to me, too."

"I suppose. But they couldn't collect enough to satisfy the bank. There was a great danger that they'd be left without a synagogue. One evening they held an emergency meeting in my office—the rabbi, the president, a few trustees, and some of the men who'd signed notes. A couple of them had already hocked most of what they possessed, to rescue the synagogue. Well, it was a stormy meeting, with arguments, and protests, and reproaches, and even tears. As it happened, that evening the Police Commissioner, an old

211

Irishman by the name of Maguire—he's been on the job God knows how many years—dropped in to see me. A very decent man, kindly, not a bit like a police commissioner, and of course a Catholic, but a Catholic as pious as they come. He asks me: 'What's all that hollering?' I tell him briefly: they can't meet the mortgage payments on their new synagogue. He stands there, thinking; then he bursts out, with his hot Irish temper: 'No, they can't do that! It can't happen!' So I tell him it's their own fault, they undertook more than they could handle. So he thinks a while, and he says: 'A synagogue, a church, it's all the same. It can't be too handsome. God deserves it.' So I ask him if he can give us any good advice. So he asks me, 'Is it a Protestant synagogue, or a Catholic?' So I look at him and say: 'Jews haven't got Catholics and Protestants. They're just Jews.' 'Oh no,' he says, 'the pious Jews are the Catholic Jews, and the temple Jews are the Protestant Jews.' 'Oh, well,' I answer, 'in that case you'd call it a Catholic synagogue.' 'Well, if that's so,' he says, 'we'll have to think of something. The Jews did the right thing when we were building St. Vincent's Hospital, they did. The Bishop praised them for it. I guess it's our turn to do something for them. You can rely on me.' And what do you think he did? Did? Why, it's still doing, if you know what I mean. He put a tax on all automobiles passing through Springbrook and vicinity! A sort of tax, an indirect tax. For the slightest infringement of the traffic regulations—and there are plenty of those—the owner of the car is fined ten dollars. No judges, no authority. That's what Maguire ruled. And the policemen kept a sharp eye on all out-of-town cars—even Connecticut cars. 'Ten dollars for the synagogue,' says the policeman to the driver. People protested, of course, but not too often and not too energetically. Who's going to stop and have an argument with the police for ten dollars? The Mayor knows about Maguire's regulation, the District Attorney, too, but not a word from them. 'Maguire's transportation boss here, and we can't do a thing.' And these ten-dollar fines have cleared half the mortgage. By the way, Mr. Grossman, have you paid your fine yet?"

"My car isn't coming till later in the day. I'll tell Steve to watch out for himself."

"It won't do him any good. You can't keep out of Maguire's

212

hands. Nobody can. That's Springbrook," said Silverstein, with a broad grin.

"No, it's America," said Grossman.

"Right, right," agreed Silverstein. "Well, it's time to go back to the store. I've talked a bit too much. I'll call Mr. Davis immediately. When would you like to meet him?"

"This afternoon, at four. I'll take a rest till then. It's been a busy day."

When he got back to the hotel he found not only Steve waiting for him in the outer room of his suite, but Miss Rosenberg, too.

"What are you doing here?" he asked.

"I just couldn't stay at home. I was too restless."

"Why?"

"Just a hunch. And I can see it was a good hunch."

"What do you mean?"

"Where were you all this time? I've been looking for you. I was out at Smith's Farm, I thought you'd be there."

"Didn't they tell you I was at Silverstein's? I left word."

"Yes, they told me. But I wouldn't go to Silverstein's. I don't want to have anything to do with him."

"Why? What have you got against him?"

"That man's a calamity for you. He's not pulling you out of trouble, he's dragging you into it, deeper still."

"Rose, what are you talking about?"

"This project that he's hung on you. You've got to get out of here. Springbrook is a trap for you. You'll fall sick here, you'll get yourself into something from which no one will be able to rescue you."

"Why do you talk like that? What's happened?"

"What's happened? This: it came a little while ago." She took a letter from her handbag, and showed it to him. "It came by special messenger. He wouldn't give it to me at first, but I told him who I was, and I finally got it from him. Forgive me for opening it. I didn't know it was personal. It looked like an ordinary lawyer's letter. But when I began to read it I couldn't stop. How do you come to get a letter like this?"

Grossman glanced at the letterhead. "It's nothing. This man is

213

trying to squeeze money out of me on a false charge. The thing is going to be looked after. I'm seeing a lawyer at four o'clock."

"So you know the contents of this letter without looking at it?"

"Yes, I know."

"And you're going to engage a lawyer, a new man, so the whole thing will become a public scandal."

"I have nothing to hide, and nothing to be ashamed of. This man is a swindler. He wants to blackmail me. The lawyer will shut him up."

"He says that he and Mike have found the right Kovalsky. That is, the wife and daughter of that Kovalsky. That's the daughter Kovalsky married off in nineteen twenty-three, in Springbrook. He went to New York to invite his family to the wedding, and there he was robbed. They took him into a dice game, stole his money, and beat him up. They have all the documents in proof of it. Yan Kovalsky was living in Springbrook at the time and that's where the wedding took place, not in another town. He came home sick, and died soon after. Yes, and this Kovalsky worked in the Yale factory."

"What has all that to do with me?" asked Grossman lightly. "Lost the money at dice? In nineteen twenty-three? Davis will have that man sent to prison."

"Who's Davis?"

"The lawyer I'm getting here, a very prominent man."

"Listen, I tell you you can't stay on in Springbrook. The whole town will get to know. I'll call up Lazar, he'll tell you what to do."

"Don't you dare to telephone. We'll suppress the thing right here. Nobody will get to know about it."

"But listen; there's something in the letter about an assault on his client Mike. You wanted to kill him. You tried to strangle him. You tore his new coat."

"Nothing to it. He provoked me. I don't remember tearing his coat, but if I did I'll buy him two new ones. I don't want to hear any more about it. Davis and Franklin will look after everything."

"But what happened? How did you and Mike meet?"

"That's enough, Rose, please. I'm tired. I've had a hard day. I've been working on my plans. At four o'clock I'm going to meet the lawyer. It's after three, and I want to take a rest."

"I won't let you go and see that lawyer."

"We'll talk about that later. Let me take a rest." He made for the door.

"And what's this he says here, that you tried to bribe him?"

"Let him go to hell!" shouted Grossman, and slammed the door behind him.

Half an hour later he came out, refreshed and cheerful. The impostor's letter, with its details about the Yan Kovalsky they had fished up somewhere, had set his mind at rest; the last doubt that they might have the right man had vanished from his mind. For he had been involuntarily impressed by their claim when it had been flung into his face: *I represent Yan Kovalsky*. But now the swindler had betrayed himself. He'd lost the money in a dice game, had he? Grossman laughed to himself: Isaac Grossman, the crap-shooter! And when? In 1923, when I was doing big business for myself and had a growing son. Oh, Davis will fix him all right. There's only Mike left. I'll send Steve to him, with a couple of hundred dollars. That will be enough. He'll come over to our side." And it was in this cheerful mood that he confronted Rose again.

"You'll come with me to the lawyer. I'll take along Silverstein, too. This lawyer is going to get the sports ground for us from the city. I must have it for my project. I'm going to do big things. There's a lot of work before us, young lady."

"I don't want to have anything to do with it."

"Oho, you'll change your mind, girlie. Wait till you get the whole plan. But now we have to hurry."

"What's the matter with you today? Why the cheerful mood?"

"I've never felt better in my life. My troubles are about over. Here's the biggest venture I've ever undertaken, and it's not for profit. You'll see, and wonder, and you'll be astounded at what your boss can do. Kovalsky Center will be a model for the entire country."

"Kovalsky Center!" Miss Rosenberg started back, pale. "I thought we were through with that."

"That's what I've decided, once for all. I'm going to take that pressure off my soul. You don't see it."

"But you should long ago have realized that this Kovalsky never existed," protested Miss Rosenberg.

"He did, Rose, he did," said her employer softly. . . .

Grossman took an immediate liking to Davis. Silverstein's warm recommendation had something to do with it, but the man's appearance and personality inspired confidence. A tall, thin man, with a long face, a long nose, a long jaw, a typical New England or Connecticut face, clear blue eyes, and a quiet, almost sleepy manner: there was about Mr. Davis a reassuring balance, a calmness of spirit, which communicated itself to his clients.

Davis glanced quickly through Bornstein's letter, and a faint and frosty smile passed across his lips, which were always slightly open, revealing the line of his too-prominent teeth.

"This letter doesn't accuse; it apologizes. I know his method. He meant at first to accuse, hoping to scare something out of you. But the moment he sees you aren't afraid, *he* becomes frightened, *he* gets scared of his own shadow."

"There's a saying in Yiddish," threw in Silverstein: " 'The thief feels his hat's on fire.' "

"Who is this Kovalsky?" asked Davis.

"Mr. Grossman once had an employee, a Pole, by the name of Kovalsky. He was of great service to Mr. Grossman in a personal matter, and Mr. Grossman never had the opportunity to compensate him as he should have done, because the man disappeared. Mr. Grossman is interested in finding him, or his family," explained Silverstein, seeing that Grossman himself did not hasten forward with an answer.

"I see . . . after so many years . . . it's very touching. But there's nothing in this letter which puts Bornstein in the wrong. It's cleverly worded. He says that his interest in the affair is purely personal, not professional. He's doing it all out of respect for Mr. Grossman, for Mr. Grossman's benefit. Since he knows that Mr. Grossman is looking for a certain Kovalsky, he takes the liberty of informing him that a certain client of his has managed to trace the said Kovalsky. He mentions a certain incident which took place in the life of Kovalsky. If it turns out that this isn't the Kovalsky Mr. Grossman is looking for, he, Bornstein, will forget the whole matter, and he'll see to it that his client shall do likewise, so as to avoid any possible public comment which might ensue from the situation. He will even undertake to dissuade his client from suing for the slight damage which he, the client, suffered at Mr. Grossman's hands. All this he does out of respect for Mr.

Grossman's high social standing, his philanthropic record, and so on. What is this damage he refers to?" The lawyer turned to Grossman.

"He provoked me during a conversation, and I lost my temper. I've already apologized. He says that in my excited condition I tore his coat. I personally don't remember it. But I'm quite ready to settle generously."

"Yes, the damage has to be made good," said Davis, briefly.

"I'll look after that," said Silverstein. "If the cat takes fright, the mouse will certainly hide in a hole."

These minor matters settled, Grossman unfolded his large plan to Davis. He was willing to deed his land to the undertaking, without compensation. He was also ready, in addition, to contribute a large sum toward the costs, and to obtain the co-operation of Grossman and Grossman, with the consent, of course, of the junior partner, Lazar Grossman. He expected to obtain certain credits from the government, because of the character of the enterprise. From the city of Springbrook he expected to get the sports ground adjacent to Smith's Farm. It was understood that the project would yield no financial profit, either for the Grossmans, or the city, or the man whose name would be attached to it.

Davis was immediately captured by the plan. A faint smile showed on his parted lips, through which his prominent teeth were visible. There was also a flicker of light in his blue eyes.

"Something like this should have been done long ago," he said. "The housing problem of the veterans here is a scandal."

He was optimistic about all the problems raised by Grossman. The city and state would, he believed, readily meet all the conditions. He for his part would gladly donate his services. But an uneasy shadow passed over his face when Grossman said that he wanted the new development to be called Kovalsky Center.

He repeated the name with some astonishment. Then he was silent. His smile froze, and his whole body seemed to be absorbed in his thoughtful silence.

"Don't do it, Mr. Grossman, for God's sake, don't do it," said Silverstein energetically, in Yiddish, then caught himself up, remembering that Davis did not understand. He continued in English. "Why should you occasion a lot of talk and speculation? You've seen what can happen. It gives swindlers what they think is an opportunity for blackmail. Since you provided the family of one of the Kovalskys with an annuity I've had any number of people coming to me, saying that they're Kovalskys, too."

"What annuity is that?" asked the lawyer.

"Mr. Grossman has been helpful to a poor Polish family here, thinking they were connected with the Kovalsky he was looking for."

"No, no, Mr. Silverstein, it isn't as you say," put in Grossman quietly. "I knew from the beginning that the Zaslavsky woman was not the daughter of the Kovalsky I was looking for. I only helped her because I was sorry for her, seeing her poverty. And she made a very fine impression on me, with her honesty."

"Yes, but you see what the result has been. The rumor spread at once that she got this help because she was a Kovalsky. Now they're coming to me from all around, from Richfield, and from Waterloo, and they argue that they're Kovalskys too. It's a common name in these parts. They bring papers, birth certificates, photographs. I haven't wanted to tell you, knowing it would disturb you. Now if it gets about that you're putting up a whole development in the name of Kovalsky, can you imagine what will happen? There'll be the craziest rumors about your relationship to the Kovalskys. What has happened till now will be nothing compared to what will happen then. It's liable to do a lot of harm to your name, and to the name of the firm. Your firm can disapprove of the whole enterprise."

"How?" asked Grossman, becoming agitated. "It's my property, the deed is in my name, it's my money—who can prevent me from doing what I like with my own property? Are you trying to scare me?"

"God forbid! I didn't mean to say they could prevent it in a direct way. But they can put difficulties in your way. Are you prepared to risk all this just for the sake of having that name attached to the project?"

"Yes."

Silverstein looked dumbly at the lawyer, whose face was expressionless.

"I want to ask one question, Mr. Davis," said Grossman. "Can the city put obstacles in my way because I want to call the project Kovalsky Center? And is it likely that it will have any objection?"

"It depends on who this Kovalsky was. After all, the project is part of the city."

"He was a poor worker who earned his daily bread at the Yale factory," said Grossman.

"The fact that Kovalsky was a poor worker is no objection. It has to be assumed that he did nothing that the city would be ashamed of."

"I don't think he did."

"And now permit me to ask you a question, Mr. Grossman," said Davis.

"Please."

"Is your feeling of obligation toward Kovalsky so deep, and so important, that you must under any circumstances stand by your resolve to give your friend's name to the project?"

"Yes, Mr. Davis, the project will bear my friend's name—" he clutched at the word supplied by the lawyer—"or else I will give it up."

"Well, that settles it. I don't see why Mr. Grossman should not be able to give his friend's name to the project. I don't imagine the city will have anything against that. It would be absurd to suppress such an important development for the sake of a name. 'What's in a name?' " The faint smile came back to his lips.

When Grossman, considerably relieved, left the lawyer's office, he said to Silverstein: "Maybe you know of a Jewish restaurant here, where I can get a good piece of fish. It's Friday, and I've got a great longing to taste a Jewish dish."

"A good piece of Jewish fish? My wife Malkah can give you that. I had no idea you were fond of Jewish dishes, or I would long ago have invited you to my home. I was sure that a man in your position wouldn't care much about Jewish dishes."

"I've still got the taste of my mother's fish in my mouth, and every now and again I get a yen for it."

"In that case you're coming home with me. Of course my Malkah's fish won't taste as good as your mother's. No one can compete with a mother."

"I don't know whether Mrs. Silverstein is prepared for two guests. I'd like to bring my secretary Miss Rosenberg along."

"She's prepared, she's prepared, Mr. Grossman. Once upon a time the house was crowded on Friday nights with young people.

219

Today she has no one to prepare for." He was silent a while. "But there's always enough for a guest or two. I'll go home and tell her. She'll be delighted. She was used to many guests, poor woman."

"But I'd like to go to synagogue first. What's Jewish fish on Friday night without a synagogue!"

"What? You go Friday nights to synagogue?" asked Silverstein, astounded.

"Now and again, when I get the feeling."

"Will you go to our temple, or to our synagogue?"

"Actually I belong to a temple, but when I want to pray I go to an orthodox synagogue, where my father, peace be upon him, used to pray."

"That means you pray with your father," smiled Silverstein.

"True, true. When I want to pray I have to pray with my father. Perhaps you'll come along, Mr. Silverstein."

"No, thanks. When I want to pray I pray alone. I'd rather go home and help my wife to prepare. Where will you be after prayers? In the synagogue?"

"Give me your home address. I have my driver here, he'll bring us to your house."

He noted down Silverstein's address and went back to the hotel.

"Everything under control. That Davis is a clever man, and seems to be a bigwig in town," he said enthusiastically to Miss Rosenberg. "We'll get the sports ground, and relief from taxes, he thinks. And the name will be Kowalsky Center. He's very much interested in the project, this Mr. Davis."

"So that's the last word?" she asked.

"Absolutely. You know very well what my interest in that project is. You've known it all along."

"And Mr. Davis agrees?"

"What's he got to agree to? He's undertaken to submit a petition to City Hall to give the project that name."

"And he believes the city will accept?"

"No question about it."

"And that's how it will be made public?"

"Certainly."

"And your mind is made up, no matter what the consequences will be?"

"What consequences? Why do you all try to scare me: you,

220

Silverstein? Who's going to stop me? Is it my money, or isn't it? Listen, I've got no time to argue with you now. I'm going to synagogue."

"Why synagogue precisely today, when I want to talk to you?"

"Not now. I'm sorry. I might come late to services."

"So what? Why must you go today? And suppose you do come late?"

"And I thought that you, my secretary, would remember the date."

She started.

"Oh yes! Yes! The anniversary of your father's death."

CHAPTER TEN

HE slept well that night, and started up in the morning refreshed and charged with youthful energy. He found Miss Rosenberg, too, in a better mood, friendlier than she had been the night before, though cool and reserved. She wanted to hear nothing of what had happened in her absence, either at the Old Poland, or at the lawyer's office, and she only made one mention of his project. She gave him a résumé of the business correspondence that had arrived in New York; there were also many letters from philanthropic institutions; and there was a long letter from his grandson Robert.

He was now quite determined, wrote Robert, to devote his life to something other than personal advancement. He was still deeply under the influence of what he had learned, on the scene, of the fate of Hitler's victims, and of the heroic work of the Joint Distribution Committee, particularly for the surviving children. He had learned of the young men and women of Israel, a new generation who had been parachuted during the war into enemy territory, to bring hope and rescue to their fellow Jews. He knew now the saga of the exodus, the flight across borders, and—after the war—the miserable freight boats, the "coffin-ships," which had carried the refugees through the British blockade to the shores of Israel— some to flee into liberation, some to be caught and imprisoned on Cyprus.

It seemed that the influence of his chaplain was still working on him, and more strongly than ever. Dr. Nathan Zimmerman came from New England. He had graduated from Harvard, majoring in psychology and the history of religion. He had served briefly with a Reform Congregation, then had volunteered, during the war, for army service, and had stayed on through the postwar period. He had been on the European front, arriving shortly after D day. He had gone through most of the heavy fighting, had helped to carry the wounded, had administered the last rites to non-Jewish as well as Jewish soldiers. Boys of other faiths than the Jewish often came to him for advice and comfort. He was held in high esteem by his superior officers because of his war record, and he was in an exceptionally favorable position to help his "boys."

I was one of those that came to him [wrote Robert]. He was working in the psychological rehabilitation department, and I needed someone badly. I told him my life story. He knew about us, he knew father's name, and yours. I told him how everything had changed for me since I had learned, on the spot and from eyewitnesses, what had happened here; and I did not know what to do with myself. I told him I wanted to go in for refugee rehabilitation work, but he advised me against it. After several talks, when I got to know him better, he said it's my nature to win people's confidence, and that this is a great and useful gift. He thinks I ought to study for the rabbinate, and take courses in psychology, and become the spiritual leader of a congregation. He says I have the capacity to move people to a personal faith. He told me that even among those who go to church and synagogue very few believe in a personal God. They simply accept the faith they inherited from their fathers, and if they keep a rabbi for the congregation it isn't in order that he may bring them closer to God, but merely as a tribute to their fathers. America, the non-Jewish and the Jewish, needs a personal religion which isn't just the religion of the fathers. Chaplain Zimmerman encourages me in these ideas, and they seem to tally with my own convictions. I can write to you a little more freely than to father, because I've always felt a bit closer to you in these matters. I remember how, when I was a little boy, you used to take me with you to the orthodox synagogue, among the pious Jews. I remember the big prayer-shawls they wrapped round themselves, and the whole impression is very vivid. Those Jews in the big white prayer-shawls aren't here any more. Hitler has wiped them out. And now the Jews of America, who escaped the Hitler holocaust, ought to believe as those pious Jews in the white prayer-shawls used to believe. Yes,

223

they believed in the God of their fathers, but that God was their personal God too. I'm sending you this letter, and I want you to show it to dad, just as I asked him to show you the first letter which I sent him. I want you to talk with him, and prepare him for my decision, which is like a lifeline which Chaplain Zimmerman has thrown out to me.

"So it seems your grandson will be a rabbi," said Miss Rosenberg, after she had read the letter.
"Yes, so it seems. Who would ever have dreamt of that?"
"And you're going to put obstacles in his way?"
"I am? How?"
"By this project of yours, which you're going to call by a stranger's name because of your delusion."
"No, it won't be an obstacle. It will help him, it will remove an obstacle from his path."
She did not pursue the subject further.

This was the happiest week end he had known for a long time. He was completely caught up in the project. He kept returning to his property to verify the details of his plan, to pace off, measure, estimate, and touch up his mental picture of the development as it would look when completed. He wanted to have everything ready for the architect on Monday. The Connecticut spring was now in full spate, the dogwood blossomed everywhere, red and white flowers sprang up in clusters among the trees and bushes of the landscape. Grossman had a special weakness for blossoming dogwood; it reminded him of the happy years when Clara was alive, and they would drive up from New Rochelle into Connecticut. And now, whenever he was struck by the beauty of a bank of flowers, or a knoll of trees or bushes, whenever he saw a charming effect in the landscape, he asked himself how much of it he could transfer to his project. When he saw the young flowers blossoming among rocks, purple jewels scattered in a stern setting, he wanted to find room on the sports ground for a rock garden, to be cultivated and cared for by the children. He would plant dogwood and magnolia, he would have forsythia and rhododendron bushes, so that when spring would come the yellow and white and red buds would break into open beakers of flame and steep the gardens in color. He saw mothers and children sitting in the shade of the laurels, and the petals of the magnolia blossoms falling on them like snowflakes.

His energies exhausted Miss Rosenberg and Silverstein. He insisted on dragging them along to the property, and making them listen to every new inspiration. He crawled through the bushes and dragged his feet through the tangle of weeds and fallen branches. He was scratched by thorns and poison ivy. And he talked incessantly about the placement of the houses, the stores, the lawns, the flower beds.

On Sunday evening Miss Rosenberg complained of a violent migraine headache. Grossman persuaded her to take a rest, and told her that he was going over to Silverstein's home for another talk. But downstairs he directed Steve to drive him to the Old Poland, and had him park the car in a sidestreet.

"Go into that restaurant, Steve. It's now eight o'clock and there aren't many customers. You'll find the waiters eating at their own table near the kitchen. Ask for Mike, the headwaiter. You'll easily recognize him: he's got thick black hair, and black mustaches. Bring him here to me. Tell him your boss wants to talk to him, and if he asks who your boss is, say that he knows. Don't mention my name in anyone's hearing. And listen, Steve. This matter remains between ourselves. Understand?"

"Yes, Mr. Grossman."

He knew he could rely on Steve to be discreet. Steve was a middle-aged Negro who, with his wife Frances, had been in his employ for many years. Steve had a grave, businesslike air, the air of a man who knows his duties. He was deeply devoted to his employer, and would have been ready to undertake the most dangerous enterprises for him, as for every other member of the family.

When Steve brought Mike out to the car, Grossman opened the door and signaled to the astonished waiter to come in and sit down at his side.

"Here," he said, "is the damage you say I did to you. I hope you'll find it satisfactory." He thrust an envelope into Mike's hand.

Mike felt the fat envelope, and a delighted smile came over his face. "Thank you, Mr. Grossman. My God! Thank you."

225

"And listen, Mike. Don't have anything to do with that swindler Bornstein. He'll get you into trouble."

"As I love God," exclaimed Mike, in Polish. "I wouldn't fool the boss, just like I wouldn't fool my own father. I thought I had the real Yan Kovalsky, the one you were looking for."

"Well, you didn't. The real Yan Kovalsky is the one who was a dishwasher, and you ought to know where he is. If you trace him for me I'll give you five thousand dollars, cash. What do you say?"

"I don't want to have anything to do with it. Bornstein told me to forget everything, or else it'll be very bad for me, because the boss's son is a big shot in the government, and if he gets to know, that finishes us. No, Mr. Grossman, I don't want any part of this business. Especially now, when you got Mr. Davis as your lawyer."

"How do you know that?"

"Mr. Silverstein made me come to him, and he told me. He scared me, he did; and he gave me a hundred dollars for the coat you tore. Shall I give you this money back, Mr. Grossman? Because I don't want to have nothing to do with Mr. Davis."

"No, keep the money. It's for having hit you. Now don't you think about my son, or about Mr. Davis, or anyone else. If you know anything about Yan Kovalsky, or if you get wind of him, you've got to tell me, and I'll pay you five thousand dollars. No one will know about it, do you hear? Because you've got to find out what happened to Yan. You're the last man who saw him, and you kept him locked in a room. You told me so yourself. Now tell me, what did you do with him?" And Grossman, in a blind fury, grabbed Mike by the shoulders and shook him back and forth.

"As God is my witness, Mr. Grossman, I haven't any idea what became of him. He disappeared, he disappeared. But I'll try—I'll go round to all the Kovalskys, I'll look into every corner, and I'll find him, if he's still living."

"All right. And the moment you get the slightest clue, come straight to me, and if he's the right Yan, you'll get the money. I'm staying on here, in Springbrook. Don't you breathe a word of our arrangement to anyone, not Mr. Silverstein, or Mr. Davis, or my secretary. But come straight to me. Just tell my chauffeur Steve that you want to see me."

226

"Yes, Mr. Grossman, I'll do everything I can, and you'll be satisfied. I beg you, don't kill me." He dashed out of the car like a man who has just managed to save his life, and as he slipped past Steve, who stood at a little distance from the door, he made a hopeless gesture, tapping his forehead with his finger.

Grossman rose early on Monday morning and plunged at once into the preparation of his notes for Frankel. According to Miss Rosenberg the architect was to arrive, with two assistants, on the ten o'clock train. Grossman was not yet satisfied with his calculations. It occurred to him that the three- and four-room apartments he had sketched did not leave space enough for decent corridors. They were too narrow, and narrow corridors he considered an obstacle to good neighborly relations. The corridors would have to be broader, even if it had to be at the expense of the rooms. He made the necessary corrections, and had finished them by the time Steve went to the station for the architect.

Steve returned alone. The ten o'clock train had brought no one. Grossman and Miss Rosenberg looked at each other. She ventured the suggestion that Frankel and his assistants had missed the express, and they would probably arrive on the ten forty-five.

"Call New York," demanded Grossman.

"Why bother them? Be patient. If there was a serious obstacle to their coming, they'd have phoned us."

But before Steve returned from his second trip to the station the door of Grossman's room opened, and he saw before him his son Lazar.

Father and son were silent. Both crimsoned, and then turned pale, while they kept their eyes fixed on each other.

"How are you, governor?" said Lazar, finally. He smiled uneasily and held out his hand.

"What are you doing here?" asked the old man, breathing heavily. "Didn't I tell you not to come?" His face was ashen gray with rage. He ignored his son's outstretched hand.

"Dad, I have something important to attend to in Springbrook," answered Lazar. "Rose, be a good girl and leave us for a while."

Rose, as pale as the two Grossmans, stood up. "How are you?" asked Lazar belatedly.

227

"Stay here!" thundered old Grossman. "I have no secrets from her."

"I know it," said Lazar. "But Rose, I want you to excuse me, this is something—"

"Stay here!" repeated Grossman. "Why did you come here?"

"Dad, let me talk. You know if I didn't obey you, and came here, it must be something serious. I came here for your good—"

"No preliminaries!" interrupted old Grossman. "Say what you have to say."

"Dad, you're not well. I've come to take you home," said Lazar firmly. He drew up a chair to the table and sat down opposite his father.

The old man was stricken dumb. The blood which had returned to his face retreated again.

"What's that?" he asked.

"I've told you. That's how it is. And I'm not saying it off my own bat. It's what Dr. Markowitch, who has been treating you for more than thirty years, says. I wanted to tell you gently, so you wouldn't be startled, but you don't let me. So I've got to say it plainly. I don't have to tell you how much it hurts me, but you don't leave me any other way. You've got to know the truth. You're not well, dad. You've got to see a specialist. You know nowadays it's easy to treat these nervous cases. You've got to go to a nerve specialist, and he'll help you to forget all your delusions and fantasies—all the things your fanatical father frightened you with when you were a tender and helpless child. This is the whole story."

Grossman remained silent. He fixed on his son a hard, angry look. But Lazar did not quail before it. He looked back sharply, steadily, till it was the old man who felt himself weakening.

"My fanatical father frightened me with his fantasies? How do you know that?" Old Grossman's glance shifted to Miss Rosenberg.

"How do I know it? From your brother—Uncle Sam. I had Dr. Markowitch and a specialist talk with him. He told them how grandfather used to terrify you with stories of hell and horrible punishments which a man must suffer after death. Grandfather himself was already sick in those days, and he unloaded on you all the fanatical beliefs that he'd brought with him from the old

228

country, he let them loose on you like a horde of black devils, to teach you to follow in his footsteps. Sam was older than you, and he wouldn't listen; the stories had no effect on him. When your father began to tell those stories Sam would run out of the house. He said that even grandmother couldn't bear it, and she used to tell grandfather not to scare you like that. You were a child, and the stories affected you. They poisoned you. But while you were in your prime, and you were active and full of energy, you were able to overcome the effects of those pictures. Now you can't do it by yourself. You're not strong enough. You've had gallstone trouble, and you've got a touch of arteriosclerosis. Sometimes it gets your heart, and sometimes it's cerebral. And then there's your living alone, since mother died. You can't fight those fears alone, they're too strong for you. You've got to be helped by a specialist before you do something that can ruin all of us. Forgive me, dad, for speaking so openly to you. It isn't easy for me, but I have no alternative. You've got to know the whole truth."

The old man stared at him frozenly. He thought of himself in his prime, in the active days of his big Miami operation: he saw himself standing at his table distributing train tickets to the ruined people whose mortgages he had bought up. He must, in those days, have acted the way his son was acting now: direct, brutal, in full assurance of being in the right.

"All this Dr. Markowitch told you," he said, heavily.

"Yes. He'll tell it to you himself. I brought him with me."

"You brought him with you?" asked old Grossman, with the same heaviness. "What for?"

"I want him to help me in this difficult task. And I also brought along Max."

"Max? Max Brown? Our lawyer?"

Lazar nodded. "I had to bring him, too."

"What for?"

"To cancel any contracts or obligations you've entered into here in Springbrook, or anywhere else, while you were sick."

The old man's lids fell, and it seemed that they became hollow, as if his eyes, under them, had sunk into his head. He said, in the same dull voice:

"Now I'll tell you the real reason why you came here to have me declared sick, and incompetent to manage my own affairs. I'll

229

tell you the real reason. No, it isn't worry over your father's health that brought you here; it's the big property in Springbrook, this valuable piece of land which you want to lay your hands on. That's why you came—and not because your father is sick." Grossman opened his eyes and shook his finger at his son, almost touching his face with it.

"Dad, dad, how can you say that? Dad!" And Lazar covered his face with his hands.

"You're sick, Isaac," said Rose, who had been sitting wordless till now. She sprang to her feet like a tiger, ran over to the old man, and burst into tears.

"You too? In the conspiracy with him? Don't you think I know that on Thursday evening you were in Long Island, not in New Rochelle? You went to him, and you told him everything."

"No, no, I didn't tell him anything."

"What did she tell me? What was there to tell me?" asked Lazar excitedly.

"Why I came to Springbrook, and what I intend to use my land for!"

"But she didn't have to tell me. You told me about it yourself! And I didn't quite understand at first. I even promised to help you. I know you've had a hard life, dad. You had to climb with bare hands and feet up the slope, and you made a great career for yourself." Lazar was speaking softly, gently. "And all sorts of things happen to a man, all sorts of incidents. I didn't want to know what this incident in your life was. But as I thought your proposition over, I could see what it all meant. You've been brooding over something, you've got the notion you've got to make good some terrible crime. There never was such a crime. It's your fantasy, and your father's influence in your life. And every day you spend in Springbrook encouraging your sick fantasy makes it worse. That's the only reason why I want you to get rid of your piece of property here. Give it away, if you like. Give it to some institution. But go away from here and have nothing more to do with it. Springbrook is poison for you, don't you see that? This project of yours—the longer you occupy yourself with it, the deeper that delusion eats into you, until it will bring ruin on you and your family."

"I won't discuss the matter with you. It's my business, and no one else's."

"No, I won't have that. It affects all of us," cried Lazar. "You brought up a family, you have certain responsibilities toward it. Let's even say there *was* some such incident in your life, which you want to atone for now—though I don't believe it—so what? Every one of us does things in his early years which he regrets in his later years. My God! Where will you find the man who hasn't things on his conscience? And if it was so serious, why did you wait so long? Why did you wait till now?"

The old man wanted to scream: "You didn't let me! Your mother didn't let me. I was ashamed to tell you about it." But he said something entirely different. He growled: "There was a reason."

"I don't want to know the reason. But if you didn't correct the thing while there was time, why shouldn't you at least forget it now? You've got to do it for your family's sake. You did something wrong in your youth—and you want your grandchildren to pay for it? Will your conscience let you? Have you thought about that?"

Certainly he had thought about it. It was for the sake of his family, for the sake of his grandchildren Robert and Louise, that he had wanted to straighten it all out. He hoped thereby to spin the broken thread again, the continuity between his father and his grandchildren, restoring unity and harmony to the generations.

This was in old Grossman's mind. But he said, "Why the grandchildren?"

"Are you so naïve, father? Do you think it will please the Hanovers to learn that you're on the search for someone you committed a crime against in your youth, to make it good? Because that's how they'll see it. You're turning the whole world upside down just to satisfy your conscience. You—" Lazar hesitated and burst out—"you give money to a poor woman, an annuity, you send out in search of Yan Kovalsky, whoever he was—if he was anybody—you're going to name a tremendous project after him. What interpretation do you think the world is going to put on all this?"

"How do you know about these matters? I didn't tell you. Who did?" He pointed accusingly at Miss Rosenberg.

231

"No! I saw Silverstein before I came to you. He told me."

"Why did you go to see him?"

"Because even what you'd told me yourself alarmed me, and I know Silverstein. I was afraid that it was too late. This affair is known all over town—it's being spoken of outside Springbrook. And suppose it comes to the ears of the Hanovers? Do you think they'll want to marry into a family with a shady past? Yes, it's come to Katherine's ears, and Louise's ears too. And they're at home, trembling lest it go further. Next week we're supposed to announce the date of the marriage, at Louise's birthday party. Imagine the newspapers getting hold of the story, all about your waiter, your Kovalsky, your shyster lawyer here who tried to blackmail you. Do you think I'm going to let you ruin my family—which is also your family? Repress this thing in yourself, choke it down, don't make my children pay for your sins. Remember, Robert will be coming home someday, he will have to start a new life. Do you think he'll be able to face his friends, do you think—" Lazar's voice rose almost to a shriek, he was carried away by his words—"he wants them to know about something that was done by his kike grandfather? I'm going to stop it! I won't let you destroy your family, and the reputation of the firm we've built up through the years with honest labor. I'll stop it!" And Lazar brought his fist down on the table.

The old man did not stir. Anguish and shame cut deep into his heart; he thought of the disgrace he had to bring on his beloved little Louise, and on Robert, who was set on a life of spiritual leadership. And yet, at the same instant, his heart was filled with bitterness against his family: always they had been strangers to him, always he had played a comedy for them. He choked back his anger and said, humbly, "If you have the power."

"I'll do everything in the world to get the power. I'll stop at nothing. And the world would agree with me, if it knew," said Lazar quietly, and grimly.

"Against your father?"

"No, for him. For the honor of the family he founded, and the prestige of our firm, which he created, and above all for the sake of my children, whom I know he loves." He almost broke down again, and covered his face.

"Isaac!" cried Miss Rosenberg, weeping.

The old man looked silently at his son, but now without anger; his eyes shone with unshed tears, and his voice was broken with genuine humility.

"What do you want me to do?"

"I want you to come home and forget all this business."

"I'll come home, but I won't forget."

"We'll find a way of straightening it out later, without all this noise," said Rose.

"It *is* straightened out," said Lazar. "Isn't he paying a pension to one Pole, already?"

"It's not the same one," said the old man, softly.

"What's the difference, this one or another? There wasn't anyone to begin with. That Polak is nothing but a fixation anyhow."

Old Grossman did not answer.

"What shall we do with Mr. Davis?" asked Rose.

"We heard about that too from Silverstein. There won't be any difficulty. Max is with Davis and Franklin now."

"So?" asked old Grossman.

"Yes. He'll stop the thing before it reaches the public. Max is advising Mr. Davis about the facts."

Grossman relapsed into silence.

"Shall I ask Dr. Markowitch to come in?" asked Lazar. "He's very anxious to see you."

"No. I'm just tired."

Grossman stood up slowly, and went into his bedroom.

A few minutes later, as Rose sat talking in low tones with Lazar, her ear, attuned to the faintest sound where her employer was concerned, caught something, a light moan of pain. She started up and turned toward the bedroom door.

"Where are you going? He's sleeping," said Lazar, who had heard nothing.

"He's not sleeping," she answered quickly, and went in.

She came out at once, mortally pale.

"Quick, Lazar, get Dr. Markowitch. Your father's got a gallstone attack."

CHAPTER ELEVEN

THERE are persons who are born without shadows; and there are persons who are born with shadowless faces. Let every separate feature be perfect in form and function, if there are no shadows to merge feature with feature, to provide the transition from line to line, the face is devoid of unity and character and individuality.

A man with such a face sat in the office of Franklin and Davis, across the table from Attorney Davis, and spoke of Isaac Grossman's housing project. He reviewed the facts which, in his opinion, made it clear that Mr. Davis could not continue with the volunteer co-operation he had promised Mr. Grossman; the entire enterprise had to be abandoned because it was the baseless fantasy of a man whose mind was unhinged; and for the sake of the family's good name the matter dared not be allowed to reach the attention of the public.

The man was Max Brown, of the New York firm of Brown, Rubin and Gray. Just as his facial components seemed to stand separate and apart, because they lacked the connecting and fusing intermediacy of shadows, so his thoughts were staccato, distinct, hard, and unshaded. In a given situation he saw only the dry and brutal facts; he had no awareness of emotions, human weaknesses, psychic accompaniments which imparted to the facts coloration and meaning. He drove only at the logical consequences of the naked facts: and—"There it is!" He marshaled before attorney Davis the bleak realities of Grossman's behavior, and indicated the "logical" results which had to follow. A suspicion would inevitably be created that in his youth Grossman had committed a crime against one Kovalsky. The crime would seem to be of so serious a character that it was bound in time to become common knowledge—and this could not but lead to the ruin of the important firm of Grossman and Grossman, to tragedy for a family which was entirely guiltless, and an abrupt end to the brilliant and promising career of Gross-man's only son, Lazar.

Attorney Davis, seated opposite, had his hand on his chin as if he were admonishing himself against a hasty word which might interrupt the flow of Brown's exposition. He listened with a profound and expressionless absorption, an image of reflective neutrality—listened, concentrated, meditated, and did not betray by the flicker of an eyelash whether he agreed or disagreed with his colleague. He continued his silence for a minute after the other had ended; then said, with the same cold and serious detachment:

"I am not a psychiatrist and therefore cannot express an opinion on Mr. Grossman's mental condition and his competence to act for himself. If, however, I may be permitted to speak as a neutral and unofficial observer, I would say that I see no symptoms of abnormality. Neither in his speech nor in his behavior did I see anything abnormal during his recent call on me. That he should want to name his projected philanthropic enterprise after a friend, living or dead, does not indicate an unhinged mind. It is on the contrary evidence of nobility of character and of a profound sense of justice. Mr. Grossman—no, it was Mr. Silverstein who told me, in Mr. Grossman's presence, that Mr. Grossman is under a certain obligation to that man. Some service had been rendered to Mr. Grossman, which Mr. Grossman had not compensated in good time. The fact that Mr. Grossman remembered his friend, even after many years, and is searching for him with the purpose of compensating him, is also not evidence of mental derangement. Again it speaks rather for Mr. Grossman's nobility of character and sense of responsibility. With regard to the annuity which Mr. Grossman created for the person connected, or claiming to be connected, with the family of the man, Mr. Grossman states explicitly that he did not do this for the sake of his friend, but because he was deeply affected by the poverty in which he found this family. This is a pure act of charity, something which is, as you know, not alien to Mr. Grossman's reputation. It would hardly be considered evidence of mental derangement. If we were to regard every act of charity as evidence of an unbalanced mind, we should, I venture to think, find little agreement with us on the part of the public—" And a barely perceptible smile hovered over Mr. Davis's protrusive teeth.

235

"In situations like this we will, of course, always find adventurers, and, I regret to say, members of our profession among them, who will try to turn a dishonest penny for themselves. Fortunately the majority of the members of our profession are concerned with protecting their clients against such intruders. But be this as it may, we attorneys are not competent to judge a man's mental condition. There are specialists for this purpose, and they would be appointed by a court. As long as I do not hear to the contrary from Mr. Grossman himself, I shall continue to regard myself as his representative in the matter of the building project, for which we, the inhabitants of Springbrook, can only feel the deepest gratitude. I have not as yet handed in the petition to the City Council, as it still awaits Mr. Grossman's signature. As long as the petition is not granted, we shall not issue any statements about the project. I must repeat that I regard myself as Mr. Grossman's representative, and I shall do everything in my power to further his project and to protect it against any interference, whatever its source and motive. I am sorry not to be able to do anything for you, Mr. Brown," ended Mr. Davis with the same barely perceptible smile.

"But in heaven's name," said Mr. Brown, after a long pause, "this 'friend,' as you call him, never existed. There never was such a person. He is the product of Mr. Grossman's fantasy. This is a fact which is testified by the family doctor who has been treating Mr. Grossman for thirty years, and by other doctors—specialists."

"We can't decide that, Mr. Brown. Only the court can decide it. We are neither doctors nor judges. We are only attorneys-at-law. You know that as well as I. And until a court rules to the contrary, Mr. Grossman is to me a normal person, as normal as you and I—and perhaps more so." Mr. Davis's smile became a little more pronounced. He was apparently pleased with this last observation; and he was still smiling as he turned to answer the telephone, which had just begun to ring.

Mr. Brown made a gesture of farewell and withdrew.

During the next few days Mr. Brown rechecked his "facts," and added to them, and then presented the results at a conference in Lazar Grossman's magnificent oak-panel office in New York.

There were present Lazar Grossman, Mr. Brown, and Dr. Marko-witch.

Both the lawyer and the doctor were close to the Grossmans, the first as the representative of the firm, the second as the family physician. Max Brown was of Lazar's age, and a school friend. Both had been brought up in the pragmatic philosophy of James, their minds fixed on the practical and useful. Brown was well built, a lover of baseball, and prematurely bald, so that the shadowless face continued up into a shadowless skull. He came of good family, had had his way smoothed for him, and had not known the struggle for life. Lazar had brought him early into the service of the firm, and had also made him a silent partner in several special and unrisky enterprises. He was Lazar's friend, but not old Gross-man's. The latter had never been able to warm to him, and the coolness had been mutual.

The case of Dr. Markowitch was very different. Henry Marko-witch belonged to old Grossman's generation. He had been brought to America in his childhood, and like Grossman senior he had known the bitterness of the early struggle. He had hungered his way through high school and college and, after a few years of practice in New York, had settled in New Rochelle. He preferred the quietness of the small town, for he was by temperament suited to family practice rather than the mass practice of the big city doctor with fixed office hours. His warm and friendly nature made him one of the most beloved figures in the better homes of New Rochelle, and put his career on a firm foundation. He was a man of less than medium height, with a mild, benevolent face and friendly gestures; he won Clara Grossman's confidence and liking on his first visit, and remained thereafter the family physician. No one was as able as he to curb Grossman's habits, and to dis-suade him from eating dishes that harmed him. He dissuaded neither by display of sternness nor by cataloguing the dangerous results, but by the unhappy smile which conveyed both his sym-pathy and his concern. Grossman made valiant efforts to obey Dr. Markowitch less from fear of sickness than from his unwilling-ness to hurt "Henry." Markowitch had been Lazar's doctor in his boyhood, and had attended Clara through her long and fatal sickness.

The conference took place shortly after Lazar had brought his father home to New Rochelle, and shortly before the date set for Louise's engagement. There were important problems which had to be solved without delay. There was a letter from Mr. Davis, which had to be answered. A decision had to be taken with regard to old Grossman. What was to be done with him? He had refused to sign the letter which Mr. Brown had drawn up for him, addressed to Mr. Davis. In this letter Isaac Grossman was to declare that "for certain reasons" he was withdrawing from his project, and was instead contributing a sum of money toward the improvement of housing conditions for the returned veterans of Springbrook. This contribution was to be considered a compensation for the abandoned project.

"He took the letter when Miss Rosenberg gave it to him for his signature, tore it into small pieces, and threw them into the wastebasket without saying a word," reported Lazar.

"He hardly speaks at all, either to me, or to Miss Rosenberg. He has retreated into himself," said Dr. Markowitch. He drew heavily on his cigarette and let out a thick cloud of smoke. "And that's bad. He has lost confidence in both of us. He won't take any of the sedatives I've prescribed for him. He sleeps badly."

"What's his general physical condition?" asked Lazar.

"Not bad. After the morphine injections the gallstone attacks stopped. He slept for two nights, because of the injections. He has no more pain. Miss Rosenberg looks after his diet. He must eat lightly, and lose weight; no fats; above all, he must sleep. But he won't take sedatives. It seems he's afraid to sleep, no doubt because of dreams which torment him. Miss Rosenberg hears him talking in the night, as if he's having an argument with someone. He keeps the door locked most of the time, and won't let anyone in for long stretches—not even Miss Rosenberg. All these are disturbing symptoms."

"What about the psychiatrist you were to bring for a consultation?" asked Brown.

"I invited Dr. Finkel and Dr. Crown, two of the best men in New York. He wouldn't admit any one of us. He locked himself in, and left us standing there, at the door. I had to content myself with describing the symptoms to my colleagues. I told them about your father's childhood years, and of the terrifying pictures of hell which his father loved to depict; also of the background of struggle in your father's later life. They were more or less agreed that this was a case of a guilt complex, with its origin in your father's childhood experience; it was brought to the fore by the shock of your mother's death, and perhaps by other difficult experiences. My colleagues also agree with my physical diagnosis of cerebral arteriosclerosis, with uinfavorable reactions on the nervous system. They are also of the opinion that no such person as Kovalsky ever existed. Dr. Crown thinks it would be best to put your father in a psychiatric institution for observation." Dr. Markowitch pulled heavily again at his cigarette.

"No, no, I can't bring myself to do that," cried Lazar.

"You'll do it, because you have to, Lazar," put in Brown. "Don't you see that if your father is in complete command of his mental faculties, as Davis insists he is, and if his project is therefore a praiseworthy action, it follows that our interference is the very opposite of a praiseworthy action, and perhaps even a criminal attempt to prevent him from his disposing of his property in Springbrook, which—it would seem—you have an eye on. And we are in this with you."

"My God!" Lazar shuddered. "He said that to me."

"That isn't all," went on Brown. "Tomorrow the whole city will be saying it—perhaps even the whole country. Public opinion will be unanimously against us—and Mr. Davis will make the most of it. Davis is a hard nut to crack. He'll fight like a lion. First—" Brown ticked off one finger—"personal publicity. Second—" he ticked off another finger—"he's no doubt interested that Springbrook should get the project. It will add to his popularity. So he'll be led to investigate your father's past—and so will the public. It will begin with the newspapers and end with the District Attorney's office. Everyone will want to know who this Kovalsky was, and what was the relationship between him and the wealthy Grossman that Grossman feels he must name a big project after him. Your father's name, and yours, and your family's, and the firm's will be dragged through the gutter. You've got to prove to the world, without delay, that your actions aren't dictated by greed, but by concern for your father."

"My God, I'll gladly give away the property in Springbrook, I've told that to my father. Let them take it, let them do what they like with it."

239

"*You'll* give it away? It isn't yours to give. You have to acquire it first," said Brown.

"How?"

"Very simply. Your father must be declared—through the depositions of reliable witnesses, that is, accepted psychiatrists—legally incompetent to administer his affairs. The court will appoint you his trustee, and then, as his only heir, you will take charge of your father's assets. Then you can do what you like with the property in Springbrook; you can sell it, give it away, abandon it; but not before. The legend about Kovalsky will fade away, and the good name of the firm, your name, and the family's will be untouched."

"But that's a horrible thing!" muttered Lazar, covering his face.

"The alternative is more horrible," said Brown curtly.

"I won't do it. Never!" said Lazar quietly.

"I'm afraid you'll have to," said Dr. Markowitch sadly. "There's nothing else to be done with your father. He won't admit me, he says I'm in the conspiracy to have him declared insane. He has the same accusation for Miss Rosenberg. The only one he admits freely is the chauffeur, Steve. He must be suffering a great deal. He has hallucinations. Without some medication he will get rapidly worse. He simply has to be taken to a psychiatric institution."

"But how can that be done?" groaned Lazar.

"The courts can compel him," said Brown.

Lazar turned two terrified eyes on him.

"Yes, yes," continued Brown, "your father did things in Springbrook which will immediately convince any court of his mental condition. It hurts me, Lazar, but I have to tell you. Here's a man who goes into a restaurant and orders the headwaiter to produce a dishwasher whom he, the headwaiter, keeps a prisoner somewhere near the kitchen; and when the waiter shows him that no one is being kept a prisoner, he takes the waiter by the throat and begins to strangle him. What do you think a judge will conclude? I'm sorry, Lazar, but you have to know it."

"How do you know all these details?"

"I made it my business to find out. When I saw that Davis wouldn't co-operate I approached it from a different angle. I went after the facts. I'd rather keep the whole thing quiet, of course, but Davis is immovable. He insists on bringing the case to court. I say you must save yourself, Lazar. Mustn't you?"

"Your father is sick, very sick," repeated Dr. Markowitch.

"And yet you see, doctor, how I persuaded him to go home of his own free will."

"In these cases it's impossible to foresee how the patient will act. Very often he'll behave normally for long stretches, his reactions will be normal, he'll listen to you, do the sensible thing— and then, suddenly, unexpectedly, you'll touch on his obsession and he'll become completely irrational. It's like a man with a localized pain: you can touch him everywhere, and he won't react, but just put your finger on that one sensitive spot and—" Dr. Markowitch made a gesture of violent repulsion.

"Besides, it's not quite true that he came home of his own free will," said Brown. "You forget that he had an attack of gallstones. We don't know how he would have behaved without that."

"And what am I to do now with my daughter's engagement? Katherine planned to have the birthday party and the announcement in mother's house—for dad's sake."

"Don't you dare to do that!" exclaimed Brown, vigorously.

"Why? Do you think there's a risk?"

"Very possibly," put in Dr. Markowitch. "We just don't know what to expect."

"There are several reasons," said Brown impatiently. "Suppose the party goes off smoothly and your father's behavior is everything it ought to be, then we're up against a problem: how will you be able to convince all the people who were there, friends and acquaintances, that your father is sick and has to enter an institution? You've got to consider public opinion and prepare it, beginning with the closest friends, even with the Hanovers. Otherwise you'll administer a very bad shock to it. Don't you agree with me, Dr. Markowitch?"

"I don't know. I'm not thinking along those lines. I'm only afraid of his having an attack. That's where the risk lies."

"What's to be done? What's to be done?" repeated Lazar. "My father not to be at Louise's engagement? It's unthinkable. He adores the child. It was for the sake of the engagement that he consented to come home. It was the mention of her name that broke his obstinacy. How can we deceive him now?"

"Suppose we were to bring Katherine and Louise to see him?" suggested Brown.

"I don't want the child to see him like this, it will upset her, just before her engagement," said Lazar anxiously.

"I don't know what his condition is, at the moment," said Dr. Markowitch. "It's two days since I was up there. I know that your father will be filled with joy to see Louise. But the effect can be negative, too. He may be so shaken that his nerves will go to pieces. I'll ask Dr. Finkel what he thinks of the idea."

"My poor father! Listen, Henry, can't we put all this off until after Louise's engagement? Let the whole thing simmer now—I don't want to spoil the child's big day."

"Ye-es, we can do that. Your father is in good hands. Miss Rosenberg doesn't go away from his door. I've never seen such devotion."

"We'll get a little time to think. I've got to get used to the situation, I've got to break myself in," said Lazar.

"Take yourself in hand, man," said Brown, putting his arm around Lazar's shoulder. "There's no other way of handling it."

"And what am I to do about Davis's letter to father?"

"Yes," said Brown. "What does he write?"

"It's a handwritten letter. Miss Rosenberg received it, and opened it as she has the right to. Then she telephoned me. Davis writes my father that the petition, and all the other papers relating to the project, are now ready for father's signature, and he wants to know when father will be ready to sign them."

Brown reflected for a few moments.

"Davis has to be informed that your father is so weak after the last gallstone attack that the doctors have forbidden anyone to approach him with business matters. Tell him that nothing can be done until the doctors permit it. Have Miss Rosenberg write that letter. What do you say, Dr. Markowitch?"

"Yes, I think that ought to be done, Mr. Brown."

"That'll give Davis something to chew on—and us time to think."

CHAPTER TWELVE

WHAT is sleep? Is it a form of being, or of not-being? Is sleep a shuffling off of the coil of the day, a rest from the yoke of the waking hours, a self-forgetting and a doffing of existence? Or is it a taking on of another skin, the entry into another air? Is it a return to the prenatal sleep, or plunging into hidden pasts, and perhaps even into hidden futures? Is it a refreshment in the Divine Spirit, a nightly ascent in nakedness into upper realms, there to understand with hidden understanding and to know with hidden knowledge the secret of our being, the justification of the burden of life?

The man without sleep is like a blind Samson, harnessed to the millstone which he drags round ceaselessly to grind—water. He is like a thresher condemned to beating everlastingly the chaff which has been emptied of the grain. Such was the condition of Isaac Grossman.

During the first two nights after his return to New Rochelle he slept under the influence of the narcotics which Dr. Markowitch had injected against the crushing pain. He was in a deep and dreamless sleep. When he awoke, and was capable of resistance, he refused all medicaments. He would not admit the nurse who had attended him at first; he permitted Miss Rosenberg to see him once or twice, and then locked her out. The only person he trusted, and permitted near him, was Steve. Steve brought in the meals which Frances prepared according to Dr. Markowitch's instructions and under Miss Rosenberg's supervision.

On the third night he slept for a while which was an eternity. The interval lost its position and identity in time and space. It had a time and space of its own, not ours, a time and space belonging to another order or sphere. In that interval he saw his victim, Yan Kovalsky. He recognized him by the black hair, soaked in anguish and clinging to his low forehead. And yet it was not Yan Kovalsky. It was his father, with the beard trembling on his chest. He knew that it was Kovalsky—and yet it was his father. He knew that it was his father—and yet it was Kovalsky. The two were fused into a unity. How this came about he could not tell, but he awoke retaining the illusion. From that moment on he was afraid to sleep. So he lay awake through the nights, and ground water. He thought, and thought, until he thought himself into the conclusion that the nearest person was the remotest, and that the one whom he had loved passionately he had now come to hate passionately. . . .

The house which Clara Grossman had built in New Rochelle was typical of the upper middle class during the prosperity years following the first World War, when money was plentiful. The decorator had had more say about it than the owner, and the craze of that time was for period furniture. The house itself was spacious, with more rooms than were needed, and every room with its own style, Chippendale-Colonial, Louis Fifteenth, Louis Sixteenth. Here and there, incongruously, a Moorish-Spanish armoire, a sideboard and chairs in the Queen Anne period, and other bric-a-brac signalizing Clara's rebellion against the decorator, assertions of her own taste, or accidental purchases at auctions. The Chippendale sideboards in the dining room were covered with Georgian silver, the walls were decorated with the French paintings which had cost Grossman a fortune. There were garden landscapes in deep violet, steeped in a damp and misty atmosphere, in Monet's style; there were several of Matisse's paintings; and all hung against a background of decorative latticework. There was a Picasso out of his worst cubistic period, which looked to Grossman like a textile design, a street scene by Utrillo, and a drawing by Pisarro. A romantic Innes was stuck in a corner. An impulse of Clara's taste, it had been exiled by the decorator to a place near the corridor. Nor was there, of course, any lack of Chinese porcelain.

With profound awe, with love and humility, old Grossman had kept the house exactly as it had been when Clara died, not permitting the slightest change. No picture, no piece of furniture, could be moved, let alone removed, though Lazar had an eye on several of them—as did, in fact, the local art gallery. Isaac Grossman also kept intact, locked in their closets, all her dresses, mantles, shawls, linen, jewels—even her housedresses and dressing gowns; he could not bear the thought of anyone else wearing them. He saw in the rooms, untouched and unchanged after her death, her taste, her intelligence, her refinement—in brief, her higher being and her superiority over him. This was the sanctuary, abandoned indeed by its goddess, but still pervaded by the divine spirit. And suddenly all this changed.

He crept out of his bed and wandered through the room in his slippers. He felt that he was in a strange house—more, in the house of an enemy. The house, with all its rooms and its furniture, took on Clara's identity, her features, her appearance. It was as though she had returned, was within arm's length of him. She sat on the French armchair, and he was speaking to her when he spoke to himself:

"And this is what I wasted my life on; in the presence of this I trembled, and dared not utter a word which might be out of keeping with the show. For this I locked myself away with my misery, my wound, my sin, and suffered agonies lest she should find out. Even my sleep was filled with dread, lest I betray by an unconscious word the crime which I had committed against a poor worker. I should have gone in search of him whom I had wronged, whatever the cost might be, however great the danger. I should have straightened it out with him before it was too late. But in my folly I was afraid of her, I was ashamed before her. I was ashamed before myself in the thought of her, and could not admit that I was capable of such a thing. I waited so long that I thought I had annulled it, wiped it out, forgotten it. And then, in the end, it was really too late.

"And what was she, after all? What is a wife from whom you must hide a secret, whom you cannot confide in, for whom, and before whom, you play the comedy of being better, richer, more aristocratic than you are? What is a son from whom you must conceal yourself and your life, to whom you cannot reveal that inmost secret of the wrong you have committed in your youth, and which you want to repair? He was always a stranger to me, just as his mother was. Always he wanted to show that he was cleverer, better educated, an abler businessman than I. He went to college; I was the son of a greenhorn, an East Side boy. That was how he treated me all his life, and so did his mother. And for the sake of this son, for the sake of the mother, shall I surrender my everlasting life, shall I for their sake let my soul go down to damnation? Ah, what my father told me is true: to be reborn as a beast of burden, a pack horse. Father!"

He sank weakly into a chair.

"Isaac! I implore you! Get back into your bed."

"What are you doing here? Why do you spy on me? Can't I be alone for a moment?"

"I'm not spying on you, Isaac."

"Then what are you doing here? Why are you eavesdropping?"

"I'm not eavesdropping. I heard you cry out, so I came in to remind you what Dr. Markowitch told you. You mustn't excite yourself. Calm yourself. Go back to bed. You're still weak. You don't want another attack, do you? I beg you, Isaac."

"I'm all right, and there's nothing the matter with me. You're only trying to talk me into it—you, and Dr. Markowitch, and Lazar. I know you're all in league to have me declared sick."

"Don't talk like that, Isaac. It hurts—" And she burst into tears.

"Why do you follow me, and listen in on what I say? I'm just talking to myself. Mayn't I do that?"

"I'm not listening. I know what oppresses you. Talk, then; talk your heart out, perhaps it'll make you feel better. Never mind if I'm listening. I know what's weighing on you, what's been weighing on you all your life."

"If you know, why did you go and report to Lazar everything I was doing in Springbrook?"

"I didn't report to him. I didn't speak about anything with Lazar. Brown had his man in Springfield. And it was Brown who persuaded Lazar to come and bring you home."

"But you too believe that there never was a Kovalsky in my life?"

"It's true, I believe that's all your imagination. There was no Kovalsky—you saw that yourself."

"If that's the case you're much my enemy as they are. You consider me insane, just as they do."

"No, I'm not your enemy, and I don't think you're insane. I think you're overexcited, and your nerves are weak. You've got to let yourself be cured. No one is your enemy, not your son, and not Dr. Markowitch. They are your best friends, and they mean well by you. You are unjust to them, Isaac."

"Then why don't they let me carry out my project—the one thing I must do?"

"Because it will awaken all sorts of suspicions, and all sorts of rumors will be spread. And that will do you a lot of harm—you and your family."

"What do people matter to me, what does their idle talk matter? And even my family—what does that matter to me? I must rescue my soul, I must save it out of a stranger's hand. Has my family ever taken thought for me? Has my wife? My son? Look at this house which she put up. This was her ambition—to show off before the world, to have French paintings, expensive furniture, a big, expensive house, to be something bigger and better than we were—that was my family. No, I had no family. I never had one. A comedy, a show."

"What are you saying, Isaac? Don't you love your grandchildren? Robert, who clings to you, and Louise, who reminds you of your wife? You always loved the children."

He sat, thinking. "Certainly I loved the children."

"Then how can you think of ruining their happiness, their future?"

"I must save myself before it is too late."

"In God's name, you've already paid your debt. And if you want to do something more for the Kovalsky family you can do it later, when you'll be well; you can do it quietly, without anyone knowing about it, so that you shouldn't expose yourself the way you did. Why should you destroy the child's happiness? You don't know how thrilled she is that you came back to town, to be here for her engagement. Calm yourself, and we'll see what we can do, discreetly." She went on, soothingly, patiently. "You might do something you'll regret. First you must come to, and be calm, and then . . ."

The old man did not answer, did not pay attention to what she said. When she had ended he said: "Go and get Steve. I need him. . . ."

Was it credible? Had she actually heard him say that he considered Clara to blame for his misfortune, for his present condition? The dry, thin lips in her withered, white face had become moist, and her restless eyes, too. A flame had started up in the pupils. It was the flame of jealousy, which she had repressed in her heart all these years, till it seemed to be extinguished: but a wind had blown on the ashes, and it had leapt up. Always she had been jealous of Clara; while Clara lived and even more after Clara's death. She had served him faithfully all her life, lived only for him. She had been more than wife: a mother, a servant—that was what she had been. She had watched over him and guarded him like the apple of her eye. He had come to her with all his problems and perplexities, his business worries, his personal worries; and she had always known, without being told, what ailed and troubled him. She had looked after his health, his peace of mind; she had assumed all his responsibilities. And he had not seen her. All that he had had in the way of tenderness, mildness, and devotion he had carried home, to the sick wife. For her he had had only his troubles, his gallstones, his black moods. It was for his sick wife, who in her egotism had seen nothing, had known nothing but her own narrow world, that he had always longed with feverish desire. And for *her* nothing but business—thirty years of it. Thus it was while Clara lived; and more so when she was dead. And *her* hope had come to nothing: he had not married her, and made her the second Mrs. Grossman. But even without marriage, she might have hoped that after Clara's death he would begin to notice her, would understand what she had been for him, had done for him; he would perceive how she had poured her heart into their relationship; it would dawn on him that at his side, these many years, there had been one whose life had been spent on him, without stint or reflection. But it was only Clara that he saw, more strongly after her death than before. True, he had not spoken of her, but his silence was a song of Clara.

Could he change now, so late, so close to the end? Would he understand now who had been his steadfast companion? Not his aristocratic wife, who had kept him at a distance, in whom he had not been able to confide, for whom he had had to play the comedian, before whom he could never be himself, Isaac Grossman; but this Rose, on whom he had vented his sick gall, his bitterness of mood,

248

to whom he had shown himself as he was, uncovering his secret wounds. But it was only to a mother that one uncovered one's wounds, one's secret wounds: not to a wife!

So she had been a mother to him, and nothing more! Then why had she snatched so eagerly at his words about Clara? Why had she wanted to follow him around, to hear him repeat what he had said? She was there at his door, in the nights, to overhear his curses, his complaints, his regret for the years he had lived with Clara. It was a delight to her to hear him, but it was anguish too. It soothed and quieted her heart, but it also brought a burning pang into it. She was even jealous of the curses that he had for Clara. He had never cursed or reproached *her,* he had never had any claims on her. With her it had been business—nothing more.

No, it was too late now. It was the eleventh hour. She could no longer be anything to him but a mother. Not that *he* had really chosen to have it so; it was she who had imposed it on him. It seemed that this was her destiny. Now she would have to uproot from her heart whatever jealousy she felt for Clara, and tread underfoot any spark of love still glowing in her. She would remain his mother, his servant, and nothing more. He was her child; she had no other children. He was her destined one—in the role which she had assigned to him, and in no other. So it would remain; but now she would have to love him more, with a greater devotion, because this was the hour of his need; she would have to shield him from his evil dreams, and from himself. She would restore his strength to him, so that he might again be the Isaac Grossman he had once been. He had no one but her, and she had no one but him. No, she had not gone over to Lazar's side, she had not helped him, she had not betrayed a single secret which the father had confided in her. She could not, in her faithfulness, lie and pretend to him; moreover, she had guarded the "secret" as her most precious possession; it was for her the one true sign of the utter confidence which he reposed in her. And she had guarded it accordingly. And yet she would have to help Lazar to this extent: she would have to help persuade the old man to accept the advice of the doctors, even against his own will, and no matter what price she would have to pay for it. He had to be cured, he had to be freed, once for all, from the delusions, the evil hallucinations, which tormented him so.

Was it possible that he did not love his grandchildren? he asked himself later, thinking back to Rose's words. Did he actually dislike them, and did he want to ruin their lives? But was it not for Robert's sake, and because of Robert's letter, that he had submitted to the homecoming, and listened to Lazar's words: "Dad, it's better that you should carry your curse to the grave with you than leave it to your grandchildren to carry"? That was what had softened him, was it not? And had he not brought home with him Robert's letter, and put it between the leaves of his mother's prayer book—the only inheritance he had let himself take from her, the sacred memento he had guarded through the years? And had not Miss Rosenberg, only now, quieted him in his outburst against Clara by the mere mention of Louise's name? Was he not looking forward with longing to the day of Louise's betrothal? Did not his heart overflow with joy that he should have lived to see that day, and was not his heart sore because it had not been granted to Clara to see it with him?

And he wanted to ruin their lives! That was what Lazar had said; that was what Rose had warned him against. But within himself he knew that it was for their integrity, for the peace of his family, that he wanted now to correct the error of his youth. He was a builder. Whenever he had looked at a building he had known instinctively whether it was solid, real, reliable, or jerry-built, speculative, dishonest. And as he looked at buildings, so he had looked at his family. There are certain buildings which in themselves are sound enough, put up on the proper principles, but they stand on unfirm ground; and a corruption seeps upward from the slimy subsoil, termites eat into the foundations and work their way into the walls. Something must be done then to save the building; and that means the drying and hardening of the subsoil, the destruction of the termites. Such was the situation now with his family, which he wanted to rescue from collapse before it was too late.

How could he possibly abandon his project? It was his child—and his masterpiece. Could an artist refuse to give life to a vision which had come to him? Could a scientist throw off an idea which held him imprisoned? The GI project was his vision and his idea. He carried it about within him. He could see the blocks of houses, the individual apartments. He could see the mothers and children, the happy fathers, filling with life the empty, abandoned property in Springbrook. He could see the little garden plots, the playgrounds. He could hear the singing and laughter. It all shone inside him like a light. How could he for a moment contemplate the extinguishing of this happiness?

And so he turned, in his sickness, with more energy than ever to the fulfillment of his project. This was his refuge from the nightmares which pursued him. He began once again to order his ideas and to correct the plans which he had brought with him from Springbrook. No, Lazar's original promise meant nothing; Lazar would not help him now. He would have to do it quietly, secretively. He would only wait until after Louise's engagement. Then he would return to Springbrook, and then he would let nothing stand in the way.

Once he had launched his underground plan of action he became calm and farsighted. He too, old Isaac Grossman, could play the conspirator. When he resumed conversations with Miss Rosenberg, he was extremely cautious, watched every word. Only Steve the chauffeur was reliable; and him he kept sending on furtive errands, warning him with dire threats against revealing their purpose, either to Miss Rosenberg or, even, to his wife. He sent Steve to Silverstein, in Springbrook; and through Silverstein he sent a message to Davis to have all documents ready for the petition to the City Council. He also sent Steve with large sums in checks to deposit in the Springbrook bank. He sent Steve on a secret errand to the building contractors Klein and Klein; and then again to Springbrook, to The Inn, to reserve a suite for May 15th. All this was successfully concealed from the watchers, who thought that the old man was dangerously sick, and over-nervous, and could not be approached.

It was not an easy thing for Lazar to go out to New Rochelle to see his father after the painful scene in Springbrook. The reports from Miss Rosenberg and Dr. Markowitch were extremely discouraging, too. Lazar was afraid of another miserable and horrible scene—if he got to see his father at all; and such a scene would be dangerous for his father. Nor would it be any too good for Lazar himself, whose nerves were badly shaken by recent developments. What ate into him now was the necessity of getting

251

the old man into a psychiatric institution—it could not be delayed any longer—and the effect this would have on the Hanovers, and perhaps even on the match. One thing was sure, he had to see his father and talk with him. Somehow he had to break it to him gently, with all circumspection, that it would be better for his health not to be present at Louise's birthday and engagement party. And how was it possible to do that? The old man looked forward with longing to the event. His granddaughter's betrothal!

Katherine and Louise, depressed by the elder Grossman's condition, had proposed a visit to him before the engagement. But Lazar had opposed it; at least, he would see his father first. Or perhaps he would accompany them. But Dr. Markowitch had forbidden him to take along Katherine and Louise.

"I'm afraid of the effect," said Dr. Markowitch. "A visit at this time can set off a chain of associations and lead to a serious upset. Neither should Katherine and Louise go alone."

"What do you mean by a chain of associations, Henry? You scare me. What associations?"

"I can't tell you, Lazar. You'd better talk with Miss Rosenberg. If she wants to tell you, it's all right."

He got a similar answer from Dr. Finkel when he consulted him on the wisdom of taking Katherine and Louise with him to New Rochelle.

"Under no circumstances," he said, and ended the brief warning with the diagnosis: "It's a classical Freudian case."

Rose was the one who disturbed him most. She said, "I can't tell you what I told Dr. Markowitch, and it's better for your nerves that you should not know. Your father's sick, and I won't let you bring Katherine and Louise to him a couple of days before the engagement. My advice to you is that you oughtn't to try to see him, either. Besides, I don't think he'll let you see him."

Lazar came nevertheless, and first had a long and urgent conversation with Miss Rosenberg in her room, explaining why it was essential for him to take the risk of seeing his father. Finally they sent in Steve with a message.

But something astonishing had happened during their conversation. Steve came back with the answer that Mr. Grossman would receive his son, not in the bedroom, where he was supposed to be, but in his den, where it was his custom to work and to receive business visitors. Moreover, Steve found his father, not in dressing gown and slippers, but fully dressed, seated at his huge desk, with a sheaf of papers before him. Old Grossman did not even lift his eyes.

"What is it, Lazar?" he said, in an indifferent tone, as if Lazar had dropped into his office during the business day with some routine question.

Lazar remained standing at the door open-mouthed. Finally he managed to stammer, "I'm terribly glad to see you, governor. Are you all right?"

"Not bad, not bad. I had some cramps these last few days. I think it was something I ate when I was at Silverstein's in Springbrook." And Grossman still kept his eyes on his papers. "Did you want to see me? Anything new? Take a seat." And he waved him with an absent-minded gesture to a chair near the desk.

Lazar sat down opposite his father. He saw that his father was working on rows of figures.

"You're pretty active, governor, aren't you? Isn't it a bit too soon? Dr. Markowitch says—"

"Oh, leave me alone with that old fraud. He doesn't know what he's talking about."

"What are you calculating there, governor? Costs?"

The old man looked up from the work. "It's still that project in Springbrook. What did you want to tell me, Lazar?"

Thus confronted, Lazar became confused, and turned pale. He had not wanted to hear mention of the project. He was determined to avoid any kind of dispute.

"Well, nothing. I wanted to see you, find out how you were feeling." He stammered. "There's nothing unusual about that, is there?"

"No, certainly not. And what else?"

"There was—something—something that I wanted to tell you." Lazar groped for words.

"Well, what is it?" asked the old man impatiently.

"The thing is this—" and Lazar pulled himself together— "Katherine and I planned to have Louise's birthday and engagement party here, in mama's house. It's bigger than ours, and it's— well—more distinguished. Also we didn't want you to have to come out to Long Island at this time. But—well—the thing is—

253

the doctors, I mean Dr. Markowitch is advising us against it. He says it'll be too much of a strain for you just now, to meet so many guests, and then all the noise, and the preparations. He thinks you ought to have no excitement just now. He says the gallstone attack was a very severe one. And it's not only your gall bladder, it's your liver generally. So we thought it would be better after all if we didn't put that burden on you, the guests, and the greetings, and the excitement, and the young people. You can imagine how miserable Katherine and Louise feel about it all, and they wanted to come here to visit you before the engagement, if you'd let them."

Grossman let his son speak on to the end. He saw the drops of perspiration breaking out on his forehead, he could hear, it seemed to him, the thudding of Lazar's heart. But he did not help him out with a word or gesture. When Lazar had ended, a shadow of a smile appeared under the old man's gray mustache. He waited, then began:

"Maybe you're really right. I understand you perfectly. Thank you for worrying about me, Lazar. Give my love to Katherine and Louise, and thank them, too. And tell them not to take it badly, and not to let it spoil the grand celebrations. I'll see Katherine and Louise after the engagement. And—my heartiest *mazeltov* and congratulations to you, Lazar." And he stretched out his hand to his son.

He watched his son leaving, slightly stupefied, and he broke into a quiet laugh.

"Now, Kovalsky, we're even. They drove you away from your daughter's wedding because they believed you'd boozed away the money which I stole from you. And me they've driven away from my granddaughter's engagement because—I'm crazy. You've been paid in full measure."

"In heaven's name, Rose, what's all this about my father being terribly sick? He's perfectly well. I found him working at his project. I must say it was a very queer feeling: he left me with the impression that we're the crazy ones, not he," complained Lazar to Miss Rosenberg.

"Perfectly well, did you say? Come with me, I'll show you something." She led Lazar back to her room, opened a drawer, and

254

took out a handful of cardboard fragments, obviously a destroyed photograph. "Do you know what this is?"

"Yes. Mother's photograph, the one that always stood on the piano in the drawing room. Who did this to it?"

"I don't have to tell you. Frances found the pieces in the wastebasket in his bedroom. I didn't want to tell you at first, but it's best for you to know everything."

Lazar bit his lips. "Beast!" he muttered.

"Your father's sick," said Rose, quietly.

"Just the same—beast!" repeated Lazar. And his eyes, as they became bloodshot, reminded Rose of his father's eyes when he flew into a rage.

The following morning Lazar stayed home late, his nerves still shattered by the recollection of his mother's destroyed photograph. At ten o'clock the telephone rang and he heard the voice of Alex Green, their auditor:

"Lazar, your father was here early this morning, just when the office opened. He asked the head bookkeeper to open the safe for him, and he took out all his papers. He also asked the bookkeeper to prepare a balance sheet as of this date, and to forward all his correspondence to The Inn, in Springbrook. His chauffeur Steve was waiting for him outside with the car."

"Did you see him, Alex? Did you talk with him?"

"I saw him as he was leaving. I spoke to him, but he didn't answer. I couldn't hold him back, you understand."

"No, no, of course not." Lazar hung up and called New Rochelle. "Rose? Is my father home?"

"No, I thought he was with you, in the office. I was just going to call you."

"I'm not in the office. I'm home. They've just told me that my father was in the office, took all his papers from the safe, and went away to Springbrook."

"How do you know he went to Springbrook?"

"He asked to have all his correspondence forwarded there. Did you see him this morning?"

"No. I only just learned that he's gone to New York. Frances told me. Earlier in the morning I thought he was still sleeping. He was awake all night, wandering through the house."

255

"All right, Rose, I'll see you later." He hung up again and called the lawyer, Max Brown.

"Max, my father's gone back to Springbrook. Took all his papers, all his stocks and bonds from the safe."

"I know it," said Max.

"How do you know it?"

"I was expecting it any day. I've got the papers ready for you."

"Which papers?"

"The petition and affidavits for the Probate Court to have your father declared incompetent to look after his affairs. It would have been better if we could have applied to the New York Courts."

"Do you think he can do a lot of damage in these few days?"

"Which days?"

"I'm thinking of postponing Louise's engagement till after the court action. I haven't consulted Katherine yet. I also want to see the Hanovers and put the whole situation before them. It's better than having them hear about it from others. I'm ready for the court, I only want to delay it a little while. We can't hide it any more."

"I agree with you, Lazar. But there'll be a delay anyhow because of the shift to Connecticut. Come over, Lazar. I want to send the papers out today."

"I'm coming, Max."

"And about the damage your father can do in the meantime: we can annul any obligations he's undertaken since the beginning of his sickness. I have all the dates. But come over at once. I'll have everything ready for you, and we can talk it over at lunch."

CHAPTER THIRTEEN

HE went to the bank and deposited his papers and valuables in a vault. He had completed all the formalities at the attorney's office; he had held a consultation with Silverstein and given him his instructions; now he asked Steve to drive him down to Smith's Farm, to make the circuit of it—as if to assure himself that the property was all there—and take him back to The Inn.

On entering the suite which had been reserved for him he found Rose in the outer room. She was engaged in unpacking one of his valises, which she had brought with her, and was putting away his suits and linen.

He stared at her in utter astonishment, as if she were a stranger. "What are you doing here?" he asked. From his tone of voice he might never have seen her before. It was filled with indignation, as well as astonishment.

"You'll need a change of shirts, won't you? And an extra suit," she answered, without breaking off. "You stole away from your own house like a thief."

"Will I never get rid of you? You aren't in my employ any more, do you understand? I'm firing you."

"All right, so I'm fired. So what? You've got to have someone around to look after your diet. You haven't come to yet from your gallstone attack. The doctor says it'll be your heart next."

"You didn't come to look after my diet. You came to keep an eye on what I'm doing. You came to spy on me. You came because Lazar sent you."

"I didn't come to spy on you, and Lazar didn't send me," she answered, calmly. "I came because you need me. Do you understand, you need me."

"I don't need you. I've got someone else to look after me. I interviewed Rebecca Cantor some time ago—a very fine girl." His

257

manner was quieter. He had obviously been taken aback by Rose's ignoring of his offensive words.

"Who is Miss Cantor?" asked Rose indifferently, and still continuing with her work.

"My new secretary. A very reliable girl, with high recommendations. She'll look after my office in Springbrook."

"Here, in Springbrook?" she asked, curiously.

"Yes, ma'am, here in Springbrook. My office will be opened on Monday, right here, in The Inn. Mr. Silverstein has prepared everything. My office begins to function on Monday, and the firm of Grossman has its headquarters in Springbrook. I don't need you any more, Rose," he said, earnestly. "You can go home. Thank you for helping me until now, and for looking after my affairs. Thank you." He spoke quietly.

"I'm not interested in your affairs. I didn't come here because of them. I came because of you. You need me, and so I'll remain. That's all there is to it."

"I can't prevent you from staying here. It's a hotel, and anyone can stay here if he has the price. But I won't have you in my office. I won't have you mixing in my affairs. Do you understand? I won't have you interfering with Miss Cantor. She's the boss now, and what she says goes. I'm dismissing you from your position. Is that clear?"

"I've told you it's no concern of mine what affairs you have, and what you do. I've had business enough in my life—someone else can have it now," she said drily, and went on unpacking his things.

Before old Judge Parker, of the Springbrook Probate Court, had had the time to study the petition of Lazar Grossman's lawyer for a court order to declare Isaac Grossman incompetent to administer his own affairs; before he had had the time to examine the testimony of Doctors Markowitch and Finkel; before he had fixed the date for the hearing, he became acquainted with the case in the columns of the *Connecticut Standard*. In several successive issues the Springbrook daily exposed the Grossman case in detail, coloring the facts and adding, here and there, notes of pathos and local patriotism. Judge Parker also heard the case discussed in his club.

Everyone knew that Isaac Grossman, founder of the firm of Grossman and Grossman, had decided to donate his property, Smith's Farm, to Springbrook, as a non-profit making GI housing development, which he would largely finance. Mr. Grossman, according to the *Standard,* was going to name the project after a dead or vanished friend in recompense for an outstanding obligation of many years ago. Isaac Grossman's only son, the younger member of Grossman and Grossman, a man of high reputation in his own right, opposed the project on the grounds of his father's mental condition. The *Standard* also managed to hint that the son's opposition was perhaps not motivated entirely by considerations of his father's health. The father had now been in Springbrook for some two weeks, in connection with the project, and no one had observed anything in his actions indicative of an abnormal mental condition. The property which Mr. Grossman had set aside for the project, the paper observed in passing, was of considerable commercial value.

Public opinion was entirely on Grossman's side. Local patriotism ran high, and the son's opposition was everywhere interpreted as nothing but financial selfishness. Judge Parker was for a time of the opinion that he ought to disqualify himself from sitting on the case, as he might not be able to remain entirely objective in view of the general excitement. The story spread at once to the columns of the larger Connecticut dailies, and was taken up in New York. After some self-searching, Judge Parker concluded after all that he would be able to act with the necessary impartiality and objectivity. However, he disqualified the testimony of Doctors Markowitch and Finkel, and appointed two local psychiatrists to examine and report on Isaac Grossman's mental condition. Judge Parker also sustained attorney Davis's objection to the demand, by the opposing attorneys, that the case be judged at once, "on grounds of the dangerous condition of the said Isaac Grossman's health," which brooked no delay. He put off the hearing for two weeks, so that the excitement might subside and the case be heard in a more calm and nonpartisan atmosphere.

During this period Isaac Grossman worked on the project with a zeal and energy which might have been the envy of many younger men. Attorney Davis had taken the preliminary steps to have the

259

sports ground turned over to the development. The Mayor and aldermen assured Mr. Davis that the petition to free the ground from city taxes would be favorably considered at the first forthcoming session of the Council. The politician who held the option also showed himself most obliging. Encouraged by the sympathy of the public, inspired by the enthusiasm of "Pop" Moses, who was now in his element, Grossman felt himself to be two decades younger. He brought contractor after contractor to Springbrook. One of them began at once on the clearing and preparation of the ground. Curious citizens of Springbrook came in crowds to Smith's Farm to watch the excavators, steam shovels and bulldozers digging, filling up, leveling off. And while this preparatory work went on in the open, under the supervision of the sidewalk architects, Grossman was busy in his offices with surveyors, map-makers, contractors, suppliers, builders. A staff of stenographers and bookkeepers had been rapidly assembled by Rebecca Cantor, well known in Springbrook for her beauty, a brunette with a magnificent head of black hair and large, dark eyes. She managed the appointments, ushering in one contractor after another, one supplier after another, and Grossman placed his orders for steel, cement, wood, bricks and other materials for his enormous project.

Miss Cantor had taken over all the office functions which had formerly belonged to Miss Rosenberg. Rose kept her word and did not enter the offices, which occupied a floor in the annex of The Inn. She remained in her room, next door to Grossman's suite. She supervised his food, looked after his clothes, reminded him of his gallstones whenever he showed an inclination to deviate from his diet, and kept track of his pills and sedatives, though he did not seem to need them. He ate heartily and slept like a log. But he let himself be "managed" out of old habit. He needed Miss Rosenberg. He was accustomed to her, as one is accustomed to an old dressing gown, or an old pair of slippers. He could not eat unless she was there, he could not sleep unless he knew she was on the other side of the wall. They did not talk business any more; he did not offer, and she did not ask for, information. Actually he would have liked very much to discuss his affairs with her—also out of habit. With his new secretary, Miss Cantor, he could not discuss anything: she might just as well have been an adding machine.

260

Spurred on by his upwelling energies, uplifted by the enthusiasm of the public, he found once again his long-lost inner peace. He was the Isaac Grossman of old. Rose observed him with secret joy, saw how he was returning even to the bearlike joviality of former days, regaining his good humor and rough friendliness. And yet...

Like an uncured dipsomaniac longing for one last drink, he longed to go back to the Old Poland Restaurant and take one last look into the kitchen, to see whether Yan Kovalsky was not there among the dishwashers. He knew perfectly well, did he not, that the kitchen was not as he had pictured it in his imagination; he had seen, had he not, the automatic dishwasher, the rooms in the corridor which were now storerooms, and yet... He was so taken captive by the picture of his fantasy, of Kovalsky in the kitchen, that the real picture could make no headway against it. The reality dissolved like a hallucination, the hallucinatory became real.... He had to fight himself brutally evenings not to go down and set out for Old Poland, to ask Mike about Kovalsky. For though Steve kept quietly in touch with Mike, Grossman himself had not seen him since his return to Springbrook.

One afternoon, in the midst of a rush of business, Steve came in and said that Mike wanted to see him. He arranged a rendezvous for that evening at nine o'clock, in the alley where they had last met.

When Steve brought Mike through the darkness to the car, Mike refused to get in. He said he would converse with him through the open window.

"Can I talk with you while he's listening, or should he go away?" asked Mike.

"Steve can stay."

"Listen, boss," began Mike. "I've got good news. That Yan Kovalsky, the dishwasher that you've been looking for, and I thought he was dead—I think I found him."

"He's alive!" cried Grossman, in a spasm of fear.

"Yes, I think that's the man. He's alive, Mr. Grossman."

"Where is he?" Grossman's heart was thumping. "Where are you keeping him?" He thrust his hand through the window, to take hold of Mike.

"Not here. He's somewhere in New Jersey. He's living with a daughter. Yes, Mr. Grossman, I thought he never got married, but he did, and he had children, he's got grown-up children. He's living with this daughter."

"How do you know it? Have you seen him?"

"Not yet, but I'm going out there to see him. A good friend of mine, he told me he met him in New Jersey. Ever since you told me to look for that Kovalsky, the dishwasher and no other Kovalsky, I said I got to find him. I don't care how much trouble it will be, I got to find him. I asked all my friends, I asked all the people I know, about that Kovalsky who worked in our restaurant. And I got him! Yes, sir, when Mike says he'll do something, he does it. And you're going to be satisfied, Mr. Grossman. He's here, and alive, as I love God. I mean, if it's the same man."

"What do you mean?"

"My friend, he said that Yan Kovalsky got very, very old. You can't hardly recognize him. He became very old, gray. You want to meet him, Mr. Grossman?"

"Certainly, I want very much to meet him," said Grossman impatiently.

"I can bring him here. I'll take off a day from work, and I'll go to New Jersey and bring him here. But it will cost me money."

"I'll look after that."

"No, no, I don't mean that. You've done enough for me, Mr. Grossman. I'll spend my own money. I'll bring him, you'll talk with him. If that isn't the Kovalsky you meant, all right, you won't give me a cent. But if it's the real Kovalsky, I want you to give me what you promised—five thousand dollars."

"You'll get it, if it's the right Kovalsky."

"But I want you to put that down in writing, Mr. Grossman."

"You won't take my word for it?"

"Sure, sure, I know you're a rich man, Mr. Grossman, and a very good man. You wouldn't do a thing like that to a poor waiter. But you know it's like this: I'm taking a big risk now. If my boss finds out that I have anything to do with Kovalsky the dishwasher, he'll throw me out of the restaurant. He's very, very angry with Kovalsky. I told you that, Mr. Grossman. That's why I want to be safe. I want you to write it down about the five thousand dollars if I bring you the right Kovalsky."

Every instinct in him cried out: "Don't do it! It's a trap!" It was as if he could actually smell the presence of rats. Again he felt like taking Mike by the throat. But he was sufficiently master of himself to conceal the impulse. He said, "I'll repeat the promise, and Steve is a witness. Is that good enough?"

"No, Mr. Grossman," said Mike, uneasily. "I believe your word, I do, as I love God. I don't need Steve to be a witness. Your word is like money in the bank. But it's like this: I'm only a poor devil, I've got nothing but my job in the restaurant. When you find out it's the real Kovalsky, you'll forget about me. You'll do everything for him, like you did for my aunt when you heard she was a Kovalsky. You'll be so busy with him, you won't have time to see me. And I'll be here without a job and without a cent. So one of these two: if it's not the real Kovalsky, I don't want anything, not even my expenses, not even what I already spent till now, looking for him. And I'll give you back your letter. But if it's the right one, I want what's coming to me. Isn't that right? I must have it black and white, or else I got to leave the whole thing, and that's all there is to it."

Grossman thought for a while. "I'll let you know through Steve," he answered.

"Well, if you're not in a hurry, I got time too," said Mike. "Good night, Mr. Grossman." And he disappeared in the darkness of the alley.

He knew it to be a trap. He knew he did not dare—and yet... In the middle of the night he started up and wrote the letter. In the morning he gave it to Steve to take, with fifty dollars, to Mike.

"Mr. Grossman, don't you do it," said Steve, with a woeful expression on his good face.

"I know, Steve, I ought not to do it. But I must. If I don't, I won't have a moment's peace as long as I live. I'll always be thinking: maybe this was it!" he answered, and felt pity for himself welling up.

Mike accepted the letter, but he sent back the fifty dollars of expense money. "Everything or nothing," he said to Steve, putting the letter carefully into his wallet.

"You see how it is now, Lazar," said Max Brown. "It's your neck or your father's. If Davis has his way, the hearing in open

263

court will not only throw a shadow over your father's whole past; it'll drag you into the gutter, as well. Davis will do his best to prove before the whole world that you have nothing but a financial motive for starting this action against your father. You're fighting for your existence now. You can't turn back. You can't have any scruples, or hesitations. You've got to throw in everything if you want to come out clean before the world."

"What do you want me to do?"

"I want you to keep out of the conduct of the case. You don't know, and I don't know, how my man got the proofs he needs. I don't know what his methods are. And it's not your business, it's not our business, see? We know nothing about it."

"All right. But one thing I'll ask of you. My mother's name must not be brought in. You mustn't dare to use what I told you about the photograph."

"That would be a strong piece of evidence against him. But I promise not to use it unless I absolutely have to. With this document which my man got out of him with Mike's and Bornstein's help, I don't think we'll have to bring in the destroyed photograph."

"You're working with that swindler who tried to blackmail my father?"

"Neither I nor you are working with him. I tell you it's none of our business what my man does. We refuse to know anything about it. Tell me, have you spoken with Rose?"

"There's nothing to be done with her. She won't testify, either for our side or for his. She says my father will need her later, and she doesn't want to forfeit his trust in her. She won't have anything to do with the business."

"We'll manage without her. Have you spoken with Steve?"

"Yes, he made this condition: he'll be a witness if Rose tells him to. Rose told him to go to court and tell everything he knows about my father. She obviously believes it will help my father."

"Will he talk?"

"I believe he will."

"That's fine. He's important."

"Yes, Max, but about the ad in the papers, that I repudiate responsibility for any obligations entered into by my father during the time of his sickness. The *Connecticut Standard* refuses to print it."

264

"That's of no consequence. People know what the situation is. If they want to have dealings with your father, it's at their own risk."

The party of the second part was also making preparations for the hearing. It was attorney Davis's view that he would need no witnesses. What his client had done for his project in the period preceding the hearing would itself be the best proof of his sanity. Moreover, Davis had the full weight of public opinion, and the opinion of every influential citizen, on his side. There was, however, one point that Davis had to carry with old Grossman—and that was, not to turn his back on the two psychiatrists appointed by the court. Grossman consented to receive them, but when they came he refused to discuss anything but his project. He kept them for two hours in the office, and with great eagerness unfolded before them all the details of the enterprise, showing them maps, plans, blueprints, drawings. Then he took them out to the site of the project, among the uprooted trees, the excavations, the mounds of dug-up earth, and showed them everything once again, this time not on paper but on the grounds. He showed them the locations of the streets: Corregidor, Bataan, Eisenhower Square, Patton Square. He showed them the places for the gardens, the playgrounds. The two doctors followed him through the mud and the weeds, and when he was through with them they realized that they had not managed to get to the point, the central issue of the hearing, to wit, the Kovalsky family.

Grossman did not appear at the hearing. He was content to be represented by Davis. Miss Rosenberg stayed with him that day, not letting him out of her sight for a single moment. She accompanied him to the office and to the building site, which was now in a fever of activity. Grossman spent a good deal of time that day with the overseers, and almost had to be prevented from taking over the job of one of the excavators which was not working to his satisfaction. He was everywhere, observed everything, understood all the details. He knew that Rose was accompanying him all the time, but he did not say a word to her, nor did she try to speak to him. At lunch, too—she was always with him at mealtimes—they did not exchange a single word. Silently she pushed the mayonnaise over when he reached for it, took away the butter, handed over the dishes he was permitted to eat. After lunch he went into his room to take a rest, and there he found his mother's prayer book, with Robert's letter, which Rose had brought from New Rochelle, stuck between the pages.

CHAPTER FOURTEEN

THE hearing took place in camera, in a quiet and sober atmosphere. Judge Parker was anxious to have both sides speak freely and without embarrassment regarding the behavior, history and character of Isaac Grossman; he felt that the presence of a public, apt to give expression to its local patriotism, would be a deterrent.

Lazar gave his version of the case in a slow, careful manner. It began, as far as he was concerned, when Dr. Markowitch told him confidentially that he was beginning to observe in the older Grossman symptoms of mental imbalance. Isaac Grossman was at the time in mourning for his wife. Some time later Lazar Grossman tried to persuade his father to take a holiday, but without success. It was only after a considerable lapse of time that he and Dr. Markowitch induced the defendant to go for a longer stay at a newly opened Grossman winter resort in Florida. It was there, however, that the symptoms indicated a more rapid deterioration of the defendant's mental condition. Dr. Markowitch and the consulting specialists diagnosed it later as an acute guilt complex associated with the fear of punishment after death, and directly traceable to the effects of what the defendant had experienced in his childhood at the hands of his extremely pious, orthodox father. Further, the defendant had developed a fixation regarding a certain Kovalsky toward whom he, the defendant, believed himself to be under a painful moral obligation.

"I am myself partly to blame," said Lazar Grossman, "for having let him come here to Springbrook to look for this Kovalsky, because he had taken it into his head that this was where the man was to be found. But it seemed to me that if he did not find Kovalsky here—which was bound to be the case, this Kovalsky never having existed—it would help him to recover his normal mental condition. This was a grave mistake. Springbrook only aggravated the delusion; and my father began to behave in a manner which encouraged swindlers to victimize him and attempt to blackmail him in connection with his search for Kovalsky, to which they attached some sort of criminal and sinister interpretation. Finally, in the grip of the Kovalsky delusion, he hit on the fantastic idea of the building development which he has undertaken in Springbrook."

Lazar then described how he had made every effort to dissuade his father from continuing with the project, which would not only absorb a gigantic sum of money, because of its dimensions, but would compromise the good name of the family because of the inexplicable dedication to a mysterious Kovalsky.

"I could not budge him," said Lazar. "He simply would not consider giving up the project. Neither would he let himself be treated. A couple of days before his granddaughter's birthday and engagement party, to which he had been looking forward with great anticipation, he left his house furtively, came down to our office in New York, removed his papers and valuables from the safe, and came here to finance and direct the project. I then felt that I had no alternative but to bring the case to court."

Judge Parker asked whether either of the counselors wanted to question the witness.

Attorney Davis rose. With as warm an expression of sympathetic understanding as he could summon on his frosty features, he began:

"Is it not a fact, Mr. Grossman"—his manner was tranquil, his voice low—"that you seek to prevent your father from continuing with this public-spirited enterprise for purely commercial reasons? Is it not a fact that two or three months ago, when your father was still in Florida, you were negotiating with a firm which offered a high rental for the property, and participation in its profits; and is it not further a fact that these negotiations were dropped because your father intended to use the property for an enterprise of a non-profit-making character?"

"I certainly tried to persuade my father not to use this property for a housing development. At the outset I was against the project on material grounds. But then I began to see in his obstinacy something definitely abnormal. My father is a very able businessman. He has an excellent sense of values. If a businessman like my father

268

takes a piece of land of enormous commercial value, obviously fit for shops and offices, and proposes to convert it into a low-rental housing development, it can only be explained by a breakdown of the mental faculties. It would serve his ostensible purpose far better, it would be much more beneficial for the veterans, if he had chosen an area outside the city. It would be cheaper, it would be more suitable. His refusal to consider these obvious facts bespeaks an abnormal condition."

"Is it not a fact, Mr. Grossman, that you were opposed in general, and apart from these considerations, to your father's philanthropic enterprise in Springbrook?"

"I am, and will remain, unalterably opposed to any project which my father will undertake in Springbrook."

"Why?"

"Because I believe that Springbrook has dangerous associations for my father's delusions. It is precisely here, in this beautifully quiet town, that his hallucination happens to find its poisonous nourishment; and I shall do everything in my power to remove every trace of Springbrook from my father's mind, and from the memory of my family. Springbrook is a very melancholy chapter in the life of our family." At this point, as he was yielding to his emotions, Lazar intercepted a warning look from his attorney, Max Brown.

"Do you not believe, Mr. Grossman, that every man has a right to his own life, the right to live according to his own lights, to bring order into his house, even though his wishes should differ from those of his family?"

"What is your meaning, Mr. Davis?" asked Lazar.

"You know that apart from the very praiseworthy public purpose of the project, the relief of the housing famine among returned veterans, your father also had something personal in mind. You know that the choice of the name Kovalsky Center expressed your father's sense of obligation toward the person of that name. The character of the obligation is known only to your father. Do you not believe, Mr. Grossman, that your father has the right to satisfy that moral demand within himself, to meet the debt which he believes he has contracted, without regard to the impression that it may produce on his family?"

"But in heaven's name, there never was such a person in his life.

It is the product of his deranged mind, it is his fixation, his sickness."

"We are not doctors, Mr. Grossman. We must leave that decision to the experts."

"Gentlemen!" The judge lifted his hand. "I must ask you not to touch on the question of the real or fictitious character of Kovalsky until we shall have heard from the experts. Have you any more questions, Mr. Davis?"

"That is all, your honor." Davis returned to his seat.

"Have you anything to ask your client, counselor?" the judge asked of Max Brown.

"Yes, your honor." Brown stood up and turned to Lazar.

"Mr. Grossman, did you ever, at any time, oppose your father's philanthropic activities which were, I believe, of a generous and far-reaching nature?"

"Never. On the contrary, as long as I remember I have co-operated with him in these activities. If we ever disagreed on the subject, it was in connection with public acknowledgment of his benefactions; he would not have his name attached to any of them, whether it was a new wing to a hospital, or an old people's home, or a synagogue, whereas I thought that my father ought to get the credit for his actions. But my father always had his way."

"Your honor," said Davis, "may I, with the permission of opposing counsel, ask Mr. Grossman a question?"

"Certainly."

"Mr. Grossman, in your opinion is the modesty which your father manifested a negative or a positive element in your father's character?"

"Very decidedly a positive element, a high virtue, which I tried to emulate."

"Thank you, Mr. Grossman." Davis sat down.

"Mr. Grossman," Brown resumed, "if you have never on other occasions opposed your father's philanthropic activities, why do you oppose this one, in Springbrook, so energetically?"

"I have already explained my motives. I will repeat that the good name of my family is endangered by the flood of innuendo and slander which this project has unloosed—and by every divine and human law my father is responsible for his family. I am sorry that on this point I cannot agree with the view of the distinguished

270

counsel, Mr. Davis. I do not know how it is elsewhere, Mr. Davis, but we are a Jewish family, and among us Jews the responsibility of parents for children, and of children for parents, plays a great role. Moreover, I accept the expert opinion of Dr. Markowitch, our family doctor, that the continuation of this project is more liable to aggravate my father's mental condition than to improve it."

"I thank you, Mr. Grossman," said Davis.

The second witness for the defendant was Moses Silverstein.

"Mr. Grossman, whom I knew for many years before he acquired his property in Springbrook, came to me with his secretary, Miss Rosenberg, and inquired after a certain Pole by the name of Kovalsky. I advised them to look up a waiter by the name of Mike, in the Old Poland Restaurant here, also a Pole, who would probably know the Kovalsky he was looking for."

Silverstein went on to relate how Mike had conducted Grossman and Miss Rosenberg to an aunt of his living in Strawberry Hill, this aunt being related to the Kovalsky family. Grossman came back from Strawberry Hill shaken by the scenes of poverty he had witnessed, and in particular distressed by the housing famine among GI's.

"I saw in this an excellent opportunity to interest Mr. Grossman, with whose philanthropies I was familiar, in coming to the help of the GI's," continued Silverstein. "It was not difficult to do this. In fact, he responded enthusiastically, all the more because it fell in with his idea of making good his debt to his friend Kovalsky. I did, it is true, try to persuade him not to attach Kovalsky's name to the project, because it was such an odd and irrelevant thing to do. But he stood by his decision, and I stopped objecting. Homes for GI's were too important to let a small matter like the name of the project interfere. Besides, I finally began to see the matter in another light: a man whose gratitude extends over so many years, who can never forget a benefaction and wishes to acknowledge it, is a man to be admired. And so I encouraged him in every way, and I am proud to have done so. I at no time saw in Mr. Grossman the slightest trace of what has been called here mental derangement, and I think it very sad indeed that his own son should try to prevent—"

"Mr. Silverstein, please stick to the facts," interrupted the judge.

"I have nothing more to say," concluded Silverstein.

Attorney Brown began to question the witness.

"Do you believe, Mr. Silverstein, that there was such a person as Kovalsky, to whom Mr. Grossman was obligated—"

"Your honor, I object to the question," interposed Davis.

The objection was sustained, and the court stenographer directed to delete it from the record.

"I have no questions to ask the witness," said Brown.

"Your witness," said the judge to Davis.

"Mr. Silverstein," began Davis, and for the first time he betrayed a slight agitation, which manifested itself in tiny red patches on his grayish face, "I understand that you arranged, on behalf of Mr. Grossman, for the payment of a pension, or annuity, to a certain person in this town. Did Mr. Grossman do this as the result of a hallucination, or a fixation, as my colleague would call it, or from some other motive? Since you are the one who arranged it, you can perhaps tell us."

"It was done out of pure goodheartedness and pity. There was no other reason or motive. He saw the wretched condition in which the woman lived; he was told that she could not find an institution for her mother, and that her son, a returned GI, was homeless. My God, if we are to consider Mr. Grossman insane for having done this, we would have to put all our philanthropists in lunatic asylums."

"Mr. Silverstein," said Davis, "you brought Mr. Grossman to me and told me of a certain person in this city who tried to blackmail him by threatening to expose certain alleged secrets of a disreputable character. Later this person took fright, and apologized to Mr. Grossman in a letter which you showed me. Will you tell the court how Mr. Grossman dealt with this person? Did he behave like a man who can easily be frightened, or did he show the self-confidence and firmness of a normal person with a clear conscience?"

"How he dealt with him? Why, he practically threw the man, who pretended to be Kovalsky's representative, out of his office."

"Your honor, may I ask the witness a question?" interposed Brown.

"Certainly."

"Mr. Silverstein, in connection with this man who tried to blackmail Mr. Grossman: was he the only one who tried to exploit the

272

Kovalsky situation on false grounds? Or were there others who came forward, either as alleged relatives of Kovalsky or on other grounds, to make claims?"

"There were many others. I can't get rid of them. Ever since it became known that Mr. Grossman is looking for a certain Kovalsky, and that he helped a poor family connected with Kovalsky, I've had a constant stream of people claiming that they are related to the real Kovalsky that Mr. Grossman is looking for. I call them the *biedny ale uczciwy.*"

"What is that?" asked the judge.

"It's Polish for 'poor but honest.' They all use that phrase. 'I'm poor, but honest.' I don't tell Mr. Grossman about them."

"Why?"

"I don't want to make him uneasy."

"Why should these people make him uneasy?"

"My God, if the man is looking for a certain Kovalsky and can't find him—no matter whether that man ever existed or not—and here people keep coming and saying they're related to that Kovalsky, it's bound to excite him, isn't it?"

"Yes, it undoubtedly is. Thank you, Mr. Silverstein."

It was now Mike's turn, as chief witness for the plaintiff.

Mike sat on the edge of his chair. His hair was stuck to his perspiring forehead. He stared about the courtroom in a frightened and uneasy way, and his voice shook. He told first of Miss Rosenberg's inquiry at the Old Poland, and then of Grossman's visit late on a rainy evening, when the restaurant was almost empty.

"Mr. Grossman told me to bring out Kovalsky; he said I was keeping him in the kitchen, or one of the rooms near the kitchen. I took Mr. Grossman into the kitchen, and I showed him that the workers there were colored. I also showed him the rooms in the corridor where we keep canned goods and other supplies. It was no good. Mr. Grossman grabbed me by the throat and began to choke me. 'Where did you hide Kovalsky, the dishwasher?' he wanted to know. You see there was a Kovalsky who worked for us many years ago, a dishwasher, and he's disappeared and we don't know where he is."

He still had marks on his throat from the assault, said Mike, but he was not claiming anything as both Mr. Silverstein and Mr. Grossman had compensated him for that, and for a new coat which Mr. Grossman had torn. He did not claim anything, but he asked the court for protection from old Mr. Grossman, because since that time Mr. Grossman had been threatening him with death if he did not produce Kovalsky the dishwasher. He was afraid that the old man would attack him some night and strangle him. Mr. Grossman was very persistent. He kept sending his chauffeur to Mike. Some nights ago the chauffeur had brought Mr. Grossman in his car to the alley at the side of the restaurant, and had called Mike out to him. Mr. Grossman had offered Mike five thousand dollars if he would produce Kovalsky. When he told Mr. Grossman that he did not know where Kovalsky was, the old man wanted to attack him again. The chauffeur Steve would testify to that. He, Mike, was so afraid of the old man that he decided to get a letter from him, repeating the offer of five thousand dollars, so that he would have the proof in black and white. He had brought this letter with him, to show the court that the man was persecuting him and was not in his right senses.

"Here is the letter," said Mike, and produced it from his wallet. "He also sent me fifty dollars as expenses for trying to produce this dead man, but I sent that back with Steve. I am poor, but honest, and I don't want to take anybody's money for nothing. I don't want anything. I only want to be left alone. Because ever since that man's been after me I can't sleep at night, and I can't work by day, as I love God."

The letter was handed to the judge, who passed it on to Lazar, asking him: "Mr. Grossman, is that your father's handwriting?"

"Yes, your honor, I regret to say it is."

"Do you challenge that, counselor Davis?" asked the judge.

"No, your honor. I accept Mr. Grossman's testimony."

Attorney Davis was completely surprised by the letter. He remained seated, the red patches on his face deepening.

"What day of the week was it when Mr. Grossman senior came to your restaurant to look for Kovalsky, the dishwasher?" asked the judge.

"It was—it was before his son came to take him home. Not Monday, not Wednesday, because Mondays and Wednesdays I don't work in the restaurant. It was Thursday. Yes, Thursday."

"It was May fifth, your honor," stated Brown.

The judge made a notation. "Any questions?"

Davis turned to the witness.

"Is it not a fact that on the day following Mr. Grossman's visit to you at the restaurant, you came to Mr. Grossman's hotel with a certain Bornstein, whom you introduced as Kovalsky's lawyer, and tried to press money out of Mr. Grossman?"

"Your honor, Mr. Grossman not only tried to choke me, he threatened me with prison if I wouldn't produce this Kovalsky, whom he said I was keeping locked up, and torturing him. . . . I knew that Mr. Grossman is a big man, and a very rich man, with pull in the government. . . . I had to do something to protect myself, didn't I? So I went to my lawyer, Mr. Bornstein, and I told him everything and asked him for protection. Mr. Bornstein also said that Mr. Grossman is a very important person, and you can't complain, just like that, that such a man is not in his right senses. You've got to have proof. And so he said he would go with me to Mr. Grossman, and he would see how Mr. Grossman behaved. My lawyer tried to calm Mr. Grossman, that was why he said that I was trying my best to find this Yan Kovalsky—not the Yan Kovalsky the dishwasher, who was dead, but another Yan Kovalsky. And when my lawyer saw that Mr. Grossman didn't want any other Kovalsky, he advised me to drop the whole business and not even sue Mr. Grossman for trying to choke me and tearing my coat. Mr. Grossman is sick, my lawyer told me, and his family would soon come and take him away. But I saw that the family wasn't coming, and nobody was looking after him, and he didn't leave me alone. He called me to him again and made me the offer of five thousand dollars, and he would have attacked me again, so I decided by myself to get this letter from him. You can see from this letter that I was not trying to get money out of him, but he himself offered me that money, which would make me rich for the rest of my life. But I am an honest man, and I have brought the letter to the court."

"Any questions?"

"No, your honor."

It was not only Mike's testimony, which had apparently been learned by heart, it was also the man himself, that left a sickening impression with the judge and with both parties to the trial. The air in the courtroom seemed to have become foul, permeated with an odor of putrescence. Both parties were glad to get rid of the witness, and the judge more than they. But there remained, after him, and as the result of his testimony, a number of massive facts—and the most outstanding among them was the letter.

A very different figure was Steve the chauffeur, modest, sad-faced, bent, who was called after Mike. He sat down like a broken man, his mournful, honest eyes fixed on space. He did not tell of the many errands on which he had been sent by Grossman. These were confidences he could not betray. But he told of the last scene in the alley near the Old Poland Restaurant. He testified that Mike had refused to enter the car, and that the conversation was conducted through the open window. There was a question of five thousand dollars, and Mike had wanted a letter from the boss, he wanted the offer in writing. The boss said that Mike could take his word for it.

"When the boss sent me to Mike the next day, with the letter," related Steve mournfully, "I said to him, 'Boss, don't you do it,' and he said to me, 'I know, I ought not to do it, but if I don't I shall have no peace for the rest of my life.'"

There was silence in the courtroom. After a pause the judge asked: "Any questions?"

No one answered.

The judge himself put a question to the witness.

"How did Mr. Grossman say that?"

"He was very sad," answered Steve, and added, in a lowered voice, "poor Mr. Grossman, like he was being followed by a ghost."

There was silence again in the courtroom. Lazar covered his face.

"I reckon I won't have to make use of your mother's photograph," whispered Brown to Lazar.

The testimony of the psychiatrists was of little interest now. Nor did they have anything substantial to report. Grossman had refused to co-operate. He had wanted to talk about nothing but his project. They had not observed in his behavior any symptoms of mental abnormality. It was, however, understandable that Mr. Grossman would conduct himself normally in all matters which did not relate to his fixation. Whether such a fixation would be the result, in his case, of cerebral arteriosclerosis, or of a guilt complex aggravated by a violent psychic shock, they could not say,

276

inasmuch as Mr. Grossman had evaded their observation and left their pertinent questions unanswered.

Attorney Davis asked: "Is not the extraordinary energy which Mr. Grossman is now manifesting in the carrying out of his project evidence of a sound organism and a sound mind?"

One of the experts answered: "In our practice we not infrequently come across cases of mental disturbance confined to one point, while in all other points the patient remains more or less normal."

The other specialist added: "This very excess of energy can sometimes proceed from a mania, or a fixation, which drives the patient ceaselessly to unsual effort."

Brown had no questions to put to the experts.

The judge took the case under advisement for a few days.

To the disappointment and indignation of the city of Springbrook, Judge Parker issued the following statement:

"The court declares that, as of the 5th of May last, Isaac Grossman has not been competent to conduct his personal or his business affairs. The court therefore appoints Isaac Grossman's son, Lazar Grossman, as administrator, supervisor, and guardian for Isaac Grossman, both as to his person and as to his business affairs and enterprises. The court further orders that the said Isaac Grossman shall be placed in an institution for the cure of the mentally sick, to be chosen by Lazar Grossman, and that he shall be kept there for an examination and observation for not more than thirty days; and that a medical report regarding Isaac Grossman's condition shall be submitted to the Probate Court of Springbrook."

"I didn't do it, neither did you, neither did Mike. It was all done by Steve, your father's chauffeur," said Brown to Lazar, when they heard the verdict.

It fell to Miss Rosenberg to conduct Isaac Grossman to the private sanatorium in the vicinity of Springbrook which his son had agreed upon. They went in the Cadillac, which Steve drove. Rose had prevailed on Lazar to give up his original intention, which had been to choose a sanatorium as far away from Springbrook as possible. She made it clear to him that if this was attempted, the old man would resist, and it would be necessary to resort to force.

Louise's engagement was put off, with the friendly consent of the Hanovers, until things had quieted down. Nor, with the deferment of young Hanover's military service, was there any hurry. Lazar came to an accommodation with the contractors whom his father had engaged for the project, and whatever material had been delivered was taken back. Only the excavators and bulldozers remained to continue with the leveling and preparation of the site on which old Grossman had expended his brief and furious effort. Lazar's prestige rose higher than ever in the business world. He received many letters expressing sympathy with his personal tragedy and approval of the vigorous measures he had taken to safeguard the good name of his family and the high reputation of his firm. Meanwhile Springbrook was repeating with sour gusto Moses Silverstein's summary of the outcome of the Grossman case: "Judge Parker is proposing to have all philanthropists declared of unsound mind, and is preparing a court order for their confinement to mental institutions for examination and observation."

CHAPTER FIFTEEN

THE private institution for the mentally disturbed went by the Hebrew name of Bethesda. That had been the name of the pool by the sheep's gate of Jerusalem where, according to the gospel of St. John, the sick and crippled came to bathe; there an angel descended from time to time and renewed the waves; and there Jesus performed many miracles. Bethesda had been founded far back in the last century, when the mentally sick had been considered "possessed" and had been treated by violent methods. An institution with tradition, Bethesda had passed through all the stages of improvement in the treatment of its patients. For Bethesda as for medical science generally, it had been a slow process of evolution, which began with strait jackets and padded cells and reached the Freudian stage of psychotherapy and psychoanalysis. Bethesda was by now a modern institution in the best sense of the word, a private hospital for a limited number of well-to-do patients. It was set in a landscape of trees and flower beds, the houses grouped about the main building, and the whole almost completely concealed by foliage. Magnificent fields and meadows occupied tens of acres on every side, laid out with paths and set with groves of lofty elms. A lake whose clear waters were fed constantly by natural springs lay in a valley hidden from prying eyes by a wall of willows whose hanging curtains swayed in the wind.

The patients, for the most part alcoholics of both sexes who had agreed to enter of their own free will, and manic depressives, strolled singly or in groups, accompanied by nurses or relatives, through the magnificent grounds. Free to pass the time as they wished, they spent their days either strolling or seated in the recreation rooms, where they were provided with light handicrafts. The women sewed or knitted, for themselves or for friends, or

279

turned out gifts for the poor in the city hospital; the men did carpentry and locksmith work. If they could not take to physical employment there was a second recreation room with reading material and gramaphone music; there would also be discussions on social and other questions, led by a member of the medical staff, and guided sometimes toward personal problems and experiences as part of the over-all psychoanalytic method of the institution. The patients were encouraged to spend their evenings together. They were free to receive visitors at any hour of the day; they could even stroll out of the grounds, or go for a ride in their own or hired cars, accompanied by a nurse or a relative. They seldom saw an attendant guard, but they were always under rigorous surveillance; when occasion demanded it, a guard would appear on the spot, as if materializing out of nowhere: he was simply a gentleman dressed in discreet and unobtrusive black, who would address the patient with extreme courtesy: "I am sorry but this is against the regulations." And if the patient showed an inclination to ignore the reminder, the polite gentleman in black, still courteous, still smiling, took the patient by the arm, but with the kind of grip which indicated that resistance was useless, and led him quietly away. Thus, within a short time, the patients learned that their ostensible freedom had its limitations, defined by others and impassable to themselves.

There were also patients who had to be kept confined to their rooms. These were the aggressive and as yet undisciplined persons, like alcoholics who tried to break through doors, extreme hysterics, or depressives with a tendency to suicide. For these there was a separate wing, divided off from the rest of the general building, and from the adjacent buildings, by steel curtains over the doors and windows. Bars were forbidden, as apt to suggest a prison to the patients, and the steel curtains were constructed so as to suggest ordinary wire network; they were, however, much stronger, and could not be torn with the bare hand. Every patient had his own room, which suggested a decent room in a country hotel; but nothing was to be found in it which a person could use in an attack either upon himself or upon another. The water in the bathroom could be made to flow only by an attendant. The patient could move freely about his room, or even walk in the neat corridor, which was, however, under constant watch. All doors had always to be open. The patients took their meals separately in their own rooms under the eyes of an attendant. They too could receive visitors with the permission of the superintendent, and also stroll in the gardens—again under surveillance.

It was the generally accepted rule in the institution that a patient entering under a court order, or by direction of a doctor, had to spend some time first in the isolation section for observation, where it would be decided whether, and when, he could graduate to the free section. On arriving at Bethesda, Isaac Grossman was accordingly placed in the isolation section. His baggage was thoroughly examined, and whatever might be used against himself or others—such as razors, suspenders, and even his hard shoes—was taken away. He was under observation by attendants twenty-four hours of the day, though he was not aware of it.

At the request of Lazar, who was now his father's guardian, with complete authority over him, Miss Rosenberg was given the right to visit the patient at all hours. She was lodged in the guest house of the institution, like a private nurse. Lazar left nearby— for the use of Miss Rosenberg and his father—Steve and the Cadillac.

Old Grossman submitted to the regulations of the institution with stoical calm. The superintendent returned his suspenders on the first day, so as not to humiliate the patient, but like every other patient in this section Grossman had to be shaved every morning by the barber who made the rounds. Miss Rosenberg could be with him from ten o'clock in the morning until after supper, and they had their meals together, at one table, as they were accustomed to do. The superintendent raised no objection when Miss Rosenberg insisted that her employer be allowed to keep by him the papers relating to his project—the plans, schedules, and blueprints, on which he wanted to continue working. The court order, she pointed out, directed that Mr. Grossman was to be kept under observation for thirty days; thereafter, if his condition was pronounced normal, he would resume his activities. Isaac Grossman heard the argument, and he steeled himself to endure whatever had to be endured, and not to lose his patience and self-control, so that he might emerge from the institution triumphant over his son, whom he regarded as his enemy.

He co-operated now to the best of his abilities; he followed all

281

the instructions, listened to the doctors, readily took the medicaments and sedatives prescribed for him. After a complete physical examination the doctors reported that apart from gallstones and an oversized liver he was free from any organic abnormality. His blood pressure was higher than normal, but not alarmingly so. His heart reacted spasmodically, but this was most probably due to his recent experiences. His physical system was sound, his athletic body well preserved, with, however, an excess of energy. They found no evidence of nervous disturbance; however, it was their opinion that the patient needed a period of rest and calmness to rid himself of his mental burden. Above all he needed plenty of sleep. They therefore prescribed sedatives, which he took obediently, and he slept well.

After the first psychotherapeutic treatments his blood pressure diminished. His pulse was normal. After the first week he felt restored to himself, calm, relaxed; the superintendent therefore recommended that he be given more freedom of movement. Miss Rosenberg was permitted to take her employer out for a drive through the beautiful countryside.

Steve drove the Cadillac. Next to him sat one of the men in discreet black. Miss Rosenberg sat with her employer at the back.

As they drove out through the gate Steve asked, "Which way, Mr. Grossman?"

"Take me to Springbrook, to my property."

"I'm sorry. You can't go to Springbrook. Turn right," said the attendant.

"Why?" asked Grossman.

"Orders," said the attendant briefly and courteously.

"Steve, drive to the right, Mr. Grossman wants to see the countryside."

The car turned away from the direction of Springbrook. The landscape unfolded like a picture gallery of green-clothed hillocks and covered valleys. The soft carpet followed the contours of the undulating land and melted into the misty blue-violet of the horizon, which in turn lost itself in a mirror of green waters.

"It's beautiful here, isn't it?" cried Miss Rosenberg.

"Yes," muttered Grossman, and fell back into a brooding silence. Suddenly he called out: "Steve!"

"Yes, sir."

"Take me back."

"Why?" asked Miss Rosenberg.

"Because I want it. Take me back, Steve."

Steve turned the car around.

"Why did you do that?" Miss Rosenberg asked the superintendent later.

"Orders," he answered, with a friendly smile.

"Whose?"

"His son's. His father must not be permitted to visit Springbrook. It happens to fall in with our regulations," he continued, still with a friendly smile. "We don't let our patients visit Springbrook or any other city. They can only ride through the country. Our patients always turn to the right, not to the left."

"That's a pity. He's so eager to see his property," said Miss Rosenberg.

"I'm sorry, but I'll have to take away his papers too—the plans and schedules of his enterprise."

"Doctor, don't do it. It's the only thing that keeps him going."

"I must, Miss Rosenberg. I let him hold onto the papers as a test. Now we are getting at the fundamental reason for his condition. The way he reacts to this prohibition to go to Springbrook points to the root of his trouble." The doctor spoke very earnestly. "He behaved quite normally as long as he had the plans of his project before him. Now we will see his reaction when this plaything is taken away from him. I'm sorry to have to distress him, believe me, but we have no alternative. It's part of our psychic therapy."

"Don't do it," insisted Miss Rosenberg. "I'm afraid. It's his only happiness." She stood there, gray-haired—not a single black hair remained in her head—and her eyes were filled with despair.

"Miss Rosenberg," said the doctor, sympathetically but firmly, "we're not here for our pleasure. We have a task to perform. We have our methods and our practice. We let Mr. Grossman keep the papers to quiet his nerves; also, the papers were not a part of the process of examination so far. Now we must deprive him of everything liable to awaken associations with his fixation. We must, in fact, change his environment. I'm afraid I shall have to ask you to stop seeing the patient. I know how painful that's going to be for you, and how much more painful for the patient; but we have no alternative. You will have to wait until the patient is some-what better, and we can transfer him to the free section. You'll then be able to see him as often as you like, and spend as much time with him as you like. You and he must submit to the regu-lations the way everyone else does. We want to help the patient, don't we?"

"It's horrible!" whispered Miss Rosenberg to herself.

"Believe me, Miss Rosenberg, there are more horrible cases than Mr. Grossman's. We have been extremely considerate, we have perhaps interpreted our regulations a little too leniently in his case. He has had privileges we usually do not grant similar cases. Now there must be a change, for his good. Look at the thing sensibly, Miss Rosenberg. We know how you are affected by Mr. Grossman's condition."

"Can I visit him again today?"

"Only today," smiled the superintendent. "About later, we'll see."

She found him sitting with glazed eyes fixed on empty space, his breath coming and going heavily. The table before him was empty. In place of the maps, plans and blueprints, there was a flower vase.

"It's only for a while, till they've finished with their experi-ments, as they call them. In a few days they'll take you to the other section. You'll be able to go about, to drive into the country. They'll give you back your papers. Be strong, Isaac; pull yourself together, so you'll be able to come through the test."

He made no answer; only after a little while the extreme misery faded from his face, and a touch of life came into his eyes, as though he were emerging from a coma.

"I'm wondering," he murmured with a smile, "whether hibiscus flowers could be adapted to the local climate."

"Why?"

"You see, the rhododendrons blossom and fade so quickly. Did you notice how they've blossomed round the lake, here in the grounds? A swimming pool with rhododendron bushes around it is very beautiful. It's a pity they fade so quickly."

"What's this sudden interest in flowers?" asked Miss Rosen-berg.

"I've always liked flowers. I used to help Clara in her garden. I

284

was thinking of making a swimming pool in the middle of the four blocks of my houses, and surrounding it with hibiscus flowers. I don't know if they've ever tried to transplant hibiscus this far north. The flower lasts through the entire season in Florida. Why shouldn't it blossom here, too? It would be beautiful—a swimming pool set in red hibiscus flowers. We mustn't let children fall in, though. We'll have to surround it with an iron picket fence—handworked."

"Isaac, I hope you'll make the first successful experiment at transplanting hibiscus, and if you don't get a prize for your project, you'll get it for your flowers," said Miss Rosenberg.

They sat opposite each other at supper. Then she prepared to go.

"Good night, Isaac. Sleep well. We'll meet tomorrow."

"Yes, ma'am," he answered, and conducted her to the door.

A nurse came out of the adjoining room, pushing a wheelchair with a patient in it. The patient was an elderly woman in an advanced stage of melancholy. She sat huddled up, her head drooping on her breast, sunk in the blackness of her thoughts.

Grossman threw a quick glance, not at the patient, but at the nurse. It seemed to him that the face under the white headcovering was familiar. He had seen it before, naked, white as chalk, the face of a corpse, with closed eyes and shaven brows. He closed his own eyes quickly and went back into his room.

That night they had to compel him to take a sedative, but his terror of sleep counteracted the drug; he lay in a lethargic twilight which was neither sleep nor waking. In this twilight he saw himself ascending a height thrust upward into a dimensionless space which was neither substance nor empty space, but consisted of tattered clouds; he was oppressed by a massive burden which brought his head down to his knees. He was not himself, or not himself alone; he was his father, and Kovalsky, too. He was twofold and threefold. The two, the three, bent under the burden, ascended the height. At his side, at their side, went Clara. She was so small and delicate. With her slender, delicate arms she helped him carry his burden. His heart was filled with fear lest she break her fragile arms. He wanted to tell her not to help him, he wanted to warn her, but his voice was soundless and she did not hear him. He exerted himself to bring forth a sound, but his throat was locked and refused to respond. Suddenly she fell, and re-

285

mained on the ground. But he had to go on. And without her hands to help, the burden fell on him with the weight of a vast block of houses. It lay not only on his shoulders but also on his heart, on his hands, on every part of him, and he was crawling on all fours, his strength draining out of him; till he and the others came to a body of water in which were mirrored red flowers; no, not hibiscus, and not rhododendron, but flames breaking out of the swimming pool. And then he saw the chalk-white face and the browless eyes of the nurse. She brought a wheelchair to him and indicated wordlessly, with her eyes only, that he was to sit down in it. He began to scream with fear—and now his throat responded, and his voice was like that of a man possessed.

The sound set off the hysteria of other patients, and the section was filled with a wild chorus of screaming voices. Two attendants appeared at his bedside. One of them covered his mouth and said, "Quick, the doctor. He's got to have a needle."

After the needle he fell into a sick sleep. The tumult in the section died down. Only here and there an isolated howling broke out, as of a tortured animal.

The next morning, when Miss Rosenberg presented herself at the closed section, the nurse at the door stopped her.

"Excuse me, Miss Rosenberg. I think Dr. Martin informed you yesterday that you would not be able to see the patient."

"But I want to see Dr. Martin."

"I'm sorry," said the nurse, politely. "Dr. Martin will be busy all morning. You will learn from Mr. Grossman junior, who gets a report from us daily, about the patient's progress." And as Miss Rosenberg turned away, the nurse added: "Oh yes, something else, Miss Rosenberg. Dr. Martin asks you to be good enough to vacate the room in the guest house, as you have no reason now to occupy it and we need it for other guests. You won't be able to see the patient for quite a while, Dr. Martin says."

She did not know where to go, or what to do with herself. Finally she decided to visit Moses Silverstein. She entered his shop and sat down, completely broken, in a chair. Silverstein was, for a change, actually serving a customer. When he was gone, Silverstein turned to Miss Rosenberg. He seemed to guess, from the despair of her face and posture, the state of affairs.

"What do you expect?" he said, "when a son maneuvers his

286

own father into a lunatic asylum so as to inherit him while he's still alive."

"What are you talking about?" she asked, astounded.

"I'm talking about your boss, Mr. Lazar Grossman."

"Lazar Grossman is not my employer. My employer is Isaac Grossman."

"If that's so, why did you help his son in the frame-up to get his father into an institution?"

"Mr. Silverstein, I haven't come here to quarrel with you." She began to weep. "There was no frame-up. Mr. Grossman is sick."

"Mr. Grossman became sick in the institution. Anyone would, after he's been tricked into an asylum by his own son. He's sick of a broken heart. We knew it would end up like that."

"What are you saying?" she wept. "There was no trickery."

"There was, Miss Rosenberg. The whole city knows it. The whole city knows that the lawyer sent a man here to that swindler Bornstein, and the two of them worked on Mike—they threatened him, they gave him money—to get that letter out of Mr. Grossman, and that was what sent Mr. Grossman to the asylum. The whole thing cries to heaven, it's an unforgivable crime—and you helped."

"I?" She started back.

"Yes, you, you. You interfered with his carrying out of the project."

"But the project *is* his sickness, it's part of his obsession."

"Who cares whether it's an obsession or a fact? He needed it for the sake of his conscience. Does it matter what led him to undertake the project if the result would have been good for him? And now? What have you got now? You've all banded together to have him locked up in the asylum, and there he's really going mad."

"Who told you that he's going mad?" she asked, horrified.

"I see it in your face. And now it's your conscience that's tormenting you."

"We had to help him."

"Help whom? Old Mr. Grossman? Or help his son to inherit him while the father is still living? Oh no, Miss Rosenberg. If you think this ends the matter you're very much mistaken. Mr.

Davis won't take it lying down. He's got all the facts now about the frame-up. We're going to make such a row about it that the whole world will sit up and take notice."

She ran out of the shop, hailed a taxi, and drove back to the hospital. The gateman asked her for her pass. When she showed it to him he said, "I'm sorry, lady, I'll have to call the office. Your card has been canceled."

The office permitted her to enter the institution only once, in the company of an attendant, to remove her belongings from the guest house.

And again she did not know which way to turn. She disliked the thought of staying alone in the Springbrook hotel. She did not feel like telephoning Lazar. She went to the railroad station in Springbrook and waited for a train to take her to New Rochelle. She would not use her employer's car because she was ashamed to show herself to Steve.

On the way to New Rochelle she decided to leave the house and move into a hotel room in New York. She would wind up her relations with the Grossman family. She no longer had any reason to be connected with them. She must begin a new life, find an interest of her own. She had given enough of her life to the Grossmans. But hardly had she entered the huge house than she was told that there had been several calls from Long Island, and she could not refrain from calling Lazar at his office. There she was told that Lazar had just left and was on his way to the house in New Rochelle. She called Long Island, and Katherine uttered a cry of pleasure on hearing her voice:

"Rose, where are you? We've been trying to reach you. Lazar is worried about you. He's coming to New Rochelle to bring you here. You've got to stay with us until they decide about father. We've got everything ready for you."

When Lazar arrived she could not restrain her impulse to fall on his neck in a storm of tears.

"I know, I know," he said, and stroked her head. "The superintendent told me. Father had a very bad night. He disturbed the other patients. He's calmer now."

"They took away his papers. That broke him completely," she sobbed.

"They know what they're doing," answered Lazar, still stroking her head. "We mustn't interfere. We can't interfere."

"They won't let me see him any more."

"It has to be that way. They told me father mustn't be disturbed by anyone, not even the people closest to him, until they're through with the examination."

"Lazar, can't we bring out a big specialist, the biggest in New York? Why don't we do something?"

"We can't do anything, Rose, until the doctors who are treating him have made their diagnosis. He's in the institution on a court order. The doctors have to submit their report. We can't do anything before that's finished."

"It's dreadful, it's dreadful," she whispered.

"Rose, we have to be patient. Bethesda is one of the best institutions of its kind in the country. Be a good girl, Rose, get some of your things together, and we'll go to Long Island. Katherine and Louise are expecting you. What will you do here alone? You won't be helping father, and you'll get sick yourself. Come. We've got to be together and help each other at a time like this."

There was nothing else for her to do. She had no other home, and she realized that it was too late for her to begin a new life.

"Lazar, they are saying the most frightful things about you, and about me, and all of us, in Springbrook," said Rose, as they sat in the automobile and she had calmed herself a little.

"I know it, Rose. The only thing they want is father's property in Springbrook. Well, I'll sell it and give them the money."

"No, don't sell the property. Smith's Farm belongs to your father. I beg you, don't sell it. He'll never forgive you," she said.

"All right, we'll see about it. Only let him get better."

Before the thirty days had run out the Bethesda Institution submitted its report to Judge Parker of the Springbrook Probate Court. The report contained little that was new. It corroborated, in general, the diagnosis already made by the private specialists. The patient suffered from an exaggerated guilt complex resulting from the education he had received in childhood. The complex had been aggravated in recent years by the psychic effects of cerebral arteriosclerosis, and by a nervous shock following the death of the patient's wife. The patient was subject to extreme hallucinations, with occasional symptoms of hysteria. The general effect was such that the patient could not be considered responsible for his actions, in spite of a surface appearance of normal activity which might in fact be the result of the nervous disturbance. The patient was liable to commit acts uncontrolled by the intelligence and harmful to himself and to those about him. On these grounds the doctors of the Bethesda Institution regarded it as their duty to recommend to the Springbrook Probate Court that the said Isaac Grossman undergo a course of treatment under the proper specialists in an institution for the mentally disordered.

On the basis of this report Judge Parker ordered that Isaac Grossman be considered incompetent to administer his personal or business affairs until, after due treatment, he should be declared cured by the proper authorities. Until such time his son Lazar Grossman was to continue in his capacity as administrator of his father's affairs, and as the guardian of his person. Lazar Grossman was further empowered to choose the institution and the doctors for the further treatment of his father.

In the dispute between attorney Brown, who wanted Isaac Grossman to be removed to an institution at a distance from Springbrook, and Miss Rosenberg, who insisted that he be left where he was, Lazar gave way to Miss Rosenberg. The excitement in Springbrook died down when it was learned that Lazar Grossman had full authority to dispose of the Grossman property in the city, and that he would probably turn it over to the city after all. The public soon forgot Isaac Grossman. Like every other inmate of Bethesda he became one of the living dead.

CHAPTER SIXTEEN

MAN is born with the sense of death not less than with the sense of life. The truth is that life is death, and life cannot be grasped without the consciousness of death.

There are three stages in a man's attitude toward death.

The first is the stage of childhood and youth. A normal child, a normal boy, is utterly unable to imagine that someday he will die. He sees death about him at every step, among acquaintances, among his family: his brother falls in the war, a grandfather or a grandmother dies. He does not deny death, death is there, but all others will die and not he. This is the stage of rebellion against death, the denial and repudiation of it for oneself.

The second stage comes with the middle years. Now a man accepts death. He has become familiarized with it. Death belongs. Many of his family, many friends and acquaintances, are now with death, and he acknowledges now that death will come for him too. But death must be evaded, the final moment must be put off as long as possible. These are the years of valor, the fullest and most energetic years. Man builds himself fortresses against death, he guards his health, does not leap into the flames any more, accumulates wealth so as to live in comfort and safety in his latter years, so as to be able to withstand as long as possible the siege of death.

Then comes the third and final stage. A man makes his peace with death. The more death grows into the man, the more it loses its mystical secrecy, that which terrified the man in his younger years. Now death is a familiar, almost a blood kin. Death is the final providor, the ultimate home, the resting place. And so with the years the man becomes ripe for death, until he realizes that this is a new birth into an eternal life.

Man dies only when he wills it. Each one of us, whatever faith or philosophic system we belong to, actively or passively, will unconsciously and instinctively seek a mother to give him birth into the everlasting life. If he finds this mother, he surrenders himself into her arms like a helpless child which lets its head droop on its mother's breast. This is what we know as the easy death. If he does not find the mother—if he has lost her, or never had one—he is afraid to die, and he fights death tooth and nail, seeing it tower above him, axe in hand. This is what we know as the hard death.

Isaac Grossman had lost his mother, and perhaps he never had a mother to bear him into death. Therefore he was afraid to die.

The doctors of the Bethesda institution declared that the "cure" for Isaac Grossman would consist in keeping the patient as comfortable as possible, soothing him, avoiding anything which would jangle his nerves or awaken painful memories. Lazar agreed. And expense did not matter.

Soon after the report the patient was transferred to the free wing of the main building. He now had his own private nurses to tend him night and day. He never caught a glimpse of a guard. Steve was always at his disposal to take him out riding, in the company of a hospital orderly. And in keeping with the regulations, he had to "turn right, never left"—that is, away from the direction of Springbrook. Eventually Miss Rosenberg also got back her pass and was able to be with him at all reasonable hours; that is, as long as she did not disturb his rest. She now moved into The Inn, in Springbrook.

When Miss Rosenberg saw him for the first time after his transfer to the free wing (the doctors had warned Lazar that it would still be dangerous for him to appear before his father) she was almost unable to recognize him. He had lost a great deal of weight. His cheeks had fallen in, there were hollows around his mouth; and his throat, which had always been full and strong, now showed two bones which protruded through the loose skin, with the Adam's apple running up and down between like a captive mouse. The eyes had sunk deeper into the sockets, and the pupils looked out from the glazed whites as from a misted windowpane. He did not look as her when she spoke to him, as he had been wont to do; he avoided her look, as though he had something to conceal.

But more than by his appearance she was appalled by the way

he bore himself. He was quiet, motionless—silenced, almost—utterly unlike the man he had been, so that she felt as though she was meeting a stranger.

"The doctors say that you're improving, and you're feeling better."

"Yes, I think so," he answered, and nodded.

"How did you sleep last night?"

"Not bad," he said, quietly.

"Dr. Martin says you can take a drive now in your car."

"That'll be nice."

"You can also stroll around in the garden, if you want to. Wouldn't you like to come out? It's beautiful outside. The rhododendrons are in full bloom."

"No, thank you." He shook his head.

"I think Mr. Grossman is too weak to walk in the garden. He'd rather sit here and look out through the window, wouldn't you, Mr. Grossman?" said the nurse, and arranged the pillow behind his head.

"Yes, Dorothy." And he nodded.

Miss Rosenberg sat wordless for some moments. Her heart was constricted with pain to see the change in her employer. She sought for some way of evoking a response from him.

"Maybe Dr. Martin will let you have your papers again," she said, and her heart beat with anxiety as she waited for his reaction to mention of the project.

He was silent. His glazed eyes were fixed on empty space.

"You'd be able to work on your project; it'll help you to pass the time," she ventured again.

Grossman was silent; his look did not change.

"I think Mr. Grossman is still too weak to start work," said the nurse. "Another day, when he feels better—don't you think so, Mr. Grossman?"

"Yes, Dorothy." He nodded.

Later in the day the superintendant, whom Lazar had asked to be somewhat more friendly toward Miss Rosenberg than he had been in the past, asked her what her impression of the old man was. She answered, in a depressed voice: "I don't know. Something has changed in him. He's another person."

293

"That's the shake-up he's had in the treatment; he hasn't come out of it."

"He doesn't react to anything. I even took the risk of mentioning his project, to see how he'd respond."

"He doesn't. We know that. We tried it, too. We put his papers on the table. He didn't look at them."

"Is this the normal course of a treatment, is it a sign of progress?" asked Rose, frightened.

"This is the natural course in his case."

"But he was completely tied up in his project, and apathy is foreign to his nature. That apathy of his terrifies me, Dr. Martin."

"You don't have to be terrified. I think the worst is over. He's coming out of his nightmares. He's making the transition from sick hallucinations to sober clarity. It's a long road, this road to a cure. There are good patches and bad ones, regressions as well as progress. He still hasn't got his feet on terra firma, Miss Rosenberg. His senses are in a mist. It's quite natural that he should seem to be atrophied and paralyzed; that is the effect of the pictures which his sick imagination conjured up. Patience, Miss Rosenberg, patience. The crisis is past. I'm keeping Mr. Grossman junior informed about his father's condition. If you like, Miss Rosenberg, you can take him out for a drive tomorrow. That is, if you can persuade him. It would be good for him."

Dr. Martin excused himself and withdrew.

Half persuaded, half forced by Miss Rosenberg and the nurse, old Grossman went out reluctantly the next morning for the first time since he had been closed in. Steve and an attendant supported him to the car, where he was placed between Miss Rosenberg and the nurse. Then they drove out of the grounds and turned right.

Rose watched anxiously for the effect which the landscape would have on the sick man. He sat there, staring mutely through the window, and no reaction showed on his face. But when they came to the top of the slope from which the big lake was visible, Grossman stretched out his hand and murmured something.

The nurse put her ear close to his lips. "He wants to go back," she said.

"Why?" asked Miss Rosenberg, in alarm.

"Probably some association is troubling him. We'd better return." And she instructed Steve to turn the machine round.

Dr. Martin was insistent that Grossman should mingle with the other patients and spend time at work and games, as they did. He did not like, either, Grossman's habit of taking his meals alone. He wanted him to use one of the small tables in the general dining room.

"Loneliness isn't good for you. You might get depressed and imagine that you're really sick, Mr. Grossman," he said. "This is a sanatorium, a hotel. Imagine that you're taking a sea voyage; you're on a ship, and you're making the acquaintance of your fellow passengers. You might even become friendly with a few of them during the trip. Make friends, Mr. Grossman. It will do you good."

Grossman made no acquaintances among the patients, despite the efforts of the staff and even of the patients themselves. But he had never made friends easily, and since Clara's death he had become a recluse. He came into the dining room attended by his nurse, sat down at the table, and stared mutely into space. He behaved similarly in the recreation room. Now and again he had the vague notion that he had caught sight of a familiar face among the patients. Now and again a patient would approach him and say: "Aren't you Mr. Grossman?" He would shake his head, or even ignore the questioner completely.

Once, however, as he sat in the recreation room, he saw a man passing through in the company of a nurse. One hand leaned heavily on the nurse, the other shook violently. Grossman recognized him at once, in spite of the change; for the man had become smaller, and walked with a stoop now. It was Judge Lapini, who had been his neighbor in New Rochelle, and with whom he had often commuted to and from the city. Occasionally they had played pinochle in the special, or discussed politics. The judge had suddenly disappeared from New Rochelle. It was variously reported that he was in California, sick, that he was taking a long vacation, that he was dead. His house in New Rochelle was sold by auction. Grossman had not seen the judge's obituary in the papers, but he had heard others say they had. And here the man was, passing through the room. Was he perhaps mistaken?

"Listen, nurse, isn't that Judge Lapini, that man who just went past?" he asked, in great astonishment.

The nurse looked about her cautiously, then half whispered to him, "This is the second year he's been here. He'll probably live here the rest of his life. Don't tell anyone. Nobody's supposed to know."

Grossman was silent.

In that case, he thought, I'll be dead here, too. I'll stay here for the rest of my life. Or perhaps I'm really dead. Why don't they begin my trial?

From the time of that incident he refused categorically to eat in the dining room.

Was there in old Grossman the will to die? Yes, the will was there, in his unconscious, but in his conscious self the fear of death grew stronger and stronger.

Frustrated by his son in the effort to correct the error of his life, to remove the defect which he carried about in him—only thus could he have restored his unity with his father—he fell deeper and deeper into a depression which drained away the stream of his energy. He became apathetic to everything about him—what did anything matter now?—but this passivity did not penetrate to his inmost being. On the contrary, deep within the storm still seethed, and he used the remnants of his strength to conceal his feelings from the outside world. After the experience of that night in Bethesda, when he had screamed his anguish out of his coma, he knew enough to contain his terror and not to inflict it on the other patients; and if it issued at all, it was in a melancholy, inner babbling of lamentation. For after the last line of rescue had been cut, the evil spirits came out of their lairs and, no longer held in check by his efforts, tormented him at their will. Medusa shook loose the locks of her head and the snakes crawled out and covered his body. Frightful chimeras, nameless pictures, wandered through the chambers of his mind, and acquainted him with torment after torment. The most abandoned images of evil, the boiling and roasting of the flames of Genennah, carried over from the years of his childhood—he had not believed that they still lived in him— awoke, the seed that had been planted in his childish mind by his

296

father, augmented by repulsive fantasies of his own invention. The feeling of a crushing burden on his chest, which was the reflex of an attack of gallstones, issued into images of everlasting subterranean labyrinths through which he dragged his faltering limbs. In every lake he saw the lake of brimstone into which he was being thrown by the punishing demons, according to what his father had told him on Friday evenings. And the rosy-blossoming, innocent azaleas, and the red begonias which Clara had loved to have in her garden, and with which he had thought to adorn a swimming pool on his project, became the leaping fires of the nether world. As long as he had kept a hold on the project as an atonement for his sin, he had been able to master, and even to wipe out, the tormenting hallucinations. But when this last protection was removed, the hallucinations ran riot and penetrated through the lethargy of his half-sleep.

Rose saw Grossman sinking deeper and deeper, from day to day, into the abyss, and she was at her wit's end.

"Lazar, we must do something," she cried. "I can't watch him falling deeper and deeper." And she wept.

"Rose, he is in good hands."

"I know, I know, but see what has become of him."

"What do you suggest? What ideas have you?"

"Let's get Dr. Crown again, the specialist Dr. Markowitch consulted but whom your father wouldn't admit to him. Can't we get him out to the institution?"

"We must ask Dr. Martin. We can't do anything without his consent. I'll call him."

Dr. Martin had no objection to having the great psychiatrist Dr. Crown examine the patient. On the contrary, he expressed his satisfaction. It was therefore arranged that Dr. Crown should come out to Springbrook.

Lazar also brought Dr. Markowitch to the consultation. Lazar himself still did not intrude on his father. The famous psychiatrist went again into the record of the patient's sickness. Dr. Markowitch again told him the story of Isaac Grossman's childhood years, as he had heard it from Sam Grossman, and of the happiness with Clara which was ended only by her death. They then consulted the reports of the Bethesda medical staff, and Dr.

Martin explained in detail the curative methods they had applied to the patient. Dr. Crown then tried to conduct a conversation with old Grossman, who did not now show the same obstinate hostility as on the previous occasion; however, he was not particularly friendly or co-operative. Nevertheless his behavior was more or less normal and balanced. Dr. Crown formed his own estimate of the patient's condition, which he afterwards gave his colleagues.

"I don't see what else can be done for the patient," he began. "The case is a clear one, classic even: cerebral arteriosclerosis accelerated by his guilt complex. We have means, today, of helping the patient. Psychotherapy ... yes, very good, but only if the patient believes in it. All our experience with psychoanalysis teaches us that a treatment can be useful only in the measure that the patient is willing to co-operate. But if his attitude to the treatment is negative, or hostile, we are wasting our time. I do not believe that it can be of help in the present case. But if we were to make the attempt, I would recommend the principle of *similia similibus curantur,* a disease is cured by a similar disease: the patient was made sick by religion. Why not try religious psychotherapy? It can do no harm. What is your feeling, Dr. Martin?"

"Why, yes, Professor Crown, we have no objections to the patient getting spiritual help from a religious representative. It certainly can do no harm. But the trouble is that the representatives of religion, when they approach a patient, especially one in a state of psychic disturbance, become representatives not of their profession, but of ours. They want to play the role of doctor, not of priest or rabbi. They want to treat the patient psychiatrically, psychoanalytically; and sometimes they are a danger to the patient, because they plant in him ideas which complicate his condition. Yes, if we could find a spiritual leader of the patient's own faith who could confine himself to his profession, and not trespass on ours, we would be happy to have him here."

They invited to Bethesda Dr. Silberman, rabbi of the New Rochelle temple, very popular in his congregation, a man of kindly spirit, a visitor in the best homes of his city. Grossman recognized him at once, even reacted with a friendly smile, albeit with some astonishment.

Dr. Silberman was an elderly man of less than medium height, with a small white beard and mild eyes. He spoke to Grossman in homey fashion, and asked him when he would pay a visit to the temple. He also brought him regards from acquaintances. Grossman smiled, nodded, but remained silent. Dr. Silberman went away sad at heart.

"I didn't know that his condition was so bad," he said to Miss Rosenberg. "What a pity! What a pity! I blame it all on Clara's death. He loved her too much, if I may put it that way. I know what a shock her death was. Pity! Pity!" And Dr. Silberman went home.

They invited Dr. Glicksman, the well-known rabbi of Temple Jeshurun in Long Island, Lazar's temple. Dr. Glicksman was middle-aged, well built and well dressed. He had the reputation of being a modern rabbi, with a two-year course of study in psychology at Columbia. He brought Grossman the regards of Louise, whom he had grounded in the elements of the Jewish faith as he had once done with her brother Robert years before. Louise was a member of the Junior Sisterhood of his temple. Everything was now ready, he reported, for the engagement of Louise Grossman and Felix Hanover. It was too bad that they had had to delay it.

"Hurry up and get well, Mr. Grossman," said Dr. Glicksman. "They're all waiting for you."

This time Grossman showed a more positive reaction. He looked at Dr. Glicksman and asked, with some astonishment, "Louise isn't engaged yet? Why?"

"They delayed the engagement for you, Mr. Grossman. They want you to be there. Louise and Katherine. They love you very much, your family."

The old man's face lit up, hearing these words, but he relapsed into silence.

Dr. Martin was particularly interested in Miss Rosenberg's report of this last encounter.

"So he reacted to greetings from his family. It's significant. It's possible that . . ." And he did not finish.

On Sam Grossman's recommendation Lazar also invited Gabriel, the pious one among the Grossman brothers, to visit Isaac. Gabriel had aged a great deal in the brief period since he and Isaac had last met. His white beard had acquired a yellow tinge, and his eyes were sadder and more depressed. His face was as wrinkled as a sponge, and the sponge was soaked with pity for Isaac.

Isaac showed more interest in his brother than in the two rabbis. He spoke very little, but his eyes lost some of their glaze, and it was evident that he was glad to see his brother. Gabriel swayed as he talked; one would have said that he was at his prayers. He began by asking after his brother's health, and then he held forth with a prayerlike chant:

"Repent, Isaac, repent." He quoted: "Repentance, prayer and charity annul the bad decree. Say Psalms, Isaac. Look, I've brought you a little book of the Psalms." He took out the book from his pocket and turned the pages. "Here, repeat this chapter. If it's hard for you to read it in the holy tongue, no matter, repeat it in your language. Tell them to bring you a book of Psalms in English, and read this chapter. When a Jew is in trouble, he recites Psalms. The Judge of the Universe will help you."

It took some time before old Grossman reacted with words. He remained mute till they believed he would not answer. Then suddenly his lips moved, and he said, weakly but clearly:

"God can't help me."

"Don't say that! A Jew daren't say that. What do you mean, the Judge of the Universe can't help you? If not He, who?"

Again there was a long interval, and then again old Grossman pulled himself together and with an effort managed to utter these words:

"Father told me that God can forgive only the sins we commit against Him. He can't forgive the sins we commit against our fellow men."

Reb Gabriel was staggered. He became pale, and his eyes grew larger.

"What is this? Have you, God forbid, been guilty of a sin against a fellow man? If so, the sin can be atoned for and made good, and the man can be persuaded and won over to forgiveness. You have not, God forbidden, stolen from anyone, have you? But even if you have, you can return the theft. You must not talk yourself into despair, Isaac. It is as the doctors say, the work of your imagination. Pray to God, Isaac, recite the Psalms. Father, peace be upon him, and mother, bright be her portion in Paradise, will intercede for you, and you will be helped because of their merit. Now they have nothing against you. Your grandchildren are Jewish, God be thanked. Repent, and give charity, and above all recite the Psalms."

After this point Grossman sank back into his lethargy, and his eyes became glazed again. The nurses gave the signal, and Miss Rosenberg led Gabriel Grossman from the patient's room.

"I wish you a quick and complete healing, with the help of God, Isaac," he said, at the door.

Grossman did not react.

A few days after Gabriel's visit Miss Rosenberg came into Grossman's room and said, "Isaac, I have good news for you. Robert has arrived."

Grossman's eyes opened wide. He was silent, then his lips moved and he began to murmur, as if he were looking for a word. or had found the word and was not able to pronounce it.

"Robert, Robert, Robert," he whispered, finally. "Arrived." His lips were contorted, one could not tell whether it was an attempted smile, or a grimace of pain. "When?" he asked.

"Last night. He came suddenly, by plane. He wasn't expected for some time, but he got an unexpected lift. Would you like to see him?"

He nodded a few times, and then got out the word "Yes."

He became silent and abstracted, and his eyes were no longer glazed. After a few minutes he signaled with his finger to Miss Rosenberg, summoning her. When she came close he put his lips to her ear and whispered, "Were they looked after?"

"Who?" she asked, puzzled.

"The people I hired for the project."

Miss Rosenberg was astounded by the unexpected question. "Yes," she answered. "Lazar gave them three months' pay."

"Good." He sighed, as if a weight had been taken off his heart.

"It was almost as if he'd been waiting for him, when I mentioned Robert's name," said Miss Rosenberg to Dr. Martin.

"It seems he had him in mind," said the superintendent. "He was thinking about him all the time, and we thought his brain was paralyzed. He fooled all of us. I think we have found the key. Bring the young man to him as soon as possible—the sooner the better. I believe we can expect a change in the patient's behavior. It's very possible that the presence of his grandson will precipitate a crisis, but we have to try it."

CHAPTER SEVENTEEN

HOWEVER violent the cataclysms which occur in the course of a man's life, the changes which ensue from them will always be within the framework of his character. It is as though man brought with him out of his unconsciousness a locked and completed unity formed according to an original model, with fixed attributes from which there will be no deviation. All the profound spiritual experiences through which young Robert Grossman had passed during his service with the American army in Germany, and during his association with Chaplain Zimmerman, had served only to bring out the inborn characteristics to which he seemed predestined. This was what saved him from a lapse into despair and spiritual nihilism, to which the vivid reminders of human brutality and vileness might have led another.

In his general appearance Robert suggested one of those great-grandfathers from whom he had a spiritual as well as physical inheritance. The two strains of his heredity mingled and were fused into a unity. For the time being his face had lost that softness which came to him from his mother, for the skin had been roughened; but the eyes still guarded the look of candor and simplicity and timidity which came to him from his Jewish ancestry, and which had such power to win the confidence and affection of those he met. The sharp nose was the legacy of some anonymous Quaker ancestor, and bespoke pioneering resolution and a strong will. You had but to imagine Robert's face set in earlocks and a sprouting black beard—he shaved every day—and his head covered with a skullcap, and you would have had the perfect picture of a young rabbi or of a student in an old Talmudical academy. Whereas if you had thrown over him a black, buttoned cloak, a black felt, broad-brimmed hat, you would have beheld a pious Quaker youth just returned from a meeting where he had declared, in the full presence of the congregation, that it was his desire to be betrothed to a certain Quaker virgin, and to ask the permission of the brethren. There was graven into his face a sadness which was drawn from both his father's and his mother's side, the recollection of persecutions for the faith, of the torture chamber and the lash. And what he had seen of the now emptied concentration camps and the crematoria seemed to have brought out more strongly the inheritance of Jewish and Quaker suffering.

And all this strove for expression on his face as he stood, in a trance of pain, before the invalid in the wheel chair, the skeleton of that massive, bearlike grandfather whom he had so loved, and asked:

"Granddad, do you recognize me?"

The old man nodded repeatedly, and at last produced a sound: "Yes, Robert."

"How are you, granddad?"

"Much better, much better," he said, slowly, and with obvious effort.

"From now on you'll get well very fast, Mr. Grossman," said the plump, motherly nurse.

Miss Rosenberg said nothing. She was struggling with the tears which threatened to pull her into hysteria.

"Are you glad to see me?" asked Robert, looking for something to say.

"Yes, very glad," answered the old man, nodding.

Suddenly Robert observed that his grandfather was beckoning him to come closer. He moved his chair.

"Tell them to go out," murmured the old man.

Robert looked up at Miss Rosenberg and repeated his grandfather's request.

"Come with me, Dorothy," said Rose.

"Dr. Martin told me not to leave his room," answered Dorothy.

"Come. I'll take the responsibility," said Miss Rosenberg firmly, and took the nurse's arm.

"It's not safe."

"I'll take the responsibility," repeated Miss Rosenberg, and practically forced the nurse to accompany her. They closed the door and stood by with beating hearts.

It took the old man a long time to formulate his words. He kept opening and closing his lips, as though he was working on something, trying to break the seal of his secret. He managed at last:

"Robert, I'm not insane, as your father thinks," he said, slowly and laboriously, but quite clearly.

"Father doesn't say that. No, granddad. He only thinks—"

The old man indicated with a motion of his finger that he did not want to be interrupted. Robert stopped.

"No, Robert, I'm not insane," he continued, in a more natural voice. "There was that man against whom I committed a wrong, I want you to know that, Robert. I must make good the wrong. I myself will not be able to do it any more, and so I want you to do it for me, Robert." And he emphasized his words with motions of his finger. "Find him, Robert, or his family. Take a pencil, write down his name."

"No, granddad," cried Robert, turning white. But he took a notebook out of his pocket.

"Write," said the old man, and the command came from the eyes and face as well as from the voice.

"Yes, granddad." Robert trembled, and obeyed.

"His name is Yan. He also had a middle name ... I don't remember ... it begins with an M. ... Have you got it?"

"Yes, granddad."

"And after the M—Kovalsky. Have you got it?"

"Yes, granddad."

"A worker, a machinist, in the Yale factory in Springbrook."

"Yes, granddad."

"In nineteen hundred and four. March. I don't remember the date. It was a Friday. Have you got it?"

"Yes, granddad."

"I took away from that man twenty-seven dollars. Illegally."

"No, granddad."

"Yes. Stole it from him."

"Granddad!" Robert tried to scream the word, but his voice failed him.

"Have you got it?"

Robert nodded.

"A poor man. All the money he had. He came to New York from Springbrook to buy things before his daughter's wedding."

"Granddad!" cried Robert.

305

"Quick," said his grandfather, looking in terror at the door. "They'll come in soon. Have you got it?"

"Yes," said Robert, bending over his notebook.

"It was in the Bowery, in a secondhand clothing store. I was a salesman there. Have you got it?"

Robert nodded.

The old man meditated for a few seconds.

"He lived in Strawberry Hill, here in Springbrook," he continued, now showing signs of exhaustion. "Have you written?"

"Yes, granddad."

"Have you got the name?"

"Yes."

"Read it."

"Yan, middle initial M, Kovalsky."

"Date?"

"March, nineteen four, on a Friday. On the Bowery, in New York."

"Good. Hide it. They'll come in soon."

Robert put away the notebook.

"Tell me that you'll do what I asked."

"Yes, granddad."

"Give me your hand."

The old man took Robert's hand in both of his, and tried to press it. But he had not the strength.

"Good. Thank you, Robert." And he closed his eyes, but held on to Robert's hand. His breast rose and fell, as if he were sighing deeply.

"Don't tell anyone, Robert. They won't let you. Tell no one, do you hear?"

"Yes, granddad."

"Good," whispered the old man. "Call them in."

Robert went to the door and let in Miss Rosenberg and the nurse.

"I hope you had a good talk," said Rose. "Did you, Isaac?"

"Yes," said old Grossman.

"I see that Mr. Grossman is tired. I think we ought to let him rest," said the nurse.

Grossman nodded.

"I'll see you again soon, granddad," said Robert, and he went out with Rose.

"How was it, Robert?" she asked, as they walked down the long corridor. "I hope he didn't tell you about his obsession," she added, noting Robert's distracted look. He did not answer, and from his silence she inferred that he knew everything, and she too became silent.

"Aunt Rose," began Robert after a while—that was the name by which the children had always called her—"will you do something for me? Will you call mother and tell her I'll be late this evening. I want to go and see Dr. Zimmerman. He's not far from here."

"Isn't that the chaplain you wrote us about?"

"Yes."

"He's back already?"

"Yes, he came back before me, and he's at his temple again. He's also giving a course at the university near here. It's only an hour away by train. I want to see him—I'll be killing two birds with one stone."

"Your dad will be waiting for you. He'll be impatient to hear what you think of your grandfather's condition."

"I'll get home in the evening, and I'll tell him."

He said good-by to Rose and set out for the railroad station.

Now he sat with Dr. Zimmerman in his study. The rabbi had the face of a man of forty and the white hair of a man of sixty. But there seemed to be more old age in the few remaining black hairs than in the white shock that surrounded them. It could be seen that age had come upon him suddenly, like a robber leaping upon his victim. But the eyes were big and lively, and their black depths seemed filled with the courage and strength to meet every adversity. They were overshadowed and, as it were, held in check by immense gray brows.

Rabbi Zimmerman listened with the profoundest interest to Robert's recital. Of all the painful experiences which young Robert had known in his life, this was the most shattering, and the most personal.

"He gave me the man's name, and the time and place of the

terrible incident," wound up Robert, and his voice choked on his tears.

Dr. Zimmerman thought for a long time, wrinkling his lofty forehead and biting his lips. Then his face lit up with a gentle and sympathetic smile.

"I think you'll have to tell all this to your father," he said firmly.

"Dr. Zimmerman, my grandfather absolutely forbade me to do that. He warned me they would only prevent me from carrying out his wish, because they think it's all a delusion. Miss Rosenberg already said it."

"You'll have to tell everything to your father, and show him what you've put down in your notebook."

"But I gave my word that I wouldn't do that."

"Robert, you'll have to break your word. A man's life is at stake, the peace of a man's soul which wants to return to its Father in heaven. You will have to do it. I order you."

"How can I?" cried Robert, desperately. "They believe he's mad, out of his mind, and here he is, struggling with himself, tormented."

"That is why you must speak, Robert. You can't do anything without your father's consent."

"And what if my father forbids me to mix in the matter?"

"Then we shall see. I'll talk to him."

"And you'll help me?"

"Certainly. Tell your father that I want to see him."

"Yes, Dr. Zimmerman."

"Now go, and God go with you."

Max Brown would have felt that his triumph over Davis, the "proud Yankee," was complete, if he had not been haunted by the fear that Lazar might spoil everything by a false step. Was Brown filled with rancor against the old man, so that it was a matter of life and death with him to keep him where he was? By no means. On the contrary, he genuinely sympathized with Isaac Grossman's condition. Apart from his professional ambition he was concerned for the good name of his friend Lazar Grossman, of Lazar's family, and of the firm; and a reopening of the case would again endanger that name. So far, thank God, everything had gone well. And now, suddenly, a man appeared on the scene, and the structure

308

which Brown had erected for the safeguarding of the Grossman name was threatened with destruction. But Brown's own reputation was now at stake, too. If old Grossman were now declared sane, Brown and his client would both be made to look like swindlers and intriguers. And who would gain anything thereby? The old man was anyhow sick, with little prospect of life. What difference did it make whether he was dying sane or insane?

At Lazar's request he had come to the conference with Dr. Zimmerman. He listened patiently while the rabbi stated his view of the case. Underneath the big, bald skull, which shone with a metallic luster, his brain worked swiftly, grinding into dust the rabbi's arguments. And when Dr. Zimmerman had ended, Brown waited for Lazar to speak.

In the couple of days which had elapsed since Robert brought the report from his grandfather, Lazar had aged perceptibly. The hair on his temples had become visibly grayer; and lines had formed on his face, the marks of sleepless nights. What his son had told him changed completely the aspect of the case, and Lazar Grossman stood before a blank wall, perplexed and helpless.

"Has anyone tried to find out whether there is any substance in your father's statements?" asked Dr. Zimmerman. "Has anyone tried to discover whether there ever was such a person as this Kovalsky?"

"We knew of the man only from father's talk, and we never took that seriously: neither we here, nor the doctors. And we had reason enough for our stand. Hadn't my father himself, with the help of Mr. Silverstein, and Mike the waiter, tried to find that fictitious person? My father settled an annuity on one so-called Kovalsky. Then there was a man who tried to blackmail him. And all this pursuit of a nonexistent Kovalsky worked so on my father's nerves that he began to have wilder and wilder hallucinations," said Lazar in a broken voice.

"But this time he gave not only the name, but the time and place."

"But in God's name, he talked himself into the belief that this man is to be found in the kitchen of that waiter's restaurant, where he works as a dishwasher, and my father went there to look for him. There you have time and place—and it's nothing but a fixation. It's part of the workings of his guilt complex, which haunts

309

him in the nights. Do you know anything, Rabbi Zimmerman, about my father's early history, and about the terror-stories with which his father tried to bring him up as a Jew?"

"Yes, I do. I talked with your father's brother, Sam Grossman, before I came here."

"You met my Uncle Sam?" asked Lazar, astonished.

"Yes, I wanted to know every possible detail of his sickness."

Attorney Brown could no longer keep quiet. "Tell us, Dr. Zimmerman," he broke in, "what reason have you, if I may ask, for looking into the history of Mr. Grossman's sickness?"

"I will tell you, Mr. Brown. As a rabbi, and a spiritual guide for those who seek my counsel—as it was sought by my young friend Robert—I became deeply interested in the Grossman case. It touches me closely in my capacity as spiritual adviser. It is—as a case—characteristic of those who have never tried to establish their own contact with God, but who have accepted Him through the intermediary of a father, or mother, or teacher. This indirect relationship to God, which is not based on a personal experience of Him but on the experience of another, I call 'father-worship.' "

Lazar and attorney Brown looked at each other. The rabbi's words sounded strange and remote.

"Dr. Zimmerman, will you be good enough to explain more exactly what you mean by 'father-worship.' Mr. Grossman and I don't understand you," said Brown.

"It is quite simple," said Dr. Zimmerman tranquilly. "My experience as a spiritual guide in congregations, and as a chaplain at the front, has convinced me that the average American businessman or professional, Jew or Christian, is so absorbed in his daily tasks that he has no time left—even if he has the will—for spiritual matters; such as seeking his own contact with God, for instance. So he accepts a ready-made God from his father, or his mother, or his religious teacher, and leaves it to father, or mother, or the reverend, to deal with God for him. This suffices as long as everything goes well. But should a crisis arise and he must seek God's help, a conflict sets in. Then, since he sees God only through the eyes of his parents, or a teacher, he must accept another's conception of God, having none of his own. But God is not static; He is not frozen into the framework of a particular generation; He is an eternal spring of renewed spiritual life; and every man must re-discover God for himself. He must be his own Abraham."

"Are we to understand, Dr. Zimmerman, that you are opposed to tradition?" asked attorney Brown with a touch of irony, and glanced at Lazar.

"No, God forbid, I am not opposed to tradition. Tradition is a form of life. It is music, the form of a hymn to God. Faith is prayer to God, the silent prayer which a man carries in his heart, his secret with God, which he entrusts to God in the hour of his need. Your father's conflict, Mr. Grossman, arose from the fact that he had not his own prayer to God but used his father's. But he did not possess his father's tradition, which harmonized with his father's prayer. The form of your father's life did not follow the tradition—it was modern. But his God came to him from his father. The environ-ment he lived in, too, was different from his father's, so that his conceptions of right and wrong, even of decency, which he drew in with the air he breathed in a free world, were also different. This is your father's tragedy. And not his alone. It is the tragedy of a whole generation, the second generation, and the third, which have had no time to find their own God and have taken Him over from their parents. Your father is not the only one who suffers from this conflict. Every spiritual leader, every psychiatrist, will tell you of similar conflicts. The particular point about your father is that he is honest to the marrow of his bones. A sensitive con-science. That is why he has taken the matter so to heart. Others with similar problems—and who in your father's generation is without them?—take them more lightly. They rely on their mothers in a bright paradise to straighten things out for them. As far as I understand your father's case, Mr. Grossman, I believe he can be helped by one who is a religious teacher. Your father's is a spiritual case. If you will permit me, and give me the possibility, I would like to undertake his treatment."

Lazar felt his interest awakening. "What do you propose to do?" he asked.

"We must first find out whether there was such a Kovalsky in your father's life, or whether it is a fiction."

"How?"

"Simply enough. Your father has now given Robert the details

—name, date, place of employment. There must be a record in the Yale factory. Has anyone ever looked into it?"

"No, of course not."

"And then again, the man was probably a Catholic, because he was Polish. He probably belonged to a Catholic church. One could make inquiry there, too."

"Dr. Zimmerman, isn't it too late?" asked the lawyer.

"What is too late?"

"This whole business you propose to start"—and Brown leaned his heavy body over toward the rabbi. "Listen to me, Dr. Zimmerman. You are a wise man, with much experience. You are the spiritual guide of many families. I believe I do not exaggerate when I say that many secrets have been confided to you, and that you consider them your sacred trust. Let us assume that inquiry will reveal that there was such a man, and there was such an incident, what good will it do? Whom will it help? The sick man? No. This Kovalsky, if he ever existed, is long since dead. It won't help Mr. Grossman here, or his family; on the contrary, it will be a misfortune for them. Do you understand where this leads to? All sorts of suspicions will be set afloat concerning Mr. Isaac Grossman's past, with consequent reflections on the whole family, on Isaac Grossman's son, on his grandchildren. All sorts of people will be provided with an opportunity to come forward with claims —as has already happened in fact. That is all that you can achieve with your investigation. Let us be realistic. Mr. Grossman senior has not long to live. The doctor says his heart has been affected. Why do you not let him die in peace? Why stir him up? Let the confession which he made to his grandson remain a family secret."

"It is precisely because I want him to die in peace that I will not let matters stand where they are. Mr. Brown, have you ever seen men die? Hundreds of young men have died in my arms. I eased their way into death, young men of our faith, and of the Christian faith. Some went with prayers which hovered like a smile on their lips, some went with curses distorting their faces; all were mortally afraid of the unknown which stared at them out of the mystery of the infinite. In the last moment of their passage into eternity they relive their lives. Their fate hangs on a hair, and it is according to the state of their conscience that they surrender to the hands stretched to them out of the unknown. If it is a clear conscience, they surrender with hope, as if into the arms of a mother. But if it is not a clear conscience, they surrender with horror, as into the claws of a demon. The life of a man trembles in the balance of his last moment before death. Reward and punishment are in us, so are heaven and hell. As the man lived, so he dies. Mr. Grossman, if you want to give meaning to your father's life, let him die in peace."

Lazar was silent.

"Are you so sure, Dr. Zimmerman, that you can restore to Mr. Grossman the peace which his sickness has destroyed?" asked Brown, in an unfriendly voice.

"That is not in my hands, it is in God's hands. Everything that faith and experience have taught me bids me make the effort, if I get permission."

"And with this uncertainty as to the issue, you are prepared to expose Mr. Grossman's family to the extremest dangers, Dr. Zimmerman?"

"I do not see any dangers, Mr. Brown. Suppose it is discovered that Mr. Grossman committed an error in his youth. It can, to begin with, be made good. My God, what is it, after all? Who of us has not committed errors? I don't see how this would in any way reflect on Mr. Grossman's family, so that for its sake we must sacrifice a life."

"Sacrifice a life? That's putting it too harshly, Dr. Zimmerman," said Brown, with some agitation.

"I can't help myself. If you will not let a man set right an error which he once committed, and you prevent him from dying in the grace of God, it is, as I see it, sacrificing a life. Our sages have said: Repent one day before your death. It is never too late to right a wrong and to die at peace with God."

"What do you want us to do, Dr. Zimmerman?" asked Lazar.

"The first thing I want is your permission to see your father, and to talk with him."

"You have my permission, Dr. Zimmerman. But it also depends on Dr. Martin, the superintendent of Bethesda. Dr. Martin informed me that my father was very weak after Robert saw him. Every visit excites him. I'll call Dr. Martin and ask him. Meanwhile I want to thank you for coming here, Dr. Zimmerman, and

313

for your interest in my father. I'll let you know of Dr. Martin's decision through Robert."

"I hope you are not going to do it, Lazar," said Brown uneasily when the rabbi had left.

"Dr. Martin won't let him anyhow. He feels that all these visits from rabbis don't do father any good. He can't sleep after them. But I've got to do something for Robert's sake. Robert believes in this rabbi as he believes in God."

"A fine rabbi, I must say, who doesn't hold with tradition. You heard what he called it: father-worship. I thought rabbis were all for honoring one's father and mother. There's something wrong with all the GI's who've come back from the war. Something happened to them. Here, in their minds," said Brown.

"Yes, you're right. It's touched Robert, too. He's not the same boy at all." Lazar spoke slowly and thoughtfully. "I'm afraid I'm going to have a lot of trouble with him."

CHAPTER EIGHTEEN

"SON, I'm sorry to have to say this, but I'm afraid that Dr. Zimmerman can't see granddad for the time being. Dr. Martin is absolutely opposed to it. Visits are very tiring for granddad, and Dr. Martin is afraid of a relapse—it often happens with nervous ailments. Granddad must have complete rest and peace. That's Dr. Martin's decision, and we have to bow to it. Tell Dr. Zimmerman that I appreciate deeply his interest, and I thank him; and as soon as Dr. Martin decides that granddad can receive guests again, Dr. Zimmerman will be the first one."

Robert trembled and turned white; but he tightened his lips and uttered no word. Was there, he asked himself, something in the rumors which had reached his ears about material motives behind the Grossman case? Could his father, whom he had worshiped all his life as the personification of honesty and integrity, be guilty of such a thing? What was he to think, after his grandfather's warning against his father, after the talk he had heard, and now after the decision to keep Dr. Zimmerman away? He went out to Springbrook. He wanted to find out more about his grandfather's actual condition. He wanted also to talk the whole matter over with Aunt Rose, for even though she too was under the same shadow of suspicion, he could not admit the consequences to himself.

"Robert," said Miss Rosenberg radiantly, "I don't know what you did with your grandfather, but your visit was like a miracle medicine. He's simply another person. For the first time in I don't know how long he slept peacefully through the night."

"Father said that visits tire him, and Dr. Martin wants no more visitors," said Robert, and there was a fiery light in his eyes which Miss Rosenberg had never seen there before.

"Why, yes, he felt very tired when you left. That's only natural, what with seeing you at last. He'd looked forward to it so. It was

bound to exhaust him. Dr. Martin expected something worse—
a regular crisis. But that night was the best he's spent here. Last
night, too, he slept well. He's out there in the garden now. He went
of his own free will. He's warming himself in the sun. Do you
want to see him?"

"I'm afraid I'm a bit too excited myself today. I'll see him another time."

"What's the matter with you, Robert?" She looked at him
anxiously, trying to read his mind.

"Nothing." His lips were drawn in a grimace of repression. Rose
knew that look.

"Robert, what has happened?"

"Nothing," he repeated; but his boyish anger was written clearly
on his face. He went on quietly: "I have a suspicion that you're
keeping grandfather here not because he's sick, but for some other
reason."

"What are you saying?" She became stony. "What other reason
can there be?"

"A material and selfish reason. Father, Brown, even you. You've
ganged up on him to keep him a prisoner in the institution."

"Robert! Do you know—wait—have you been talking with Mr.
Silverstein?"

"No, I haven't seen him. But I'm going to. I've heard of him.
And I want to see Davis, too. I want them to know my opinion
about the whole business."

"Have you gone out of your mind, Robert? Accusing your father
of such a crime! And is that what you think of me, you stupid
boy?" The tears started to her eyes. "If that's the case, I've had
enough. I'm through with it all." She made a motion as if to
leave him.

"If it isn't so," he asked, holding her arm, "why won't father
let Dr. Zimmerman see him? Forgive me, Aunt Rose, I didn't
mean to include you—that slipped out."

"Your father won't let Dr. Zimmerman see granddad? I didn't
know about that." And now the tears ran over, and she freed herself and walked toward the gate.

"Don't go away, Aunt Rose, I beg you." He followed her. "I
didn't mean you, you see. Forgive me. I don't know what I'm saying. I'm going out of my mind."

316

The boyish voice, familiar, intimate, touching deep chords in her heart, made her stop. "Come," she said, and led him to a shadowed corner of the garden. "Sit down with me on this bench, and tell me what's happened."

"When I saw granddad he told me everything that he has on his conscience: about the man he wronged, about the money he took from him, how much it was, where it happened, and when. He made me write it all down in my notebook, and he made me promise that I would right the wrong, because he was no longer able to do it. He also made me promise that I wouldn't tell anybody, not even you, because you all consider him mad. But, Aunt Rose, he isn't mad. He spoke sanely and normally, just as you and I are speaking. I went away to Dr. Zimmerman and confided in him, and Dr. Zimmerman made me tell father all about it. Father still tried to convince me that granddad is mentally ill. He told me about granddad's behavior in Springbrook, and about a letter he gave a waiter there, and about the project which granddad wanted to name after that man. He also told me how granddad, in a fit of insanity, tore up grandmother's photograph, and other things like that."

"Listen, Robert. About the photograph. Imagine this: after your visit I found a photograph of grandmother on the table near your grandfather's bed." Her voice trembled. "The one he tore up, you know, was the big one, of grandmother in her Spanish costume. It used to stand on the piano. It seems your grandfather hated that photograph. The one I found is an old one, of grandmother when she was a girl. I don't know where he's been keeping it; he must have had it with him all the time. But he took it out only after your visit."

"Poor granddad! He took grandmother with him into the lunatic asylum," said Robert.

"You know, this gave me the first inkling that your grandfather is not sick. He knows what he's doing. You reconciled him to his family."

"Have you told father?"

"No, not yet."

"Why?"

"I just don't know." A slight blush appeared on the old-maidish face, like the reflection of a sunken sun.

317

"Enough!" said Robert. "You know, I asked dad to see Dr. Zimmerman. Dr. Zimmerman left everything and came to the city, when father invited him. I wasn't there at the interview, but father had the firm's lawyer there as though this was a business transaction. Dr. Zimmerman told me what happened. He tried—Dr. Zimmerman, I mean—to show them that the first thing they had to do was to find out whether there ever was such a man as granddad talks about. But they couldn't see it. All they think about is the danger to the family's reputation—but that's something *I* can't see. Must they sacrifice grandfather's peace of mind, his very life, for the sake of the family? My God, what's happened to dad? Is he so eaten up by materialism that he has no feeling left for right and justice?"

"Don't speak like that about your father. I know your father. It's not a matter of business. It's the honor of the family, which grandmother raised so high, that matters to him."

"Family, family! I can't bear that word any more."

"Don't talk like that, Robert."

"I feel poisoned, Aunt Rose."

"Tell me what happened after that."

"There's nothing more to tell. Dr. Zimmerman begged father to let him see granddad. Just think, Aunt Rose. Dr. Zimmerman is doing all this out of the goodness of his heart. He's putting all his work to one side. I'm certain that he can help granddad. I've seen him help scores of our boys who came to him half crazy, ready to commit suicide. He straightened all of them out. Dad won't let him see granddad because he's afraid! He's afraid Dr. Zimmerman will cure granddad."

"I don't understand it," murmured Rose. "I think your grandfather would want to meet Dr. Zimmerman. I remember the letter you wrote your grandfather about him. Your grandfather would like to thank him for everything he's done for you."

"What makes you say all this, Aunt Rose?"

"Your grandfather once asked after him. In fact he mentioned something about wanting to meet him."

"But they won't let it happen."

"Let me speak with your father, Robert. I'll call him and ask him to speak with Dr. Martin and have him give Dr. Zimmerman a permit."

"Dad won't do it. Brown won't let him."

"He'll have to do it," said Rose, firmly.

"And suppose he won't."

"In that case we'll go to Davis. We'll tell him everything, and we'll prepare an appeal from the court's decision."

"Are you ready to do all that?" asked Robert, startled.

"Certainly. If your father will refuse me I shall have to suspect him the way you suspected me." She rose. "Meanwhile, Robert, don't do anything which might lead to a public scandal. Don't go to Silverstein. Leave everything to me. Come—do you want to see your grandfather? He's sitting in the garden."

"No, Aunt Rose. I'm too upset. Another time. I'll go and see Dr. Zimmerman."

"Wait. Let me talk with your father, first," said Rose, and went to telephone.

She spoke to Lazar decisively. She demanded that he call Dr. Martin without delay and have him issue the permit to Dr. Zimmerman to see Lazar's father. The old man had himself asked for it.

"I see Robert has been with you already," said Lazar.

"Yes, he has. And I know everything. And I want to tell you, Lazar, that you've got to let Dr. Zimmerman see your father if you don't want to lose your son—after having lost your father. And me, too," she added, "if that matters to you."

"Very well, very well. If that's the way you feel about it I'll call Dr. Martin; but I don't want the rabbi to start any investigations. Brown won't stand for that. Neither will I."

"Mr. Brown is your misfortune, Lazar. But we'll discuss that later. Call Dr. Martin. Robert is waiting here. Then I'll go and get Dr. Zimmerman."

Dr. Martin issued the permit, on condition that Dr. Zimmerman should make this a "pastoral visit" for purely religious psychotherapy, without reference to the patient's particular mania which was responsible for his confinement in Bethesda. The rabbi agreed to stay strictly within his own professional field, and to speak with the patient as a religious teacher, and not as a psychiatrist.

Dr. Martin himself, accompanied by Robert, led Dr. Zimmerman into Grossman's room. Robert introduced the rabbi to his

319

grandfather, who smiled sadly and, with astonishing clarity, thanked Dr. Zimmerman for the good influence he had been in his grandson's life. Dr. Martin and Robert then left Dr. Zimmerman with the patient.

"May I speak to you freely, Mr. Grossman?" asked Dr. Zimmerman.

"Yes, yes."

"And put a number of questions to you?"

"Why not?"

"You don't have to answer them if you don't want to, Mr. Grossman. I am neither a lawyer nor a doctor. I am only a rabbi, a religious teacher, or a spiritual guide, if you like."

"I shall answer if I want to, and if I don't, I won't," said Grossman.

"Good. That's the way I want it. May I begin?"

"Ask."

"Do you believe in God, Mr. Grossman?"

"What do you mean?"

"Do you know that there is a God who rules the world?"

"What kind of question is that? Of course I know there is a God who rules the world."

"How do you know it?"

"How? Am I not a Jew? I was brought up in the Jewish faith, and when I was a child my father taught me that there is a God who rules the world."

"Your father taught you?"

"Certainly. When he came home evenings from work he would barely have opened the door before he asked: 'Has Isaac said his prayers?'"

"And he told you that you must fear God?"

"Ah, how he frightened me about that. For the least sin, like omitting the benediction over a bite of bread, or for failing to wash your hands, you would be boiled and roasted in hell."

"Did he tell you that we ought to love God?"

"Surely. He kept hammering into us that we ought to thank God for every mouthful of food, every drink of water. We must never stop praying to Him, he said, never stop repeating the prayers in the *siddur.*"

"Or else—"

"Or else it was fire and brimstone down there."

"But you yourself, did you not find out without your father that there is a God set over the world?"

"Why did I have to find it out for myself? Didn't I already know about it? I had it driven deep enough into me, with terrible stories, and threats, and blows."

"Mr. Grossman, you are, as everyone knows, a builder of hotels and theaters and developments. Did you get that profession from your father?"

"From my father?" A smile hovered over Grossman's lips. "Not by a thousand miles. If my father had had his way I would have been a Hebrew teacher, or something in that line. I tried my hand at all sorts of work until I found what I was best fitted for."

"Mr. Grossman, if you found that you could make more money in some other line, would you change over? Pardon me for asking this question."

"No, I don't think I would. I've always loved my profession. I've always wanted to fill vacant places with buildings. It's as if God created me for this purpose."

"So you tried, for the sake of your livelihood, to find what you were best fitted for. Wasn't it just as important for you to find God for yourself, and not to rely on your parents in this regard any more than you relied on them in regard to your livelihood?"

"Yes, it may be so, but I never gave it a thought," said the old man.

"Every man must find out for himself that there is a God set over the world, just as he must find out other things for himself. For instance—forgive me for this question—did you love your wife?"

"Yes, certainly I loved her. What kind of question is that?"

"Did you love her because your father told you to love her, or because you understood that your father loved your mother?"

"That's a bit childish. I did not love her because I was told to by my father, or because my father loved my mother—my poor mother. I don't know, as a matter of fact, whether my father was aware of her devotion. He believed that's how things ought to be, and that settled it. I loved my wife because I wanted to love her. My mother didn't like the match, as it happens. She thought I could do much better. But of course I did not listen."

321

"Good, my friend. Thus it is with love of God, too. When we discover for ourselves that God is there, love follows of its own accord. Have there not been incidents in the course of your long life when you felt, either immediately, or soon after, as though you had been touched by God's hand? Has it never seemed to you as if God had turned His glance from all the world, from the whole of creation, upon you, leaving everything else to look upon you from heaven, to occupy Himself with you alone, and with your fate? Think back."

Grossman meditated.

"Yes, there have been such moments. I think there have. For instance, when I saw my wife for the first time. I think it was the touch of God's hand."

"That is it, my friend, that is it." The rabbi's face lit up with joy. "Were there other such moments in your life?"

"There were. Of course. In my family life, in business, in other situations. You're up against a blank wall, there's no way through or round—that's what your common sense tells you, and you must retreat—and all of a sudden something comes, something from deep within, and says: 'Don't trust your common sense.' And I do the opposite of what my common sense tells me, and it turns out that the inward feeling, not the common sense, was right."

"That was the hand of God that guided you, my friend. Have you ever prayed?"

"What kind of question is that? On the New Year, and on the Day of Atonement, I always said prayers in the orthodox synagogue where my father had prayed. But for the rest of the year I relied on my mother. She would say all the prayers for me."

"I don't mean saying prayers. I mean praying. Has there never been an hour of need, of misery, when you prayed to God to help you?"

Grossman sank back into his memories.

"There have been such moments. When my wife got her first heart attack. It was probably my fault, too—or so I thought. I prayed to God in my heart: Do not leave me alone in the world, I cannot live without her. And she recovered. Then I thought to myself that perhaps it was my prayer. But I couldn't say for sure. I didn't believe I was worthy of God's help; but I thought that perhaps He had helped me for the sake of my mother."

"You do believe, then, that there is an ear which listens to our prayers, and a power which can help us. That is what we call God. And what do you think, Mr. Grossman—is this God whom you and I believe in, whom everyone, all the world, all the peoples of the world, believe in, is He a just God?"

"Certainly He is a just God."

"And good?"

"That I can't say. I believe there is a God, and that He is a just God, and that He judges us according to our deeds, as my father taught me."

"Did not your father teach you that if a man has sinned against God, and prays to Him with a pure heart, and repents, and promises not to sin again, God will forgive him his sin?"

"Yes, my father taught me that on the Day of Atonement God forgives all the sins committed against Him in the past year; but only the sins against Him, like omitting a prayer, eating with unwashed hands, even desecrating the Sabbath. But never the sins we have committed against our fellow men. The sin of man against man God cannot forgive. Only the man sinned against, the wronged man, can do that." And a cloud settled over Grossman's eyes, as he sank into thought.

"And so your father set a limitation on God? I shall not enter into a dispute with your father. I believe that all human beings belong to God, that all our deeds come up before Him, and that He alone can forgive us. 'What man is without sin?' Every one of us sins, against God, against our fellow men. And all the sins, like all the good deeds, are assembled in one place. When a man sins against a fellow man, he sins likewise against God. For how do we know of sin and virtue, evil deeds and good deeds, if not through God's commandments? Yes, God is a clearinghouse for all our deeds. He can pay one sinner with the sin of another, so that in Him all accounts are straightened out."

"God is a clearinghouse? I never thought of that," said Grossman, brightening, as if the word had awakened his hope.

"But suppose we grant your father's view, that God cannot forgive us our sins against our fellow men. Suppose we grant that God is just, not good. When He sits in judgment, His sentence, as you say, is a just one. Very well. Now imagine that you are a judge. God has appointed you a judge. And a man appears before you, saying, 'I have sinned against another man. I have wronged him. I cannot right the wrong because the man is no longer about, he has disappeared, or he is dead. I have done everything in my power to find him, but in vain.' If you, the judge, are convinced that the guilty man has done everything in his power, if, further, he has paid in full measure for his sin, and has done good, and is prepared to do good further in recompense for his sin, would you, the judge, condemn that man to destruction, or would you comfort him? Would you not say: 'I know you committed the sin. But I also know that you exerted yourself to the utmost to right the wrong. Go home and beg God to forgive you. And if God forgives you, the man will forgive you too.'"

Old Grossman listened with the closest concentration. He actually imagined himself in the situation described by the rabbi: he saw himself as a judge, he saw a man before him, he thought long and hard. The man before him was himself, and he himself was the judge.

"Yes," he said, softly, "it seems to me that I would act as you say."

"And you, the judge, would not punish him?"

"No. I would command him to compensate for the sin with good deeds."

"You would forgive him?"

"If it were up to me."

"Do you think, then, that you are more righteous than God, and a better judge than He? If you, a human being, a thing of flesh and blood, believe that your sentence is a just one, and you would not leave the sinner in torment, why should you believe that God is cruel enough to let a man suffer for a sin which he has tried to set right, but which it was beyond his power to set right?"

The old man was silent, as if he were holding counsel with himself. After a while he said, "Robert told how, when you were a chaplain during the war, you saw many of our sons through the gates of death. Do you believe in reward and punishment in another world?"

"Certainly I believe. If I didn't, how could I have been a chaplain? This is the hope—no, not the hope, the certainty, which young people who sacrifice themselves for us on the very threshold of life take with them when they leave us: their eyes are turned on us at the last moment, with this certainty in them. How could I confirm their certainty, and deepen their comfort if, God forbid, I did not believe in this truth? It is all that they have."

"If God rewards us for the good deeds we do on earth, He must punish us for our wicked deeds. And if there is a paradise, as you assure our boys when they die, then there must be a hell."

"The reward and punishment I believe in is not physical. All people have their idea of the life beyond this—I mean, of course, all those that believe—and it is based on the conceptions that they have of this life. That is a mistake. We do not know how it will appear to us, and in what manner we will come to know our continued existence in another life. And we Jews may not imagine that which is hidden, or seek to investigate it—it is written so. We believe there is an everlasting grace of God which never abandons us. This grace is made more manifest to us as we throw off the external trappings which accompany the soul. We then learn to cleave to God through other emotions than those we have known in our earthly life. And we then are steeped in the light of the *Shekhinah,* the indwelling, as that condition is called among us. All souls, even the souls of sinners, reach finally the stage of communion with God's being. Perhaps we must first pass through a process of purification, a restoration of that which we have lost, a removal of the stains left upon our souls by our sins. For all souls, even of sinners, are a part of the Divinity above, and all are gathered in the end under the wings of the *Shekhinah*. God is a Father of mercy and grace, as Moses taught us."

There were many long pauses, many long silences, in the conversation. Old Grossman thought hard. Then, turning his big, watery eyes on Dr. Zimmerman, he asked: "Do you think, rabbi, that sinners, such as have not been able to right the wrongs they have committed, will also be admitted at the gates of mercy in the world to come, as my mother, peace be upon her, said?" And the old man stammered with anxiety.

"Our sages have taught us this saying: 'Where the true penitent stands not even the saint can stand.' This means that when a sinner repents he is higher than a saint who has never sinned."

"Are you an ordained rabbi?" asked Grossman suddenly.

"Certainly I am an ordained rabbi," answered Dr. Zimmerman in some astonishment.

"I mean, are you authorized to answer religious and ritualistic questions, and to pronounce judgments, like a real rabbi?"

A smile passed over Dr. Zimmerman's face, but he answered firmly and earnestly: "I am a rabbi and a teacher in Israel; with the attestations which have been issued to me by my teachers I have the right to declare clean that which is clean, and unclean that which is unclean. And according to the judgment rendered here below, it is a judgment rendered above, as our sages have taught us."

The old man pondered this reply, then smiled and stretched out his hand. "I thank you, rabbi."

"I see you are tired. It's enough for today. We'll meet again."

"I thank you, rabbi. And come again, soon." And the old man put his hand before his eyes.

Dr. Zimmerman called in the nurse, then took his departure.

That evening Grossman refused the sedative which his nurse handed him. "I'm going to sleep well without that," he said. "Yes, I shall sleep, let me be."

The nurse passed the word to her relief to keep a special watch on the patient.

He did not sleep that night. There passed ceaselessly before him not the hallucinations and horrors which usually lay in wait for him on sleepless nights, but memories of things that had been in reality, faces of men and women he had known. He made a moral accounting with himself as he reviewed his actions while he asked himself: "Why has God punished me so?" He understood the wrongs he had done in the course of his life's activities, wrongs which he had never acknowledged as such. There stood before him, with terrified eyes and distorted lips, the men whom he had robbed, through the bank, of their last possessions and their last hopes, in the Miami crash, sending them back to their homes with a railroad ticket and saying: "That's all I can do for you." He no longer dismissed his conscience by saying that they would have done the same to him if the positions had been reversed. No, he knew that he bore the responsibility for his actions, no matter what others would have done in his place. It was not "business"; it was sin, even though according to business usage. And there were other deeds which lay like burdens on his shoulders, far

326

heavier than the wrong which he had done to Kovalsky. And when the latter pushed himself forward and stood before him, the haunting presence which had been the shadow in his life, Grossman pushed him away again, and said, "You I have paid full measure. In you God has punished me for my sins." And he thrust away from him the hands that wanted to cling to him.

He wanted to pray to God; not to repeat prayers, to go through the long, hard prayers in the book, as he had done with the Psalm which his brother had picked out for him in the little Psalm book, beginning with the words: "He that dwelleth in the secret places of the most high." He wanted to pray with his own words, and he began:

"God, have mercy on me. Let me not die before I have righted the wrong. . . ." And he wept.

CHAPTER NINETEEN

ON the following morning the nurse found her patient considerably changed, both in appearance and bearing. He was very tired, very weak, and hollow-eyed with sleeplessness. Yet within the sockets the eyes themselves no longer had their glazed look; they were informed by an unwonted brightness. His spirit, too, belied his physical condition. He had regained a great measure of self-assurance, and he showed a will power which the nurse had never observed in him before. She could no longer issue instructions; the commands came from him. He demanded a change of food; he was going to eat what he liked. No milk, he said, but coffee; and he had always loathed cocoa, even when he was a child. And how was it, he asked, only half in jest, that this great institution of Bethesda didn't know how to prepare a real man's meal, and had nothing better to offer a patient than soft-boiled eggs, milk-toast, and similar dishes fit only for children?

And what was worse, he positively refused to touch the pills which he was supposed to take after every meal.

"Take them away!" he said sternly.

He would not submit to interrogation by the visiting doctor.

"Send Dr. Martin in!" he ordered.

Dr. Martin listened first to the nurse's report: how the patient had slept badly in the night, how she had even heard him weeping, and how, this morning, he had become downright unmanageable.

"There's your religious psychotherapy!" muttered Dr. Martin. Then he went in to Isaac Grossman.

"You simply mustn't overexert yourself," he began, at once. "You've got to relax, take up some easy occupation, Look, Mr. Grossman, why don't you try and take up some light manual work? Occupational therapy—it's been a great help to so many patients here in Bethesda. We've got the very finest equipment, and first-

328

class instructors. Choose your own craft. Believe me, you need something to help you pass the time. Get to know some of the other guests, visit with them. It doesn't do you any good to sit brooding by yourself, or listening to sermons. You don't need spiritual psychotherapy, you need work, play."

"I need to be let out of here!" answered Grossman abruptly. "Why do you keep me here? Am I a criminal, that I should be held a prisoner?"

"Mr. Grossman, calm yourself. Do you know why you are here? For your own good. The day will come when you'll bless us for what we're doing for you. You're not in a prison, and you're not in an asylum. You're in a sanatorium, a health institute. Your son can take you out whenever he likes. I'll talk it over with him."

Dr. Martin walked toward the door.

"Listen, doctor. Give me back my papers. I want to go over them again."

"What papers?"

"The plans of my project, which you've taken away from me."

"I can't do that, Mr. Grossman, without your son's permission. I'll talk it over with him. Meanwhile you've got to calm down, Mr. Grossman."

And Dr. Martin went out of the door, giving the nurse a quick look of warning and admonition.

He reported at once to Lazar, by telephone.

"Mr. Grossman, I regret to advise you that this rabbi—Dr. Zimmerman, is it?—hasn't done your father any good. On the contrary. The only effect has been to throw your father into a state of excitement and confusion, and reawaken his guilt complex, together with his hallucination, which we'd managed to weaken. He's back in his old condition, and it looks as though we'll have to isolate him again."

"That's terribly disturbing news, Dr. Martin, and I can't tell you how bad I feel about it. I suppose I'm to blame. But my son, and Miss Rosenberg, were so insistent to have Dr. Zimmerman see my father. And Miss Rosenberg only just phoned me to say that the rabbi's visit did my father a lot of good. She says that after the visit my father was much livelier, and much more active."

"Livelier? More active? Well! Perhaps she meant too lively, too active. It's very clear that the rabbi didn't know where to stop.

He didn't talk to your father like a rabbi at all, but as if he thought himself to be a professional psychiatrist. And the result is that he completely confused him, and precipitated a crisis. As for Miss Rosenberg's report, Mr. Grossman, I must tell you that it's my intention to stop her visits. Your father needs relaxation and rest; he has to forget, he has to occupy himself with something. All Miss Rosenberg does for him is remind him of his past."

"Do what you think best, Dr. Martin. And yes—the rabbi phoned me, too. He wants to see me and tell me of his visit with my father. Wouldn't you like to be there too, Dr. Martin?"

"Yes, by all means. I have something to say to him. He completely ignored my instructions. And he left after the visit without seeing me."

"Perhaps I ought to have him meet me at the Institute; I could arrange it for four o'clock this afternoon. I'm sure he'll be eager to come when he hears that you'd like to have his report. I'll bring my lawyer Mr. Brown, too. He's also got something to say to the rabbi."

"Very good, Mr. Grossman. I'll be ready for you."

"Thank you very much, Dr. Martin."

Dr. Zimmerman showed no eagerness whatsoever to come that afternoon to Bethesda.

"I have no time today," he answered on the telephone. "I can't make it until tomorrow afternoon. Three o'clock. Dr. Martin will have to be patient."

"Dr. Zimmerman, there's no time to be lost. My father has taken a turn for the worse. He refuses to follow the doctor's instructions, and he won't take any medicine, since your visit."

"That's quite natural," said Dr. Zimmerman, very calmly. "I was expecting just that."

"But what are you talking about, Dr. Zimmerman? My father's absolutely out of hand."

"That's an excellent sign," answered Dr. Zimmerman, in the same tranquil tone. "It proves that the spiritual psychotherapy is working."

"Dr. Zimmerman—"

"A little more time won't make any difference. Your father has been getting the right medicine and it's taking effect. Tomorrow at three then. Please be on time. I must be back at home by five."

One glance at the set faces which confronted him the next day in Dr. Martin's office was enough to make it clear to Dr. Zimmerman that he had not been called in to give his impressions of old Grossman's condition, but for the quite different purpose of passing judgment on him. Very significant was the presence of attorney Brown. But Dr. Zimmerman had already suspected what was afoot from Lazar's resentful tone of voice in their conversation of the previous day. However, he greeted the three men cordially, and took his place at the table. Dr. Martin was at the head, as if presiding at a meeting. Dr. Zimmerman passed one hand through his gray mop of hair, with the other took out his watch from his vest pocket and laid it on the table, and launched at once into his talk.

"Gentlemen," he said, tranquilly, "I am sorry to have so little time to give you. Nor is there much for me to report. I gather from what Mr. Grossman junior told me that my spiritual psychotherapy has, with God's help, produced effects in the right direction. This in itself proves that Mr. Grossman senior is in his right mind. True, he suffers from a guilt complex, but not in a dangerously acute form. His sensitive conscience, his profound feeling for justice, which many businessmen, and for that matter many of us professionals, would be all the better for, plays a certain role in this complex. As regards his obsession, or *idée fixe,* it is only an hallucination to the extent that he believes the man in question to be still alive, and that the wrong which Mr. Grossman committed against him can be made good in person. But as regards the substance of the case, I am completely convinced that there is not the slightest element of hallucination in it. The one thing that has to be done is to establish the identity of the man, so that Mr. Grossman may make restitution to him personally, or to his relatives if the man is no longer living; or, again, general restitution by way of a humanitarian enterprise dedicated to the man's memory. Only in this way can we allay his conscience, so that he will be liberated from his fears and hallucinations."

The three listeners looked blankly at each other for a while.

"And how will you do this?" asked Lazar.

"How will *I* do it? *You'll* do it. All of us will do it. We must look for the man in question among those who must have had some contact with him—the Catholic priests, for instance, or the

331

old employees of the Yale factory. We must do everything in our power to find that Kovalsky, or his heirs," answered Dr. Zimmerman.

"Dr. Zimmerman, I won't let you revive all those slanderous stories about my father. I won't let you destroy the prestige of my family. And I warn you, rabbi, I will take the necessary steps if you make any efforts in that direction. My father may be sick, but he has never been dishonest. Is that clear to you?" Lazar's voice had taken on a sharp edge.

"Mr. Grossman, I thought that you were interested in restoring your father's peace of mind and spirit."

"I am; and I need no one to remind me of it. But I will see to it that the cure is conducted only by qualified medical men. Rabbi, you have stepped out of your competence. I think Dr. Martin has something to say to you about that—as well as Mr. Brown, my attorney."

"Indeed? Where exactly have I been at fault?" asked Dr. Zimmerman of Dr. Martin.

"Dr. Zimmerman, did you say to the patient that he is in a prison?" asked Dr. Martin.

"No, I did not say it. Was that what the patient said?"

"Yes. To me, personally."

"Excellent! First class!" And Dr. Zimmerman rubbed his hands with satisfaction.

"What's first class about it, Dr. Zimmerman? Do you really think that Bethesda is a prison?"

"God forbid! Bethesda is one of the finest and most progressive mental institutions in the country. The only pity is that it's limited to the rich. But tell me, Dr. Martin, shouldn't we interpret the patient's strong feeling that this is not the place for him as a sign of his unclouded intelligence?"

"What is the method you have been using, Dr. Zimmerman? Haven't you overstepped the limits of your competence and profession, and tried to treat the patient as if you were a qualified psychiatrist? I know that not a few of your colleagues have taken that liberty."

"Doctor, I will tell you frankly that I don't know where the competence of my profession ends, and that of yours begins. But I will try to explain my method to you. We spiritual leaders have, in fact, only one method. Our sages have told us: 'Judge not a man until thou art come in his place.' This is the rule I have followed, Dr. Martin. I put myself in Mr. Grossman's place.. I myself committed the error in my youth, and I myself wanted to rectify it while there was yet time, because I feared God's punishment. And what I desired God to do for me, I desire Him to do for Isaac Grossman. And I brought calmness to Isaac Grossman, in the grace of God, according to my faith and my conscience. Here you have my method, Dr. Martin."

"Dr. Zimmerman, we who undertake to cure the sick study for many years; we must obtain a diploma testifying to our competence and conferring on us the right to practice. The science we study is a positive and empiric science. We treat the sick not according to our subjective perceptions, but according to the nature of the sickness, and the laws laid down in the book. You, without the necessary training and knowledge, have overstepped the boundaries of our profession."

"I understand quite well, Dr. Martin, that medicine in all its branches is a positive and empiric science. Who doesn't understand that? But that applies only to organic sicknesses. When it comes to psychic diseases, to sicknesses of the soul, the case is altogether different. That kind of sickness cannot be treated only according to the book. Perhaps there is no such book. For sicknesses of the soul the psychiatrist, no less than the spiritual guide, must use one method—the method of the eternal conscience. The center of gravity of treatment lies more in the spiritual being, in the moral foundation, of the healer than in the patient. There are others, I know, who drag the patient into their own sick condition. Just recently I was confronted with the case of a qualified psychiatrist who uses the psychoanalytic method to persuade his men patients to divorce their wives. This man has broken up more families, ruined more homes, than he has cured patients. And do you know why? Because he himself had divorced his wife."

"I see you are something of a humorist, rabbi—at the expense of our profession," said Dr. Martin.

"No, I am not a humorist, and certainly not at the expense of your profession, Dr. Martin. I have the profoundest respect for your profession, Dr. Martin, and I say that soberly and earnestly. Unfortunately there are found in your profession—as in others, but to a large extent among psychiatrists—men who have no business there, who have sneaked in, as it were, and who make dishonest use of the Freudian method and theory. With all my admiration for Freud's discoveries, which have really opened a path into the secret depths of man's nature, I have to say that his theory, after all these years, is still in the speculative stage. Its influence has been greater in literature than in medicine. True, it has focused a strong light on the close relationship between our sexual instincts and our general behavior; it has directed serious scientific research into a field which our conventions have kept closed to us. But on the other hand it has also admitted to that field—as I have already mentioned—men of dubious character, who have exploited the theory for the purpose of awakening unnatural sexual impulses in their patients. And now, gentlemen, with your permission—" And Dr. Zimmerman rose.

"One moment, Dr. Zimmerman," exclaimed Brown, who throughout all this had been listening intently, and had made occasional entries in a little notebook. "There's something I must ask you."

The rabbi looked at his watch. "I still have a minute or two." He seated himself again.

"What is your interest in this Grossman case, rabbi?"

"What do you mean?"

"I mean simply, what is Mr. Grossman's sickness to you?"

"I am interested because it's my business to be interested."

"You mean you are being paid for it. By whom? By your congregation? You are a rabbi, Dr. Zimmerman. You are associated with a certain congregation, and you have certain obligations toward it. The congregation pays you for the time that you devote to your profession. You yourself have just told us that you have very little time; you're a busy man; and I can quite believe it. And still you're spending a good deal of time on this Grossman case. What is it? Have you your congregation's permission to deflect all this time and attention to something which, I am quite sure, is not of the slightest interest to your congregation?"

"I really should not answer that question. I should, instead, ask you to consult the trustees who are authorized to speak in the name of the congregation. However, I will answer you, Mr. Brown. That's the name, isn't it? Brown? Certainly a rabbi is

334

the employee of his congregation; he has been engaged to direct its religious and spiritual affairs. But a rabbi is not only employed by his congregation; to be exact, he is employed by God, and as God's employee, if I may so put it, he must serve everyone; he must bring comfort, faith and hope to all who need it, and whom he encounters on his path, irrespective of their standing— to the rich and the poor, to the Jew and the Christian. Isn't it the same with a doctor who happens to be in the street and sees a man fall down, sick? Your father—" he turned to Lazar, "is the sick man I found lying in the street—cast out. He needed spiritual comfort and cure, whether he belonged to my congregation or not. In the same way I used to bring spiritual help to Christian GI's on the battlefield."

"Mr. Isaac Grossman does not need your help," exploded Lazar, in a rage. "Mr. Grossman is in trained hands; he is being treated by skilled men who use tested means, and not by rabbis who meddle in things outside their profession."

"Gentlemen, please—" cried Dr. Martin.

Brown detained Lazar by the hand. "One more question, Dr. Zimmerman, before you leave."

"Yes?"

"Have you the legal right to practice this spiritual psychotherapy, as you call it? Have you a diploma from some qualified person?"

"Yes, from Moses. With his authority I am a rabbi in Israel, like every other rabbi—with his authority and that of my seminary."

"Rabbi Zimmerman, you are pleased to be witty: but this is a serious matter. You realize, I hope, that Mr. Lazar Grossman can bring action against you for having made his father gravely ill by presuming, without authority and qualification, to treat him as if you were a doctor."

"What is this? A grand jury?" asked Dr. Zimmerman, with a smile. "You threaten me first with my congregation—and then with legal action. I shall not be frightened off. I've been under fire. But let me make a last statement, before I leave. Dr. Martin—" he turned away abruptly from the attorney—"I respect your profession, your institute, and your personal integrity. It was not my intention to cast any reflection on any of these; and if

335

any word of mine has been so ill-chosen as to seem to contain a reflection—and this may have happened in the course of this rather lively discussion—I ask your forgiveness. But with all the respect due to you, and to the colleagues who have assisted you in treating Mr. Grossman, I can't pass over the fact that Mr. Grossman is a victim of 'the book' which you mentioned a little while ago. I mean, of the theory of the complexes into which doctors divide our various psychic sicknesses—like the 'father-complex,' the 'mother-complex,' the 'Hamlet-complex,' the 'Oedipus-complex.' You've taken the patient and you've put him into a cage which was prepared for him beforehand. This time it's the 'guilt-complex.' Certainly there is a guilt-complex. But it's not a delusion. It is a reality, doctor, a factual thing which goes by the name of 'conscience.' Nobody dared to admit the possibility that Mr. Grossman had in fact committed that act, that error, which had to be corrected; such a possibility would have destroyed the 'complex' into which he was fitted, not only by the doctors but by his own son. What was it Mr. Grossman junior said just a few minutes ago? 'My father may be sick, but he has never been dishonest.' In the depths of your heart, Mr. Grossman, you would rather have your father sick than confess that he once committed a crime. Left completely to himself, alienated from his own, with a guilt-complex on his conscience—to use your phrase—he went out like a driven animal to find that man. Is it any wonder that he fell into the hands of swindlers who took advantage of his condition, and of his panicky fear of punishment in the world to come? The ones who spread this net before his feet are being investigated.

"This is where you come in, Mr. Brown. It was you who pulled tight the net, and delivered the hunted animal into the waiting hands. That animal, Mr. Grossman, is your father, a human being like you and me. A father helps a son to correct an error which he once committed; he does not thrust him away into outer darkness. Why should not a son stand by his father in *his* hour of need? You, Mr. Brown, tried to frighten me by talking of the courts, and of my congregation. You understand, I take it, that your threats will not deter me from fulfilling my tasks as a rabbi in Israel—from freeing a human soul from its torments and restoring it to the security and peace of its relationship to God. And I pray

with all my heart, Mr. Brown—and you also, Mr. Grossman—
that when your conscience will awaken, as I hope and trust it will,
you will find a comforter to bring you the peace and faith which
you will need then as much as Mr. Grossman needs them today."

Rabbi Zimmerman left the room.

CHAPTER TWENTY

DR. ZIMMERMAN soon made it evident that threats were not going to swerve him from his line of action.

Within two days a council of war assembled in Moses Silverstein's office to map the strategy of the war between the Grossmans, father and son. Rose Rosenberg, who Silverstein had hitherto regarded as a dangerous enemy agent, attended. She had offered her services of her own accord. She had sought out Silverstein and confessed to him that recent events had completely transformed her outlook. She had grievous suspicions that Lazar was not actuated by motives of love toward his father; she had even darker suspicions, amounting almost to certainty, that attorney Brown, commander-in-chief of the opposing forces, was a dangerous intriguer, more dangerous than the ugly little lawyer who had tried to blackmail old Grossman. She was eager now to join the Zimmerman-Silverstein forces, and she was doing it on her own initiative.

Silverstein listened, weighed the matter, and was wholly convinced when she promised to bring to the forthcoming council the enemy's son Robert, who was all for his grandfather and against his father. Robert won his way instantly into Moses Silverstein's heart. The mere fact that he was a GI was enough to open the way for him; but on top of that Silverstein found in him a moving resemblance to his own dead son.

Dr. Zimmerman suspended his university lectures for a period and almost severed contact with his congregation, in order to concentrate on the war for the liberation of Isaac Grossman.

He opened the council session with businesslike directness.

"The first point," he said, "is to see to it that no word of our intentions reaches the other side. Our investigation is top secret.

Brown is capable of throwing a monkey-wrench into the search; he's capable of anything, in fact."

"What do you mean?" added Silverstein. "That man would as soon frame you up as look at you. I'll bet whatever you like that he already has a man here in Springbrook snooping around. I was pretty careful when I had my conversation with Father McCray; and I warned him not to discuss the matter with strangers, and not to give a hint to anyone what I was seeing him about. Father McCray is an old friend of mine; I told him the whole story, and he'll help us. But things aren't so bright with the Yale factory."

"You've already spoken with the Catholic priest, and visited the Yale factory?" asked Zimmerman, surprised.

"Certainly I have. Did you think I was going to take all that business lying down?" And Moses Silverstein snatched at his pince-nez, which threatened to dance off his nose. "Do you know who started me off? Those people themselves! When I saw that lawyer Brown and Mr. Grossman junior had to trap the old man into signing a document before they dared to go to trial, I said to myself: 'Maybe there's something in what Mr. Grossman senior has been saying. . . . Maybe there was a Kovalsky who once lived here, in Springbrook, and worked at the Yale factory. What would it cost me to begin a little investigation? So I went round to the Yale factory and asked them to let me look through the employment records. But they laughed at me. 'Kovalsky?' they said. 'You'll find him, all right. You'll find dozens of Kovalskys. You're looking for a needle in a haystack. Round the beginning of the century, and especially at the time of the Russo-Japanese war, we had a big immigration from Poland. Lots of them settled here in Connecticut; most of them on the land. But quite a number came to work for us. Kovalsky is a very common Polish name. And we had dozens of them.'"

"Well," said Dr. Zimmerman, knitting his brows, "we've got an answer to that." He turned to Robert. "Did you find anything along your line?"

"Yes, sir. In 1904 there were working at the Yale factory three Yan Kovalskys with a middle initial of M. I picked them out of several dozen other Kovalskys. One of them—" he took out a slip

339

of paper—"was Yan Mieczyslav, another Yan Maczek, and the third Yan Matheus. All three were locksmiths."

"That narrows it down to three. Good. We've got to get the right one; it won't do to confuse old Mr. Grossman by suggesting the wrong middle name. Now, Mr. Silverstein, you asked Father McCray about the Kovalskys in the Catholic cemetery, I suppose. What's the report?"

"The same thing, of course," answered Moses Silverstein. "Father McCray looked through the register—dozens of Kovalskys. Of course I didn't have the middle initial; that makes a big difference."

"We can't afford a mistake," said Dr. Zimmerman, thoughtfully. "We can't rely only on the similarity of the middle initial. It's got to be the one man, and no other. What do you suggest, Mr. Silverstein?"

"Father McCray has had this parish for something like twelve years. He didn't know the old-timers personally. Before him there was a Polish priest, Father Hanecky, who emigrated at the turn of the century. He's still living. He's at one of the old folk's homes maintained by the Catholic church in this vicinity. This old Father Hanecky, according to Father McCray, knew every family, every man and woman, every child, in his parish. He knew many of them from the old country. Now if this Kovalsky that we're looking for was a good Catholic, Father Hanecky was sure to have known him."

"Well, then, that's it!" exclaimed Dr. Zimmerman. "There's our lead! Our Kovalsky married off a daughter in March, 1904. Where would the marriage take place? In the Catholic church, of course, Father Hanecky's church. Mr. Silverstein, call up Father McCray, find out where that retreat, or old folk's home, is. I think we're on the right path now!"

His enthusiasm spread to the other members of the war council. With bated breath they listened to Silverstein's inquiries, and saw his face light up.

"It's not thirty miles from Springbrook," said Silverstein, putting down the telephone. "Near a place called Kent. The home is administered by nuns. Old Hanecky is too weak to carry on with parish work, but now and again he comes on a visit to his congregation. He served it for more than forty years. If we could get

340

hold of a car, Father McCray is ready to go with us at once to Gethsemane—that's the name of the Home. We could bring Father Hanecky here."

"Robert! Your grandfather's car is here, at The Springbrook Inn," said Miss Rosenberg. "What are we waiting for?"

"I'm coming with you, Robert," said Moses Silverstein excitedly.

"No, no, you stay here," ordered Dr. Zimmerman, "in case something goes wrong. I'll go with Father McCray to bring Father Hanecky. I think he'd like to have me along."

The rabbi's forebodings of an approaching time when Lazar himself, and others, might need religious psychotherapy were intensified on his return home from the agitated conference in Dr. Martin's office. He found Katherine in her room, silent, depressed, as though she had been the recipient of crushing news. She was not crying—no one had ever seen her cry—but she was stony with some inner sorrow. Only in her eyes there was a little flame, a signal which frightened him. She did not seem to notice his entry.

"What is it?" he asked, at last.

She did not reply.

"What has happened?"

"A lot! You've sacrificed your family for the sake of the Hanovers. You won't have the Hanovers—but you've lost your children."

"What do you mean?"

"Robert's just been here. He put a few things in a bag and went away. He won't live here. At first he wouldn't even talk to me. But when I insisted, he said that he didn't want to live in this kind of house. He won't have anything to do with us. He said terrible things about you."

"It's all the fault of that blasted rabbi. I'll have him in court."

"You will not."

"Why?"

"Your own children would testify against you."

"My children?"

"Your son. He said he'll stop at nothing in this fight with you."

"He said that?" Lazar turned white. He remembered that he had said the same thing to his own father.

341

"Yes. And he told his sister that for the sake of having her marry a Hanover you wouldn't let your father right a wrong which he committed in his youth. You were afraid that it would reflect on the family. And the result was that your father fell sick. And what do you think Louise did? She telephoned Felix and said she didn't want to see him any more; she was in love with someone else. Now she's in her room crying her heart out into her pillow. She won't let me come in. Your children accuse you of having confined your father to a mental institution for your own egotistical purposes. They hate you for it."

Lazar stared at his wife. "But you know it's not true."

"I don't know it. Sometimes I think there's something in what they're saying," she answered shortly.

He started. "So you too suspect me!" he cried.

"It isn't easy to understand, is it? Why did you stand in the way of your father's project?"

"You know as well as I do. To protect the good name of the family."

"The good name of the family.... It makes me sick to hear that. You see where it's landed you. You're the one who's managed to bring a bad name on us. Besides which, you've lost your son and your daughter, and our best, most faithful friend, Rose. And perhaps even—"

"Even what?"

"I don't know, I don't know. I can't make up my mind." She rose suddenly and ran from the room.

Lazar remained standing as if in a stupor. At last he murmured, "Why? Why? What have I done to deserve this?"

He lay awake all night. All night he stared at the ruin of his family life. He kept repeating: "Why? What have I done that I ought not to have done?"

He was unable to find fault with his course of action. It seemed to him that he had prevented his father from committing one folly after another; and then, when he had discovered that his father was mentally ill, he had sought the help of the best doctors and had faithfully followed their instructions. He had done all that lay in his power in order that the good name of the family and the sacred memory of his mother might remain unbesmirched.

342

His father's plans had exposed them all to the gravest dangers. But what in particular had he done to awaken such ugly suspicions in his son, his daughter, and his wife? And then, toward morning, a light suddenly dawned on him. He had it! He should never have thought of selling the land. He should have given it at once to the city! That would have quashed effectively all the slanderous talk about his selfish motives. Or perhaps it would have been even better to add his own signature to his father's petition immediately after he had obtained the full power of attorney over his father's affairs! Yes, he should have thrown himself into his father's project, placed his firm and all its connections in its service, contributed his own funds—and then, in the end, have given his father's name to the completed project. *That* would have been the cleverest, the wisest thing to do! And why had he not done it? Not, God knew, because he wanted the property for himself. He had not thought of himself at all. It had only been his businessman's instinct which had revolted against the idea of using this particular property for a GI homes development. It was unsuitable. It was too expensive. He had said so to his father; and every businessman would agree with him.

"But don't you see, that's the whole trouble!" he admonished himself. "You looked only at the business side of the enterprise. You were blind to the emotional element which was attached to it for your father."

Yes, he saw it. He saw the things he had done which he ought not to have done. And not only with respect to the project, but with respect also to his father's spiritual breakdown. For he had measured his father's need and misery with the same measure— the common sense, practical business, measure; that was why he had turned the problem over to his attorney, Brown, who of course had proceeded according to the strict letter of the law.

"Now why did I do that?" he asked himself, proceeding step by step. "Why didn't I, instead, make a search for that man, that Kovalsky? Why did I prevent father from finding his peace of mind? Because I believed the doctors? Because I thought that Kovalsky was an hallucination? Or was it because I *wanted* to believe it? It suited me better to believe it. It's better to have a sick than a dishonest father. You don't have to be ashamed of a sick father. So I wanted him sick rather than dishonest. And I *made* him sick. I brought on his mental breakdown—No!" He started away violently from this conclusion. "No! I did what every honest man would have done. I have nothing to reproach myself with. I didn't do it only for my family's sake, and certainly not for my own sake. Because I still don't believe that such a person ever existed!"

An interval passed, and a small voice suggested: "But suppose such a person did exist? Ought you to stand in the way of a search for him?"

There was no way out of this impasse. In despair he made one resolve. Come what might, he would renew without delay his father's Springbrook project. And this thought alone brought him a little measure of repose. He would go and see Silverstein and attorney Davis. He would ask to have the petition renewed, and he would put his signature on it. And he would proceed to reorganize the work.

Then after another interval. . . . No, he would not go to Silverstein, that slanderer who had befouled his name. Perhaps he ought to take Max Brown along.

"No, you won't take Max along. You've got to detach him completely from this business. That was your great mistake to begin with. You'll go alone to Silverstein. You'll go to Dr. Zimmerman, too, and ask him to return your son to you."

The voice was quiet, but insistent.

"That," he returned, "I'll never do."

"You will do it. For the sake of your family. And before you do that you'll go to Rose, and ask her to help you."

That voice coming out of the night rang strangely like Katherine's.

On the very day of the "council of war," and before Dr. Zimmerman had returned from the trip to Gethsemane, Moses Silverstein was able to score, or at least to record, a decisive victory over the enemy forces. Miss Rosenberg herself, who had left for her hotel, returned unexpectedly to Silverstein's office bringing with her a "prisoner"—none other than Lazar Grossman. And in Miss Rosenberg's and Silverstein's presence the prisoner declared—or implied—that he was capitulating: he was prepared to carry out

344

his father's development project on the very property where it had been started.

Astounded though he was by this sudden and unexpected turn of events, moved though he was by Lazar's repentance, Silverstein could not suppress an angry mutter:

"Your father isn't sick. It's you who've made him sick."

Lazar's face had visibly aged since Silverstein had last seen him. His hair was a shade grayer, his figure a little less upright, and his manner was humble.

"Let us rather say," he murmured, "that all of this made him sick, the doctors, the specialists, and perhaps I too. And possibly you, Mr. Silverstein, are not altogether without blame, if you will let me say so. Didn't you too believe that the whole affair was a delusion? You admitted, in court, that you didn't believe such a thing had ever happened to my father; and your testimony carried a lot of weight with the judge, because he and everybody else knew that you are a friend of my father's."

"That's true. I admit I thought it was all a delusion. Who could have imagined such a thing in reality—" And Silverstein pulled himself up, with a frightened glance at Miss Rosenberg. Had he admitted too much to the "enemy"?

"You may speak openly, Mr. Silverstein. Mr. Grossman knows that Dr. Zimmerman is on his way to Gethsemane to find out all the details from the old priest," said Miss Rosenberg.

"He does?" exclaimed Silverstein. And instead of addressing Lazar, who seemed to be sunk in a stupor of contrition, he asked Miss Rosenberg: "And what does he say to that?"

"He says that if it turns out to be true, if his father's story is factual, he will do everything possible to right the wrong which lies so heavily on his father's conscience. He will ignore, he says, any effect it will have on the reputation of the family or the firm. He's of course prepared, in that case, to sign a petition to Judge Parker declaring Mr. Grossman senior to be in possession of all his normal mental faculties, and fully competent to conduct all his business and personal affairs. He is ready, in fact, to take his father out of Bethesda tomorrow."

"We shall know a great deal before long," said Silverstein, contentedly. "Dr. Zimmerman must be on his way back. Mr. Grossman, here's my hand in sign of friendship. Let's forget the past—except insofar as it has taught us something we ought never to forget. Neither of us believed that your father, whom all of us knew as a model of honesty and nobility of character, could have been mixed up in an affair of that kind. What does it prove? That even the best of us carries about with him secret wounds, inflicted during the years of our struggle with life. The only difference is that while the rest of us are only too ready to bury the secret, to ignore it, Mr. Grossman would not, and perhaps could not, bury and forget the evil of his past. Believe me, when a man achieves the moral heights now achieved by your father, he has done something rare." And Moses Silverstein launched, after his wont, into a long and scholarly discourse.

Dr. Zimmerman burst into the office with a happy countenance, and stopped dead when he saw Lazar Grossman. Behind him was Robert who, perceiving his father, remained standing at the door. Dr. Zimmerman recovered his composure immediately. The happy look returned to his face, and understanding at once what had taken place, he took Lazar's hand and pressed it vigorously.

"Mr. Grossman, I am happy to see you here, and to congratulate you. I am thoroughly convinced that with God's help your father will very soon be a normal man again. We have the facts now—and they prove that your father was not suffering from a delusion. We've brought a witness—Father Hanecky—who knew the man in question. Father Hanecky is in Springbrook now, and he has the whole story. Tomorrow we shall inform your father of everything. I think we can all congratulate ourselves."

Lazar nodded slowly, as if still unable to grasp the reality.

"So the thing did happen," he murmured. "It did happen."

"Yes, Mr. Grossman, it happened. Your father was in the right, and all of us were in the wrong—" Dr. Zimmerman generously included himself. "If your father will be in condition to meet Father Hanecky tomorrow, the last details will come out. We must telephone Dr. Martin. What is the latest report on your father?"

"Dr. Martin told me that they put a sleeping draught into his food, and that's been helping him to sleep."

"Tell Dr. Martin to leave it out today. We want your father at his most alert tomorrow. He's facing the big test. Meanwhile, it won't do us any harm, either, to take a good rest. Robert—" he turned to the young man, who had been standing silently at the door all this time—"you take your father home. He looks tired."

"I don't want to go home," said Robert. "I'll stay over at The Springbrook Inn. I want to see Dr. Martin in the morning. And Mr. Davis, too."

Dr. Zimmerman did not press his point. "I'll tell you what," he said. "You might as well use the morning for something else. Go over to the Yale factory and get a copy of Kovalsky's working card. Yan Mattheus Kovalsky, 1904."

He put his hand on Robert's shoulder and drew him out of the office into the store.

"Robert," he said, in a low voice, "remember—honor thy father. He meant well. Do you hear me, Robert?"

"Yes, sir."

Lazar, Robert, and Miss Rosenberg went together to Springbrook Inn.

Among the disillusionments which Robert, like so many others of the younger generation, had suffered, none had hit him harder than the loss of faith in his father. Robert had idolized his father since childhood; unable to live without a God, he had begun by lifting his father to that role. There are certain natures which may be classified as planetary, which have no light of their own but reflect the light of the parent sun to which they are attached. Such a nature was Robert's, and the sun about which he had circled, and in whose light he had basked, had been his father. Everything about his father had been exalted in his eyes; and in particular he had idolized his father for the role he had played in the war, and for the nationwide reputation which it had won him. But when this sun and center had failed him, when he had fallen out of this gravitational field, he had been drawn at once into that of Dr. Zimmerman. But for this fortunate circumstance he might have fallen into the lightless void.

Even with this change of orbit he had only half meant the bitter things he had said about his father, and these he had mostly picked up hastily from Moses Silverstein and others. He had never believed that his father had been actuated by motives of personal greed. But he did accuse his father of social motives on behalf of Louise. His father had inherited from his mother a

347

weakness for "Society," and he had indulged this weakness in planning his daughter's marriage. But if the words "upper" and "lower" had ever any social meaning for Robert, that meaning had been destroyed for him by what he had learned in Germany. For there all Jews had been reduced to one level and they had achieved equality in death. It was this that Robert wanted to say to his father.

But as the three of them walked toward The Springbrook Inn he remained silent. He was not blind to the change which had come over his father. The sunken cheeks, the new touch of gray in the hair, the unwonted stoop—these worked on him, awoke his pity, and loosened the bitterness which had gathered in his heart.

"We must call up Katherine," said Rose as they came into the apartment. "She must be quite miserable, waiting for news. Then I'll order up dinner."

"Robert!" Lazar addressed his son for the first time. "Call your mother."

"Yes, dad."

They could all hear Katherine's anxious, excited voice: "Robert! Where are you? Where is your father? He left the house early this morning, and I haven't heard from him."

"We're in Springbrook, mother. Dad is with me. Everything is all right. Rose is with us, too. We're going to stay here overnight, and we'll be home tomorrow. And we'll be bringing someone with us. I can't tell you everything now. Wait—father will talk with you."

With the ice broken between father and son, Robert found some of his old feelings reawakening. Finally, as they sat waiting for the meal, he took up courage.

"Dad, there's something I want to tell you. Dr. Zimmerman and I once visited a DP camp where they still had a number of people from the old concentration camps. We met there a clever Polish Jew who had been through everything except the very last stage of the crematorium. And this Jew told us a story—I don't know whether he meant it seriously, or whether it was a kind of parable —I don't know—Dr. Zimmerman had to translate it for me. This Jew said that the crematorium in his concentration camp had a door just high enough for a man of medium height to go through

348

without stooping. And if the man being led into the crematorium, to be burned up, was too tall and had to stoop, they wouldn't let him go through. He was taken away, and had his head cut off. That was because Hitler insisted that all Jews were of the same height, you couldn't have some Jews taller than others. This Polish Jew—he was a very bitter man, and God knows he had reason to be—told us this story when we were talking about American Jews. He said that we American Jews oughtn't to think ourselves better than other Jews. Hitler made us all equal."

Lazar looked steadily at his son, and answered, "I know what you're thinking, Robert. You're thinking it was because of Louise, and her marriage into the Hanover family, that I let all this happen. You're wrong. It wasn't Louise I had in mind. It was you."

"Me?"

"Yes, you. I was thinking of your having to confront your friends at school, and later in life, in society; your having to meet with old boyhood friends; and how you would feel, how you would face them, if they should know about your grandfather. That's what I had in mind."

"How I would face them if they knew about grandfather and the story of Kovalsky? I would feel proud! My grandfather was a man who could not rest, could not spend his last years in peace, because of a sin he had committed in his youth. And this grandfather moved heaven and earth trying to make good the wrong. He became sick, he almost lost everything, because he was determined to right that wrong. And now I can also say that we, his near ones, weren't afraid of the harm it would do us, the effect it would have on our reputation. We went to his help, and we stood by him right through. We cured him. We made him whole. And that's more than many of my friends would have done; they prefer to enjoy quietly the plunder which their grandfathers have accumulated for them."

Lazar looked long and wonderingly at the boy. Was this his son?

"That's enough now," broke in Miss Rosenberg. "I think that's the waiter coming. If you are as hungry as I am—"

CHAPTER TWENTY-ONE

LAZAR and Dr. Zimmerman brought to Bethesda the news which completely transformed the Grossman case. Dr. Martin listened to the report with the closest attention.

"Your father is an astonishing person," he said at last, to Lazar. "I am ready to believe anything about him. Certainly I am ready to believe that we've been entirely wrong. And yet all the symptoms supported our diagnosis, and in nine hundred and ninety-nine cases out of a thousand we would have been correct. Your father's case is the thousandth. But it's not the only time he has surprised us."

"How is the patient today?" asked Dr. Zimmerman.

"That's a surprise, too. After your last visit, everything pointed to a new and severe crisis. But just when we expected something close to a collapse, there was a sudden change for the better. He's quieter now, and calmer. To be honest, I'm more afraid for his heart now than his mind."

"What do you mean, Dr. Martin?" asked Lazar uneasily.

"There's been a sudden indication of spastic nervousness. I wouldn't call it organic—yet. No. But it can develop into that. His blood pressure fluctuates between very high and low."

"Do you think I can take him home, doctor?"

"I don't see why not. We can do very little for him here. From all the symptoms, I judge that he would be just as well off at home."

"Dr. Martin, do you also feel that Mr. Grossman is strong enough to go through an investigation of his case today?" asked Dr. Zimmerman.

"As much as any other day. The fact is, of course, that any kind of excitement will react on his condition, sometimes favorably, and sometimes unfavorably. As I said, he's a bit unpredictable. As far as his mental condition is concerned I believe the reaction would be favorable. You say you've brought the old priest to Springbrook. Where is he?"

"He's waiting for us to call him."

"Then do what you think best. The patient is in your hands, Dr. Zimmerman," said Dr. Martin, smiling. "You've won."

"Not yet, Dr. Martin. The patient is in God's hands; and you've been the instrument of God's help," Dr. Zimmerman returned. "Meanwhile, I shall ask Miss Rosenberg to see the patient and prepare him for the great event."

The most recent turn in Isaac Grossman's condition, on which Dr. Martin had commented with cautious optimism, was connected with a curious change in outlook resulting from Dr. Zimmerman's long discussion with him. The sense of guilt had not actually diminished, but it had diffused itself over large areas outside the Kovalsky case. The whole of his life, it seemed to the old man, was tinged with a melancholy moral imperfection. That which had pressed with such anguish on a single point—a single day in his early manhood—was spread over all his past activity. A quiet and thoughtful sadness touched with hope had replaced the piercing agony of the Kovalsky memory.

Miss Rosenberg found her employer dressed in a business suit, ready to go out in the company of his nurse. He was seated at the window, staring out into the garden.

"Good morning, Isaac. How do you feel?"

"It's you, Rose!" Grossman turned. "Where have you been these days? I was beginning to think you'd run out on me."

"Really! Well, at least it shows you missed me. I thought since Robert came you had no more use for me. I wanted to find out— so I went home for a couple of days. How do you feel?"

"Very good. Where's Robert?"

"He came with me. He's waiting outside, and he wants to see you, of course. Shall he come in?"

"Certainly."

She called through the open door. "Robert!"

The boy came in at once.

"Hello, granddad! How are you feeling?" He ran over to his grandfather's chair.

"I'll leave the two of you," said Rose. "I know you've got things to talk over without me."

"Don't go, Rose," said Robert. "I've got things to tell you, too."

"No, I won't go. I'll wait in the garden."

"Robert, where were you these last few days? Why didn't you show up?"

"I was busy, granddad. I was very busy."

"With what?"

"Didn't you ask me look into a certain matter?"

"Look into a certain matter?" repeated old Grossman. "What matter?"

"Granddad, have you forgotten? You asked me to find out all about that man."

"Oh, Kovalsky?" Grossman started up.

"Yes."

"What have you found out?"

"Well, I'm not sure. You'll have to tell me. Listen, granddad." Robert hesitated. "Was that man's name Yan Mattheus Kovalsky?"

Grossman trembled, as if an electric current had passed through him. With a sudden, vigorous movement he turned his chair from the window and looked up with starting eyes at his grandson. He seemed to have lost his breath for a moment.

"What was that? Say it again."

"Yan Mattheus Kovalsky."

"Again! That middle name!"

"Mat-the-us!"

"Write it down."

"Here, granddad. I have the copy of his working card." Robert drew from his pocket the document which he had obtained from the Yale factory with the help of attorney Davis. He passed it to his grandfather's eager and trembling hand.

Grossman looked hard at the words, then closed his eyes. He opened them again, stared again, then covered the paper with his hand. After a while he began to mutter, and reread the name several times.

"Yan Mattheus—Mattheus—Mattheus—where did you get this?"

"At the Yale factory where Kovalsky worked. Where you told me he'd been working."

"Where is he?"

"Granddad, I don't know. You'll have to ask Dr. Zimmerman."

"Rabbi Zimmerman?"

"Yes, granddad. He was the one who helped me."

"Where is Rabbi Zimmerman? Is he here? Send him in at once." And Grossman got up excitedly.

"Wait a moment, granddad. Of course he's here. I'll call him."

Robert stepped outside and beckoned to Dr. Zimmerman.

"Hello, Mr. Grossman. How are you?"

"Never mind how I am. Where's Kovalsky?"

"We've found him!"

"Can I see him? I want to see him at once."

"Easy, Mr. Grossman. You're not too strong yet, you know. You've got to take this calmly."

"Don't play around with me, rabbi. I've got to see him—at once."

"That isn't possible, Mr. Grossman. We've found him—that's true. But you can't see him. He's here—and he isn't here."

"Dead!"

Dr. Zimmerman nodded.

Grossman sat down again, and stared silently into space.

"Mr. Grossman, what did you expect after these many years? You must have known all the time that he could hardly be among the living. Think back. Weren't you always aware, in some part of your mind, that the man was dead?"

As if answering an inward voice, Grossman murmured "Yes."

"When you met him you were a boy, and he was in middle age. He was marrying off his daughter. I don't think you ever really expected to find him again. We do not live forever."

"Yes," murmured Grossman.

"As long as we know that the man lived once—and we know exactly who he was, and where he's buried."

"Where?" Grossman started again.

A pleased look came over the rabbi's face. "He's buried here in Springbrook, in the Catholic cemetery."

"Can I visit his grave?" asked Grossman heavily.

"Yes, certainly. That's what I came for this morning, to take you to visit his grave."

"Will they let me go?"

"Who's going to stop you?"

"The people here."

"Mr. Grossman, you are a free man. You are not a prisoner, God forbid. This is a sanatorium, a place of rest. You're a paying guest here, and you can leave whenever you like. You've rested long enough, and you can return to your home as soon as you feel like it."

"I'm free?" repeated Grossman. "I can go home as soon as I want?"

"Yes, Mr. Grossman."

"And what will Dr. Martin say? And my son?"

"Your son is here too. He came for you."

"Lazar? No. I won't go with him. I'll go with you, Robert." And the old man turned with a frightened look to his grandson.

"All right, granddad. We can go together to your house in New Rochelle. I'll stay with you."

"No, we'll go to The Springbrook Inn. I want to take up the work on my project."

"Whatever you say, granddad. I'll help you."

"Good! Good! But the first thing is to go to Yan's grave."

He rose again, as if to leave the room at once.

"Mr. Grossman, you've got to take it easy. You've had excitement enough for the moment. And you've got to see the priest first, anyhow."

"What priest?"

"Kovalsky's father-confessor. He knows the whole history of the case. He spoke with Kovalsky. He'll tell you what you ought to do for Yan. He'll show you Yan's photograph, too."

"What? Yan's photograph?" Grossman had fallen back into his seat, and his eyes filled with tears. His voice began to tremble. "Take me to the priest. Please, let me speak with him." He was almost sobbing.

"Yes, we'll do that. We came for that purpose, Mr. Grossman. But first take a rest. You mustn't do too much at a time. The priest understands, and he'll wait. He doesn't expect us before this afternoon. And now I'll ask Dr. Martin to come in."

"No, no, not Dr. Martin. Call my nurse. Or wait, call Miss Rosenberg. Please."

"As you say, Mr. Grossman."

"And you, Robert, stay here too."

"Yes, granddad."

"Thank God! We've got past the first shock," said Dr. Zimmerman to Lazar and Dr. Martin, who had been waiting in the corridor. He passed a handkerchief over his perspiring neck and forehead. "He took it fairly well, considering his weakened condition. Ask Miss Rosenberg to go in; and now perhaps she can give him a sedative. I think I could do with one myself. Dr. Martin, have you a room where I could lie down for a few minutes?"

A little while later Dr. Zimmerman returned to the patient's room. Rose and Robert were with the old man.

"Mr. Grossman, if you're feeling too weak for the trip, we can have Father Hanecky come here. And we can leave the visit to the cemetery for another day. Dr. Martin thinks the effort and the shock will be too much for you."

"No, no, not a bit of it. I feel very well. And I want to see Yan's grave. You promised me I would." The old man's voice was laden with such anguish that Dr. Zimmerman thought it better to give way than to run the risk of awakening new suspicions.

"Good. We shall go together. Robert, get your grandfather's car ready."

"It is ready, rabbi. Steve is downstairs with it."

Dr. Zimmerman turned to Grossman. "Father McCray of Springbrook and Father Hanecky will meet us at the cemetery.

The group went down into the garden—old Grossman, Rose, Robert, Dr. Zimmerman. Steve was standing with a broad, happy smile at the open door of the car. Grossman seated himself at the back, between Rose and the rabbi. Robert sat in front with Steve. This time there was no guard; and when the car issued from the sanatorium gate it turned left, in the direction of Springbrook, and there was no one to correct the "error." This was the first real sign for old Grossman that he was actually free. . . .

A second car followed the first at an even distance. It carried Lazar, Dr. Martin, and Grossman's nurse.

The Catholic cemetery lay on the other side of the city, in the direction of Boston. A high wall covered with little climbing roses interwoven and shot through with branches of honeysuckle surrounded the green slopes which were thickly sown with gravestones, crosses, and stone figures of human beings and angels.

At the door of the little chapel near the gate stood Father McCray, a solidly built man in the middle forties; and near him, in his shadow and as if in his protection, a frail, silver-haired old man, with a pair of childlike blue eyes set in a fantastically wrinkled face. When old Grossman was helped from the car the two men stepped forward and greeted him—first Father McCray in a hearty, friendly voice, and then Father Hanecky with a silent, protracted handshake.

"Yanush lies in the Kosciusko Alley," quavered Father Hanecky.

"I know, Father Hanecky. I've got the record," answered Father McCray. He took out a card: *Polish Corner, Kosciusko Alley, Plot 26.*

"We always called him Yanush," said the old priest to Grossman, placing himself at his side. Grossman nodded silently, and in silence walked toward the slope. And the others were silent with him.

Father McCray led the procession through a number of narrow alleys, till he came to the Polish Corner.

"This is the section where all the Poles are buried," he said. He stopped before a grave hemmed in on all sides, and almost sunk into the earth. On the narrow stone at the head, still legible, there was the inscription, in Polish: YAN MATTHEUS KOVALSKY. *Born 1865. Kutnowsky Community. Died 1922.* Below these words were others, by this time illegible.

"This is it, Mr. Grossman," said Dr. Zimmerman softly. "Here lie the earthly remains of Yan Kovalsky. The immortal part of him is with God. Is it not, Father Hanecky?"

"According to our Catholic faith," said the old man.

"And according to ours," said Dr. Zimmerman.

"I performed the last rites for him," went on Father Hanecky.

"I buried him in this place. It was during the Easter week of 1922. A few months later his widow and daughter and son-in-law returned to Poland, which had been liberated in the first World

356

War. They promised to send the money for a fine tombstone, but I never heard from them again. I suppose they fell on hard times. This tombstone was put up by the local Sokol. They always do that. A modest stone, but good enough in God's eyes. Not that God needs the stone at all; He knew the man and received him into His mercy."

Miss Rosenberg stood close to old Grossman, her arm under his, and she watched him intently. He stood there motionless and earnest, but on his face there was no sign of nervousness or fear. His lips were closed, his eyes fastened on the worn and faded inscription. But after a while his lips began to tremble, and Miss Rosenberg turned her face quickly to Dr. Zimmerman, who took Father McCray's arm and led him away from the grave. Father Hanecky followed immediately, and after him Robert. Miss Rosenberg remained with Grossman at the graveside. His lips continued to tremble, but no sound came from them.

Dr. Zimmerman turned back and said quietly: "Mr. Grossman, wouldn't you like to go home now, to New Rochelle, or to The Springbrook Inn?"

"No, I want to talk with Father Hanecky," said Grossman, in a clear, unshaken voice.

"Another day, perhaps," suggested Dr. Zimmerman uneasily.

"No, now. Isn't there some place nearby?"

"You can come to my rectory," suggested Father McCray. "We have all the records there, Father Hanecky's papers, the files of Polish compatriots, photographs of weddings and other ceremonies."

"I want my son to come along. I want him to know that I've never been out of my mind," said Grossman.

"Good. Robert will bring him to the Rectory."

"Let him go for Moses Silverstein, also. He too has to be there." He turned away from the grave and said to Miss Rosenberg, "There's nothing more to hide now. They can all know."

They were all assembled in Father McCray's rectory: Grossman, flanked by Rose and Robert, Dr. Zimmerman, Moses Silverstein, the two priests; and, somewhat withdrawn, Lazar. Isaac Grossman's mood had changed again. He was still earnest, but

357

the sadness had gone out of his face, and there was a long-absent freshness and freedom in his motions.

"I knew Yanush," began Father Hanecky, "from the day of his arrival in Springbrook. He came here with his wife and daughter. The circumstances were these: at the turn of the century, when the big reaction set in in Czarist Russia, a great migration of Polish peasants and workers began, to America and Canada. It followed more or less along the lines of the Jewish migration. The Catholic Church decided to send along a priest with every larger group, to look after its spiritual interests in the new country and to hold it firm in the Catholic faith and in its memories of the beloved fatherland. I was a young priest, and the Bishop of our diocese chose me to accompany one of the groups. The place of my mission was Springbrook, where we already had a large settlement. I came before Yan Kovalsky's group, and so I was able to help him. We arranged for Yanush to learn the trade of locksmith, and I got him a job at the Yale factory, where we'd placed a number of Polish immigrants.

"But Yanush—God forgive me—brought with him from the old country a weakness for drink. He was a nice quiet man, as a rule, a good Catholic, a good husband and father, and he bothered nobody. But when the big thirst came on him there was no holding the man. Indeed, he wasn't the same man any more. He'd lift his hand to his wife—which he wouldn't dream of sober. The poor woman came weeping to me more than once. And he would take things from the house and pawn them. It was bad, it was very bad. Now I'm telling you this not to besmirch the poor man's memory, or to put him in a bad light. God forbid that I should offend the memory of one of my flock. I only tell it so that you can get the picture of what happened on that Friday in the spring of 1904— the day before his daughter's wedding—when he went to New York to buy himself a suit and attend to some other matters in connection with the wedding. Now you might wonder why he had to go to New York. We had shops enough in Springbrook, didn't we? Well, that's what I want to explain, and that's why I've had to tell you about his weakness for the bottle. Among other things, he wanted to see some relatives in New York and invite them in person to the wedding. But he also went to buy a stock of whisky from an acquaintance of his, thinking to get a bargain. Well, I advised him, since he was going to the city, to get himself a new suit of clothes, something decent to lead his daughter to the altar in. It is a principle with us that every marriage which we sanctify within our church should be celebrated in a solemn and festive way. We insist that the father who leads his daughter to the altar shall be dressed as befits the importance of the occasion, in a dark suit, with a white tie, and with a flower in his button-hole. We also insist that photographs be taken of the bride and bridegroom, and of the in-laws, and of some of the guests, individually and in groups. The photographs remain within the family as a sacred reminder of that great day. They bring a touch of solemn festiveness into the workaday life of the family, they impart a sense of importance, are a comfort and a source of strength in a time of trial. You will wonder, rabbi"—and the old priest turned to Dr. Zimmerman, who sat, like the others, transfixed by the priest's words, "you will be astonished, when I tell you what some of these wedding photographs have done to strengthen people in a time of despair, restoring their courage, or holding them back from some rash and evil deed. Once a gentleman, always a gentleman.

"And this well-established custom I wanted Yan to follow. I told him that on his daughter's wedding day he would be, and he would look like, a 'Pan,' a personage of dignity and importance. He would be wearing a dark suit and a white tie. Of course they often hire a suit for the occasion; but Yanush wanted to kill two birds with one stone. He decided to buy himself a secondhand suit which he would be able to wear on Sundays; you see, he hadn't a decent suit of clothes to come to church in on Sundays. His daughter, who worked, contributed something. And so he went to New York. In the first store—that was before he came to yours, Mr. Grossman—it was a store on Grand Street, he didn't find what he wanted. You see he told me all the details. He told me that it was a miserable, wet, snowy day—that unforgettable day, poor Yanush—and the second store he went into was yours, Mr. Grossman. And there he found what he wanted, the kind of suit that he could wear to the wedding, and on Sundays to church. It was a dark suit. Right, Mr. Grossman?"

Grossman thought hard.

"I don't remember that," he said. "Very possibly."

359

"Yes, a dark suit. That's what he told me when he came back, so bitterly disappointed, from New York. It was a fortunate thing for him that he had friends and relatives in New York who could give him the money for the return trip. He thought, of course, that the family wouldn't believe he'd lost the wallet. They'd think he'd spent the money on drink. Things like that had in fact happened to him before. But this time I knew that the story he told us was a true one. I went home with him. I calmed his wife. I calmed the bride. And I assured them that in spite of everything Yanush would conduct his daughter to the altar in becoming attire. Not just a dark suit, but a frock coat! And that is how it was. Would you like to see how he looked on that day? I have the photograph. I made it a practice to keep in our files a copy of every wedding photograph taken in our church."

And Father Hanecky stretched out his hand to Father McCray and took from him a photograph, which he held out to Grossman.

"This is it. The wedding of Celina Kovalsky and Joseph Grabski, solemnized March 18, 1904."

If the heavens had opened, and an angel of God had descended before him, Isaac Grossman would not have been more astounded and uplifted than when he looked at the photograph.

There, in the picture, stood a Polish aristocrat, in frock coat and white tie, with a white carnation in his buttonhole. The hair was neatly parted in the middle and smoothly combed to each side. The mustaches were curled up in a fine, triumphant curve. At his side stood the bride in her white batiste dress, with a wreath of forget-me-nots on her brow, a long veil falling over her shoulders, and a bouquet of white lilies in her hand.

In that one instant a fiery hand erased from Isaac Grossman's brain the image of the dishwasher, the lost and despised drunkard of the Old Poland, who had haunted him ever since his return to Springbrook.

"This is Yan Kovalsky?" he said, after a long pause, and shook his head.

"Yes, Mr. Grossman. This is Yan Mattheus Kovalsky, with his daughter Celina, at the wedding ceremony on March 18, 1904."

Isaac Grossman relinquished the photograph, which was passed from hand to hand in silence.

"And this photograph," continued Father Hanecky, "helped

360

him to conquer the evil spirit which had entered him. From that time on he drank no more. He died of cancer. And a short time after his death, as I told you, his family went back to Poland. And they left Yanush here, in Springbrook."

A long silence fell on the group, to be broken at last by Grossman.

"What do I owe you, Father Hanecky?" he said, in a normal voice.

"What do you mean?"

"For this." He indicated the photograph.

"Five dollars," said Father Hanecky, smiling.

"Why five dollars?"

"That's what it cost to hire the frock coat and striped trousers for Yanush. Today, I understand, a wedding outfit comes to ten dollars. In my day it was only five. You got a coat, trousers, a vest, and a white tie. But you had to supply your own shoes and stockings. I think, if I remember rightly, that you were also entitled to a white shirt, and a flower for his buttonhole; but Yan's family supplied that."

"What Mr. Grossman means," put in Dr. Zimmerman, "is, what can he do for Kovalsky, by way of restitution?"

"What can he do? Kovalsky has no family here. And for Kovalsky himself he can't do anything. All his needs, if he has any, are supplied in heaven."

"Couldn't you suggest, Father Hanecky, what Kovalsky would have wanted done for him after his death? Perhaps a handsome tombstone, or the like?"

"A handsome tombstone? Yanush was a modest fellow. I think he's content with the stone which the Kosciusko branch of the Sokol put up for him. I don't think he'd have liked to arouse the envy of all his friends and comrades who are buried near him. He might have—let me see—yes, he did tell me once, when he was sick, that if he had money he would leave it to have a Requiem Mass celebrated for him one the name day of his patron saint. Here we have a solemn mass for all the dead of our congregation on All Saints' Day."

"What would that cost?" asked Grossman.

"What?"

"To fulfill his wish about the Requiem Mass?"

361

Father McCray leaned over and whispered something into the old priest's ear.

"Father McCray says it will cost a bed in St. Vincent's Hospital, in the name of Kovalsky," said Father Hanecky.

"Mr. Grossman will add a new wing to St. Vincent's Hospital, in Kovalsky's name," called Moses Silverstein from his corner.

"No, I don't think he would have liked that. It would have been outside his imagination to have a whole wing named after him. He would have been ashamed before his brothers of the Sokol, who are buried with him. No, that's not for our Yanush," said Father Hanecky.

"And do you think, father, that he will be content with this, and he'll forgive me for the sin I committed against him?" asked Grossman, mournfully.

"He forgave you long ago, Mr. Grossman. Do you know what Yanush said to me when he came back from New York? He said that in the store where he found the suit he wanted, there was a young man. And these are his very words: 'When I came back to his store, all broken up, this young man looked at me with such *litosh'* "—the old priest used the Polish word—" 'with such pity in his eyes, that it touched my heart. He comforted me, and said I would surely find the wallet.' And as a matter of fact, Yanush afterwards suspected that the young man had taken the money, but that someday he would bring it back. He felt that this young man had a conscience, and if he took the money, it was because of great need. And you see—" concluded Father Hanecky—"he was right."

Grossman was sunk in thought a while. Then he said, "I said that to him? I don't remember. Perhaps I did, perhaps I did." Then suddenly, as if to change the subject, he added, "And what can I do for you, Father Hanecky?"

"For me? What is there you could do for me? I have everything I want." The old man shrugged.

"I'll tell you what I'll do. I will give one of your churches a fund to supply wedding garments for poor parents who are marrying off a child, and to supply them with photographs of the ceremony. I'll have Miss Rosenberg look after that at once. I liked your explanation about the pictures. I think we too ought introduce that custom. What do you say, Rabbi Zimmerman?"

"Thank you, Mr. Grossman," said Father Hanecky.

"*You* thank *me?*" And Grossman smiled strangely.

"Yes, Mr. Grossman. Not for the fund, but for what you've done for us."

"What have I done for you?"

"A great deal." The old priest reached out his trembling hand and took Grossman's. "You have opened our eyes for us. You have taught us how to repent and how to make amends for our sins before we face God's judgment. Tell me, rabbi, what is it in your faith that does so much to awaken the conscience? No, not conscience, that isn't the word. It's something else. I remember that in Poland the Jews used a Hebrew word for it. What is the Hebrew word?"

"*Nemoness,*" said the rabbi.

"Yes, yes, that's it." The white head nodded several times. "I remember now, how Jews used to say: 'On my *nemoness.*' That was how our Jews in Poland used to talk."

"Our sages taught us, Father Hanecky: 'Repent one day before your death!' It was from his father that Mr. Grossman inherited this sleepless *nemoness.*"

Two days later Isaac Grossman and his son Lazar sat in attorney Davis's office. They had come to sign the renewed petition to the City Council.

"Mr. Grossman, do you still insist that the project shall carry the name of Kovalsky?"

"No, Mr. Davis. Call it by whatever name you will. It's all the same to me."

CHAPTER TWENTY-TWO

ISAAC GROSSMAN did not return to New Rochelle or to The Springbrook Inn that day. He chose of his own free will to spend a few days in Bethesda, recovering from the strain of his experiences. When he felt rested he moved to The Springbrook Inn. He had made his peace with God, and therefore with his fellow men. No trace of resentment remained in him against his son, and he never again mentioned the wrong which had been done him. Everything had become clear, everything was now self-understood, and words were superfluous.

But he had no desire to return to his home. Lazar, who came out to discuss with him his plans for the future, made a brief attempt to persuade him to go back to his home. His father would not hear of it.

"I have a task to perform here," he said.

"But you don't have to be here for that purpose, governor. And you don't have to exert yourself. We've got men enough that we can turn the project over to, and you can rely on them to carry out your instructions. I'm giving this project top priority in the firm's affairs."

"No. I shall stay here," said the old man, determinedly.

"And what about the house in New Rochelle?"

"Get rid of it. I don't need it any more."

"Get rid of it? The house Clara built?" exclaimed Rose, astounded.

"Do you want it? You can have it," said Grossman, half seriously.

"Thanks a lot. Is that your way of getting rid of *me?*" asked Rose, smiling. "I thought the house was to be a wedding present for Louise. I think you once told me that Clara's house ought to remain in the family."

"I don't think Louise would want it," put in Lazar. "What will she do with it? After the wedding Felix will be going up to Harvard, and she'll go with him, of course."

"Well, well!" laughed Rose. "They got over their quarrel quickly, didn't they?"

Lazar threw a quick, meaningful glance at her. He did not want his father to know of that incident.

"Of course they did."

"What happened?" asked old Grossman.

"Nothing, governor. Young people. They quarrel and they make up. Tell me, governor, why do you want to get rid of the house? It was mother's home, and it's yours."

"I have something in mind," the old man replied. "I'll sell the place, and I'll turn the money over to Dr. Martin for a new section for his sanatorium—a section for poor people. It's a shame that people without means can't get into Bethesda."

"What are you going to do for a home?"

"What I'll do for a home?" The old man smiled, and said softly, and half as if to himself, "They say that God looks after the old, and takes them to Himself, when they have nowhere to go."

"Dad, what are you talking about?"

"I mean it. Well, the house! Lazar, that house belongs to another age, and another generation. It doesn't fit into these times. The two of us, she—" he pointed to Rose— "and I, the oldsters, will spend the remaining few years in hotels. What do you say, Rose?"

"If you'll let me, Isaac."

"And now," he said briskly. "What about the construction work?"

"We're ready to start again, governor. The building contracts you made have been renegotiated; I paid the contractors damages, and the work will start shortly, under our name. We're only waiting for the city permits. There's a special meeting of the Council today, to take up the matter."

"And what about the staff I got together here."

"We've rehired all of them, including that new secretary of yours who ought to be Miss Springbrook. Are you satisfied?"

"Lazar, I want Robert to be drawn into the project. I want to

365

have him here tomorrow, when I'll discuss the plans with Frankel. I think it's time the boy took up something."

"You'll have to do the persuading, governor. Robert has his own ideas. I'm afraid I've lost whatever authority I had over him. I believe it has passed to Dr. Zimmerman."

The morning following this conversation the architect Frankel arrived with his chief assistant, Douglas, to renew the study of Isaac Grossman's plans. Robert came too, at his grandfather's request. The four men set out in the car in the direction of the sanatorium.

"Don't stop at Bethesda, Steve," said Grossman. "Continue to the right—you remember, the way we used to travel."

They reached the hillock which had always been old Grossman's furthest trip from the sanatorium, and from which he had always asked to be driven back. This time he stopped the car, but now the group got out, and, leaning on Robert's arm, Grossman drew the others after him to the side of the road.

"Now," he said. "Look at that landscape." And he pointed to the lake.

The lake lay like a brilliant mirror at the foot of the further hill, and the green woodland was reflected perfectly from its surface. It was a hot June day, and a faint mist had thrown the world into a kind of dream. The dogwood had long since faded. Here and there an isolated fruit tree blossomed, but for the most part the rosy tint of laurel flushed the landscape. A few cows stood dozing under the wide spread of an old elm, lazily chewing the cud. Not a human soul was to be seen among the scattered little houses half buried in green.

"You see that lake," said Grossman, at last, "that lake, and that hill overlooking it?"

"Yes, of course," said Frankel.

"Good, bear it in mind. Now, Steve, take us back to Smith's Farm, on the side of the sports ground."

When they arrived, he made the group get out again, and he pointed to the little wood at one end of the sports ground.

"There," he said, "under that little wood, I want a lake. I've been told there are plenty of springs nearby which can be made to feed the lake. It won't be as big as the other, but big enough to

366

reflect the trees, and the whole hill. And——" with this he turned to Robert—— "I want you to plant rhododendron bushes round the lake, violet and purple bushes, and azaleas, coral and scarlet, and laurel, to be reflected from the lake. Your grandmother loved red colors."

"I think you'll have to do that yourself, granddad."

"We'll talk about that. And now, my friends, we can go home. I can explain the rest on paper."

When he had dismissed the architects from his office, he asked Robert to remain behind.

"Robert," he began, "I want you to take up this project of mine. It's for GI's, and it ought to mean something special to you. I want you to work with your father and Frankel, and to see that all my plans are carried out."

"Granddad, you'll have to do that yourself. You know that nobody but you can do a thing the way you want it done."

"Robert, I don't know if I'll have the strength for it."

"Of course you will. Now, with all your troubles behind you, you'll be your old self again in no time."

"Perhaps. Perhaps. All the same, I want you to take this up. It's your task, no less than mine."

"Granddad, I'm afraid this isn't in my line. It doesn't awaken my interest."

"Robert, I understand you. I know why you feel you can't take an interest in our profession, and it's my fault. I myself didn't understand the significance of my profession. I thought of it as a means of making money. If I had only known in my youth what I know now, toward the end of my life, my life would have had another meaning. I want you to profit by the experience which has come to me so late. I have been like a man thrust out in the darkness; and a hand was stretched out to me and guided my passage in the night——"